INVADED

JENNIFER M. EATON

INVADED © 2018 Jennifer M. Eaton

Copyright notice: All rights reserved under the International and Pan-American Copyright Conventions. No part of this book may be reproduced or transmitted in any form or by any means, electronic or mechanical, including photocopying, recording, or by any information storage and retrieval system, without permission in writing from the publisher.

This is a work of fiction. Names, places, characters and incidents are either the product of the author's imagination or are used fictitiously, and any resemblance to any actual persons, living or dead, organizations, events or locales is entirely coincidental.

Warning: the unauthorized reproduction or distribution of this copyrighted work is illegal. Criminal copyright infringement, including infringement without monetary gain, is investigated by the FBI and is punishable by up to 5 years in prison and a fine of $250,000.

Published by Galactic Razor
Cover by Christian Bentulan

For my son,

Who wants to read this book, but he can't.

Not until he's 18.
No, make that twenty.
Scrap that, make it thirty.
Forty five.

Gah! No, he cannot read this book EVER.

Hey, Tall Boy, is that you, reading this?

STOP IT!

I'm watching you...

[Insert evil mommy glare]

1

Detective John Peters squatted beside a bloodstained patch of sand. He tuned out the news helicopters circling the bridge overhead. The overturned tractor-trailer and the smashed blue sedan straddling the guardrail above would make for a decent headline, but they always wanted more. He could feel their cameras zooming in, looking for the body they'd been promised. But deceased accident victim, Tracy Seavers, was no longer there.

"Dead girls don't just get up and walk away." The off-duty EMT, first on-scene, folded his arms. "I'm telling you, that girl was lightyears past CPR."

The odor of diesel engines carried on the late-summer breeze as another firetruck arrived on the bridge. Circumventing the body's last known location, John blotted out the noise and concentrated on the conundrum at hand.

"There was nothing I could do for her." The EMT shaded his eyes, squinting at the collision scene above. "I heard the other girl screaming, so I climbed the hill to see if I could help."

John nodded. The roommate, Laini Hanson, was damn lucky she'd stayed in the car. Too bad Seavers hadn't done the same.

He crouched in the space between the impact-site and a pink, size-nine loafer lying sideways in the sand. A trail of footprints led into the trees where a few uniformed officers directed doe-eyed interns on search and rescue procedures.

John sighed, surveying the reckless clusters of college students as they left holes in their search patterns any seven-year-old could avoid. If they hunted for their keys like they searched for a missing person, they'd never get out of their goddamn houses in the morning. But he couldn't be particular about personnel when there were so few cops left in the district.

The detective in him hoped one of them would shout they'd found the girl. That's what every cop wanted: a clean wrap-up. But this wasn't going to be so simple, especially with this team.

John walked beside the prints: one foot bare, the other displaying the zig-zag pattern of the lost pink loafer. The steps were narrow, the un-shoed foot dragging with a possible limp. He glanced up to the bridge, where a tow truck started to haul the sedan off the guardrail.

The EMT was right. Chances were slim Seavers survived a twenty-six-foot fall, especially after being hit head-on by an eighteen-wheeler. But if the woman hadn't walked away on her own, someone had taken a great deal of effort to make it look like she had.

His phone vibrated. John glanced down at the screen. He only followed one informational feed—the one he wasn't supposed to have access to. The message wasn't much of a surprise.

PAC Southern NJ.
Live accident scene intersection of 295 and Locust.
Police/News. File 39740. Code One.

John gritted his teeth, wishing he could get his hands on File 39740, but unless he gave up being a detective and joined the FBI, an all-access pass to government secrets wasn't coming any time soon. The only certainty was federal agents were on their way.

Bastards.

His gaze returned to the EMT as John slipped the phone back into his jacket pocket. This guy's testimony didn't matter anymore. Tracy Seavers's disappearance wasn't a crime or even an elaborate hoax. This...this was something else.

And now it was a race to see who'd find Tracy Seavers first.

John moved toward the trees as his partner, Art, dismissed the EMT. The breeze shifted the canopy, casting spotty shadows over the teams mulling through the brush. Their search patterns were too concentrated. Yes, Seavers was hurt, but she had a head start on them. They needed to move deeper into the woods.

Art jogged up alongside him. A shirttail had come untucked from his pants. "We joining the search already? You don't want to grill anyone first?"

John shook his head. "Saw everything I needed to see."

"So, you think someone took her body?"

Someone definitely took her body. The question was, where did they go with it?

The roiling in his chest quickened.

Calm down. She couldn't have gotten far. We'll find her.

John stopped walking and rubbed his chin as two canine squads entered the woods. The dogs lowered their tails and walked in circles. One barked and headed into the forest before stopping and spinning around a tree. It was going to be a long day for those guys. Like the EMT pointed out, *Dead girls don't just get up and walk away.*

The guy had no idea how right he'd been.

John drew in a deep breath and expelled it slowly, soothing his disquiet.

This had happened before. Once. Five years ago.

But that time, John had been the dead person who got up and walked away.

2

The normally soothing sound of the evening crickets cut through the night, louder than they'd ever been. Pushing damp, matted brown hair from her eyes, Tracy Seavers's vision cleared as she limped up her porch steps.

She squinted, shielding her eyes from the entry light as a wave of nausea hit. What in God's name was wrong with her? She covered her mouth and breathed deeply through her nose until it passed.

She didn't have time to be sick. With McNulty breathing down her neck every day, she'd barely had any time to prepare for her interview on Thursday. She'd be damned if she was going to let another promotion slip through her fingers.

Taking three more deep breaths, she steadied herself and drew the keys from her pocket, but the deadbolt fuzzed and shifted. Grabbing the chamber with her left hand, she scraped the hole three times before the key glided into the lock. She'd opened this door a million times. It shouldn't be so hard, no matter how out-of-it she was.

A shooting pain lanced her hip as she stepped over the threshold and dropped her jacket and keys on the floor. Being home should have been settling, but the hallway seemed to close in, stifling her.

McNulty had coughed when he leaned into her office yesterday. If that asshole gave her the flu, she was going to make his life a living hell when she got back to work.

Hazarding another step, Tracy eased her bare foot to the floor. Her legs ached worse than any workout on the treadmill. It seemed like she'd been walking for hours. Days. But where had she been, and how had she lost a shoe?

She rubbed her eyes. Remembering shouldn't be hard. She just needed to focus.

She'd gone to work. That's where she'd been. But she had no idea how she got home.

Pulling her hand from her face, she grimaced. The coppery tinge of what looked like dried blood came into focus, and the folds of her shirt were caked in mud. Maybe she'd gotten into it with McNulty in the parking lot—gave that prick the whooping he deserved.

She stumbled forward, her head spinning. "Jesus!" She grabbed the table in the entryway until her legs stopped tingling.

"Laini?"

The pendulum of the grandmother clock in the hallway ticked in answer.

Maybe she should call Jason. He could come and sit with her for a while, until whatever this was passed. Was that too much to ask of a guy when they'd only been on four dates?

She wiped the dampness from her forehead. If she were smart, she'd have him take her straight to the doctor. She patted down her pockets, not finding her phone. Shit. She probably left it on the table in her rush to get out to work this morning.

Tracy staggered into the kitchen, leaning on the walls. She limped toward the dinette, hitting the flashing *play* button on the answering machine as she passed. Maybe she should just go to bed and hope for a do-over tomorrow.

She slipped into a chair and rested her head on the kitchen table as the machine announced: *"Tuesday, August 29th."*

"Hey, baby, it's Mom."

As if anyone else would call on the landline. Mom had bought that machine for them so she could leave messages when Tracy wasn't home. Laini didn't even know how to work the damn thing.

"Just reminding you about tomorrow. Don't you dare try to get out of your birthday breakfast. I'll be there at six to start cooking. Tell Laini she's welcome, too."

Laini would be so disappointed if they had to postpone Tracy's birthday celebration. It was one of the few times in the year when they ate breakfast that didn't come out of a box. But right now, Tracy didn't think she'd be able to keep a glass of water down, let alone, a three-course meal.

"See you in the morning," her mom's voice continued, fading into another beep.

"Tuesday, August 29th," the machine announced again.

"Hey, Tracy." The male voice startled her.

She lifted her head and stared at the machine. Jason? A long pause hung in the air. Why hadn't he called her cell?

"Listen," he continued. *"It's like this. It's been fun and everything, but, umm, I-I don't think this is working out. So, umm, yeah. That's it. Sorry."* He puffed out a breath. *"Oh, umm, happy birthday, I guess."* He whispered something that sounded like "idiot" before he hung up.

The beep at the end of the message dragged on longer than usual as a solid weight balled in her stomach. Did that asshole purposely call a number he knew Tracy wouldn't answer to avoid dumping her in person?

She groaned, ignoring the ache as her nails dug into a layer of dirt caked in her scalp. Saturday they'd had dinner, laughed, and gone back to his place for the night. What had gone wrong? She rubbed the back of her neck and cringed, hitting a new sore spot.

Another goddamn birthday without a date. Why couldn't she ever get a break?

The machine beeped again. *"Monday, September 4th."*

Tracy blinked twice. September fourth? Was the machine broken or something?

"Laini?" Mom's voice broadcast from the speaker. She sniffed like she'd been crying. *"Laini, please pick up the phone. It's Carole."* Tracy straightened. *"Laini, please..."* The message cut off. Laini must have answered.

September fourth?

No. It was August 29th. Tomorrow was Tracy's Birthday.

The machine clicked off.

The date didn't matter. Mom had been crying. Tracy needed to find out what was wrong.

She rifled through the unopened mail on the table, looking for her cell phone. Dammit! She didn't even know her mother's number to call her back without her cell. Moving another stack of envelopes, the edge of a newspaper caught her attention.

When was the last time they'd had a newspaper in the house?

Tracy pulled the paper out from under the mail, and her eyes widened over a photo of herself on the front page. It was the publicity shot for her volunteer work at the animal shelter last year. Her gaze flicked to the caption:

Body of Thirty-Year-Old Woman Still Missing.

Body? That had to be the misprint of the century. Laini must have peed herself laughing and grabbed a copy. She probably planned on framing it.

Tracy skimmed to the date, and she nearly dropped the paper.

September fifth.

She closed her eyes, forcing herself to breathe. How could it say September fifth? She pressed her temples. No. It was impossible. She couldn't have lost a week of her life. Where had she been? And why was she so sore?

She stood and the room spun, slamming her back onto the chair. The sound of breaks squealing echoed through her mind, followed by a sickening crunch. The taste of dirt and a sticky, coppery goo filled her mouth. Bile rose from her gut as the room skewed again. She grabbed her stomach and heaved. The world became a swirl of blue and white, then brown and muddy yellow. A pounding drummed her ears.

Clawing at the table, she breathed deeply, scrunching her eyes closed until the nausea passed. Her vision cleared, but a dull hum droned through her mind, as if a dense fog hung in the kitchen, forcing all sound inward.

Whatever this was, she shouldn't be alone. She needed help. Fast.

Focusing on the landline beside the refrigerator, Tracy drew herself up slowly, continuing her steady breaths. She could make it to the phone if she...

The front door opened with a squeak.

"What the hell?" Laini's voice carried from the foyer.

Thank God she was finally home!

"Laini?" Tracy's call came out in a whisper as the pounding behind her eyes deepened. She rubbed her forehead, trying to stop the pain, but it only got worse. Forcing herself from the kitchen, she stumbled down the hallway.

Laini stood by the front door, staring at Tracy's jacket on the ground.

"Laini?"

Her roommate stepped back, eyes wide. A Starbuck's cup fell from her grasp and crashed to the floor. The contents spilled across the hardwood. Her lips formed an 'O' as she stood, frozen and staring.

Tracy clutched the wall behind her. "Why are you looking at me like that?"

Her roommate's lips contorted, forming several words, but no sound left her mouth. Her cheeks paled.

Tracy slipped to the ground. Her hand fell on her leg, landing on a foot-long tear in her pants with a matching crusted scab beneath. "W-what?" She stared at the grime still coating her hands. "What happened to me?"

"Tracy?" Laini took short, clipped breaths. Her eyes filled with tears. "You're… not… but you…"

Slipping the rest of the way to the floor, Tracy reached out to her friend. The pounding intensified, blocking all other sound. The world pressed in, making it hard to breathe. Why didn't Laini help her?

The door crashed open and Laini ducked, holding her head as three men in riot gear stormed into the foyer. She screamed as one of them pointed a gun at her before centering the weapon on Tracy.

"Wh-what?" Tracy held her head down as the men shouted to each other. Black boots stopped inches from Tracy's face before a firm grip hauled her up like a rag doll. Pain lanced her skin from all angles.

One of the men talked into his shoulder. "We've secured the P.A.C. Prepare for transport." He handed a syringe to someone standing behind her.

Transport? "Wait," Tracy whispered.

Something pinched her neck and a burn crept through her skin. "What? Why? Who are you?"

"That's my friend!" Laini jumped to her feet. "Where are you taking her?"

Two men dragged Tracy out the door and carried her toward a black van.

"What do you mean she's been exposed to something?" Laini's voice blared through the evening sky as Tracy's world faded to nothing.

3

John perused the morning headline as he walked toward the municipal building: *Government Coffers Picked Clean.*

Yeah, he bet they were picked clean. Dirty politicians will do that to a state. He tucked the paper under his arm and ripped the *Office Space for Rent* sign from the front entrance.

Were they serious? This building wasn't scheduled to close for another twelve weeks. There was no way he was working with real estate agents walking through his office all day.

Consolidating the precincts was bullshit. The majority of John's team was already staffed with volunteer labor. They had to draw the line somewhere.

"You still killing trees?" Art pointed to the newspaper as John passed.

"News isn't news if you have to read it on a computer screen." John dropped the paper on his desk. "We need to reevaluate the search regimen. Seavers is about to turn up. I can feel it."

More like he knew it. Seavers must be awake by now. She was probably wandering around, bewildered. He remembered those first few hours. The panic, the confusion, the pain. No one should go through that alone.

His stomach twitched and cooled as if he'd just chugged a Slushie. He'd find her. He wasn't giving up.

The news had sensationalized Tracy Seavers's disappearance for the first week, which helped rally troops for volunteer search parties. But now that political corruption had taken center stage, the plight of a single missing girl was no longer the community's top concern. They were losing search volunteers every day. Soon, it would be just him and Art again.

Staff Sergeant Biggs opened his door. "Peters, Commings. My office." He disappeared inside.

Art groaned as he stood. John pulled the door closed behind them as his partner sat in one of the two chairs in front of the sergeant's desk.

"Tracy Seavers has been found," Biggs announced. "Alive, believe it or not."

"What?" A ball lodged in John's throat. "Where? When?"

"Last night in her house. She showed up out of nowhere."

The swirl in John's gut tightened. "Can I talk to her?"

Not that the sergeant's answer mattered. John needed to get to Seavers before the FBI dragged her to a containment center.

"I wish I could say yes." Biggs twisted his lip in distaste. "We expended a lot of manpower on this case. I'd like some answers, myself." He threw a pencil across the desk. "The Feds already picked her up and took her to a hospital for observation."

A hospital? Yeah, right. It was probably more like a cage.

John dragged his nails through his hair. He'd stopped watching the house after the first week. What an idiot he'd been. He could have been there, helped her, explained what was going on. Instead, he'd let the government swoop in and grab her right out from under him.

Now Tracy Seavers was alone with doctors who knew too much, and nowhere near enough. She'd have been better off alone in the woods.

John dropped into the other chair and pounded his fist on the desk. "Dammit!"

Biggs raised a brow. Art failed to cover his grin.

"Sorry," John muttered. He breathed slowly, forcing a calm to run through him.

It was okay. He still had her address. The Feds would have to let her go sooner or later. An unofficial visit from the local police wouldn't be out of the question.

Biggs dropped a manila file and a flash drive on the desk. "New case: Diana Worth, twenty-six, from Haddon Township. Single mother of two. Found dead outside a pizza shop."

John's gaze shifted from the folder to Biggs. "Haddon? That's Schnell's and Anderson's precinct."

"Haddon laid off its detectives and ten patrol cops yesterday."

"You gotta be shitting me," Art said.

Biggs lowered into his chair. "I wish I was. Right now, you two should be thankful you have such a good track record." He pushed the folder toward them. "Let's make short work of this, gentlemen. I have a feeling this is going to be a long week."

4

Tracy blinked, but darkness surrounded her. An odd sense of openness churned in the air, as if the space would have dwarfed her bedroom.

Someone moved beside her. "She's awake," a man's voice said.

"Proceed," said another.

"Hello?" Tracy said. "Hello? I can't see anything."

Someone touched her arm. She tried to pull away, but some sort of clamps kept her tight against a soft surface. Oh God, she was tied down!

She pulled against the bindings. "Where am I? What's going on?" Something cold covered her arm. A shriek wrenched from her throat.

A woman's voice: "Relax. Just breathe through it. You'll be fine."

Tracy gulped. Her heartbeat thumped in her ears. "Why can't I see?"

"It's only drops. It's for everyone's protection. We need you to relax." The woman tapped her shoulder.

The second man's voice: "Enough talk. Let's see if we can draw it out."

Draw it out? Draw what out of where?

"Clear!" A third voice shouted, and a buzzing surge thundered through Tracy's body. Her back arched, lifting her from the bed before she fell back down.

"Again," the second man's voice said.

Tracy tried to cry out, but another sizzling torrent coursed through her. She fell back to the bed, shaking. Tears streamed from her eyes.

Her world shrank, lost in a dark prison of pain and uncertainty as the next jolt riddled her body. Nothing existed outside the excruciating bubble that coursed, prodded, and burned her from within. Each jolt created its own eternity of dark madness, until she fell to the bed again, gasping.

She panted, gripped her bindings, and waited for the next surge to flood her. They'd listened to her scream, but they hadn't stopped. Where was she, and why were they doing this? No. The why of it didn't matter anymore. She only needed to survive. And she *would* survive.

Sweat ran from her forehead and down the sides of her face. Her heavy breaths drowned out any other sound as a cool cloth covered her forehead.

"Please make it stop," Tracy whispered.

"You're doing fine." The woman pushed damp hair from Tracy's face.

"Negative reaction from the Ambient," the third voice intoned. "Looks like we're in the clear."

"I'll decide when we're in the clear," the second man's voice said. "This is not our typical scenario. I want the same phase two prod we'd administer if we'd stimulated aggression with the shocks."

Shocks. Is that what they were doing, shocking her as if her heart had stopped beating?

"That's not our protocol," the woman said. "There's no precedent to put the patient through phase two."

Tracy cringed as someone took three steps along what sounded like a tiled floor. The bindings bit into her wrists as she tried to shrink away, sensing the man stood closer to her.

"We have no precedent of an entity mobilizing a class five host within minutes of death, either." Another step. "I'm not clearing this one until I'm completely sure."

Entity? Class five?

"Please," Tracy whispered, "would someone please tell me what's going on? Why are you doing this?"

The hand lifted from Tracy's forehead. "How many rounds of tests will make you sure?" the woman asked. "There's just so much the human body can take."

The man snorted. "She's already dead. We'll take this as far as it needs to go until I'm satisfied that thing inside her is not a threat."

"Thing inside me?" Tracy sniffed, holding back a sob. "Would someone please tell me what's going on?"

A light touch cupped her cheek. "Hold tight," the woman said. "This is going to be a very long day."

5

Diana Worth's eyes pleaded to John from the photograph pinned to the corkboard. There was nothing he could do for her, of course, but he could give her family closure by nailing the asshole who took the twenty-six-year-old mother from her two young children.

Dammit, what had happened to those kids? Were they still with their grandparents?

Not that they were his problem, but he'd gone with the social workers to pick the Worth children up from daycare. He and Art had stayed in the parking lot, invisible but present, in case the killer made a second appearance. The red, puffy eyes on those kids had nearly killed him.

John gulped down a burning swig of coffee, then another. What he needed was a solid lead, not erroneous conjectures.

His gaze drew to the second photo, to the lines outlining Diana Worth's body in front of the pizza shop. No harsh angles, no apparent impact from a quick dump of the corpse. Her killer had even placed her hands over her heart.

John tapped his fingers on the table. "The perpetrator cared about her. I'd stake anything on it."

Art slumped into the chair beside him. "Forensics said the examination was conclusive. This was a random mark."

Then why take the time to bring her back to the exact place she'd last been seen alive, especially a place so public? "I don't buy that. You shouldn't, either."

"I don't buy it because you don't buy it." Art leaned closer to the pictures. "But I don't see what you're seeing."

"At a bare minimum, he's imprinting…using her as a substitute for someone else."

Art twisted his lip skeptically. Nothing new.

"Call it a sixth sense." John took another sip of coffee as his *actual* sixth sense swirled down from his lungs and wrapped around his stomach.

John blocked out the ethereal movement. Diana Worth was a woman with no known enemies. He'd failed to uncover an obvious motive, and they had no leads.

"Everyone in this case had an alibi," John said. "It's almost too perfect."

Art folded his arms. "Too perfect is right. Almost planned."

Nodding, John continued to stare into the photo. Diana was smiling, but there was just a touch of sadness in her eyes. Something wasn't right…something she kept from everyone.

What was it, Diana?

What could be so far removed that no one else was aware of it?

John leaned back in his seat. "The ex-husband."

Art looked up from his coffee. "His alibi is rock solid. He was at a dinner party with his neighbor in California."

"Don't care," John said. "I want to talk to him again."

6

Searing light burned through Tracy's eyelids. A wave of nausea swept over her before sinking into the background.

The sound of male voices carried through her fog. She tensed. God no! She couldn't take any more!

Gripping the cold bars beside her bed, she peeked through her lashes. The rush of joy from being able to see dissipated as she took in the pock-marked, tiled ceiling above, and the large double window to her left. A vase of peach carnations sat on the sill, casting a shadow across the white blanket covering her chest. To her right, a tacky brown striped curtain hung a foot away from the bed.

A hospital?

Tracy shifted her weight and grunted, unable to move. Gray belts with buckles connected her wrists to the rails alongside the mattress. She stared at the thick bindings as the last foggy dregs of slumber left her. Sweat beaded at her temples. Part of her had hoped the last several days had been a bad dream.

The last few days... Were they even days, or were they months? Years?

But she could see again. That was good. At least she hoped it was good. Maybe they wanted to watch her reaction when she saw them coming for her.

God, this was insanity! She had to get out of here.

"Help!" She yanked at the restraints. "Someone, please, help me!"

A man in a tan khaki uniform whipped around the curtain and pointed a gun at her, steadying the weapon with both hands. "Calm down, ma'am."

Her eyes widened. "Calm down? You're pointing a gun at me!"

"I told you to calm down, ma'am."

This guy thought intimidation would work? The sight of a gun was nothing compared to the living hell she'd been through. "Don't tell me to calm down. You can't do this to me."

Another man rounded the corner, tucking a pen into the inner pocket of his oversized black suit jacket. "At ease, lieutenant," he said. "She's been through enough."

The lieutenant didn't falter. "Not until we call an all-clear, sir."

Suit-guy pursed his lips, running his fingers through spiky, blond bangs. Tracy might have considered him attractive if she weren't his prisoner.

"I'm glad you're awake." Suit-guy took a step closer. "Do you know your name?"

He had to be kidding. She was tied up, and he had the gall to ask *her* questions? "Who are you? Where am I?"

The man with the gun re-set his footing.

Suit-guy stiffened before a smile formed on his lips that didn't quite touch his eyes. "All in good time. What I need right now is your name."

Tracy tried to blink away the haze coating her thoughts. Yes, she knew her name. She just couldn't recall it at the moment.

She yanked at the bindings again. The bed shifted, but the bands seemed to tighten. "Why am I tied up? What's going on?"

"The restraints are for your protection." Another man walked around the curtain. Same suit, same haircut except for a scattering of gray at the temple and deep lines around his eyes. He moved with a sense of precision that made Tracy's skin crawl.

"Protection from what?" The rasp in her voice startled her. "Who are you people?"

Suit number one flipped a badge out of his back pocket.

Number two did likewise but shoved it back in his jacket before she got a good look. Not that she would know what she was seeing, anyway.

"I am Special Agent Clark. This is Agent Green," the older man said. "Can you remember your name?"

That voice. Tracy's stomach twisted, and she fought the need to shrink away. She'd probably have nightmares about his voice for the rest of her life. The voice of the man in the dark, the one demanding test after painful test.

Was that why he was here now? To administer more pain? To see how she reacted when she could see what was coming?

But he didn't move toward her. He simply stood, staring in her direction, expressionless.

"Your name," he repeated.

Could that really be all he wanted?

She could tell him her name. That shouldn't hurt anything.

Her name. Yes. This was an easy question. Everyone has a name. Her lungs tightened and she gasped for breath. Her heart started to throttle. Why the hell couldn't she remember her name?

Agent Green held up his hands. "Calm down, Miss. There's no reason to panic."

"No reason to panic?" She pulled and the bed shifted toward the right this time. "Do you have any idea what this man has put me through? And now I'm staring him in the face, I'm still tied down, and you expect me not to panic?"

They stared at her. Clark folded his arms. "Your name?" he said, more insistently.

She closed her eyes and breathed deeply. A slow exhale calmed her enough to form a coherent thought. "Tracy. My name is Tracy

Seavers." Good. She knew her name. Everything would be fine now. Peeking out at them from beneath her bangs, she eased out another breath.

Clark nodded. "That's correct." He turned to the guy in khakis. "We can take it from here. Keep a guard by the door."

The lieutenant nodded and placed the gun in his holster.

Tracy swallowed the ball building in her throat as he disappeared behind the curtain. "So you knew my name already? What is all this?"

Green tilted his head. "What is the last thing you remember, Miss Seavers?"

She glared at Clark. "Other than being tortured?"

"Before that," the younger, kinder-looking agent said.

Her pulse throbbed within her ears. "I don't know." She lifted her head from the pillow. "Please tell me what's going on."

"First things first. What is the last thing you remember before being brought here?"

More questions. She shouldn't have been surprised. The younger one may have looked kinder, but he wasn't. He was with the maniac calling the shots. For all she knew, Green was one of the people flipping switches while they electrocuted her.

Tracy closed her eyes and took another steadying breath. She wanted to rip these guys apart and claw her way out of this nightmare, but tied down, her options were limited.

They weren't asking much of her. She only needed to tell them where she was last. She could do that.

Couldn't she?

Clenching her jaw, she wracked her brain. She certainly didn't remember anyone bringing her to this god-forsaken place. What was she doing before this?

She'd had breakfast with Laini. Then they went to work together like any other day. They got into the car and...

Biting her lip, she opened her eyes. "We were driving on 295, heading to work. We got a flat tire. Laini never changed a flat, so I got out of the car and..." And then what? The next thing she could remember was stumbling up to her front door and being carted away by men with guns. In-between there was nothing.

The agents' blank expressions crept inside, causing the hair on her arms to lift.

"That was over two weeks ago," Clark said.

She jolted, but the restraints kept her close to the mattress. "I couldn't have been unconscious that long. What happened? Where's Laini?"

Green raised a hand. "Your roommate was treated for lacerations and whiplash and then released."

Laini had been released, but not Tracy. Tracy came here. To be tortured.

She settled back onto the pillow, feeling the weight of the unspoken elephant of a secret pressing against her chest.

Clark fiddled with his sleeve. "Technically, Miss Seavers, you were not unconscious. You were in a state of transition."

The pressure shifted to her stomach. "Transition?"

Green glanced at Clark, then to Tracy. "You've only been in this facility for a week. You were missing for eight days, then you showed up at home, unexpectedly. I'm told you gave your roommate quite a fright."

Laini's wide, shocked eyes fizzled up from somewhere deep within. She'd dropped her drink to the floor. A faint sheen hung over the memory, as if watching TV through dirty glasses. "I went home. Where was I before?" Tears streamed down her cheeks. "I don't remember anything."

Clark motioned to the younger agent. "I've heard enough to clear her. Let's get those restraints off."

Agent Green unclasped the buckles. She rubbed the red indents the straps left on her skin and eyed the handle of Green's gun peeking out from beneath his jacket. She had a bad feeling she wasn't walking out of this hospital any time soon.

But she felt fine, like waking up after a good night's sleep.

What could possibly be wrong with her? Had she been delirious? Imagined being tortured?

A thread of her dark hair fell into her eyes. She looked through it, not wanting to stop massaging her raw wrists. "Are either of you going to tell me what's going on?"

Clark dragged the chair up beside the bed and sat. He twiddled his thumbs before raising his gaze. An odd expression crossed his features, a combination of disgust and caution.

He straightened. "When you got out of your car, you were hit by an eighteen-wheel tractor trailer traveling at seventy-two miles per hour."

Her forehead dampened as she fisted the cool bedrails. "That's bull."

"Your body was thrown over the embankment, landing in a construction site twenty-six-feet below the highway." His neck tensed. "The doctors surmise that you probably broke most of your ribs. X-rays show that your lungs were punctured in seventeen places."

Gaping, she ran her hands over the thin, striped hospital gown covering her chest and held up her arms. "Look at me. If that was two weeks ago, I'd be in traction."

Clark smirked. "You'd be dead."

The air seemed to suck from the room.

"But you said I went home." And maybe she had.

There were trees.

Dogs barking.

She had to get away from them.

They'd hurt her if they found her.

But it wasn't the dogs that she'd been afraid of.

Tracy glanced at Agent Clark. Somehow, even then, she'd known there was something terribly wrong. She'd stumbled through the woods for days, hiding under bushes and finally making it to the one place she thought she'd be safe. Home.

Clark stared back at her, his face a mask of incredulity compared to Green's attentive eyes.

Her sigh stole the silence from the room. "I remember just bits and pieces. Like flashes."

Green reached for her hand, but she recoiled before he touched her. His gaze darted to Clark, then back to her. "Spotty memory lapse is normal."

Normal for what? The elephant in the room had inflated to blimp-size. No one wakes in a hospital with no doctors. No one. Maybe this wasn't even a hospital.

And maybe these guys weren't cops. They'd called themselves agents. But agents of what?

She re-gripped the bedrails. She could run again, but even if she got past these two, she'd never get away. Not with the itchy-trigger-fingered lieutenant outside.

Clark's eyes narrowed. "You were pronounced dead by an off-duty EMT who witnessed the crash."

She froze, gaping.

He drew a small tablet out of his jacket and showed Tracy an aerial picture of a bloody body wearing her favorite pants suit. One of Tracy's pink loafers lay in the sand to the right, almost out of the picture.

Oh shit.

"The EMT made his way up the embankment to help your friend." He showed another photo of Laini with a bandage on her head. Tears streamed down her cheeks. "Your body went missing before the coroner arrived."

Her gaze darted from the tablet to the stoic agent. "What?"

Clark tapped his knuckle on his lower lip. "There is a moment before a person dies when the brain gives up and realizes it's over. At that moment, the human mind becomes susceptible."

A pause hung in the air, sucking all other thoughts from her mind. "Susceptible to what?"

Agent Green shifted in his seat as the older agent stood and walked toward the window.

Leaning against the glass, his eyes trained on something outside, Clark continued: "Seventeen years ago, the United States government entered into an accord with a race of non-corporeal beings we call Ambients. The accord gives them asylum in our country, and the right to take human hosts whose bodies are beyond repair."

He turned, his gaze lancing Tracy. She sat frozen, waiting for the punchline.

She glanced at Agent Green, hoping to see a smile on his face, but his lips formed a line, his expression unreadable.

Clark took a deep breath. "Initial scans proved positive. You are now an Ambient host."

Tracy seized her knees through the covers. This couldn't be happening. "I don't believe you. That's ridiculous. Things like that aren't real."

The older agent inclined his head. "Denial is also normal. That's why we are here, to try to assist with the last phases of transition."

Transition into what? Things like this only happened in the movies or in books. None of this made sense.

"The Ambient Custodial Division of Homeland Security monitors every hospital in the United States, watching for miraculous recoveries. Your case has been on our radar screen since news of your body's sudden disappearance hit the web. After all, a corpse can't leave an accident scene on its own."

She clutched her legs tighter. "So, they made a mistake. Obviously, I wasn't dead."

"Ms. Seavers, no one can explain why you are alive right now with holes in your lungs, or how half the bones in your body reset without the help of an army of medical practitioners. You got up and walked away from an accident scene."

She panted as if she'd run up a flight of stairs. "So, I'm a fast healer. That doesn't mean there's something inside me. Joke's up. I want to go home."

She grabbed the bedrails and shook, trying to lower them. Clark gently nudged her back down to the mattress. Not like she put up that much of a fight.

"There is nothing for you to worry about at this point, Miss Seavers." Agent Green stood. "Most entities are benign. Many hosts barely even recognize there is something inside them."

Something inside them—something inside *me*.

Wait a minute. The blankets crinkled in her clutched fists. "*Most* are benign? What does that mean?"

Clark held up a hand before Green could answer. "That's enough for today."

"Enough for today?" She sat up again. "You can't tell me there is some kind of parasite inside me and expect me to just accept it."

"No, not completely. Right now, we need you to digest what we've told you. We'll explain more tomorrow." He looked past the curtain. "Doctor Morris?"

Tomorrow? Was he out of his mind? "Screw tomorrow. I want answers now."

A man with wild, gray hair and a lab coat moved into the room. Tracy balked when the light from the window fell on the syringe he held at his side.

"Now wait a goddamn minute!"

She pushed away from the bed. Clark and Green were on her before she could protest further, forcing her back onto the mattress. The burn crept through her skin before she felt the needle.

The room wavered, and they released her.

The gray-haired man shined a light in her eyes. "You are a lucky girl," he whispered.

Clark's voice muffled through the growing hum in the room. "Your findings so far, Doctor?"

Her vision clouded as the man scratched his long, messy hair.

"We've seen no signs of aggression, even after the extensive stimulation you ordered." He cleared his throat.

Stimulation? Was that the electrocution? The water pouring over her face? The sirens blaring in her ears? God, had she imagined any of that?

"The Ambient is very strong, but benign." The doctor became a blur. "It must have been desperate to conscribe someone with injuries this extensive."

"Meaning?" Green asked.

"I'm not sure the patient will ever fully heal, even with the Ambient's help. There was too much damage to her internal organs."

"We'll have to explain her options tomorrow."

Options?

Agent Green leaned down, squinting as he looked into her eyes. Darkness crept in from all sides, hiding all but the agent's concerned expression before fading to nothing.

7

John leaned on the steering wheel and stared at the front door of 355 Spruce Street. The conservative split-level rancher seemed quiet, as it was every night. There was no sign of the welcome home banners Tracy Seavers's mother had purchased on her credit card three days ago. Whatever the government had been feeding Mama Seavers and the roommate, Laini Hanson, must have been enough to give them hope.

But the bastards already had Tracy for a week. That was four days more than they'd kept John, and more time than they needed for their psychotic shock tests.

John's stomach tightened in an otherworldly grip. His hands spasmed as if he could feel the electrical charges surging through Tracy Seavers's body.

He shivered. The memory was too new, even five years later. If John hadn't been tied down, he'd have electrocuted a few doctors' asses and seen how they liked it. The pricks.

And to think that they might be doing that again, to an innocent woman—but why would they keep her for so long?

His gut turned to stone.

"Don't even think that," he whispered.

There was no reason to dwell on the worst. If Seavers was a host, and the Ambient fought back, proving it was strong enough to do harm to a human being, the creature would have been executed, and the mother and roommate would probably be planning Tracy's funeral.

It was all one big, autocratic mess.

The more John thought about the day he'd woken up, tied to a table, the more he wondered, had those guys *hoped* for a fight?

Why torture a creature they were supposed to protect under the accord?

A disposable coffee cup appeared in front of his window, blocking John's view of Seavers's house. John rolled down the window and snatched the cup from his partner's hand.

Art walked to the passenger side and got in. "I know I ain't half the detective you are, but it didn't take much for me to figure out I'd find you here."

"You always told me I was predictable."

"Yeah, but it's usually in a good way."

"Meaning?" John took a sip of his coffee. There wasn't enough creamer.

"Meaning the Worth investigation isn't going well. You admitted it yourself."

"Tell me something I don't know."

"What you don't know, or are just plain ignoring, is that you're not a hundred percent with me on this one."

And what Art didn't know was that John lay staring at the ceiling at night, kept awake by visions of a beautiful brunette screaming. How could he focus, knowing what that poor girl was going through? But his partner was right. He really wasn't as sharp as he should be.

Art turned, placing his elbow on the dash. "They found the Seavers girl. She's not our problem anymore."

John set his cup into the coffee holder between the seats. "I know that. It's just…" The boulder in his stomach twitched, poking his ribs. "It's complicated."

Art pursed his lips, enhancing the deep lines in his face. "I ain't gonna get all fatherly on you, but you know I'm here if you need to talk, right?"

John sighed. He wished he could talk to Art. He wished he could talk to anyone. But who would believe what he'd been through?

The mass in his gut splintered and bubbled up into his chest. John rubbed his sternum and fought back a smile.

"Any chance you gonna tell me what's so funny?" Art asked.

John let his smile burst free. "Just that when you're right, you're right." He turned on the engine. "Seavers will turn up eventually, and we'll get our answers then."

Art folded his arms. "And?"

"And until then, Diana Worth is the only woman in my life. I swear."

8

Tracy tapped her plastic fork on the edge of her melamine plate. The ten cubes of yellow gelatin they'd given her for breakfast rolled through her stomach like frozen dice.

What was going on at home? What did they tell her mother? Laini? Work?

She straightened. The promotion interview was today.

She had to get out of here!

Wait. Not today.

Her appointment was two weeks ago. She'd missed it.

All that hard work practicing interview questions with Laini, shot to shit.

Tracy rubbed her face. She'd missed her birthday, too. She'd been unconscious. Missing. And to top it all off, Jason broke up with her on the phone. Asshole.

Tracy groaned, pushed aside the remainder of her gelatin, and rested on her folded arms. This had to go down in the record books as the worst birthday week—or weeks—of her life.

She rubbed the back of her neck and shivered. What did any of that matter? There was something *inside her*. The whole idea was almost impossible to get her head around, but as more of her memories came flooding to the surface, something seemed *off*.

She ran her hands over her lap. A little over a week ago she'd stumbled up to her front door, dizzy and hurt. She'd been hit by a truck a week before that, but now there was barely a bruise on her.

She closed her eyes and rubbed the bridge of her nose. No one at the hospital would speak to her past a grunt or two. The guy in the lab coat ignored her questions while he took his readings this morning. So far, no one even hinted at being the person who would "explain more tomorrow," as she'd been promised.

Was it worse than they thought? Was she going to die anyway? Or did they find out it was all a mistake?

Or maybe they had no intention of letting her go. Maybe they were going to study her to find out more about this thing inside her. Maybe…

Her heartbeat pulsed in her ears. Tracy took in a slow, deep breath. She needed to keep calm. They said they'd come. For now, she had to believe that.

She covered her mouth and yawned. Whatever they'd given her had knocked her out for the entire night. When she woke, she slipped into the jeans and T-shirt she found on the table beside her bed: not her own, but a perfect fit, oddly enough.

After Dr. Morris checked her blood pressure and flashed the light in her eyes, he okayed her to walk around, which equated to exploring two hallways of locked doors that formed a circle opening to the unadorned common room where she sat now.

A single white-clad guard stood sentry at the nearest exit, with another stationed at the exit leading to the other hallway. Both doors, she'd learned, led back to her room. Pushing her tray to the edge of the table, she paced the shiny, gray tiles before sinking into a plush orange couch opposite a television the size of Montana mounted on the wall.

Pictures of protesters shouting and holding signs filled the screen. Some people seriously needed to get a life. Being kidnapped, tortured, and chained to a hospital bed without even a phone call was something to protest.

Grabbing the remote control, she turned up the volume on the TV. "...the municipal building since the decision was made public last night."

A female reporter shoved a microphone at a uniformed police officer. "What is your response to this landmark decision in South Jersey?"

South Jersey news. At least they hadn't taken her far from home.

The officer shook his head. "All I know is thousands of good cops got laid off this morning. And whoever decided it was a good idea to consolidate four counties into one precinct with a quarter of the manpower has got to be out of their minds. How is any cop supposed to protect and serve if the people they need to help are over an hour away?"

The camera cut back to the news anchor. "That was former patrol officer Peter Goning, repeating the sentiments of many in reaction to New Jersey's decision to combine Burlington, Camden, Gloucester, and Atlantic counties into a single police district."

Tracy snorted. Yup, definitely local. At least there'd be fewer speed traps to deal with on her way to work.

The gorilla at the door nodded as Agents Clark and Green entered.

Finally. Now maybe she'd get some answers so she could go home. She lowered the volume on the television.

"Feeling better today, Ms. Seavers?" Agent Green smiled, taking the hard-backed chair next to her.

"I guess."

"Dr. Morris says your recovery rate is phenomenal, all things considered."

Tracy shifted her weight. His enthusiasm unnerved her. "Yesterday the doctor said I might never completely heal."

"Inconsequential. Today's data shows otherwise." He inched even closer. "Have you felt it move, yet?"

A shiver riddled her spine. "It can move?"

"Let's not worry about that right now." Clark tapped on his phone before shoving it back into his inner jacket pocket. "I'm sure by now you have an interesting list of questions."

Of course, she did. But where to start? *Did you take Torture 101 in college? Where did you get your personality from, an Alfred Hitchcock movie? And, of course, what have you guys been smoking to come up with something crazy like coming back from the dead?*

Clark's eyes narrowed. She shrank back, just like she had in the dark between rounds of electricity.

Damnit, she needed answers. *Real* answers, not all this vague shit they'd been feeding her.

Steeling herself, she readied for the worst. "Can you explain what this thing is that you think is inside me?"

"Your scans are conclusive, Ms. Seavers," Clark said. "We don't think. We know."

She gulped. "Then what is it?"

"We already explained. It's an Ambient."

She rubbed her temples. "You say that like I'm supposed to know what that means. Is it some kind of leech? Am I still going to die?"

"Not today, Ms. Seavers, and not likely anytime in the near future—at least from any injury or illness that can be healed by an intelligent, non-corporeal being."

She shuddered. "Non-corporeal?"

Green shifted his seat closer, his eyes beaming. "These creatures are beyond anything we've encountered before. They exist in a nearly gaseous state and are barely visible to the naked eye. Modern science still says their existence is impossible, yet here they are." He held out his hands, like she was a prime example of the find of the century.

But she didn't want to be anyone's prize specimen. She just wanted all this to be over with.

Tracy dropped her hands to her lap. "I still don't understand what this thing wants from me."

"Your lungs, quite simply." Green reclined in his chair. "They can't breathe our air. It's the perfect symbiotic relationship. You needed healing beyond human medicine. The Ambient provided that—is still providing that. And in exchange, it uses part of your lung capacity." A smile burst across his face. "It's all pretty amazing, if you think about it. I mean—"

"Green." Clark held up a hand, his gaze squashing the younger agent's excitement. "I'm sure Ms. Seavers has more constructive questions."

Her gaze shifted back to Green. "Last night you said that *most of them* are benign. What does that mean?"

Clark shot the younger agent a chilly stare before turning to Tracy. "In other countries, Ambients are hunted like animals and put down. The ones that are here understand what a privilege it is to live unencumbered in the United States. There are a few, though, who take advantage of our hospitality."

This just got better and better. "What do you mean by *take advantage?*"

"Benign entities sink into the psyche and play nice. Malignant Ambients manifest the second their host wakes up. Their presence overwhelms and destroys the brain cells that hold memories. They can walk and talk and carry out normal human functions, but they can't even remember their names."

"I remembered my name. So that's good, right?"

"Yes, that's good. We ran every test we had to tempt your Ambient to react. We were ninety-eight percent certain you were clear at that point. After testing, if the patient remembers who they are, statistically, they are safe."

"Statistically? Either I am, or I'm not."

"We can make no guarantees, Miss Seavers." His phone rang. He brought the case to his ear. "Agent Clark." His expression hardened as he listened. He glanced at Tracy. "I need to take this. I'll be right back." He stood and walked past the guard at the door.

The news report on the television showed a scene of people milling about the Art Museum steps in Philadelphia. A regular day for anyone else, but the start of unending hell for her.

She rubbed her face. "I don't get it," she said. "If these things are intelligent, why would they want to live in our bodies if they're forced to the background? I mean, that's not even living, it's just surviving."

Green nodded. "You're right. From what we can gather, they are extremely long-lived. Earth is a transitory holding ground for what's left of their species until they can find a suitable home."

Oh, God. So now they were talking about alien life forms? "I don't want to be something's temporary housing."

Apparently done with his call, Clark returned to his chair. "Understand, Ms. Seavers, that you owe this being your life. And as long as they play by the rules, they are protected by the Ambient Accord."

The set of his eyes, the turn of his lip, told her something about those protections disgusted him. But his stance promised he would abide by them, Tracy be damned.

"Screw your goddamn accord," she said. "I never asked for this."

He handed her a card, as if not even listening. "You will need to stay in the hospital for routine monitoring before we sign off on your release, but after you leave, if you ever get uncomfortable, or feel like you've lost time, contact me and you will be evaluated for an extraction."

Tracy leaned forward in her chair. "Extraction? You can take them out?" She stood. "Then do it now. I don't want this thing inside me."

He shook his head. "Sorry, the accord gives the Ambients rights. Like I said, as long as they abide by the rules set for them, they are American citizens."

"What about my rights? This is my body!"

He stood, pointing at her. "Your rights terminated when your brain fired off the chemicals that ended your life and let the Ambient in. Without that entity, you'd be in a coffin right now and we wouldn't be having this conversation."

"So, what, I'm supposed to be thankful? Happy that there is some kind of, of *thing* inside me?"

Clark's eyes narrowed. "There is an option, but it's not ideal."

She tensed at his lowered tone. "I'm listening."

"Extraction is painful to both the Ambient and the host. The accord is clear: we cannot harm an Ambient living within the agreement's parameters. But—"

Tracy gulped. "I'm still listening."

"We could kill you again. A bullet to the temple should suffice and give you the least amount of discomfort." His expression didn't change, as if he suggested they share a cup of coffee or eat a piece of pie. "That would be too much damage for even an Ambient to heal. It will leave, find another host, and let you die like you wanted."

A cool breeze from down the hall chilled her open mouth. "How is that an option?"

"Until you heal enough that your body can survive on its own, it's your only option." He held up his hands. "As we said, you should be dead. If you'd rather follow fate's plan, we can accommodate you."

The younger agent fidgeted in his seat. "Let's not be hasty. Most people don't even know the Ambient is inside them. They just feel odd movement from time to time." His gaze darted between her and Clark. "Being nervous is understandable, but statistically speaking, there's really nothing to fear."

Nothing to fear. Tracy hugged her shoulders. Easy for him to say.

Green appeared at her side. "What you need to do now is rest and get your strength back so we can re-assimilate you into your old life. What's happened is a miracle. You'll realize that eventually."

Eventually. That was a pretty big word.

They left after a speech about national security and keeping her situation to herself.

Even if she did tell anyone, who would believe her?

She was dead, or she was supposed to be dead. And by some ungodly twist of fate, this creature had snatched her body.

Dozens of science fiction scenarios flooded her mind. She sat, covering her face with her hands. These things couldn't all be bad, right? The president wouldn't have signed an accord if they were some kind of nasties out to destroy the world.

Unless the president was one of them. She puffed a heartless laugh.

Damn all those science fiction movies!

She rubbed Clark's card between her fingertips. She could call him if there was a problem—he could make this thing go away. Maybe that was the answer. Wait a few days until she was completely healed, then call the number on the card, say something happened to break this stupid accord, and they would get rid of this thing for her. She didn't care if it hurt. She just wanted this all to be over.

Tracy's fingers froze. Her hands grew cold as something within her trembled.

Clark hadn't seemed all that concerned about killing Tracy if she'd rather die. What kind of person could suggest such a thing with a straight face?

The kind of man who could stand there and watch while an innocent woman was tortured, all to *stimulate* the creature who had taken refuge inside her.

Yes, that was the kind of man Clark was.

A deep chill crept across her skin and drifted away as quickly as it had come. For some reason, extraction scared her more than knowing her body wasn't her own anymore.

9

John stared into his cold cup of coffee and tapped a pencil on his desk. Headlights lit up the wall to his left as someone pulled out of the municipal parking lot.

A light flicked off past the reception area and a lone set of footsteps echoed through the hall.

Soon, he'd be the last one there and he could finally be alone to think. Well, as alone as possible, all things considered.

John fingered the evidence bags scattered across his desk. His theory about the Worth murder had nothing to do with this meaningless shit he kept examining. The body wasn't dumped. Diana Worth was placed in front of that pizza shop. Respectfully. There was more to this story to piece together.

He leafed through the crime scene photos, stopping on a picture of Diana's final pose. "He was careful when he dropped her. Like he cared."

"There's no sign of a boyfriend and we've already grilled the shit out of the ex-husband." Art walked into the room and replaced John's coffee with a steaming cup. "That's decaf."

"I hate decaf."

"Yeah, well, I'm not brewing a fresh pot and Starbucks is

closed." Art looked down at the photos. "You really think our guy knew her?"

John rubbed his eyes. "I'm not really sure what I think anymore."

"You two still here?" Sergeant Biggs leaned into the room.

John glanced at the clock. It was nearly eleven p.m.

Biggs's face remained hardened. "I appreciate the dedication, but you're no good to me if you fall asleep behind the wheel on the way home. Call it a night, gentlemen. Now." He headed for the exit.

Art shrugged. "You heard the man. Let's get some shut-eye."

John rubbed his eyes again. Maybe sleep wasn't all that bad an idea.

He stood. "I want to look at the crime scene again in the morning. Meet me there at six."

Art groaned. "You know, the Surgeon General recommends eight hours of sleep a night."

John grunted in response, gathering the evidence.

Art shook his head. "Fine. I'll bring the caffeine."

Leaving the coffee on his desk, John headed down to the hallway toward the case-file lockers and deposited the evidence.

A single light shone through the hall from the doorway marked *Data Accumulation*. There was only one other person in the office even more sleep-deprived than the detectives. John leaned his head through the door. "Hey, Emmerson."

The data analyst looked up from her computer screen. Several strands of graying blonde hair had escaped from her haphazard bun.

"Rough day?" John asked.

"Every day is a rough day lately." She smiled. "At this hour, I'm guessing this isn't a social call."

"Guilty as charged. Can you run Tracy Seavers's name again?"

Emmerson nodded. Her fingers blurred as she typed on her keyboard.

She leaned toward the screen. "Same as the last fourteen times I ran her name for you. No credit card usage, no cell phone, nothing."

At least no one had filed a death certificate, which meant the Feds still had her. Bastards.

John had only been their *guest* for three days after he woke up, and that was three days he'd rather forget. A faint tremor rolled just beneath his navel. John rubbed his stomach in soothing circles. He wasn't the only one who'd rather forget.

John thanked Emmerson and turned to leave, running right into his partner.

"You gotta stop obsessing over that girl," Art said. "How many times do I have to say it?"

"I know, I know." John held up his hands. "She's not our problem anymore."

Art was right, of course. He should be preoccupied with Diana Worth.

He *was* preoccupied with Diana Worth, but until he knew for certain whether or not there was another Ambient in the area, he couldn't let this go.

But he had to. With the kind of injuries the EMT attested to, Seavers would have been considered a Class Five host: a body beyond repair. Her entity was probably struggling to heal such extensive injuries. That was the only reason he could think of for the Feds to keep Seavers for so long. For all he knew, they could have taken her to their main custodial facility in Washington. If they had, she wouldn't be needing those welcome-home signs.

Shit. He gritted his teeth against his own stray thoughts.

Diana Worth's family needed closure—the kind of closure that only a focused detective could deliver to them. He wasn't giving up on Tracy, but he had a job to do.

Art gave him a shove toward the door. "Biggs will have our asses if he finds out we're still here."

"No worries," John said. "We're leaving."

10

Tracy sighed as her mother opened the car door for her. "I'm not an invalid. I told you, I feel fine."

Her mother's nose flared. "You were missing for a week. I thought you were dead." She closed her eyes and took a deep breath. "When they called and said you were alive, I almost didn't believe them. I thought it was a joke because they wouldn't let me come see you." She wiped her nose. "You needed experimental treatment. Top-secret government kind of experimental treatment!" A sob broke free and she looked away. "They told me you almost passed away three times from some kind of crazy flu virus. Did you know that?"

No, but dying had crossed her mind more than once. Could those tests possibly have been as painful as she remembered?

Tracy shivered. Shit, she wished she could block the insanity of those days out of her mind.

Her mother turned back to her. "I keep expecting to wake up and find out this was all a dream and you're still gone." She shoved her hand forward. "So, get over yourself and let me help you."

This must have been a nightmare for her. Her mom had always prided herself on taking care of *her girl*. She probably thought she'd never get another chance to be a mother. And maybe, after everything, a mother was exactly what Tracy needed.

Tracy took her mom's hand and hoisted herself from the car. She wouldn't admit it, but the ache in her legs did make it hard to walk after sitting for a while. The doctors said some discomfort was to be expected after such a remarkable healing; nothing jogging a few miles in the park couldn't work out.

She winced as a pain shot up her shin. Maybe she'd start out on the treadmill, just in case.

They walked past a sparkling silver Toyota in the driveway. A single crystal shard hung from a long, clear string attached to the rearview mirror: the same type of charm that had hung from her roommate's windshield before the accident. Laini had wasted no time in getting a new car.

Then again, Tracy had been gone for almost a month. A girl had to get around somehow.

She took in the yellowing leaves on the tree in the next yard. Last time she'd been here the kids were still on summer vacation. Had she really been gone so long?

Every part of her tried to deny what the agents had said. The whole thought of an alien race that you couldn't see, it was ridiculous. But they'd shown her the X-rays. She'd seen where her Ambient had repaired more fractured bones than she could keep track of, not to mention, that faint hue that had shown up alongside her lungs. The shadow that moved freely within her.

She shuddered. Was this why her muscles twanged when she walked? Was her body trying to drive that thing out of her?

The door opened and Laini appeared. "I thought I heard something!" She threw her arms around Tracy's shoulders. "It's so good to see you." She leaned back. "And it looks like you've lost weight. That's cheating!"

Tracy laughed. "Yeah, that's why I walked in front of a truck: to lose weight."

Laini hugged her again. "Damn, girl, you scared the shit out of me, you know that?"

"I think I scared the shit out of myself." In more ways than one.

Her mother helped her inside. "That nice Mr. Kremmer called this afternoon."

Tracy cringed. Her Mom had been talking about Miles's ass since the company picnic last year. She couldn't get it through her head that Tracy couldn't date her boss.

"Seems to be, they've already fired two people that they brought in to replace you. I told him not to worry, that you'd be back as soon as the doctors cleared you to work. He was thrilled!"

Of course, he was. Miles wasn't the type to pick up and do someone else's work. It was nice to know she still had a job, though.

Walking through the house, Tracy scanned the light fixtures and glanced at the television. Clark said they'd be keeping an eye on her. Did that mean cameras? Bugs? Was her every move going to be recorded for the rest of her life?

And if she did tell someone, would Agent Clark come barreling in to arrest her, Laini, Mom?

A tremor ran through her. The not knowing, it was horrible.

"I'll get some coffee brewing." Laini headed toward the kitchen. "I got some apple turnovers to celebrate."

Apple turnovers: Tracy's favorite. There was some chocolate syrup in the refrigerator. She could warm the bottle up, drizzle some over the pastry and...Tracy blinked.

"What?" her mother asked.

"Oh, nothing. I was just craving chocolate syrup."

Her mom's brow furrowed. "Doesn't chocolate give you a headache?"

Tracy nodded. "Yeah, I know. Weird."

Setting her hand on the wall in the foyer, Tracy stared at the floor where she'd fallen weeks ago. There was no sign that she'd been dragged away by uniformed men with guns. The table where she always dropped her keys was pushed slightly to the left, but other than that, home was exactly how she left it.

Well, maybe a touch cleaner. Good old Mom.

Tracy walked into every room, checked behind every door, and flicked every light switch on and off. A giggle flittered through her lips as she sat on her bed with a bounce.

Her mom propped herself against the doorframe. "Are you sure you're okay? You're acting like you've never been here before."

Springing from the mattress, Tracy stared at her indent on the comforter.

Dread slithered through her.

She'd certainly been here before, but the thing inside her hadn't.

She rubbed her temples. Thinking this way was going to make her psychotic.

Her mother continued to stare, her brow furrowed.

"I'm fine. It's just been a while, you know?" Tracy smiled. "Come on. I smell coffee, and a turnover has my name on it."

Laini slid a pastry onto a plate as they entered the kitchen and placed the cookie sheet back on the stove. She couldn't cook to save her life, but she had that reheating thing down pat.

Mom sat behind a plate while Tracy grabbed the chocolate syrup and some milk from the refrigerator.

"Thanks," Laini said, grabbing both from Tracy's hands.

Frowning, Tracy clutched the syrup to her chest.

"Umm, are you gonna let that go?" Laini asked.

Tracy's fingers had whitened around the bottle. "Oh!" She released her grip and fought the desire to grab the bottle back and hug it.

What the hell? A tingle fizzled over her cheeks, as if something moved beneath her skin. *Oh God!*

"Dude," Laini said. "You just turned pale as a ghost."

"She's right." Mom stood and helped Tracy to her seat.

Sweat beaded Tracy's brow. She breathed deeply, and the tingling subsided. "Wow, that was weird."

"You should rest," Mom said. "You've been through a lot."

Tracy sighed. "Rest? I've been cooped up for weeks. I want to get out. Do stuff."

"But, Trace," Laini said. "You look like you got—"

"Hit by a truck?"

Laini shifted. "Well, yeah. Don't rush it, okay? Not having a roommate sucked. And I don't want to be hauling your ass back to the hospital."

Fat chance of that happening. She wasn't going anywhere near that place ever again.

She took in another deep breath and the tingling disappeared. Maybe that was it. She had to remember she was breathing for two. Extra deep breaths once in a while. If that's all it took, she could do that.

"That's it," Mom said. "I'm bringing you up to bed. Laini, help me."

Tracy's roommate appeared on her other side, and she and Mom hoisted Tracy up to a standing position. Taking another deep breath, Tracy held out her hands. "I'm fine, guys."

"No, you're going to bed." Mom tugged her arm. She'd used *the voice*, and Tracy knew better than to argue. Within five minutes, she was tucked into bed and feigning sleep, just like she'd done as a kid.

"I can't help but worry," Mom whispered outside Tracy's door.

"I get that," Laini said, "but you're going to make yourself sick. Go home and get some rest. I'll keep an eye on her."

After a short argument, Tracy waited for the front door to open and close. When the sound of Mom's car faded into the distance, she sat up in bed.

She was home. Safe. The last thing she needed to do was lie around and feel sorry for herself. She needed to get back to normal. The sooner the better.

When the sound of music and the thump of Laini's sneakers on the treadmill carried through the air vents, Tracy padded down the steps, grabbed her keys, and headed out to her car.

After being cooped up inside for so long, the steering wheel tingled like sweet freedom. Normalcy. That's what she needed. And chocolate. Yes, chocolate.

A chocolate croissant and a chocolate latte with an extra pump of chocolate syrup. Oh! Maybe two pumps!

Salivating, Tracy pulled into a free spot on Merchant Street, a few blocks from The Treehouse Coffee Shop. She turned off the car and grabbed her purse. The succulent smell of coffee quickened her step. Maybe if she asked nicely, the girl would give her three pumps of syrup. She skidded to a stop, studying a crack in the cobblestone beside her right shoe.

Chocolate again. What if this craving was all in her head? What if the headaches came back? It wasn't worth the risk. A nice non-migraine-inducing chai tea would do fine.

11

John shoved his hands into the front pockets of his jeans and stared at the red bricked sidewalk. This was his third trek up and down Merchant Street today. The shopkeepers were probably starting to worry that he was casing the place.

The familiar bricks, old-fashioned black lampposts, and decorative railings soothed him and gave him a clean slate to think. Ever since leaving Audubon after high school, he'd found himself drawn back to the smells, the sounds, the small-town atmosphere, and to the very streets where he'd hung out as a kid.

Somehow, the comfort of home washed away the deluge of unnecessary data riddling his mind. It brought him back to the basics, back to when times were easier.

The muscles in his legs contracted and he stopped. His shoe hung in midair over the sidewalk. He struggled to place his foot down, to no avail.

John grimaced. Sometimes, living with another person inside your body had its drawbacks.

"Dak, what's wrong?" he whispered to himself.

His Ambient swirled along his ribcage without answer.

"Okay, buddy. Can I please put my foot down?"

He fought against Dak's hold until the Ambient gave way and John stumbled forward, tripping into a poor, unsuspecting girl. She toppled backwards and fell on her ass. The entity chuckled inside him.

Glad you think it's funny. John offered the girl his hand. "I am so sorry. I'm a klutz sometimes."

She grumbled beneath a blanket of dark hair shrouding her face. Ignoring his hand, she pushed herself off the red bricks and stood.

Deep blue, startlingly familiar eyes challenged him as she swiped her bangs behind her ear.

John blinked, soaking them in. "Do I know you?"

"Really? That line is older than both of us put together." She shoved past him, clutching her purse.

Feisty. I like this one.

Shut up, you. To the girl, John said, "I'm sorry, I know this sounds crazy, but I'm sure I know you from somewhere."

"Nice try." She continued on her way, her purse gripped against her right shoulder.

John's gaze fell over the girl's smooth contours as she navigated the cobblestones circling the decorative bars hiding a trash can. Dirt clung to her pink slacks, highlighting a perfectly rounded ass.

He'd gladly have dusted her off if he hadn't made such an idiotic first impression.

She glanced back at him, her blue gaze latching on for a moment. He'd looked into those eyes before. The familiarity, the sense of need filled him.

"Shit," John whispered. "That's Tracy Seavers."

He began walking after her. Dak quickened his pace.

She stopped suddenly, and before John realized it, he slammed into her again.

Her purse thumped to the sidewalk, and those bright eyes turned to fire. "What in God's name is wrong with you?"

"Let me explain." John reached for her bag the same instant she did. A sizzle of warmth shot through his hand as their fingers touched.

Dak quaked, enjoying the energy expelled by one of his own kind, confirming what they both knew had to be true: Tracy was no longer alone in her body.

"I'm sorry, but I *do* know you." John handed Tracy her purse. "I helped coordinate the manhunt when you went missing."

She clutched the bag to her chest. "You helped look for me?"

"First of all, let me prove I'm not a complete nut bag." He drew his badge from the inner pocket of his blazer and showed her. "I'm a cop."

"A badge doesn't prove you're not a nut bag." She looked toward the concrete and a small smile began to form. "But thanks for trying to find me."

"It's my job."

Idiot. She's cute. Tell her you felt compelled to find her.

He slipped the badge back into his pocket. "You recovered quickly. What's it been, three weeks?"

Three weeks and three days to be exact, but who's counting?

John called up his concerned detective face. "No one could figure out how you walked away after an accident like that."

Of course, John knew. And it killed him. Her gaze seeped into him, her eyes betraying the horror of those missing days. John wanted to step forward, take her into his arms, and let her cry the tears he'd been forced to keep inside five years ago. But he needed to be cool and collected, nothing more than a cop showing interest in his previous case. The last thing he needed to do was spook her.

"You have a good memory." She took a step back. "It, umm, wasn't as bad as it looked—the accident, I mean." She looked over each shoulder.

"Apparently not." But they both knew it was. Shit, he wished there was an easy way to ease into this. He took a steadying

57

breath. "Anything odd happened afterwards, maybe involving a guy in a suit with a really bad attitude?"

Her fists kneaded the fabric of her bag. "Yes, but how…" Her eyes widened. "Are you one of them? Are you watching me?"

"No, nothing like that."

She shrank back. "Then how do you know about the guys in suits?"

John lowered his voice. "They were there when I woke up, too."

Her jaw fell to a wide gape. "You have one of these things inside you?"

He cleared the distance between them and struggled against placing his hand over her mouth. "Not so loud. You know, national security and all that."

She nodded. "I'm, umm…" Her lips formed half a smile. "I'm Tracy."

"I know." He reached for her hand and shook. "I'm John."

And Dak. We're thrilled to meet you!

John looked toward the pavement. "I'll introduce you in a minute. Let's give the poor girl a second to breathe."

"Who are you talking to?" Tracy stepped toward him. Her lips formed a perfect circle. "Oh my God. You can actually talk to it?"

"Yeah. His name is Dak."

Tell her how nice her ass swings when she walks.

"He says hi."

Her lips parted before she looked away. So much for not freaking her out.

John pointed down the street. "There's a coffee shop right over there. Would you like to sit for a few minutes and talk? I'm sure you have questions."

She clutched her bag with both hands. Her eyes didn't meet his. Smart girl. Even under normal circumstances, a woman alone should be cautious. If more people second-guessed strange guys they ran into, maybe less of them would end up dead.

John held out his hands. "You have every right to be nervous, and yes, in the interest of transparency, I do have a gun, but that's for protecting the peace, I swear." He called up his best smile. "It's really uncommon to run into someone else in our situation. I thought you might want to talk. The Tree House coffee Shop is down the street."

She nodded. "Yeah, I've been there."

Her stance relaxed slightly, but her darting gaze told him she was still judging her escape routes.

Make that a *very* smart girl.

"If your experience was anything like mine, I'm guessing you have almost no information other than you should be dead, and keep your mouth shut."

"Yeah, that was pretty much it." She tucked a strand of long brown hair behind her ear. "I was actually already headed to the coffee shop. I'd love some company. Would you mind?"

Of course he doesn't mind. He's hopeless and hasn't had a date in months.

"I'd love to."

John slid into the chair opposite Tracy. The coffee house was slow for a Friday. Two other couples chatted near the door, so they'd chosen a table in the back where they could speak without anyone hearing.

Tracy settled into her chair and arranged her two chocolate croissants and double chocolate muffin beside her triple-pump chocolate latte. John suppressed a grin. With a figure like hers, that had to be either nerves, or an alien craving she was trying to feed.

She cleared her throat. "So, wow, how long have you had one of these Ambient things in you?"

Dak cringed, causing a flutter through John's chest. "Dak doesn't like that word. He prefers entity."

She lowered her eyes. "Okay. Please tell him I didn't mean any offense."

"No harm done. Dak and I have been together for about five years."

She leaned back. "Seriously? That's a long time."

"It's not all that long. It's not like I'm counting the days or anything."

"So, it's not bad? You don't hate being a freak?"

Freak?

John narrowed his eyes. "I don't feel like a freak at all. Well, only when people catch me talking to myself." He waited for the droning hum of the coffee machine to abate. "To be honest, I feel incredibly lucky. I mean, my number was up. I was dead." He took a sip of his drink. "There were three bodies on the ground. I was the only one to get up. Dak could have chosen any one of them, and he chose me. I owe him my life."

A smug warmth filled him. Dak's emotion, not his.

Tracy's shoulders hunched as she shifted her weight. "How did you, you know, die?"

Images of blood, noise, and sirens flew through John's mind. Dak blocked the visions out, saving John a relapse. The last thing he needed was to have to go through another round of sitting on a couch and talking to a shrink about his feelings.

"I was shot three times in the chest at point blank range." He tapped the lid of his latte, giving Dak time to keep his emotions at bay. "It's funny. I always wore a vest on duty. I was running late that morning and I forgot."

The color drained from Tracy's face. Her hands slipped to the table. "How horrible."

"Yeah, it wasn't a red banner day for me."

She curled up the edges of her napkin. "When you woke up, did they torture you?"

Shit. He half hoped the Feds had given up on that. Fucking bastards.

He nodded. "Short burst electrocution. Dak told me later that he'd been through that before. He knew not to challenge them."

John waited, gauging her expression. They had her for over two weeks. Why? What had they done to her?

"Tracy, did your entity fight them?"

"I don't think so. But they kept on…" She sniffed and blinked away a tear.

John gulped. Could they really have tortured her for two weeks straight?

This girl must be a fighter. He'd been ready to crack after a few hours. No one should be forced to go through something like that, either human or entity.

They sat in silence as Tracy finished her first croissant. She cleaned her fingertips on a napkin. "How long did it take before it started talking to you?"

"I'm not sure. At first, I thought the agents were full of shit. I didn't feel any different. But then I started to have strange cravings."

"Like chocolate?"

He nodded. "But mine was broccoli. It looks like your cravings are much more fun than mine." John smiled. Those first cravings seemed like a lifetime ago. "After that, I started to feel emotions. I knew when he was happy, excited, scared. I started talking to him and these feelings that weren't mine flooded me. That went on for a long time, then suddenly there were words. Single words at first. But now he's completely fluent, and hard to shut up at times."

Hey!

"It's cool, though. He's my friend, and I'm never alone."

Tracy cringed, then offered what appeared to be a forced smile. "That doesn't sound so bad."

She gulped back what may have been a fresh round of tears.

John struggled against reaching out and caressing her cheek.

He remembered the struggle when he'd first found out he wasn't alone. Damn, he wished he had someone like himself, who could have let him know everything would be fine.

Please touch her.

John looked over his shoulder and whispered, "It's not appropriate."

"What's not appropriate? Is he talking to you, now?"

"Yeah. He wants me to touch you so he can feel your entity. I've explained to him that humans don't go around touching each other."

She adjusted her sweater, twirling her finger around the top button. "If you touch me, can he talk to whoever is inside me?"

Only one way to find out.

"He says maybe." He reached out his hand to her. "Is it okay?"

"Just my hand?"

"Yeah, that should be enough."

She slipped her fingers into his. Their touch heated as Dak seeped through his skin and into Tracy.

Tracy drew her hand back. "Oh my God! What was that?"

"It's okay. That was him." Dak swirled back up his arm and into John's chest. The entity rattled like he might burst.

There was only one thing that might get him that juiced.

Dak sparkled, confirming John's suspicion. The Entity inside Tracy was female.

"It felt like something was crawling inside me."

"Don't think of it as him inside you. Think of it like him reaching out his arms. He can't actually leave me. He needs me to breathe."

"They explained that at the facility, that they use our lungs."

John nodded. "They need oxygen to survive, but carbon dioxide is pure poison to them, even in small doses. They don't have a way to separate the good from the bad, so that's why they need a host." He shifted in his chair. "If their host dies, they have to move at unbelievable speeds to find a new one. It's like running a marathon while holding your breath. If they don't find a new body, they die, too."

Tracy rubbed her hands across her face. "But why are they here if they can't breathe our air? Where do they even come from?"

"Dak told me he came from some sort of transport made of vapor. He doesn't remember anything before that ship. Seems like they were on there for a long time."

"The Federal agents said them coming here was just temporary until they find a new home. Do you believe that?"

John took a sip of his coffee. "From what he's told me, yeah, I do. But Dak's been here for decades. I think temporary is relative."

She shivered. "It all seems so crazy."

"Crazy and wonderful once you get used to it." Even more wonderful to talk about it with someone. He remembered all the questions he had those first few weeks—questions he didn't get answers to until Dak was strong enough to talk. John could be that bridge for Tracy, helping her to not feel so alone.

Her fingers slowly traced the edge of her mug, her lips slightly parted in thought. John could stare at those lips for hours.

There are other things you could be doing to her for hours.

John held back a smile. *Down, boy.*

She sat back and ran her hands over her shoulders. "Does your entity talk to you a lot?"

"Sometimes more than I'd like."

That's not very nice.

"When I'm working, he's usually good about keeping quiet, so I can think. But I still know he's there." John shifted in his seat. "I feel little jerks and spasms all the time. Occasionally he'll get excited and slam me into a pretty girl." He grinned, but her eyes only widened. Maybe it was too soon for her to know that the entity could sometimes take control. "Don't worry. It doesn't happen often. It seems to wipe him out."

She looked to the side, as if digesting that thought. "You keep calling it a him. You know it's male?"

John's gaze lowered to Tracy's cleavage.

Her entity is probably still wrapped around her lungs. If you touch her there, it will be quick and easy access for me. It's a win for both of us.

"He's definitely male." And to Dak, "Please stop."

What? You thought of it, first.

A young couple entered the coffee shop, giggling as they approached the counter. The girl kissed the boy on the cheek and took one of the tables upfront, well out of earshot.

"I don't know if mine has a name," Tracy said.

"She has a name, she's just not strong enough to tell you yet."

"She?"

"Yeah, Dak thinks she's a girl."

"Does he know her name?"

Again, John waited for the spinning of the coffee machine to subside so he didn't have to shout. "Maybe if I hold your hand again, he can get a better feel, maybe even talk to her." He reached out his hand. "Would you like to try again?"

She nodded and grasped his hand. Her eyes shut as if she expected it to hurt.

Slowly, John directed. *Don't scare her.*

Dak reached out, part of him anchoring to John's lungs while the rest of him flowed past his skin and into Tracy, again. Warmth flooded him as he inched further through their contact.

Tracy sighed, and her head fell back slightly. John gulped, a pang of jealousy seeping in as her beautiful lips parted. He wanted to trace her cheek with his fingertips, connect with her in a human way while Dak met her entity for the first time. Shit, she was gorgeous.

Dak retracted with a slam and information flooded John's mind.

He took a moment to sort it all out. "Dak got a name, but it's hard to pronounce. I'll do my best." He chewed his lip. "A-don-na."

Close enough.

"Adonna," Tracy repeated. She stiffened. "I just got a flash of heat."

"That's usually happiness. She's glad you know her name."

"Wow." She shivered and hugged herself. "Hi, Adonna."

"Dak says that she's really weak. Healing their host seems to take a lot of energy. It might be a while before you guys can get to know each other."

Tracy looked to the table before returning her gaze to John. "Tell him to tell her: thank you for saving my life."

John shook his head. "He doesn't have to. She lives inside you. She can hear your thoughts."

"Everything?"

"Yeah, pretty much."

"So, no privacy?"

John shrugged. "You're going to have to get used to that. It's an adjustment, but I can't imagine how I ever lived without Dak."

How sweet. How about you throw some of that love at the pretty girl? You can start by rubbing your hands all over those perky boobs that you're already fantasizing about.

How about you learn to keep it in your pants?

I don't have any pants, but maybe if I could get you out of yours...

You're incorrigible. "Do you have any other questions for us?"

She dabbed a few muffin crumbs from her napkin. John didn't remember her eating the rest of her pastries. Then again, the first time Dak forced him to eat broccoli, he ate a whole bag so quickly that John didn't even remember tasting it.

Tracy leaned back in her chair. "Questions, yeah, probably thousands, but I'm drawing a complete blank. I can't believe I ran into you. I mean, what are the odds?"

"We got really lucky. There aren't any other hosts in the immediate area. None that we've found, anyway. They seem to be concentrated more in the cities."

"Then why is there an Ambient research facility in South Jersey?"

"I actually asked the same question." John sipped his coffee. "Dak pointed out that people don't always die in the city, and the entities have less than a minute to find a new host. They don't have the luxury of being choosy." He sat back. "Every PAC in the tristate area gets sent either where you went or the big facility in Philadelphia. I ended up in Philly." His fists tightened, remembering how his screams echoed through the antiseptic triage room. Dak rolled, soothing him from within.

"PAC?"

John shook off the memory. She didn't need to know that he still had nightmares about his *orientation*, even five years later.

He met her gaze. "Possible. Alien. Carrier."

She looked away, rubbing a raised, red rash on her wrists. Apparently, they still restrained hosts until they were cleared for assimilation. Bastards.

Her bangs fell over her eyes, shielding her from him. She probably felt like she needed to hide from the world. He needed to help her believe everything was going to be all right; that she could trust him and Dak.

A deep pain gouged the bottom of his throat. This was the opportunity Dak had been waiting years for, but John wasn't sure he could go through this again.

You're going to let her go, aren't you?

Was he? Tracy had been right about one thing. The odds of them finding each other out here in the suburbs were astronomical.

Could he make this work? Or would it end badly, like last time, with each of them in tears?

Dak tried to help drive the memory back, but Amy's face still pushed through. Her brown eyes. The way her lips trembled when she cried in the movie theater. The way her long, blonde hair arched around her face when she straddled him in the bedroom.

John shook his head, clearing the memory, the pain.

It wasn't your fault.

It wasn't anyone's fault. That didn't make it hurt any less.

You can try again. Tracy is perfect.

Sunlight reflected off a picture frame, casting a bright glow in her dark hair. Yes, she was pretty. And Dak was right. It had been far too long since his hands had roamed across warm, silky-soft skin. But it wasn't worth the risk.

Dak gelled and stiffened within his chest.

Chill, buddy. That doesn't mean I wouldn't like to see her again. John reached into his jacket and pulled out a business card. "Tell you what, give me a call anytime you want. We'd be happy to talk. It's not all that often that Dak gets to see one of his own kind. Once Adonna is talking, it'd be great for the four of us to get together."

Tracy laughed, and covered her mouth. "I'm sorry. *The four of us*, that still sounds so strange."

"Strange has turned into my new normal."

She stared at her napkin before easing her gaze to his eyes. "I'm glad I ran into you."

Dak swirled and flipped inside him.

John tried to hold back their grin. "So am I."

12

Tracy crunched the last slice of bacon and watched the Pillsbury Doughboy dance across the television screen. The remainder of yesterday seemed to go by in a haze, part stewing over the changes going on inside her body, and part wondering how her life would change once Adonna was strong enough to speak.

She shivered. Someone was going to start talking inside her head. God, would she be able to handle it?

John certainly didn't seem to mind.

John. Now there was a rare specimen of yumminess. And so darn sweet. She fingered his business card in her pocket. She definitely needed to find a reason to call her unexpected alien-host mentor. The sooner the better.

Mom sat beside her, sipping tea while she read a magazine, leaving Laini with a pile of dishes that probably would have sat for hours if Mom hadn't come to make breakfast again.

Mom cooked, and the girls cleaned. Those were the rules, but Mom still had Tracy on light duty. Which meant if Laini wanted to eat something that wasn't wrapped in paper, she had to risk ruining her manicure.

"Did Tracy tell you she met a guy yesterday?" Laini dried off her hands with a towel, a stack of sparkling clean dishes piled in the rack behind her.

The magazine fell to Mom's lap. "Do tell."

Tracy flopped back on the couch. "He's just a guy."

"Just a guy, my left butt cheek," Laini said. "She's been on cloud nine all morning."

Mom straightened. "Really? Fess up. Tall, handsome, muscular?"

Despite her attempts to hide it, a smile crept across Tracy's lips. "All of the above."

She could still hardly believe her luck: running into another person with an entity inside him. Her skin tingled, remembering the heat in his touch. Not really him, or not completely him, Dak had a lot to do with it, but the connection, the warmth that had spread through her. It was like nothing she'd experienced before.

"What's his name?" Mom asked.

"John."

Tracy grabbed a throw pillow and hugged it in her lap. Laini threw the towel back toward the kitchen—not noticing or not caring that it landed on the floor—and sat beside her on the couch, just like when they'd talked about boys they met in high school. Mom being there wasn't an issue, not even when they were growing up. Mom *got it.* One of the fringe benefits of having a kid at fifteen was that you were still young enough to be friends when your daughter became an adult.

"John. I like it," Mom said. "That's a nice, strong name. What does he do for a living?"

"We're not dating or anything, but he's a cop."

She nodded. "A good, law-abiding man. Good for you. Do you have anything in common?"

Tracy hugged the pillow tighter. "More than I ever expected."

The television commercial cut out and the camera zoomed in on an anchor woman. *"South Jersey is reeling this morning after a* woman's body was found inside her parents' home on Trellis Avenue. The police have identified the victim as Twenty-nine-year-old Melissa Harpoona of Evesham Township."

"Holy shit!" Tracy raised the volume and straightened as a deep thickness settled into her chest. Her mind glazed over as images of police cars and bystanders flashed across the screen.

Melissa Harpoona: Cheerleader. Most likely to succeed. Homecoming Queen. There were probably a few more titles, but the numbness flooding Tracy overtook any sense of reason. Melissa had sat beside her in Homeroom. They'd barely said five words to each other through all of high school, but now she was dead.

A deep void formed in Tracy's stomach and twisted. How could someone she knew be dead? Murder happened to *other people*.

Memories of pep rallies, field trips, and times she'd seen Melissa in the school hallways flooded her. Melissa was the envy of everyone. There wasn't a girl in school that didn't want to be her.

Until now.

Laini turned her gaze from the screen. "I am totally creeped out. We used to ride the school bus with that girl."

Tracy crossed her arms and hugged herself. "I know."

A short car ride did nothing to help Tracy struggle with the unexpected grief filling her world. She parked her car beside the bus stop where Melissa waited on many a school day morning. The quiet surrounding the 'caution children playing' sign seemed stifling, alarming. Down the road, police cars parked beside barricades, keeping news vans off what Tracy expected was Melissa's parents' property. She vaguely remembered Melissa waving to her mom as they passed on the way to school; and now it was a crime scene.

Tracy's body seemed to float down the block until she settled in front of the black and white barriers surrounding the front lawn. She stared at Melissa's mailbox, the bushes along the walkway, and the old-fashioned swing on the front porch that Melissa would never sit on again. She'd only been Twenty-nine. It wasn't fair. It wasn't right.

"Tracy?"

She jumped, nearly knocking into the barricade. A strong grip steadied her as she looked up into John's brown eyes. Damn, they really were as beautiful as she remembered.

"John, w-what are you doing here?"

His grin sloshed her into a wallowing pool of mush. "I'm a cop, remember? This is my case."

"You're investigating the murder?"

A wisp of his dark hair shifted over his brow as he nodded. "One of the more unseemly parts of the job. What are you doing here?"

She shrugged. "I knew Melissa. We went to school together."

"Were you friends?"

"No. We barely even talked." In fact, she was a bitch, come to think of it.

"So, why are you here?"

Good question. "I don't know. I felt like I should come, you know?"

His eyes searched hers, tickling the part inside that made her feel like a foolish teenager again. He flinched, and his gaze carried to his side. Had Dak said something to him? How was she going to handle it when Adonna started doing the same?

He slipped his hands in his pockets and turned toward the groups of people gathered along the street. "Do you know any of these people?"

Tracy glanced past the barricades into faces she'd never seen. "No, why? Are they suspects?"

"At a crime scene, everyone is a suspect."

She jumped. "Why?"

"Many killers will return to the crime scene. They enjoy the aftermath, the attention, knowing that they were the cause of all this." He waved his hand through the air. "Occasionally, they come for the fun of it. They think they're outsmarting me." He turned back to her. "But they're not. I pick them out in eight out of ten cases."

Tracy shivered, imagining one of these people with a knife, a gun. "That's pretty sick."

"That's why people call them psychos." He propped himself up against the barricade. "So exactly why are you here, again?"

A flush whipped through her chest. "Wait a minute, you don't think I'm a suspect, do you?"

"Well, you *did* show up." He raised a brow before a smile crept across his lips. "No worries. I'm just doing my job."

Tracy relaxed, but only a little. Her eyes traveled over the remaining onlookers. Could one of them actually be a criminal? "So, do you question everyone who shows up to gawk?"

"Nope, just the pretty ones." He closed his eyes and looked away. "Sorry, that was probably the worst line you've ever heard."

A warmth spread through her middle. "Well, it was better than the, 'I'm sure I know you from somewhere' line."

A man in a suit leaned out Melissa's front door. "Peters, we need you in here."

John straightened. "Duty calls. It was really nice seeing you again, although I wish it was under better circumstances."

"Yeah, me, too."

13

Dak twitched, spiraling through John's chest. *That went well.*

"Yeah, I guess." John walked toward the Harpoona residence.

Why didn't you kiss her goodbye?

"We barely know each other." His phone rang. He didn't recognize the number but swiped the bar to answer anyway. "Detective John Peters."

Tracy's voice answered. "Oh, so it's detective? You didn't mention that."

He released the doorknob and looked over his shoulder. Tracy was still beside the barricade, holding a phone to her ear. "Yeah, well, they haven't let beat cops wear jeans and blazers on the job yet, but I hear they're working on it."

The wind carried her long, dark hair to the side. "You said I could call you any time."

He tried to hold back a childish grin. "Yeah, well, I'm kind of working right now."

She tucked her unruly hair behind her ear, adding a slight swing of her shoulders. "Okay, listen, this is going to sound completely impulsive and insane, and this is probably the worst place ever to do this, but I wanted to ask if you'd like to get a bite to eat or something some time?"

Whoa. Did she just ask you out?

Quiet. And, to Tracy, "You mean, like dinner?"

"Dinner would be great. Thanks for asking."

For a moment, the weight of the crime scene lifted. Someone inside called his name again. They could wait. "How about we meet at the Villari's in Sicklerville. Tomorrow at 7:00."

"That sounds great. I'll look for you in the bar."

"Sounds like a plan. See you tomorrow." He clicked off the phone, biting back a grin as he grabbed the door handle.

She's going to think you're an idiot for not picking her up. Who asks a girl to meet them somewhere?

"A cop working on multiple murder cases with practically no staff, that's who. And she barely knows me."

"Talking to yourself again?" Art Commings waved his hand-held tablet as he strode toward John.

"Just working some stuff out in my head."

He'd go insane if he didn't speak out loud. Sometimes it was easier to pretend Dak was standing beside him.

John motioned to Art's computer pad. "What have you found so far?"

Art pointed to the back of the house. "Same M.O. as the last one, but Forensics says most of the incisions on the body didn't take place in this location."

Shit. If this was the same guy that killed Diana Worth, the press coverage would explode, and these poor girls' families would suffer for it.

Dense humidity and the coppery tang of blood hung in the air as he followed Commings to the rear of the home. A couch and two recliners faced a flat screen television. Staff Sergeant Biggs crouched near the white tape marking the floor where Melissa's father had found her body.

Sergeant Biggs snapped off his disposable gloves and adjusted his tapered collar as John approached. "Forensics missed you this morning. They said it wasn't the same without you yelling at them."

The tape hadn't been blocked correctly. There was no way the girl's neck was that long or her head that small. "I hope you told them to bite me," John said.

He worked to settle the roiling in his stomach. Freaking budget cuts were giving murderers the upper hand. There weren't enough detectives left to work the caseload, let alone cops walking the beat. Melissa deserved better. If he hadn't been questioning the last victim's husband, he would have been first on the scene and made damn sure nothing was overlooked.

"The blood patterns don't compute." Art pointed at the coppery stains on wall. "This asshole sliced her up somewhere else, but not enough to kill her. Torture maybe?" He glanced toward the rear of the house and pointed to the small, yellow cones on the floor marking dark smudges on the carpet. "It looks like she walked through the back door on her own. She was alive when she got here."

John took a deep breath, detaching himself from the life that had depended on the blood now soaked into the rug. He couldn't dwell on Melissa. It was too late for her. The only good he could do for her and her family was to find the bastard who did this.

The pressure behind John's eyes told him Dak wanted him to look away. Anger boiled in his mind as Dak tried to block himself from the images contrived from the tape marking the ground, the deep stains marring the once-white carpet.

John didn't allow the darkness in, but keeping Dak's volatile emotions from flooding his subconscious was always a problem. Even receded, Dak's agitation boiled to the surface.

"He did her right here." Art folded his arms, looking at the outline on the floor. "The bastard cut her up somewhere, forced her to walk back home, and killed her in her own living room with her parents asleep upstairs."

John's hands shook as he tried to hold in the heat emanating from Dak's anger. "The parents didn't hear anything? How is that possible?"

"You ain't really asking me that, right?"

"It was a rhetorical question." John squatted beside the lines showing Melissa's final pose. He ran his fingers in the air above the line where her face would have been. "Why didn't you scream for help?" John spoke to the lines, as if Melissa could answer from the grave. He crouched closer to the floor. "She was gagged."

"What?" Biggs said. "The body wasn't gagged when we got here."

John pointed to the carpet. "Look at the indent here. It's deeper, less soaked with blood."

Art squinted, probably pretending he saw what John pointed out. "Yeah. So?"

"So, she was gagged. That's why her parents didn't hear anything. Forensics didn't mention an indentation in the back of her hair?"

"Not that I'm aware of," Biggs said. "Shit. I should have made the team wait for you before removing the body."

"Interesting that the bastard took the gag with him."

"Trophy?" Art asked.

John stood, his gaze following along the edge of the blood beneath the tape. "Her throat was cut, yes?"

Biggs nodded.

"He severed her vocal chords. Since she couldn't scream anymore, he removed the gag and watched her die."

"Psychotic dick," Art murmured.

John stood. "It turned you on, watching her bleed out, didn't it?" Light shone through the back door. He imagined the creep slipping through and taking a moment to glance back at his handiwork. "But there were two more people in the house." He glanced back to the stairway that led to the bedrooms upstairs. "Two more people you could have killed."

"We have no reason to believe he'd look for another victim," Biggs said. "Looks personal, like she was a premeditated target."

John's gaze carried over the splatters of blood drying in the carpet fibers, over the lines marking the unnatural spread of her legs, and the final resting place of her hands. Oh, she was definitely the target.

And everything about the woman who'd died last week, despite the robbery consensus, had reeked of premeditated assault as well. Although he hadn't been able to prove that, yet.

Dak shimmied inside him, an erratic clatter within his ribs, as if the Ambient tried to hide beneath John's organs. The entity settled again, allowing John to regain his focus.

A slight chill touched his cheek as he walked through the back door and followed the red flags their team had placed along the path leading to the woods behind the house. John eyed the indents that they believed were footprints and the break in the shrubs beside the trees. "An easy getaway. But you knew that, didn't you?" The flags shifted in the breeze, a line of perfectly uniform soldiers. Maybe too perfect. "The parents were asleep. There was no reason to rush. You wouldn't have been so careless to leave tracks."

Dak shivered as John sauntered to the opposite side of the yard, taking in each blade of grass, each small rock, and each flower in the garden.

Bingo.

A row of marigolds lay on the ground in the middle of the floral border surrounding the property, their fluffy yellow heads smashed into the brown mulch. John looked back toward the house and to the woods. "You didn't really go into the woods where they marked the escape path, but you made it look that way, didn't you?" He turned back toward the house. "Commings!"

"Yeah, what you got?" His partner ran toward him, his white collared shirt untucking from his polyester pants.

John raised an arm, a warning for Art to keep his distance. "I need a team out here to block off this area. He didn't enter the woods where you first thought." He pointed to the right. "He entered right there."

"How do you know?"

"Because deer and rabbits don't crush plants like this. I need a mold. We might get a shoe size."

"A mold? Seriously? Wouldn't a digitally modulated image be better?"

"Nope. You know I'm old-fashioned. Take as many images as you want and then get me a mold." Crouching brought John closer to the flowers. A thin piece of light wood with a red and blue stripe rounding the edge stuck out from the darker mulch. "And get me an evidence bag. I think our perpetrator may have dropped something."

14

"You asked him out?" Laini threw a pillow at Tracy. "You have got to be kidding me."

Tracy bit back her grin. "It just kinda happened."

"But damn, girl, at a crime scene? You have way more balls than I do. I don't believe you did that."

"Me, neither, but when I saw him heading to that house..." John was maybe the only person she'd ever meet who understood what Tracy was going through. If he walked out of her life, she'd be alone with the entity inside her, lost to her own fears. She couldn't let him walk away before she'd made sure she could see him again. "I was afraid I wouldn't have the guts to call him later, and you know how it is. Sometimes guys act interested and then conveniently forget your number."

"Tell me about it." Laini shifted one foot under her butt. "Was it weird, though, seeing Melissa's house again?"

"Very weird."

Everything about today was kinda morbid, but she needed that link, that assurance that her life could still be normal, that everything was going to be okay. As crazy as asking John out right then seemed, she'd do it again. In a heartbeat.

Her gaze met Laini's. "Did you know that murderers come back to the crime scene? Anyone there could have been the killer."

"Yeah, I heard that on TV. That's why you wouldn't catch me anywhere near there."

Tracy shifted her weight. Each face refocused in her mind. "They all looked so normal. It could have been any one of them."

"Scary." Laini pulled her knees up and hugged them. "It almost makes you want to lock the front door and never come out."

Tracy nodded. Except now, for some reason, she wanted to go out more than ever.

15

"Fed up, that's what it is," Art said, throwing an evidence bag across the table at John.

"Come on, think. Melissa Harpoona and Diana Worth." John tacked their pictures onto a bulletin board. "Do they have anything in common?"

"Nothing. *Noth-ing.*" His partner crossed his arms.

John frowned. "Who crawled up your ass and died?"

Art baulked and closed his eyes. He grimaced.

"Hey, man, what's up with you?"

Art shook his head, shifting his graying hair. "It's nothing. Just not getting enough sleep."

Sleep? Art had been in the precinct far longer than John. Nothing phased the guy. Not until now, at least.

But they didn't have time for outside distractions.

A flash of Tracy Seavers's sparkling blue eyes crossed his thoughts. That tight-fitting T-shirt that showed off those round curves.

Dak fizzed like a soda, but John pushed the memory aside. It was bad enough Art was unfocussed. The last thing John needed was to be sidetracked by a nice rack.

Art leaned against his palm, stretching the skin around his right eye. "Could it be possible that your instincts are wrong, just this once?"

Could they?

John stared into Melissa Harpoona's eyes, then Diana Worth's. No. They were connected. He could *feel* it.

"I'm not ready to give up on the possibility, so I need you to think." John pointed at the war board. "What connects them?"

Art threw his hands in the air. "They're both blonde. I don't know. Nothing else matches. One is a mother, the other is single. One hung out in bars, the other was on the PTA. Other than them both being murdered, it's a dead end."

Sergeant Biggs entered the room, folder in hand. "Coroner's report came back, gentlemen. I think you'll find this interesting." He tossed the file to Art. "As Peters suspected, Melissa Harpoona was also raped."

Obviously. John gritted his teeth. He didn't need a goddamn autopsy to tell him that. "Give me something I can use."

"There you have it," Art whispered, shoving the file toward John. "Preliminary DNA match. You were right. This was the same asshole that killed Diana Worth."

Two murders—one short of a serial killer. Shit.

"Prelims have been known to be wrong, but let's act like this is the official report from the lab." Biggs turned to John. "You're up, Peters. Do your magic and nail this scumbag."

John ran his fingers through his hair. "I know we've got a great track record, but that was when we had cops working the beat; when I had a team of people to bounce ideas off of."

"What am I, chopped liver?" Art asked.

Biggs snorted. "This is an ugly one, Peters. I need to know you're in the game."

"When the hell haven't I been in the game?"

Biggs held up both hands, but his gaze didn't waver.

John stared back with Art shifting nervously in his periphery.

The Sergeant turned away. "Just give me this scumbag's ass on a platter." He yanked the door shut behind him.

Taking a deep breath, John turned to his friend.

Art suppressed a grin.

"What?" John asked.

"Nothin'. Just another day at the precinct."

16

Tracy fidgeted with her purse. Why were barstools so uncomfortable? She adjusted her ankles, trying to prop her heels on the bar below her. The dress and heels were probably a bad idea.

What had gotten into her, asking a guy out like that? Thank goodness he'd said yes, or she'd have felt like a complete oaf. But was he really interested, or only being polite?

And what about her? Was she really attracted to John, or just grabbing for someone who could help her through the insanity that had entered her life?

She sipped her drink. None of it mattered. At this point, they were only friends. But could they be more? A little shiver ran down her spine. The thought certainly didn't disgust her. With those broad shoulders, chiseled cheek bones, and that adorable dimple that somehow begged to be kissed, she was surprised he didn't have a girlfriend.

The heat within her chilled. He never actually said he *didn't* have a girlfriend. For all she knew, he was married. Did he have a ring on? Idiot. She never thought to check.

A tweak of pain spread behind her eyes and she massaged the

area between her brows. Maybe she'd overdressed for a friendly dinner, after all.

Across the bar, a woman laughed. Her hand splayed over a bosom much too large for her low-cut blouse. The man she was with barely glanced at her. Well, that wasn't true. His eyes stayed perched on her hand, as if willing her fingers to fall so her breasts would tumble over the bar top. Tracy imagined the scene in a perfume ad: An overly-boobed woman and a ruggedly-handsome man—hell, even his hair seemed to flow as if it were painted rather than combed. The man licked his lips, the desire in his eyes more apparent as they lingered on the cleavage bared for his amusement.

What would it take to have a man look at her like that? She glanced down at her un-noteworthy boobs. Probably about ten grand and a plastic surgeon. She sighed. Not that she wanted guys to senselessly lust after her, but a brief glance once in a while wouldn't be so bad.

She didn't have what it took to attract and keep a guy. They all left her, again and again. Four dates was her current record. Jason almost made it to five, if he'd stayed around long enough to take her out for her birthday. Asshole.

Since she'd turned thirty, relatives had started to whisper at family parties when she'd shown up alone. Most of her younger cousins had already married. A few of them had kids.

What was it about marriage and children that meant a life was complete, anyway?

She puffed out a breath. They meant everything…everything that Tracy didn't have.

Her three recent breakups scrolled through her mind before she stopped herself. Rehashing every moment of those nights wasn't helping. She'd done nothing wrong. None of the break-ups made sense. She'd even slept with a few of them.

Jason almost made her consider giving up on guys all together

—until a cute police detective flashed his dimples over a cup of coffee.

If John wasn't attached, could she make this work? Could he be the one to break the trend, or was this relationship doomed before it started, like everything else in her life?

The woman across the bar reached for her drink. Luckily, her boobs didn't become front page news. Her date glanced across the bar, his gaze falling on Tracy.

His intensity sucked the air from the room, riveting her to her stool. The noise of the bar receded, dulling behind a hum epicentered within. Something swirled in her chest and her heart went still.

Everything stopped.

The man tapped a box against his palm and slipped something between his lips. The room came alive again and he returned his attention to his date.

What the hell just happened?

Someone slipped onto the stool beside her. "Sorry I'm late."

Tracy jumped.

"Whoa there. Sorry," John said. "What were you so intent over?"

Tracy fixed her hair, steadying herself. "Oh, umm, nothing. Staring into space. Sorry."

The guy on the other side of the bar threw a few bills beside his empty glass and grabbed his date. At least the side-show was over. Tracy turned and froze anew. John's hair hung loose around his temples, free and relaxed. Her gaze slid down his gray blazer and over jet-black jeans covering what looked like well-oiled boots. He'd definitely dressed to make an impression. Damage done. If he had a wife, she certainly wasn't on his mind at the moment. She glanced down to his bronzed hands. No wedding band and no tan line. Score!

"So, are you ready to get something to eat?"

"Sounds good. I'm starved."

The hostess walked them up a long stairway to the second level and seated them beside a window overlooking a lake. Three Canadian geese floated across the still water. Beautiful.

John pulled out Tracy's chair, shifting the long mauve tablecloth as he helped her into a seat. Drop-dead gorgeous and a gentleman. Her luck was definitely on the mend.

He tugged on the lapels of his blazer as he took his seat. A guy like this probably had girls lined up. What was she thinking? Why invite disaster by going for someone so far out of her league?

The waitress rattled off the specials and left them to read the menus. Tracy perused the seafood section. Lobster Ravioli. Her tummy rumbled. Decision made.

"So, now you know I'm a detective, what does the lovely Miss Tracy do for a living?"

Uh-oh. Small talk had never been her strong point. This is where she'd normally confirm her one-way ticket to no second date. She took a deep breath. "Well, technically I'm still on medical leave. But it's back to work tomorrow."

John placed his menu to the left of his plate and took a sip of his water. "And where's that?"

"Olson's Soup. I work in the marketing department."

"Does that mean you make television commercials?"

She wished. "No. I do layouts for magazine ads."

"That sounds like fun."

"Yeah, I guess."

A waitress lumbered up the stairs with a tray of food. Why didn't they have an elevator for those poor people?

Tracy drew her attention back to John. "It's kind of uneventful. Nothing compared to a murder investigation."

His lips parted, and his gaze lowered to the table. Whoops. Bad move. She shouldn't have mentioned his job.

John's eyes settled on the floor to the right before returning to her. Dak again? "My job is usually pretty uneventful as well. Investigations like the one I am working on are rare, thank God."

"I'm sorry, I didn't mean to bring it up. We don't have to talk about work."

"No, it's okay. I know that television glamorizes what I do. It's natural to be curious."

His eyes strayed right again. Did Dak really talk to him all the time? If she and John did end up dating, she'd have to get used to that. John had a demanding job, and another being inside his head. That had to be a lot on a person.

She could see them on a date in two years, both staring into space while the aliens inside them yacked up the night, and neither she nor John would need to say a word. Or would Dak and Adonna need their hosts to talk to each other? The whole idea seemed so strange.

The waitress came and took their orders. John ordered a half carafe of wine and poured each of them a glass, filling his only half way. "I'm sure you have more questions for me about Adonna, so shoot."

Fantastic! Like he'd read her mind. She checked over her shoulder. The closest table with guests was on the opposite side of the room.

Tracy folded her hands on the edge of the table and leaned toward him. "What was the hardest thing to get used to?"

"Other than hearing voices in my head?" He laughed. "We still struggle a bit with…" He glanced at the tablecloth. "I guess you'd call it cultural differences."

"What does that mean?"

"Well, Dak is extremely tactile. He's used to reaching out and touching if he comes across someone he wants to meet. Even after five years, he still can't seem to understand personal boundaries."

He tapped the table with his fingers. Tracy tried to imagine what Dak might be saying to him. God, how would she ever get used to that?

John's gaze trailed to Tracy. "Can you sense any more of Adonna?"

She shook her head. "Barely anything. If Dak hadn't confirmed she was in there, I might have thought those agent guys were dipping into the contraband or something."

John nodded and took a few bites of his salad, his eyes staying centered on his plate. Had this been a normal date, she'd think she was failing miserably, but she kept reminding herself that there were three of them at the table. Well, technically four, but one of them wasn't up to talking yet.

His brow rose. His eyes closed a few times, as if something was frustrating him immensely.

Maybe some*one*, rather than some*thing* was vexing him from the inside.

John took a sip of wine. His hand shook slightly. "Dak was wondering if you had a boyfriend."

A little swirl tickled her stomach, a sensation that had nothing to do with her Ambient. "*Dak* was wondering?"

A smile shot across his lips. Could he get any cuter?

"Maybe I was wondering, as well," he said.

Her eyes burned, and she blinked before they teared. Tonight was getting better and better. "Nope. No boyfriend. Why, is Dak looking?"

"Dak is always looking." He glanced to the right and whispered one word she couldn't hear.

"What's he saying?"

"Now *that* I won't repeat." The cutest blush spread over his cheeks. "He's way more forward than I would ever be."

"Go ahead. Tell me."

He shifted his weight. "I-I can't."

Hmmm, intrigue abounds. "Come on. I understand it's him and not you."

John's eyes softened, almost as if a sense of relief eased his tension. Could he be as happy as she was to have found another host to talk to?

"No," John said. "He's teasing me all the time about certain things, but I am who I am, and he's going to have to deal with that." The edge of his lip twitched. Maybe John was getting teased at that very moment.

Their conversation turned to delicate banter over dinner. Talking, always the worst part of the date, flowed freely. John and Dak eased her into feeling more safe and secure than she'd felt in a very long time. Was it possible that she could fall for a random guy she ran into on the street? Well, she supposed it wasn't really random. Dak had thrown them together, but chance had brought them both to that same sidewalk at exactly the same time. Funny how fate worked.

John held her hand as he walked her to her car. The heat from his skin singed her palm, bordering on painful. John didn't seem to notice.

It must have been Dak. She gripped a little tighter and the sting became a tingle. Her heart fluttered. What was this curious alien really thinking? And could she ever be as comfortable being a host as John was? The detective seemed to take it all in stride. Hopefully it wouldn't take Tracy five years to accept and adapt to her new normal.

"This is my car," Tracy said.

John shifted his weight, his gaze carrying over her car and into the woods. "We had a great time tonight." His lips turned up into an almost-grin. He shook his head.

"What's wrong?"

"It's weird being able to say *we*. I usually have to hide Dak. Being with you: someone who understands, someone I can talk to, it's...I don't know. It's such a relief to be with someone I don't have to keep secrets from."

Tracy ran her fingers across his chin. Each touch, no matter where she placed her fingers, sizzled, tingled, and popped. What would it be like to strip off that blazer and hold him to her?

His gaze lingered on her lips before rising to her eyes.

"What's wrong?" she asked.

"This is the part of the night where my dates usually make a run for it."

Now *that* she found hard to believe. She ran the back of her fingers across his cheek. "I'm not running."

The color in his eyes deepened. He grabbed her hand, taking it from his face. "I'd really like to see you again." He glanced to the side. His whole body tensed.

"What, is Dak not interested?" Not that she thought that was true. She could feel the entity's heat, but she knew he'd said something to knock the strong, hardened police detective off kilter.

"On the contrary," John said. "If he had a body, I'd be peeling him off you right now."

A giggle burst from her lips. The sound surprised her. She warmed deep within. "I would definitely like to see you again."

"How about tomorrow night?" John gaped and stepped back. "No, that's a bit soon, umm…"

She squeezed his hand. "Tell Dak next Friday would be better for me. I'm going back to work tomorrow."

John nodded. "Dak said it's also appropriate for the guy to pick the girl up on a second date. I mean, if you're okay with that."

She was so glad she wasn't into the whole alpha-male dominant thing. What were the odds of her coming across a rugged, strong-on-the-outside guy, a cop no less, with those cute, quirky, not-so-sure of himself qualities that she had always found so endearing?

"I'm totally okay with that." She gave him her address and he typed it into his phone.

"Great. We're looking forward to it."

We're. The word still seemed a little odd. How long until she started to think of herself in the plural?

He brought her hand to his lips, placing a warm kiss on her knuckles. "Until Friday, then."

Wow, could he get any sexier?

17

The fluorescent light above Tracy's workstation buzzed. The air conditioning kicked in, dropping chilled air from places unseen. Tugging her sweater around her shoulders, she stared at the pile of proofs on her desk. They must have gotten tired of filling in for her somewhere around a week ago. Now these jobs would be behind schedule. It would be her fault, even though she had two superiors perfectly capable of spotting incorrect PMS codes and potential issues with the bleed.

Sighing, she grabbed the top proof and immediately noticed the lack of a cover sheet. Colonel Olson would have a cow if he'd heard someone hadn't followed company process. She grabbed the next job and the next, all without cover pages. How hard was it to grab a sheet from her desk tray? She reached for the cover sheet bin and found it empty. Idiots. God forbid someone made a few copies while she was gone.

She turned her chair to her computer, called up a blank cover sheet, and sent fifty copies to the printer. This was going to be a long day.

"Seavers!" Resident sales asshole, Scott McNulty, called to her as she passed his office. "Hey, welcome back. Good to see you."

His gaze remained fixed on what looked like football stats on his computer screen before he finally turned. "Any idea when you'll have my East Coast campaign ready? We can't let that fall behind. I handed it in early to make sure it was done. But then, you know." He waved his hand up and down like that could sum up being hit by a truck and out on disability for a month.

"I'll get right on it." She passed him by and looked over her shoulder. "I'm going to do the ones that were handed in correctly first. As long as you did your paperwork, I should have it done today." Tracy smirked as she reached the copy room. That pig never did his paperwork, even when the forms *were* on her desk. Served him right.

She snatched her copies off the machine and fanned through them. The pages warmed her fingertips. Closing her eyes, she touched the sheets to her cheek until they cooled. Strange, how something so simple could give her peace.

Tracy fanned through the copies again, concentrating on the words as they flashed past her eyes. So interesting how they were all the same. She plucked one of the center sheets out of the pile, placed it in the top paper tray, and pressed the green copy button. She giggled as an exact duplicate shot out of the side of the machine into the paper sorter. How fun!

She replaced the sheet and pressed the copy button again and again. Over and over, a warm duplicate appeared on top of the growing pile.

"Umm, Tracy?"

She jumped, spinning toward her boss, Miles Kremmer, standing inside the entrance to the copy room. His wide eyes fixed on her, then to the three-inch thick stack of copies in the sorter, and the mass of paper still in her hand.

"You okay?" he asked.

She tucked back a loose bang. "Yeah, I'm fine. Just making some copies."

He moved around her and placed his hand on an uneven stack

of papers several reams high, and then another right next to it. He held up a piece from each pile, both cover sheets. There were thousands of them.

Something deep in her gut sank. How long had she been in there making copies? Not that it mattered. She couldn't let on that there was something far more wrong with her than a recent car accident. "I-I needed cover sheets."

His brow furrowed. "I can see that." He pulled out a chair from the table beside the wall. "Why don't you sit down for a minute? You look a little pale."

She took the seat and Miles reached for the copies in her hand. She clenched her fingers, refusing to give them up.

The furrow in his brow grew deeper and she released her grip. They were copies, for goodness' sake.

But they were hers!

The room spun. When her vision cleared, she was on the floor, half-supported by Miles.

Within two hours, she was home, tucked in bed.

"Anything I can get you?" Laini asked.

"You already picked me up from work. You better get back before you get fired."

Laini placed Tracy's cell phone on the nightstand. "Call if you need anything."

Tracy's mind had already begun to fog by the time her roommate had closed her door.

A dog barking roused Tracy. The sun shone on her nightstand as her alarm clock changed from 10:12 to 10:13.

She startled herself the rest of the way awake. It was morning already? She'd slept an entire day?

Rubbing her temples, she replayed the incident in the copy

room over and over. Dammit. Maybe going back so soon wasn't such a good idea.

Tracy schlepped to the kitchen, popped a choco-bliss coffee cup into the machine, and put a piece of bread into the toaster. Her stomach rumbled, and she tapped her fingers on her thigh until her coffee mug finished filling. She sipped warm, sweet heaven, but her stomach only growled louder.

Setting her mug down, she grabbed a sleeve of chocolate bars from the cupboard. Laini wouldn't mind if she borrowed one. She ripped open the wrapper and shoved the chocolate into her mouth. While the toaster's timer ticked, she tore into another bar, and a third by the time the bell finally dinged.

She settled onto the couch with her toast, coffee, and the rest of the sleeve of chocolate. The small pile of Hershey wrappers on the counter in the kitchen caught her attention. She couldn't possibly have eaten all of those.

But she had.

Or someone inside her had.

Chocolate. Photocopies. Oversleeping.

What next? She rubbed her eyes. Setting her drink on the end table, she perused the collection of paperbacks piled bedside the lamp. One with an embossed silver dragon on the cover called to her. She settled in to the soft cushions, opened the book, and lost herself until the front door opened and Laini came in.

Tracy glanced at the clock: 5:32 PM.

Holy shit! She'd been sitting there for seven hours!

She set the book beside her and tried to get up, but her legs buckled. She fell back as tingling waves rolled up and down her calves.

Laini stopped in the kitchen and fingered the empty chocolate wrappers. "I guess you're feeling better?"

Tracy shook her head. No, she was not feeling better at all.

18

John's grip tightened on the steering wheel. Despite falling into bed early last night, his eyes blurred and stung as if he'd partied his ass off.

He got out of the car and grimaced at the lone police car parked in front of the municipal building. The dozens of cars that used to call this building home base had been placed in storage last week. They'd probably be repainted and sold at auction. He shook his head. No one benefited from police layoffs.

He ripped the *Office Space for Rent* sign off the door and threw it in the bushes. It landed on the previous sign he'd thrown there a few days ago. They'd give up sooner or later.

Art Commings handed him a coffee as he walked through the lobby.

John grimaced. "Hand-delivering the java? Must be bad news."

Art took up stride beside him, waving a folder. "Alexandra Nixon, thirty-six years old from Marlton. Single, last seen by her neighbor at about six p.m. Sunday night getting into her car. *Dressed like a tramp*, he said."

Snatching the folder, John pushed the door of the war room

open. He took a sip of the coffee before setting the paper cup on the long, laminate-covered table. "Is she a prostitute?"

"Unconfirmed, but we don't believe so. She lives in a pretty ritzy neighborhood. Works in upper management at Stockton and Alberts. She's a six-figure executive."

John opened the folder and withdrew her picture. "She's a brunette."

"Yeah, so I guess our guy isn't only looking for blondes."

"If this is even our guy. Don't be so quick to jump to conclusions." John rubbed his chin. "So, she's been gone two and a half days. Is there any past history of disappearance?"

"None. Employer says she's always on time. She missed several meetings on Tuesday, one jeopardizing a deal she'd been working on for months."

John picked up the photo and placed her beside Melissa and Diana on the war board.

"Her friends say she's a partier. Spends a lot of time in bars."

"Could she have known Melissa Harpoona?"

"We couldn't find any connection."

John rubbed his chin, staring into each woman's eyes. Diana had been found on the walkway in front of her favorite pizza shop. She went missing and died the same day. Melissa had been gone for three days before being found in her parents' house.

How did Alexandra connect, if she connected at all?

John placed both palms against the board and stared into Alexandra's eyes. "Where are you?" he whispered.

The last two victims didn't show up on the radar until they were already dead. This could be completely unrelated.

But it wasn't. Deep down, he knew.

If their perpetrator kept up his MO, she was probably dead already. But if she was dead, why hadn't anyone found her? He'd made no attempt to hide his victims yet, why start now?

The woman's eyes reached out to him, begging. He dove deep

into her gaze. There had to be a connection. Something. Her irises came into clear focus.

He leaned back. "Green."

"Green?"

"They all have green eyes."

19

Tracy tugged at her hair, considering the even higher pile of ads waiting for her approval that morning. Miles had given her an extra two days off, but he'd made no attempt to lighten the workload for her return. She considered the tower of photocopied cover sheets sitting on the edge of her desk. At least the results of her copying spree hadn't gone to waste.

She grabbed the first job and stared at the graphics. Her eyes blurred slightly, and she rubbed them. McNulty walked past her cubicle, glanced at her, and snorted. Asshole.

Like it wasn't bad enough that everyone had stared at her as she walked through the door this morning. But after Monday, she couldn't blame them. The whispers started instantly: *the mad copy machine addict, back for another go at the Xerox.*

She sighed. How long would it take for everyone to get over this new little tidbit of office gossip? She'd be the resident freak until something else happened to garner their attention. Office life was going to suck until that blessed day arrived.

Tracy checked the margins and PMS colors on the *Parent One* ad campaign and scrolled her name on the signature line. Her gaze carried over the remaining ads and to the hallway.

What was out there other than the copy machine that she could play with?

Play with?

She shook the fog from her head and grabbed the next ad off the top of the pile. It had been too long since she'd been in the office. She needed to retrain herself to focus.

At least that's what she wanted to believe.

Something twitched in her stomach and she ran her palm over her abdomen. Her eyes stung, and she blinked back welling tears. The truth was hard to ignore. Adonna was waking up.

But Tracy would be fine. She could do this.

20

John turned right, pulling onto Route 42 heading toward Winslow. According to dispatch, they'd sent two patrol cars to answer the call after a maid at a local motel found a woman's body tied to a bed. Fifteen minutes later, another call from the neighboring building reported shots fired. Why it took them over an hour to get this information to him, he didn't know.

John gritted his teeth and did his best to not linger on the incompetency. The longer it took him to get there, the more chance of the evidence being compromised. He had the best shot of finding something useful in a fresh crime scene.

Dak shook, bouncing between John's temples. John conjured every happy thought he could come up with, doing his best to calm his friend down.

I don't want to look at the body.

"I have to, buddy. It's my job."

But they all look the same. I don't understand, if blood is so important to you, why does it come out so easily?

"It's just the way it is. Would you mind giving me a little quiet to think?"

Police tape cordoned off the parking lot of the Royal Dove Inn.

He'd investigated a missing person at this establishment a few years ago. Interesting layout for a South Jersey hotel. One of the few places that boasted a front and back door to each unit. His gaze carried over the top of the building and traveled along the vast expanse of woods behind the building. This piece of the puzzle wasn't new. There were trees behind the pizza place, as well as the Harpoona's residence.

Not a coincidence.

Sergeant Biggs flagged him down. "Looks like one of our guys may have shot someone fleeing the scene but the suspect got away. Commings had them tape off some blood in the trees." His gaze carried to a patrol car leaving the scene. "Everyone not directly involved here is already searching the perimeter. This asshole is bleeding. We'll find him."

"Where's the cop who shot him?"

"At Winslow Township Municipal. I'm heading down there now. But *you* I want in that crime scene."

John nodded and headed toward the open police-guarded door to room number twenty-five.

Forensics had beaten him to the scene and were still processing the victim when he arrived.

One of them held up a driver's license between his gloved fingers. "Alexandra Nixon."

John nodded. Giving them room, he took a quick scan of the body and the splash of blood on the wall before he slipped out the sliding glass door.

Art stepped out with him. "That's all? You're not going to yell at anyone for trampling evidence?"

"Why bother?" He saw what he needed to see. The amount of blood and the position of the body told the story.

He stared past the narrow rear parking lot and into the forest —the same forest their perpetrator had stared at. The trees were important to him. It was probably something more than an escape route, something John hadn't figured out yet.

The change in length of event for each murder didn't add up. One night for the first victim, three nights for the second, and five nights for the third. Was he getting more comfortable, or was it something completely different?

"You wanna see the blood in the woods?" Art pointed to yellow police tape shifting in the breeze behind some brush.

John held up a hand, silencing him.

In the room, Forensics prepared to load the body into a bag for transport. Only her right leg and foot were visible at this angle. John turned his attention back toward the trees. "He had her tied up for days. Raped her repeatedly. He took his time."

Art shifted beside him. "How did you get that from a one-minute walk through?"

John continued to scan the trees to either side of the flapping yellow tape. "The abrasions on her wrists, under the ropes. Signs of struggle but time to heal in between. She had some quiet intervals. Maybe he left her during the day and came back each night."

"Shitbag," Art whispered.

The wind picked up, breaking a piece of the marking tape, leaving it to fly free. The murderer was out there somewhere, gloating.

What was his after-murder ritual? Did he sit alone and have a cup of tea? Did he go somewhere public and watch the news? Or did he stew over what he'd done, remembering every second, maybe even relishing it?

"Some of those lacerations on her stomach have a few days of healing," John whispered. "You cut her a little bit each day, didn't you? You liked to watch the blood spill across her skin. Why? Was it power? Did it make you feel strong? Did you get off on it?"

His partner chewed his cheek beside him. "You get freaking scary sometimes, you know that?"

Inside, Forensics picked items out of the carpet and placed them inside small plastic bags. Over the next few days, they'd find it was remnants of past guests. The killer only left behind what he wanted them to find. That part he'd been consistent on, but eventually his arrogance would lead to a mistake, and John was more than ready to call this bastard on it.

However, he had to find this nut bag *before* he made that mistake. Tonight, this lunatic would be out looking for his next victim. The only way to stop that now would be to keep every green-eyed woman within a twenty-mile radius locked tightly in their own homes. And since that wasn't likely to happen anytime this century, he had to work faster than ever.

"Let's take a look at the blood you found." John stepped off the back patio square.

This is making me hurt. Can we think about something more pleasant...like Tracy?

It's my job to save lives. I can't do that if my mind is on a woman.

Art slipped his hands in his pockets and strode silently beside John as they walked toward the trees, scanning the asphalt and the surrounding parking spaces.

Until a week ago, John had given up on dating. After Amy, he'd had a few first dates, but never any second dates. After a while, he had no dates at all. How could he try to have a serious relationship with someone who couldn't understand what it was like to have a completely different person inside him?

That's why Tracy and Adonna are perfect.

John bent to get a closer look at a pile of stones near the curb. *You haven't even officially met Adonna.*

But I know she'll like me. What's not to like?

John straightened and headed into the woods. Dak had gotten better and better at distracting him; and Tracy was too tempting a diversion.

Damn, those eyelashes, those lips…

"Penny for your thoughts." Art came up from behind.

John grimaced. He needed to keep his focus on the case. "Our guys rattled him. Somehow, we caught him off guard and he panicked. Ran straight into the woods, rather than one of his well-calculated exits."

"So, you do think this is the same guy?"

John crouched beside a scattering of crimson-stained oak leaves. "Yeah, I do." He straightened. "I need to talk to the cop."

Stopped at a red light, John rubbed his burning eyes. His shoulder ached like he'd taken a beating. It seemed like he'd hardly slept at all, but he couldn't remember lying awake last night. Maybe he slept too deeply, or in a bad position. He massaged his shoulder. Coffee. He definitely needed more coffee.

Dak fizzled to the surface, swirling below his hand, relieving some of the ache. *Please feel better, John. I'm looking forward to you having the sex with Tracy tonight.*

John straightened. "Jumping the gun a little, aren't we? It's only a second date."

Come on, she's perfect. You know she is. Don't you want to touch her?

The light changed, and he pulled onto a neighborhood street. "You told me Adonna was too weak. She probably won't be able to do whatever it is that you guys do to each other."

I can give her joy even if she's too weak to give in return. And remember, I feel what you feel. A human orgasm is almost as good as the real thing.

John snorted at his friend's probably un-intentional snub. But Dak had done what he did best...distract John. He had to admit, there was a light in Tracy's eyes when she smiled. There was something about the innocence wrapped up inside the outwardly modern woman that made him want to pull her into his arms and protect her from the reality of this godforsaken world.

A shimmer ran through his stomach that probably had little to do with his Ambient. Not to mention the tightening in his pants. "I really like this girl, Dak."

I know. That's why we should have the sex.

"It's too soon. I don't want to scare her off. And I'm also in the middle of a multiple murder investigation. I don't have time to—"

The car stopped suddenly. John couldn't move his foot from the brake pedal.

He glanced at his rearview mirror into his own eyes. "Get your foot off the brake, Dak."

Thank goodness there was no one else on the residential road.

His hands shook under Dak's fury. *Don't you dare ruin this for us. Tracy is a one-in-a-million chance. You like each other. Why would you even think of not going after her?*

"The timing is bad. Don't you get that?"

The timing is always going to be bad. She's not Amy. It's going to be different this time.

Was he really using his job as an excuse to avoid being hurt again? Maybe.

His leg relaxed and he removed his foot from the brake. Dak was always more amicable once John bent to his way of thinking. But then again, it was probably easier for Dak to live within his host when John took the time to consider things from his Ambient's perspective.

"I'm not going to do anything to ruin our chances with Tracy."

I need this, John.

"I understand, but you need to remember that there is a human girl involved. One with feelings. I can't just *do her* in the back of my car so you can get your rocks off."

Every muscle in his body tensed. Dak didn't say it, but his entire being screamed *why not?*

"How could you have lived in three other people all these years and not learned anything about humanity?"

An empty stillness encompassed him for several seconds.

I want you to be happy.

"I want you to be happy, too. Give me time, okay?"

Dak slipped deeper into John's psyche as they drove into the Winslow Municipal parking lot. John parked between Sergeant Biggs's Chevy and a black and white patrol car. An *Available* sign stood on the front lawn. He'd thought this building had been closed already. With the number of empty spaces in the parking lot, it certainly wasn't the police hub it had been six months ago.

Voices shouted from the rear of the building. One of them was his boss.

"I told you, I shot him," a uniformed officer yelled in Biggs's face; not the best thing for a cop to do if they wanted to keep their job.

John placed himself between the arguing men. "I'm Detective John Peters. Is there something about this case I need to be made aware of?"

The officer who had spoken, Doogan from the badge on his shirt, shifted his bulky form. John knew the type: tall, muscular, and used to using his size and uniform to intimidate people. He'd been no different at his age.

"Forensics thinks the blood in the woods was from the girl," Doogan said. "It wasn't. I shot the fucker. I saw him fall."

John raised his hand. "You were one of the first officers on the scene? What did you see?" A flutter ran through John's stomach. Dak must have been nervous about having to hear about the murders again.

Doogan thrust his chest out. "We answered the call. We found the girl and I saw a man running into the trees. I identified myself as a police officer, but he kept running. I took two shots and he fell."

John raised a brow. "You shot a man in the back?"

"No." Doogan's eyes darkened. "I shot a cold-blooded-killer in the back. We combed the woods, though. Once the blood trail stopped, there was no sign of him."

"Did anyone else see the suspect?"

Doogan shrugged. "No, but I pegged the bastard. I know I did."

Spoken as if he was proud of shooting an unarmed man. Idiot. But maybe they could use this to their advantage.

John turned to Biggs. "Have we checked local hospitals?"

"Of course." Biggs gave him that *'I'm not an idiot'* look and held out his hand to Doogan. "I'll need your gun and badge."

The cop's face reddened. "Seriously?"

"You know the rules. Desk duty. Should be temporary."

He slammed the weapon and badge into the sergeant's hand. "This is bullshit." He scowled and stomped away, grumbling colorful obscenities.

Biggs shook his head and flipped Doogan's badge over in his palm.

"Do you think he saw the killer?" John asked.

"Inconclusive. They are running a DNA scan."

John tapped his finger against his bottom lip. Maybe the perpetrator was starting to get sloppy, after all. John would need to meet with Forensics, and then get Doogan into a room alone where he wasn't peacocking in front of a superior. This might be the break he needed.

John glanced up to the clock on the wall. One-fifteen. Hopefully he'd have enough time to make a dent in this case and still make his date with Tracy. Dak shimmied, but remained silent. Maybe his friend knew the inevitable. This was going to be a long night and John had a feeling Tracy wouldn't be a part of it.

21

Tracy's cell phone chimed. She put the last dabs of mascara on her lashes then grabbed her phone.

The caller ID read: *John*.

"Hey, you. I'll be ready soon." Silence answered her. She bit her lip as her stomach sank. "John? Is everything okay?"

"Yeah. Listen, I'm sorry. I was hoping I'd be able to get out on time, but…"

But. There was always a *but*. Tracy closed her eyes to ward off the tears. She'd hoped John would be different.

His sigh permeated the line. "There's been a development in the case. I don't think I'll be good company tonight. I'm sorry."

Tracy ran her hands over her skirt. She instantly felt sorry for thinking bad of him. The guy was involved in a murder investigation, for goodness' sake. "That's okay. I hadn't really started getting ready yet." Well, she still had to put on lipstick, so it wasn't a complete lie.

"Listen, I don't want you to think we're trying to get out of this or anything."

We're trying. The plural barely even sounded funny anymore.

"Can we get together tomorrow, maybe for lunch? I'm sure I

can squeeze in at least an hour. We really want to see you. I've been trying to explain to Dak that the timing has been bad."

"It's okay. Really, I understand." And she did, oddly enough. Usually, Tracy got bad vibes from some guys, but John's were good. How could she feel threatened by a man trying to save people's lives? "How about we meet tomorrow at a Starbucks or something?"

There was a brief silence. "Dak still says I should be picking you up for a second date, but if you could meet me, that would give us some extra time. My schedule is going to be nuts until this case is closed."

Until he caught the killer, he meant. Funny how he worded it so it sounded like another day at the office. "Name the place and I'll be there."

"How about the Starbucks on Route 42? Do you know it?"

"Northbound? Yeah, I do."

"How about one o'clock?"

"I'll be there."

She hung up the phone, slammed her makeup box shut, and slid it across the bathroom counter. She wasn't mad that John had cancelled her date, but disappointment was inevitable after looking forward to seeing him for an entire week.

Her skirt shifted around her hips. A weightless sensation came over her, mixed with an air of giddiness.

Adonna? It certainly didn't feel like her own emotion.

She turned her waist again, and the fabric glided back and forth. Did her Ambient maybe like to dance? Was that why the movement of the fabric sent tingles up her spine?

Tracy placed her hands on her hips and stared at her reflection. Well, why not? No one said she needed a date to go out and enjoy herself, right? She tousled her bangs and grabbed the hairspray as the radio on her nightstand cut to the news: more about the murders, and a warning that the killer was still on the loose.

"*Local law enforcement advises women to use caution when traveling alone,*" the announcer said.

Well, she wouldn't have been alone if she hadn't been stood up. She stared at her reflection. She hadn't been stood up. She'd been postponed. Big difference. But she still wanted to go out.

"Laini!" She walked down the hall and into the living room.

Her roommate sat with her feet up on a recliner and a book in her hands. "What's up?"

"Let's go out for a while."

Laini set her book down and folded her arms. "Don't tell me the cop dumped you already."

"No. He's stuck on a case. We're meeting for lunch tomorrow, instead."

"Instant make-up date? Three extra points for Inspector Gadget." She pushed her footrest down. "He must like you."

Tracy's cheeks heated. The thought had occurred to her, but she wasn't ready to get her hopes up. After all, he didn't even kiss her yet. Disheartened, she pushed the thought aside. "So, what do you think? Are you up for a drink?"

"You know what, why not?"

A few swipes of lipstick and a short car ride later, they settled onto a set of stools at the Shoreline Bar and Grille. Two couples swayed to a slow song on an otherwise empty dance floor. A few girls sat at tables along the wall. Not really the party Tracy was hoping for.

Laini leaned toward her. "There is no way I'm dancing unless I can hide in a crowd of people. Let's get that perfectly clear."

"You'll get no argument from me." She glanced back at the door. "Do you want to leave?"

The bartender wiped his hands on a towel. Deep mocha biceps

stretched the short, black cotton sleeves of his T-shirt as he rested his elbows on the bar. "What can I get you ladies?"

Laini's mouth snapped shut before falling open again. "I'll, umm, have…" She stared at him until he laughed.

Cute bartender. Hmm. For Laini's sake, they could stay for a drink or two.

"Get her a bay breeze," Tracy said. "I'll have a white wine spritzer."

He threw the towel over his shoulder. "You got it. I'll be right back."

Tracy handed Laini a napkin. "You're drooling."

She covered her bright pink cheeks with the small white square. "Oh my gosh, he had blue eyes. Did you see his eyes?"

"Sorry, I didn't see the ebony god's eyes because they were too busy undressing my best friend."

Laini's gaze widened. "Do you think so?"

She turned toward the end of the bar as the bartender bent over to grasp a glass. His tight jeans left little to the imagination. Dang.

"I am so going over there and talking to him." She stood.

"But he'll be back with our drinks in a minute."

She tapped the napkin on the counter. "If I don't go ahead and do it, I'm gonna chicken out."

Laini straightened her skirt as she skated down to the end of the bar. Adonis flashed her a million-dollar smile as she lolled over the far side of the counter toward him. He better not just be working up a good tip. Her roommate deserved better.

Laini never complained as much as Tracy did, but they were both in the same boat: thirty, single, and no prospects. Well, Tracy had one now, but she wasn't quite ready to put her handsome detective on the marriage radar yet.

Tracy jerked up in her seat as if struck by an electric current. A swirl moved within her, jittering. She took a deep breath and rubbed her stomach as someone stepped up to the bar beside her.

A deep southern drawl filled her ears. "One of us doesn't belong here, and I don't think it's me."

"What's that supposed to mean?" Tracy turned toward the blue eyes of the guy from the bar last week. Mr. Intensity. The stale air touched her tongue as she gaped.

"This place is usually a tramp-fest," he said. "You don't look much like a tramp."

That had to be the worst line ever. "Really? What do I look like?"

"A nice girl."

Wow, that was even lamer than she expected. "And I suppose you're looking for a nice girl?"

He laughed and ordered a gin and tonic from a different bartender. "Nope. I was looking for a tramp."

Tracy could feel her eyes widen, not expecting that kind of honesty.

He gestured over to the table of girls. "Except for that group of kids who came in with fake ID's, the pickings are pretty slim tonight."

"So you came over to talk to the nice girl?"

"Yeah, well, I figure if I can't get laid, I might as well have some friendly conversation."

Damn, was this guy candid or what? "Conversation is as good as sex?"

"Not always. Sometimes the conversation is better."

She tried to control the dumbfounded stare that she was sure had plastered itself across her face as he drew a small box from his pocket and tapped it into his palm. The contents shook against the metal sides of the container until a small, thin toothpick appeared. He shoved it between his lips and ran his thumb over the embossed picture on the front of the case.

Tracy raised an eyebrow. "You don't strike me as the toothpick type."

He shrugged. "Do I strike you as the smoking type? 'Cause I use these to curb my much nastier habit."

"You use toothpicks to quit smoking?"

"Yeah. The patches worked great, but it was harder to curb the habit of having something in my hands and mouth."

"Good for you." That sounded stupid, but she could never relate to people who smoked. She'd never even been tempted to try.

Across the bar, Laini and the cute bartender spoke over both the drinks he'd made. Had Laini forgotten she'd come here with somebody?

The southerner tapped the top of the tarnished box. Twice his brow arched as he glanced in Tracy's direction, as if there were something about her he was trying to figure out.

Uncomfortable under his stare, she centered her attention on the metal box he passed back and forth between his hands. "That looks like an antique."

His brow rose. "Actually, it is. My daddy and his daddy before him used this very same box to carry their toothpicks. I never in a million years thought I'd carry it in my pocket like they did. But here I am, the third generation of toothpick dweebs." He handed her the box.

The picture on the front showed an embossed peach with a red and blue circle around it. "Does this symbol mean something?" She handed the container back to him.

"Yeah. That's the symbol of my family's plantation in Georgia."

"You grow peaches?"

"Me? No. My family did a long time ago. This little box and a few thousand toothpicks to fill it are all that's left of those days. I think that land is an outlet mall now or something."

"Oh, I'm sorry."

He grimaced. "No worries. That was long before I gave a damn about any of it." The container reflected the lights above the bar as he slipped the tin into his pocket. "I do remember running through those trees as a kid, but not much else about the place." A sense of calm coated him, as if the memory of the trees gave him peace.

The plantation must have been like a magical playground. Her earliest memories were of the countless daycare centers she'd been left in. She'd never even seen a park until she was twelve. But her mom had worked hard to make the best of their time together. Tracy had always been thankful for that.

The peach-guy eased onto a bar stool as his gaze dropped over her. "Dressed like that in a place like this. Let me guess: some asshole stood you up." His gin and tonic arrived, and he took a sip.

"It wasn't like that."

"It never is."

What was she supposed to say to that? Tracy's personal life was none of his stinking business. "What happened to the blonde you were with last week?"

His head tilted back, and he laughed. "Yeah, I thought you looked familiar." He shrugged. "That, well, that really didn't work out." He reached for his drink again but hit the glass instead. His drink sloshed across the counter, soaking Tracy's blouse.

"Oh, crap, I'm so sorry, darlin'." He grabbed a few napkins and turned toward her. He hesitated and handed her the white squares. "Maybe you should do that yourself."

She laughed and dabbed the drink from the front of her shirt before taking the extra napkins he offered. The tips of their fingers touched and a jolt of electricity shot up her arm.

She dropped the napkins, forgetting about her outfit.

He stared at her, wide-eyed. "What in Sam Hill was that?"

Her fingers still tingled. Her hand hummed. Something inside Tracy shook, like pure glee waiting to explode with nowhere to go.

This guy had an Ambient inside him, and from his expression, he either had no idea he wasn't alone, or he'd never touched another host. Ho-lee-shit.

She dried herself off, still undecided about what, if anything, she should say. John had a badge to hide behind, and he was sure to flash it before he mentioned Dak so she wouldn't think he was out of his mind. All she had to show this guy was a wet blouse.

When she placed the damp napkins down on the bar, the southerner was in exactly the same position, staring at her. His beautiful blue eyes quaked. His lip trembled.

"My name is Tracy." She held out her palm.

He stared at her fingers as if they might bite him.

"Sean," he finally said. He didn't take her hand.

Might as well try to ease into this. "Did you feel something strange when we touched?"

"Shit yeah." His gaze lingered on her fingers, her wrist, her arm. "What was that?" He reached out toward her but drew back. "Why do I feel like I'm going to die if I don't touch you again?"

Every molecule in her body cried out. She inched toward him, but the pressure in her mind, in her blood, in her very being, coaxed her even closer.

Like she would die if she didn't touch him? Yes. Exactly like that. But why? She didn't feel that way about Dak.

Sean took a deep breath and grabbed her hand. A new pressure dove through her skin. An Ambient. Not gentle and searching like Dak, but strong, demanding, needy. And sure as hell not afraid to take what it wanted. A firecracker exploded in her chest and she clenched her teeth to keep from crying out.

Sean pushed her away. "Fuckin' A." When his eyes returned to her, they were filled with a hunger that sent a chill to her core.

She stumbled from her stool and stepped back despite an inner push to climb on top of him and comingle his body with hers.

Wait. *Comingle?*

Her sense of reason wavered as the chill was replaced with heat. She blinked and shook her head. The fog subsided before rushing back and prodding her toward him.

Tracy staggered forward, and Sean grabbed her shoulder. A deep pressure formed under her skin beneath his grip. A silent curse crossed her lips. Why did she have to wear sleeves?

Shaking her head again, she tried to steady herself. Why did she care if she had sleeves on or not? Tracy stiffened. She didn't care, but the being inside her—the one who craved skin to skin contact—did.

Oh, shit.

Sean's eyes never left hers as he threw a few bills on the bar top, took Tracy's hand, and pulled her to the door.

Wait! Tracy blanched, realizing the word she'd tried to scream hadn't left her lips. And she was walking. With him. Toward the exit. *Laini!*

The female bartender shouted to them. "Sir, you left two twenties here."

"Keep the change," Sean shouted over his shoulder, quickening his pace.

Tracy matched him, the swirling heat inside her driving her forward through a fog. A dull hum drove out all but the sensation of their entities stroking each other through the touch of their fingers.

They walked toward a blue sedan and Sean opened the passenger side door for her.

No! I am not getting in that car with you!

But her body ignored her, slipping into the leather seat and reclining.

Sean glided into the driver's seat and closed the door. His gaze combed over her as he moistened his lips. Tracy's gut clenched, but the thought of his mouth not being on her drove her to madness. A burning sensation rolled over her skin and she leapt toward him, assaulting his mouth with her tongue. He growled, a deep guttural sound of need that shook her entire body as his tongue jammed between her lips.

A wave of nausea swept over her, but the swirling need pushed it back. She tried to shove him away, to scream, but her body moved on its own, as if she weren't even there.

Need, the deep, ethereal voice boomed within Tracy. Her own voice, but yet, not.

Oh God!

Want

No! Don't want! Stop this!

Tracy slammed her hand against the steering wheel, wishing she could push it out of the way so she could cover more of his skin with hers.

She bit at his lower lip as he pulled her blouse out of her skirt and rubbed his hands over her stomach.

Tracy tried to wince away, but the tingle of the touch overtook her, driving her consciousness deeper down, as if she'd fallen into a pit.

More.

Her silent scream filled only her mind as her own hands unbuttoned her blouse and released the clasp between her breasts.

Sean's eyes widened, and she guided his head to her chest. He smiled before her breast disappeared into his mouth. He sucked deeply, driving her Ambient to a mad fury as Tracy fought against the steering wheel to mount him.

He growled, his eyes dark and menacing as he shoved her off him and back to the passenger seat. He crawled over the shift between the seats, driving his tongue deep into her mouth. She sucked greedily, all sense of reason gone. She reached between his legs. She needed to touch him, feel how much he wanted her.

No! Adonna, no! I don't want this. You need to stop. Jesus, please stop!

The swirling ball inside her shuddered, weakening. Tracy willed her fingers to claw at Sean, to beat him off, and they twitched.

They twitched!

Adonna slipped away in a whoosh. Tiny tendrils of energy shot through Tracy, stinging her muscles, trying to regain hold.

Tracy pushed with all her will to keep the Ambient from taking control again. But Sean's merciless grip dug into her arms. She screamed into his mouth, tears streaming down her cheeks.

A slam against the window startled them both and the door opened. Tracy tumbled out as the Ambient receded in a whoosh, releasing her as Tracy stared up into Laini's fiery brown eyes.

"What the...?" Her friend turned to Sean. "Who the hell are you?"

Tracy's legs wobbled as she grabbed her roommate. "Come on. We have to go."

Laini held her up and they stumbled from the car. Each step seemed harder than the last, as if the blood running through Tracy's body was reaching out to the man who still sat in the car with his forehead now resting against the steering wheel.

"This is not cool," Laini said. "This is so not cool!"

No, it wasn't cool. Tracy had been taken over. Her body had been used without her permission, and she could do no more than watch. The helplessness, the powerlessness.

Her knees gave way as Laini dragged her to the passenger side of her Toyota.

"Stay with me, girl," Laini whispered, opening the door and helping her inside.

When Laini eased behind the steering wheel, she brought her cell phone to her ear and engaged the power locks. "Yo," she said into the phone. "We're in the parking lot of the Shoreline Bar and Grille and some psycho just attacked my friend." She turned the keys in the ignition.

Oh, shit. She'd called 911.

"No!" Tracy jolted up in the seat. "It's okay, let's just leave."

"Like hell it's okay." She pulled out of the parking spot and the wheels screeched as she pressed the gas pedal. "He's driving a—" She looked over her shoulder, back toward Sean's car.

"No!" Tracy repeated, snatching the phone and clicking the *off* button. "It's not like that. It's okay."

Tears had formed in Laini's eyes, but she still drove out of the lot. "You're crazy. You are freaking crazy. I know you didn't leave a bar with someone you just met. That is soooo not like you." She sniffed. "I saw you with a guy and a few minutes later I looked up and you were gone. I know you weren't drunk because you didn't even have your drink yet." She wiped her nose. "Then I find you outside in that asshole's car, obviously fighting him off you."

"It's not what you think."

She pulled into the bustling parking lot of a pizza place and parked. Laini turned, shaking. "Then what the hell was it? What's going on?"

Well, you see, Laines, I have an alien inside me, and so did the asshole. They used our bodies without our permission. God, even if she could tell Laini, she'd never believe her.

And what the hell *had* happened?

Was Adonna finally waking up? Was she starving for contact like Dak seemed to be? She thought about John, working late trying to make all of South Jersey safe again. How had she repaid him for his dedication? By grabbing the first guy she found in a bar.

She covered her face. No, it wasn't her. It was Adonna. The Ambient saw something she wanted and decided to take it, Tracy be damned.

Laini propped her arm on the steering wheel, her eyes set and defiant. How could Tracy explain without telling her the truth?

"Things have been really weird since the accident. Sometimes I don't even know who I am anymore." Tracy covered her eyes as tears streamed from her cheeks. "I don't know what to do."

"Dude," Laini said. "I can't even imagine." She shuffled closer and hugged Tracy. "I'd be totally weirded out, too, if I'd lost two weeks of my life; but hooking up with a guy you've never met is not the answer. You would have hated yourself tomorrow."

Hated and then some.

Laini leaned back. "Maybe you should talk to someone? You know, professional help?"

Tracy straightened. "I do *not* need a shrink."

"Okay, okay, I'm sorry, but I'm worried about you. I lost you once. It sucked. I don't want to lose you again."

She doesn't want to lose me.

Tracy didn't want to lose herself, either.

The silence between them hung like a veil the rest of the ride home. The pained look on Laini's face as Tracy slumped off to bed stung like a lance through her chest. They'd been inseparable since middle school, like sisters. There was no one Tracy wanted to confide in more. But how could she ever talk to anyone about this?

John's warm smile seeped into her thoughts. He'd understand. Maybe he was the only one who could. Explaining this night without ruining her chances with him was the problem.

She rubbed her eyes. What was she going to do?

22

John checked his hair in the rearview mirror. He blinked, hoping to lessen the puffiness around his eyes. He looked like he hadn't slept in months. Maybe this case was getting to him more than he realized.

You look great. Let's get going

Glancing through the Starbucks windows, he wondered if Tracy was ticked off about last night. What if she didn't show up?

You won't know unless you get your ass in there.

"All right, all right. I'm going already."

He slipped through the door, and stopped in the vestibule. Tracy stood at the counter beside a bag and two drinks. A smooth warmth flooded him. He paused for a moment, drinking her in. He sure as hell could get lost in that smile.

"Hey, guys," she said. "I decided to order and have it ready when you got here. I hope you don't mind."

Touch her.

No.

Please?

John kissed her cheek. A slight zap tickled his lips as Dak reached for Adonna. Dak recoiled inside him. *Something wrong?*

She's exhausted. Worse than before.

John took the coffee and followed Tracy toward the back room. "Are you guys okay? Dak seems to think Adonna is tired, like she's exerted herself or something."

Tracy flinched as she sat opposite him. "Maybe she did. I think I felt her last night." She shifted in her seat, brow furrowed. "No. I know I felt her last night. She…" She closed her eyes and looked away.

"What?" John set down his drink.

Tracy gulped and met his gaze. "Words popped into my head. I don't think they were mine."

"What were the words?"

"Need. Want." Tracy bit her lip.

Was she thinking about me?

"What were you doing when you heard it?"

Her eyes darted to the side. "I was, umm, in the car."

A twinge of panic rattled through John. What was she thinking? "In the car? Last night? Alone?"

"No. I was with my friend Laini. We went for drinks."

John dragged his fingers through his hair. "Please tell me you didn't go to a bar. That psycho is still on the loose." His gaze darted to her eyes. Blue. Maybe a hint of green, but not the vivid emerald of the victims. He let his tension scale slip from a ten down to a six.

"Psycho, not psychos?" Her lips thinned. "Oh, God, are all those murders related? Is it like a Jack the Ripper thing?"

He held up a palm. "We're not releasing that information yet. But they are asking everyone to use caution. Especially in public places like bars."

"Oh, please. I was with Laini, and nothing happened."

She slipped her fingers around his hand. A tingle shot into his wrist. A new sensation. Dak fizzled and seemed to draw back with a slight amused twist. Maybe Adonna wasn't quite so tired after all.

But that didn't explain the odd set of Tracy's shoulders—like some important speck of information was being withheld. Maybe she suddenly realized how much danger they could have put themselves in. Or was it something else?

The cop inside him sucker-punched the regular guy on a date. He *would* find out what was wrong, once he got her to relax and open up to him.

"I wish you'd be more careful." He tightened his grip on her, giving Dak an avenue to reach through him to her skin. His Ambient took immediate advantage, sliding through the embrace.

John warmed when Tracy's lashes fluttered. She didn't flinch, she just seemed to enjoy the sensation of Dak spreading into her. At least she'd finally accepted what they both were, what all four of them were. Maybe this could work out, after all.

"I know I may seem overprotective, but please, don't go out at night. Not until we have this guy behind bars."

Dak withdrew his touch and John released Tracy's hands. Dak sank away from the top of John's awareness, nearly disappearing. John hoped it was alien satisfaction, not a problem with Adonna.

"We were fine and in a public place." Tracy took a bite of her croissant. Her arm jiggled as her leg bounced under the table.

If she was a suspect, he'd already have concluded she was lying. But about what? "I doubt the murderer cares about public places."

Her eyes trailed away as she chewed the inside of her cheek. She wasn't listening, or if she was, she was blowing him off. How many times had he seen this? Human nature would never change. No one ever thinks it will happen to them.

Dammit! How could he make her understand?

He placed his other hand atop hers. "Listen, I'm sorry, but I deal with the aftermath of this animal every day. I see things that are too horrible for even the media to know about."

She took another bite of the croissant, her gaze stitched to her napkin.

John balled his fists, rubbing them on his lap. What would he do if something happened to her because she hadn't listened to him? He'd never be able to live with that.

Dak shook inside him.

John scratched his brow. "You can't understand what it's like, waking up every day and wondering if he's struck again. At this point, I don't even wonder anymore. I just wait for the bad news." He sighed, staring at his still-wrapped sandwich. "Every time I get a call, a little part of me dies. Another woman is dead, and it's my fault."

Tracy's eyes widened. "Your fault?"

He slammed his fist on the table. "It's my job to find this bastard. My job to stop him. Every day he's still free is my fault."

A passing employee stuck his head in the quiet room. His gaze centered on the only couple seated in the small space.

John waved him away. "Sorry."

He needed to get a hold of himself. Maybe he really hadn't been sleeping well.

Tracy reached across the table. "Hey, no one blames you. And you have to be getting closer, right?"

John shrugged. "A beat cop shot a suspect fleeing the scene yesterday. That's why I couldn't see you last night. We were combing hospitals, but we came up dry."

She leaned back. He could see the disappointment in her eyes. She blamed him as much as everyone else did.

"Then why are you here?" she asked. "Shouldn't you be gathering evidence or something?"

Crumpling his napkin in his fist, he did his best to ward off the implication that he hadn't done enough already.

She was right, of course, since the asshole was still out there, possibly choosing his next victim right now while he was here drinking coffee.

Dak swirled beneath John's left shoulder, relieving some of the tension centered there, while John's gaze wavered over Tracy's somewhat haggard expression. Her lips tightened.

Her gaze was on him, yet she seemed distant. Distracted. Yes, he'd definitely rather stare at her than look at crime scene photos, but what was going on in that pretty head of hers?

His Spidey senses were tingling on overload. Something was up. Unless his cop side was overreacting.

Again.

Shut up, Dak.

But his Ambient friend had a point. Maybe she'd noticed John's reactions to Dak and was giving them time for their internal conversations as well as this outward exchange with her.

Yes. That was it. He needed to stop thinking the worst every second of the day. Dak was right. He needed to learn to turn the detective off and be a regular guy once in a while.

A flash of the photographs pinned to the war board raced across his mind.

Three young women whose lives had been cut short.

A police department cut to a skeletal team.

He was the only chance those women had to see justice. If he didn't solve this case, another woman would be added to the board. And another. And another.

Who was he fooling? He wasn't a regular guy. Too many people were counting on him.

He wished things were different, though. Tracy was the first real chance for him and Dak since Amy, and Dak deserved this.

So do you.

Yeah, maybe he did.

John returned his gaze to Tracy. "Dak, he—he likes your company." John laughed and shook his head. "Hell, I admit *I* like your company." He took her hand. Her fingers felt so fragile in his. "I love that we don't have to hide anything from you. I know it might sound stupid, but keeping secrets like this can get to you after a while." That, and everything else going on in his life. He tightened his grip, suddenly afraid she might let go. Then he released her before she thought he was some kind of idiot. He stared at his fingers, suddenly missing her warmth.

Her brow pinched, then softened as if she made a difficult decision. "Listen, I get that this might not be the greatest time for you to start a relationship, but I want you both to know that I understand. Right now, the most important thing in your life is finding this killer before he hurts someone else. Don't worry about me." She gripped his hand. "Find this asshole so we can get back to the rest of our lives."

His heart fluttered. The rest of their lives?

Dak swirled a loop inside him, causing John to gasp.

Down, boy. That's not what she meant.

How do you know?

The smile drained from John's face when a tear streamed down Tracy's cheek. She wiped it away.

"What is it?"

She shook her head. "It's not fair. It's stupid of me to even be here, bothering you. You have much more important things to worry about than me."

So, there *was* something else. So much for the overactive cop instincts. "Tell me."

"Never mind. It's a bad time." She stood, grabbing her purse.

"No. Wait." John was holding her wrist. He didn't remember standing or grabbing her. "You can't do that. Dak will be crazy worrying about you."

She snorted. "Dak?"

He lightened his grip. "Okay, and me, too. Please, talk to us."

She nodded and eased back into the chair. "There's something I didn't tell you about last night."

John tensed. Maybe he didn't want to know, but he was glad he wouldn't have to stew over what was really bothering her. "I'm listening."

"I didn't just hear Adonna last night." She took a deep breath, then released it slowly.

John twined his fingers between hers. "Whatever it is, it's okay."

She drew away. "No. It's not okay. She took me over. It was horrible."

"Took you over?"

"Like a goddamn puppet." Tracy wrapped her arms around her shoulders. "She was controlling me and there was nothing I could do about it."

"What happened?"

"I was in the bar with Laini like I said, and there was this guy there. All of a sudden, I had no control of my body." She wiped another tear from her cheek. "Adonna threw me at him. I tried screaming, I tried fighting, but it was like being stuck in a nightmare. She wanted that guy, and there was nothing I could do about it."

That doesn't make sense.

John's face flushed as he profiled the scene, imagining Tracy flinging herself into another man's arms. He fought his hands from forming fists.

"And that's not all of it," Tracy continued. "He had an entity inside him."

John flinched. "What?"

Dak stiffened.

Shit. Was this the Ambient equivalent to getting cheated on?

Hold on there, buddy. We don't know what really happened, yet.

"How do you know there was an Ambient inside him?"

She shivered, staring at the pile of napkins between them. "There was this zap when we touched. Like an electric shock. The guy felt it, too. It looked like it scared him."

Dak?

An initial touch. Like a hello. If that's all it was then it's no big deal.

"But then the guy grabbed my hand, and whatever it was inside him crawled into me and, like, exploded." She shivered again and rubbed her arms. "I feel disgusting. Violated."

John poked the empty void inside him. It was like Dak had simply melted away to nothing. Apparently, exploding was a lot more than an initial hello. Shit.

He stroked her hand, surprised when Dak didn't reach for her. Tracy wiped her nose with her other hand. If she had no control, how far had it gone?

John calmed the fire brewing in his own thoughts. She wasn't his. Not yet, anyway. That didn't stop him from wanting to pummel this jackass, though. "How long did she have control?"

"Not long. Laini came and it was like Adonna snapped and lost control. All of a sudden, I was me again."

"Dak, I need your input on this one."

A swirling fizzle rose to the center of John's chest. *I really don't want to talk about this, John.*

I need you, buddy. Come on.

Dak shimmied a little higher in John's chest. *Adonna probably used all of her energy to take control. She might sleep for weeks now.* He pulsed. *If it were me, I'd be too scared to take my host over again, knowing it would tire me that much.* Another swivel. *Touching the other entity must have been very important to her to take that kind of risk.*

And the other entity wasn't Dak. His friend twitched and sunk low again. Damn, that had to hurt.

He looked up into Tracy's wide, expectant eyes, wishing he could chase away her fear.

"What did Dak say?" she asked.

John shifted his weight. "Well, we've already explained that these things are tactile, but it sounds like they said a little more than hello."

Tracy flinched.

"Dak said she probably won't do it again if she got tired

enough that she faded out. It sounds like that is pretty frightening for them."

"Frightening for them? How about frightening for me?"

"I understand."

"No, you don't. You can't."

"Unfortunately, I can." He took a deep breath and stared at his coffee lid. "A few years ago, I blacked out on the scene of a house fire. When I woke up, I had my face in an oxygen mask. I was covered in soot and the arm on my jacket had burned completely off." John grimaced. "And someone was patting me on the back, calling me a hero. Apparently, I dragged a family of five out of that inferno." He looked up at her. "Dak saved those people, not me." Pausing, he chewed his upper lip. "I know he did a good thing, but it took me a long time to trust him again. I still don't think he can comprehend why I had a problem with it."

And he probably never would. There were things about humanity that Dak couldn't grasp, no matter how hard John tried.

"As soon as you're able, I suggest sitting down and having a talk with Adonna. I can't imagine she would knowingly put you through that kind of stress." He lowered his hand. "These beings don't have the same moral system we do. She probably had no concept that what she did was wrong, or that she scared you."

Tracy's brow furrowed. "So, you want me to *talk* to her?"

"It's worth a try."

She nodded, and John's phone rang. *Commings.*

"I have to take this."

So much for their second date.

23

Tracy washed her face in her bathroom sink and blotted herself dry with a towel.

This wasn't something she could disregard. She'd been taken over, pushed away, and replaced by someone else. Some*thing* else. John seemed to think that it wasn't a big deal. But it had been a huge deal. How could she ever feel safe knowing the thing inside her could take control at any moment?

Her gaze drew to the folded business card on the vanity: 1-800-Federal-Agent. She could do it, call them. Tell them what had happened.

A shiver ran through her. Her heartrate increased. Not her reaction, but definitely a reaction from within.

Talk to her, John had said. As insane as it seemed, could it be that easy?

She leaned toward the mirror. "Listen. You and me are going to have to get along. I mean, I get being attracted to someone, but I am not interested in having sex with some disease-ridden guy I met at a bar."

A jolt ran through her, a confused jumble of frazzled movements.

Tracy focused on her reflection. "What about John? He's great. A cop. And he's really nice. I think he and Dak really care about us. We've got a great chance with them, so let's forget this ever happened."

Mine.

Dread crept to Tracy's core.

My what?

Tracy pushed away from the mirror. John had said Dak started with single words, but that sounded like her own voice. Her own thought.

Mine.

What did it mean? What was it about Sean that had drawn Adonna out? And why hadn't she reacted to Dak like that?

She rubbed her hands over her slacks. Maybe she should find a way to contact Sean. His Ambient had reached into her. There was no hesitation. None. A tingle ran through her, remembering the thrill of the Ambient's touch. How strong, forceful.

Tracy balked. It wasn't a thrill. Not at all. It was horrifying. She didn't want to see Sean again. Ever. In fact, if she did see him, she'd run in the other direction.

Wouldn't she?

Her hands shook. Her reflection stared back at her. Different. Pale.

She couldn't live like this. Grabbing the card, she strode to the kitchen and slipped the phone out of her purse.

One call. That's all it would take. Agent Clark would remove Adonna like a squatter in the park. An Ambient taking control of a human had to be against the accord. That should be enough to warrant ripping this thing out of her.

Her hand trembled. She didn't even know if her body was healed enough to live without Adonna's help. This call could be suicide.

And if she *was* healed enough, what was involved? Was it hard to get one of these things out of your body? Would extraction hurt? Agent Clark had said all her personal rights terminated the second Tracy died. He flat out said she belonged in a coffin. Would it be easier to kill her to set the Ambient free?

Her head spun, unable to hold on to a single question or form a clear thought. She tucked the card into the zipper compartment in her purse and dialed John's number instead.

"Tracy, what a nice surprise."

Some of her fear slipped away as she soaked in his voice. Someone shouted his name in the background.

"Is this a bad time?" she asked.

He puffed into the phone. "Nope, give me a second." The sound in the background decreased. "What's up?" His voice echoed, like he'd stepped into a stairwell or empty hallway.

She glanced at herself in the mirror. "I tried talking to her. There's nothing. How can she be strong enough to take control of my body and not be able to talk?"

There was a slight hesitation. "Like Dak said, she overexerted herself and is paying for it now. Consider it Ambient traction."

Tracy tightened her grip on the receiver. "I really need to talk to you again. I'm scared. I realize we don't know each other that well and I shouldn't be dumping on you, but I need to talk to someone."

"Hey, it's no problem. I completely understand." His name echoed through the hallway again. John cursed under his breath. "Listen, I'm really sorry, but I can't get away right now. How about lunch again tomorrow? You name the place, I'll meet you there."

"I guess I can go to wherever you are. I know you're busy."

"That would actually help. I don't mean to be a dick, but things are a little tense at work."

Tracy rubbed her forehead. What a bitch she was. She shouldn't be so self-centered. "I'm sorry. You're busy. Never mind."

"Whoa, whoa, whoa. Be careful there, you're gonna give Dak a coronary." He laughed. "I do get a lunch break, you know. How about Kyle's pizza in Winslow?"

"I've never heard of it."

"Best pizza in South Jersey. And they are also quiet between eleven and twelve. We can sit in the back and not have to worry about roving ears. Can you meet me there at eleven? I'll text you the address."

She tucked a strand of wayward brown hair behind her ear. Could she wait an entire day? Live like this, wondering if this parasite inside her was going to hijack her body again?

Tracy took a deep breath and let it out slowly. She needed to talk to someone who could help her understand. She needed Dak.

"I'll meet you there at eleven."

24

John handed Tracy a slice of pizza.

"I can't believe they had this all sitting here at the table waiting for us to arrive." She juggled the sagging plate, saving the pizza just short of falling to the table.

"Being a cop has its privileges sometimes." He slipped a slice onto a plate for himself and sat back in the hard booth.

"Anything new with the case?"

John chewed his first bite of pizza. Did Tracy really care about his case or was she making small talk? Maybe she was as scared as everyone else and wanted this over with.

He swallowed. "Nothing I can report. We're still reviewing evidence."

So many people were counting on him. Even though it was only Sunday, Friday was screaming toward him, and he was no closer to solving this case now than he was last week at this time. This jerk was playing with them; and John, unfortunately, was letting him frolic to his heart's content. There had to be something linking all the clues. He just hadn't found it yet.

Wiping his hands on a napkin, John conjured up his best grin. "I'm guessing you didn't want to meet to talk about my job."

She set her pizza down and dabbed a nonexistent stain from her lips. "How do you do it—live your life knowing that something can take you over at any time?"

John shrugged. "Dak and I have trust. He's never given me a reason to worry."

"But he took you over once. He could do it again." She twisted the napkin between clenched fists. Interesting.

"But he hasn't." He covered her right hand with his. Dak tickled across the edge of her skin, playing politely. "I know it's hard to believe right now, but in time you'll have the same trust with your entity. They aren't all that different than you and I. They just don't have bodies."

Her lips thinned. She fingered a burned bubble in her pizza crust before her eyes returned to his. "Could I maybe talk to Dak?"

"He's here."

She licked her lips. "What is it like, being in there, all alone?"

It sucks. John's boring.

Stop it. "He said it's hard sometimes."

That's not what I said. A sparkling warmth spread through John's belly, a sensation he long ago equated to Ambient laughter.

"I don't get why he does it. How can he live someone else's life and not his own?"

Dak's voice whispered inside him. "He said it's not bad, and other Ambients, the weaker ones, have a tougher time with it. A lot of them can't even speak to their hosts."

She nodded, sucking her lower lip into her mouth. "Could he take you over right now? Talk to me with his own voice?"

"No," John answered. "It takes an awful lot of energy to control a body. Last time he was quiet for days. Immersed, he called it. To him that's like hell. Imagine your most talkative friend, and then take away her voice. She'd go nuts."

"But, in theory, he could."

"Tracy, you need to stop dwelling on this. You're going to drive yourself crazy over nothing. Are you sure there was no response at all when you tried to talk to her?"

Tracy blanched.

Maybe there was a reaction, but if so, why not tell him?

She covered her eyes, her hands trembling. "It's like she's not even there. I don't understand. I feel so alone. Even you, the one person who should understand, doesn't." Tears streamed from her eyes. "I don't think I'll ever be as comfortable as you are with all this."

John reached for her but pulled back. If he touched her, Dak might try to comfort her himself. The last thing she needed was to prove just how invasive these entities could be.

You're being ridiculous! Go to her. Hold her!

His own heart twisted. He wanted to trust Dak, but in this one instance, he knew he couldn't, and the last thing he wanted was to make things worse for Tracy. "I don't know how to help you other than letting you know it will get better. You need to give it time."

"I'm done giving it time. I'm alone, and I'm scared."

John splayed his hands. "Dak and I are right here. We're proof that this can be an amicable relationship."

She tossed her palms up. "Relationship. There's a kicker. I'll never have one of those."

"What do you mean?"

"I'm going to be alone, forever, because I'm a freak."

"We've already told you you're not a—"

"Dammit, you're in the same boat I'm in, and I don't even think you're interested."

"Tracy, I'm here, aren't I?"

"Yes, but you're here for Dak. You said he was interested, but all I get from you is this weird, standoffish vibe; like maybe you're being nice to me because Dak likes Adonna and you're not interested in me in the slightest."

"Tracy, this isn't just about Dak." He motioned to the food. "He doesn't even like pizza."

He cringed as the words left his mouth. That was the best he could come up with?

John drew his fingers through his bangs. "Look, if I'm distracted, you need to understand that my job is all-encompassing sometimes." He dropped his hand and sighed. "I wish to God that we'd met at a quieter time in my life but..." But so many things.

Dak screamed inside his head, but John blocked him out.

Damn, he liked this girl, but was he ready to take a chance again? Was it possible to have a relationship with four different personalities battling each other? He wanted to be strong and independent, as sure of himself as he led others to believe he was, but deep down, he wanted someone else he could depend on. Someone he could talk to. Someone who could understand.

He sat back and considered her smile as he walked in to the coffee shop yesterday, and how she'd preordered lunch. Shit, if she hadn't already proven herself to be everything he wanted and more.

Tracy was right, though. With an Ambient inside you, nothing was assured. She was here, now, but tomorrow she could be gone, leaving him no better than crap flushed down the toilet. She'd come to him for help, but how can he help her if he hadn't even gotten his own shit together.

She wiped her nose. "You should see the look on your face. You look like a scared rabbit ready to run."

"That's not what I'm thinking." But it was. He wiped the sweat from his palms.

"I want to talk to Dak. Now."

John startled. "It's not like he ever left."

Tracy rested her arms on the table. Her gaze centered on his eyes, looking into him rather than at him. "What's going on? How does John really feel and what isn't he telling me?"

John's brow lifted. "Umm, hello." He pointed at himself. "I'm right here."

"I said I wanted to talk to Dak."

"Yeah, well, you gotta kinda go through me. What do you mean by…"

I can't take it anymore. I'm sorry John.

A huge pressure overwhelmed him. Everything that made him John rolled into a little ball and sucked away from his eyes and into a void. Dak surrounded him, encompassed him. He sank and felt Dak above him where the entity normally seemed below. He tried to claw at the darkness, fight his way back to the surface, but finally gave in, exhausted. The sensation of his body reclining in the chair surrounded him. He could feel it happen, but he was no longer in control.

Dak stretched John's neck and grinned.

"Hello, Trace. It's me."

The sound of his voice with someone else's words sent a flurry of anxiety through John's core. He screamed without sound. Could Dak hear him?

Tracy's eyes widened. Her mouth formed an 'O'.

John's lip turned up only on the left side. He cringed, the movement seeming awkward. Wrong. Dak propped their left elbow on the edge of the table, pushing back the half-eaten pizza. "Why do you look so surprised? You asked to talk."

She shivered as if the temperature dropped thirty degrees and wiped her brow with the back of her hand. "Wow. You did that so fast. So easily."

"Yeah, well, John is freaking out, so let's make this quick before he has a heart attack."

You better believe I'm freaking out. That is my goddamn body, Dak. Give it back. Now.

Her gaze crept over John's face as if searching for him. "He's hiding something. Something that scares him. Something about me."

Dak shifted John's weight to rest on their other arm. "We've been through a lot."

"I can see that, but I think it's more than this investigation. I mean, he may be the nicest guy who's ever shown an ounce of interest in me, but I'm tired of getting hurt. I need to know if there's any chance for us. All of us."

A smile shot across John's lips. He fought to make it a grimace, to gain control back, but Dak was too strong.

Dak plopped both arms on the table. "Well, I'm going to be honest with you and not try to sugarcoat things like you humans always seem to."

Don't you freaking dare!

"You're nice and all, and I think you're great for John, but all I see when I look at you is Adonna. If John is holding your hand, I'm not even paying much attention to what the two of you are talking about. I'm reaching inside you to touch the part of you that does interest me. Adonna is amazing—tired and a little lost, but still amazing."

The entity tapped John's fingers on the edge of their water glass. "I feel every emotion that floods through John's body. It's annoying at times, because he's almost always focused on work, and let's face it, what the guy does is deeply disturbing. But every once in a while his mind wanders, and I feel a flood of positive energy from him." John wished he could crawl into a hole and die. "He's thinking of you, Trace. Sometimes I think you are the only joy he's felt since…"

Don't.

Tracy cocked her head to the left. "Since what?"

Dak studied the woodgrain in the table.

Please, Dak. Don't tell her.

Dak looked up to Tracy. "I'm the only person in the world who he can't hide his feelings from. I know it's pretty soon for a human, but I think John could be on the road to falling in love with you."

Oh, crap. That was even worse.

Pressure pushed John down as if a giant hand squashed him from above. He thrashed phantom limbs, screamed with a silent voice. But it was like he didn't exist, like a phantom memory or a forgotten nightmare.

Dak leaned toward her. "If you care for him at all, you need to ask him about Amy. You deserve to know why he's so scared."

The void, the weightlessness, the pressure zapped away. Everything that was John flew through a swirling vortex, stopping with a numbing crash. He blinked and his eyelids responded. He grabbed for his temples and his hands did his bidding. John was in control again. He sat for a moment, just breathing.

Jesus Christ, Dak.

Sucks, doesn't it?

John drew in a deep breath and let it out slowly. Yes, it did suck.

He shuddered. Dak lived like that every day. Cognizant, but helpless to John's every whim. How did his friend not go insane?

It's the price I pay for the use of your lungs.

But they were John's lungs. His. Not Dak's. Dak was a guest. And guests don't take over their host's homes.

Your heart rate is through the roof. You need to calm down.

"Don't ever do that to me again."

Tracy sucked in a breath. Her hands slid off the table.

"Next time, let me translate." Son of a bitch. That was not cool. Not cool at all.

John clutched the side of the table and took a few more quieting breaths before he risked meeting Tracy's gaze.

She sat with her hands in her lap, her eyes strained. "I'm not sure if I should laugh or run screaming. They really can take control of us anytime they want."

His heart continued to pummel his ribcage. He'd been a prisoner in his own body and there was nothing he could do about it.

He wanted to give Tracy some comfort, but right now, he was the least comfortable he'd ever been since meeting Dak.

"Can all of them do that, then?"

John shook his head. "They tell me it's not common." Because any sane person would have them yanked out.

I would never hurt you, you know that.

You fucking took me over!

Someone had to.

Clenching his teeth, John rubbed his eyes and counted back from ten slowly. "This isn't exactly how I'd expected this lunch to go."

She laughed in that pitiful way girls do right before they dump your ass. "Me either. I'm really sorry." Standing, she gripped her purse.

"Leaving already?"

She nodded, her eyes closed. "I'm not feeling well all of a sudden."

Is this because I talked to her? She asked. It wasn't like I...

"Shut up, Dak." John stood, grabbing her arm. "Hey, are you all right? Because this wasn't normal. Really." He shook his head. "I don't want Dak scaring you. Just because he's an ass doesn't mean your..." He glanced toward a couple of women who took a table close to them. John threw money on the table and gestured to the door. "Your *new friend* probably won't be anything like him."

She wiped the damp edges of her lashes. "But that's the thing. She already is. That's probably why he likes her so much." She rubbed her forehead. "God, this is crazy."

"I get it. Believe me, I totally get it."

"I think I need to digest this all. I'll call you, okay?"

She'll call him. Great, just great.

John held the door as she passed through. She got into her car and pulled out of the parking lot without looking back.

He let the door go and stood on the sidewalk, staring at a

crack that eddied toward the pavement. A deep pain welled in his chest. His teeth clenched so hard they creaked. Dak remained blessedly quiet as an ant dragged a hunk of bread ten times its size into the crack and disappeared.

Gone. Like everything else that mattered to him.

25

Tracy drummed her fingers along the edge of her laptop, allowing the gentle cadence to drown out the voices of the men gathered around the office's main conference room table. The first twenty minutes of every meeting innumerably equated to a complete waste of time. No, you idiots, your precious football team were not going all the way this year. Like every other season, they would fail miserably, leaving you moaning and groaning and rooting for someone else come Super Bowl Sunday.

"What do you think, Seavers?" Scott McNulty jostled her from her thought. His eyes narrowed as everyone's gaze fell on her.

Tracy knew McNulty would be pissed about her taking her time approving his ad campaign. And now he was looking to publicly humiliate her, drawing her into a conversation she'd normally avoid. These idiots bonded over their stupid sports teams. She couldn't say what she was really thinking.

Why senseless knowledge of sports statistics gained you professional momentum, she didn't know. But Olson Soup was no different than any other place she'd worked. Inevitably, jerks like him always seemed to climb the corporate ladder. Infuriating, but it also put her into the habit of listening to sports radio for a few minutes before any major corporate meetings.

She sat back in her chair. "Well, I think the new quarterback looks pretty good. If the defense can protect that bad shoulder of his, I think we have a shot this year."

Her answer earned a few appreciative slaps on the table. McNulty simply turned in the other direction, ceding his ground. Ignorant bastard.

"Good afternoon, Gentlemen." Colonel Marshal Olson blasted into the room, followed by Executive VP of the World, Kyle Olson, a kid barely out of college, but nonetheless heir to the Olson's Soup empire.

The sales team jumped to shake Marshal's hand. Their enthusiasm waned as each greeted Kyle. Idiots. It wasn't like the boss was going to go out and get a new son.

The room began to settle. Hands started to fold as all the good little soldiers faced the end of the table where Marshal shuffled papers from a black leather binder.

Kyle dug his fingers through his hair, blinking red, puffy eyes.

"The baby isn't sleeping through the night, yet?" Tracy asked.

Like a room of robotic soldiers, all eyes turned to her.

Bite me, assholes. Women can play corporate politics, too.

A light smile touched Kyle's lips. "That obvious, huh? He actually gave us three hours in a row last night."

"Well, that's a step in the right direction."

McNulty twitched. She could almost see the steam floating from his ears as he tried to think up useless statistics about babies.

"I bet you'll be getting five hours in no time, then six," Tracy said.

"That sounds like heaven." Kyle rubbed his eyes. "And thanks for the tip on the zinc, by the way. It cleared Nancy's cold overnight. I'd be dead if I had to take care of both of them without any sleep."

"Yeah," McNulty nearly shouted. "Ya gotta keep that wife

healthy so she can take care of the kid. You got no business changing diapers."

Check, and mate.

Tracy reclined as Kyle straightened—in one simple movement, transforming himself from daddy's little boy, to Mr. Olson Jr.

"Actually," Kyle began, "I was thinking about what a trooper she is. She's working from home, taking care of a newborn, getting less sleep than me, and she's still doubling your sales numbers this quarter. How do you figure that?"

Oh snap!

McNulty nearly peed his pants last year when the boss's son announced he was engaged to Nancy Treven, the only competition for top-performing salesperson on the Olson team. Little did we know there was already a miniature bun in the oven. Too bad Nancy wasn't conferenced in for this meeting. She would have loved hearing her new husband rub McNulty's nose in it.

Invariably, the boredom of the Monday meeting set in. The sales guys gave their spiels, butting heads with marketing on how to increase sales in the next quarter. The same old boring, stale ideas bounced around the room.

It was a waste of Tracy's time to have to sit there through all of this bickering. She was the layout person. Once they made their decisions, they could call her in to bring their ideas to fruition, which basically meant doing the same exact thing she'd done for the last five campaigns. "Because you're all a bunch of blithering idiots who couldn't sell a can of soup if one hit you in the face in the middle of a football field filled with starving people."

Everyone was looking at her. She was standing.

All by herself.

In the middle of the conference room.

Oh, shit. She'd said that out loud!

Colonel Olson gazed at her over the tops of his glasses.

"Sit down, Tracy," Miles hissed under his breath.

Stunned, she slumped into her chair. The gaze of each member of the sales team bored through her. Miles slouched as if he could avoid the boss's stare by slipping under the table. Kyle Olson's lips pressed together as if suppressing a grin.

The colonel pushed up his glasses. "What exactly do you mean by that Ms, umm…"

"Seavers," Kyle completed his father's query.

How many meetings had she sat in this very chair wanting to tell all these blowhards off? But you don't do that! What had gotten into her? It was like a sudden jolt of adrenalin had shocked her to her feet and ran off her tongue.

Something swirled in her chest. Adonna. *Oh shit.*

The CEO and his son still stared at her, awaiting her answer.

She grabbed the arms of her chair, gathering her thoughts. The Ambient may have jolted her the first time, but Tracy had only said what she was thinking, and her thoughts were still sound. Maybe she'd been silent for too long.

Taking a deep breath, she stood. "I look at it like this: sales have fallen steadily each quarter."

"It's the economy," McNulty said. "People aren't buying soup."

"People still have to eat," Tracy pointed out. "They're buying soup. They just aren't buying *our* soup."

"She's right," the Colonel said. "Campar's soup division is up fifteen percent. Why is that, Mr. McNulty?"

McNulty paled. "They-they're dropping prices."

"Even their sales prices are higher than ours," Kyle pointed out.

Tracy nodded. "But that doesn't keep them from leveraging sales and promotional space. Have you seen their displays in Ace Markets and FoodShop?" She pointed at the table. "Olson's Soup, year after year, has failed to combat the competition at point of sale."

The Colonel set his glasses on the counter. "I'm not getting into dirty advertising. My family founded this company on certain principles that I refuse to overlook."

Tracy settled herself under his gaze. "I'm not asking you to.

But you should use those principles as leverage. Olson's Soup is made from all-natural ingredients. More natural spices and less salt. It's good for your family. Plain and simple." She stiffened as Kyle's right eyebrow shot up. "Clean, simple, and back to basics. Olson's Soup. It's good for you."

Kyle dropped his pen and looked at the ceiling.

The Colonel's nose flared. "You're suggesting a complete change in marketing strategy."

"Yes. Yes, I am."

The Colonel's hands fisted. "I've invested one-point-five million dollars on easy to open packaging for the Fast and Easy promotions. You do realize that."

Tracy nodded. "Yeah, well, everyone is using the new canning technology. It doesn't set you apart anymore."

His eyes narrowed as he slowly stood. His gaze flicked from his son to Tracy's boss. "Kremmer. My office. *Now*." Colonel Olson slammed the door behind him as he left the room.

Miles turned to her. "Your job is layout, not to piss off the owner of the company. What the hell is the matter with you?"

Tracy shrugged. She refused to say she was sorry. This company was run by too many men stuck in the stone ages. If this alien inside her was going to help her stand up for herself, maybe this whole Ambient situation wasn't such a bad thing. This was a long time in coming.

But as Miles left the room, the reality of the daggers shooting her way set in. Kyle Olson rested his forehead on a shaking fist. His ears burned an angry red. McNulty sat back in his chair and folded his arms, a triumphant smirk leached to his lips.

Sweat soaked through Tracy's shirt as her small victory melted into spiraling defeat. She closed her laptop and bolted from the room.

Where the hell was she going to find another job in this Godforsaken economy?

26

Art handed John a coffee as he passed through the war room door. "Happy Monday."

"Seriously?" John snatched the cup. His partner should know by now that happiness on the job equated to a killer behind bars. Until then, he'd better keep the coffee flowing.

"You know, a day off wouldn't hurt you once in a while. Might make you less cranky."

John whipped around, ready to show him how cranky he could be, especially since Dak had fallen into a sleep-like state after their argument yesterday afternoon, leaving John alone to brood over being taken control of; but Art's wry smile eased some of the tension in his shoulders.

"I'm not the bad guy, remember?" Art said.

John drew in a calming breath. "I know."

Art tapped on his handheld computer. His lips thinned and his eyes narrowed as he stared at the screen, evoking deep lines around his puffy eyes. His partner hadn't been himself the last few weeks, as if his age caught up with him all of a sudden.

"Looks like you haven't been getting much rest either."

Art shoved his handheld in his back pocket. "Yeah, well, I have this partner that doesn't believe in weekends." He opened his lips to continue but seemed to think better of it.

"And?" John queried.

Art held up his hands, then laughed. "Never could pass anything by you."

John waited, raising a brow.

"My Dad's been under the weather. Doctors say it's his heart."

Shit. John knew what that was like, but Art had to be in his late-fifties. It seemed almost unfair that someone so much older than him still had their parents.

John shook away the thought. It didn't matter how old anyone was. Losing a parent was hard.

It was six years and two months since the night his sister had called. John didn't meet her at the hospital like she'd asked. He'd been on a big case—the kind that gets you promoted. He figured he'd visit his dad the next morning before work.

He didn't get the chance.

There weren't too many decisions he regretted in his life, but that was probably at the top of his list.

"When was the last time you saw your dad?" John asked.

"Last night."

John nodded. Art was always ten times smarter than John in certain areas. "If you need to go, just go. Leave me a message or something. Family comes first."

"But—"

John's pointer finger cut him off. "Promise me."

A half-hearted grin crept over Art's lips. "You'll have me believing you're trying to get rid of me."

"Sure. As you're so fond of pointing out, you're all I've got. You think I want to have Biggs as a partner?"

"Now that'd be fun."

John took a sip of his coffee and set the cup on the table. A thin tendril of steam rose from the hole in the lid. Like every other day, he gave his first few minutes to Diana, Melissa, and

Alexandra—a few quiet moments where he stared into the eyes of the pictures tacked to the bulletin board.

Come on, ladies. Give me a hint. What connects you? Where is this asshole? Where does he eat breakfast? Where does he fill his gas tank? Where does he buy his... "Wait a minute."

Art perked up. "What?"

"Milk."

"Milk?"

"Wasn't there a Wawa receipt next to Diana Worth's body?"

Art pulled a digital image out of a folder and slid it across the table. "Yeah. Milk and bread. Paid in cash. We already checked security tapes at the time of the date stamp. What are you thinking?"

"Melissa Harpoona had a piece of a receipt tucked into her cheek."

"Yeah, but it was only a few numbers. Price per gallon or something." He slid out another image and handed it to John.

John pointed to the photo. "Bingo."

Art's brow rose. "You wanna tell me what's his name-o?"

"It's the same ink. Wawa gas stations also have convenience stores."

"Shit," Art whispered. "How the hell did we miss that?"

"Wawa links at least two of them."

"Wawa links everyone. There's a convenience store at half the intersections in the state. It's a dead-end."

"Not necessarily." He pointed to the full receipt. "I want to know the price of gas at this Wawa on the days surrounding Melissa Harpoona's murder."

"You think both receipts came from the same Wawa?"

John nodded. "I think our boy finally left us something to work with."

27

Tracy had been in the middle of packing up her desk when she'd been called to Mr. Olson's office. For all her bravado that morning, she now stood before the solid oak door with his name on it, afraid to step forward.

Adonna spun through her stomach, boosting her confidence as she knocked.

"In!" Was the only response.

Such a charming man.

She pushed the door open and squinted as the sunlight from huge windows on two sides of the corner office accosted her eyes. Two mallards flew past the glass and landed in the drain pond behind the building. Olson didn't even look up from the paperwork fanned across his dark cherry wood desk.

"Sit."

She gulped. "I prefer to stand."

He looked up, his gaze latching to hers. Tracy reminded herself to breathe.

Colonel Olson had patsies to fire people. He never did it himself. He must be pretty pissed off at her. Part of her didn't care anymore, but the other part, the part that liked to be employed, cared a lot. How long would Laini be able to float her if she couldn't pay the rent?

A chair squeaked to her left and Kyle Olson closed his laptop. He leaned on the edge of the large conference table that wouldn't have fit in her living room, let alone in an office. A bemused expression crossed the younger Olson's face as he looked at her. He'd never been an ass before, but maybe he was his father's son after all.

"Tracy Seavers." The colonel leafed through a paper file. Why the man didn't use the perfectly good computer sitting beside him, she didn't know. "You've worked for me for four years."

"Four and a half."

That gaze froze her again. When would she learn to keep her mouth shut?

His right hand formed a fist. "In four and a half years, I've never heard your voice, and today, out of the blue, you stand up and disavow a million-dollar ad campaign."

The twist in her stomach turned to a swirl. Her muscles relaxed, sparkled. She straightened her posture. "Well, I suppose someone had to do it."

His ears reddened. He stood slowly, trembling as if he might explode. "I am not dealing with this, this…" He closed his eyes and took a deep breath. "One-point-five million dollars," he grumbled, pushing past her and out of the room.

Tracy stared at the door as it slammed shut.

Kyle coughed, suppressing a chortle between pressed lips as he opened his laptop. "My father and I have been looking through your college transcripts. Pretty impressive stuff."

She stared at him. "You can do that?"

He motioned to the chair opposite him. "Public record, these days. You can get pretty much anything with someone's social security number."

Tracy glanced back to the door.

"Don't worry about him, he's probably on his way to fire the HR director."

"What? Why?"

"Because the girl we have sitting in the corner doing layout is more qualified than every marketing executive we have, combined." He tapped on his keyboard. "With your background, why did you take a position as a layout designer?"

Tracy shrugged. "I got out of school and no one was hiring."

He scanned his laptop. "I see you worked five internships, one at Campar."

"Yeah, I could find plenty of people to hire me for free, but I kinda needed to eat. I got offered a job here, so I took it."

He nodded, his gaze centered on the screen. "Is there anyone else in this company that's going to explode in a business meeting someday?"

"What do you mean?"

"Is there anyone else as overqualified for their job as you are?"

Tracy shifted her weight. "I heard Rebecca in Customer Service is a packaging engineer."

He stopped typing for a minute. "Seriously?"

She nodded.

Kyle shook his head as he started typing again. He muttered something that sounded like 'not anymore, she's not,' before he closed his laptop and reclined. "I've been trying to get my father to agree to a new promotional direction for months. I told him we needed something direct and honest that could appeal to every household in America." He folded his arms over his laptop. "Clean, simple, and back to basics. Olson's Soup. It's good for you."

Tracy gaped, hearing her own words.

"I like the way you think, Ms. Seavers, and I need someone who's not afraid to say what's on their mind."

"You need someone for what?"

Kyle walked to the windows and stared out. "I want to make changes. Stir things up a bit." He turned toward her. "I want you to pack up everything you need from your desk this afternoon and move into office eight."

She flinched. "Isn't that the office next to yours?"

He nodded. "I need a partner in crime, Ms. Seavers. You up for it?"

Tracy opened the sliding glass doors on her small balcony and breathed in the crisp, fresh air. Wait until Laini heard about this!

The swirling in her stomach intensified as she looked out over the manmade drainage-area-turned-lake. The sun sparkled over the water, a little piece of heaven right outside her window.

She rubbed her stomach and her skin warmed beneath her touch. Today of all days, at exactly the right moment, she'd found the courage to speak her mind. Her stomach sparkled, as it had in Colonel Olson's office. Then the warmth spread through her again.

Tracy gulped and placed her hand on the balcony rail. "Adonna, was that you?" Her stomach clenched and released. Tracy's knuckles whitened on the rail "Did you do this? Did you help me?"

Another pair of mallards flew across the water, trailing lines behind them as they landed in the manmade lake, but her stomach remained silent.

Tracy pressed her palm against her abdomen. "Thank you," she whispered.

A few tears welled in her eyes and she wiped them away. *An amicable relationship,* John had called it. This must be what he meant. Dak gave him strength when he was weak. A friend, who was always there, providing far more than moral support.

More tears formed, and she let them fall as she grabbed her cell, pressed the text button, and chose John.

Hope your day is going as good as mine.

John: Hey you!
John: Sorry about what happen Sunday.

She smiled at his texting skills before she typed:

It's okay. I feel better now.

Tracy tapped her foot as the three little dots popped up on her screen, showing he was typing. Then they stopped. Then they started again. Did he keep changing his mind or was he being interrupted?

John: Been thinking about you.
John: Would love to see you agn.

Her heart jumped in her chest. She closed her eyes and breathed a sigh of relief.

John: Lunch tomorrow?

Lunch. Her enthusiasm drained. The little part of her who hoped for more than friendship wanted more than that. Was he playing it safe on purpose? But then again, she couldn't expect him to be available every moment. Not until he was done with this case. If she liked him as much as she thought she might, then she'd have to get used to this.

Lunch=Yes
   Starbucks Pennsauken? I only have an hour lunch.

John: Too far. Meet halfwy? Merchantville, RT 537?

Hmmm. That was about fifteen minutes from work. It would be cutting it tight, but she'd take what she could get.

Perfect. I have good news to share.

John: Great! We look forward to it.

Tracy nodded.

So do we.

28

"Are you actually texting?" Art asked from across the war room table.

John shrugged, scrolling through his countless typos.

"Since when does the old-fashioned golden-boy embrace simplistic technology?"

John glanced up at him. "Do you have a point hidden inside that smug grin of yours?"

"No. It's nice to see you might actually have a social life." Art folded his arms. "Is it that girl from the coffee shop?"

"Yes, if you have to know." John set his phone down.

"Things getting serious?"

"We've only known each other a little over a week."

Art threw up his hands. "Hey, I proposed to Emily on our fourth date. I'm a firm believer in love at first sight."

John decided not to mention that she'd filed for divorce six months later.

Sergeant Biggs pushed through the door, handing Art a sheet of paper. "Here's the info you wanted on Wawa. Everything okay in here?"

John furrowed his brow. "Fine here. Is everything okay out

there? That's the second time you've hand-delivered findings to us."

Biggs shrugged. "I can't expect Emmerson to do all the research and deliver data, too. If she quits, we're dead."

And any other precinct—the kind with budgets—would be more than happy to snatch up a top-rate data analyst like her. "Good move on your part."

Art handed the paper to John. "You were right. The price of gas on the day of Melissa Harpoona's murder matches the receipt the scumbag shoved into her mouth."

John stood. "Either that, or she shoved it into her own mouth." He leaned against the corkboard, staring into Melissa's eyes. "You knew he was going to kill you. You gave us a clue. You wanted to tell us something in the only way you found possible."

"Peters?" Biggs moved beside him.

John broke Melissa's gaze. "I want to see the police records of every resident within a five-mile radius of that Wawa."

Biggs arched his brow. "Yeah? You and what army are going to review them all?"

John clenched his teeth and steadied himself. "Fine. Make it a two mile radius, and I'll take an army of three. You, me, and Commings." He pointed at each man. "It's Monday already. This asshole is choosing his next victim. I, for one, want to find him before the next girl disappears."

29

"Only you could mouth off at the boss and end up with a promotion." Laini grabbed a fortune cookie from the pile in the center of their kitchen table and chucked it at Tracy.

"I know. It's crazy. I really thought I was going to my exit interview and then all of a sudden Kyle is setting me up in the next office."

"Oh, so it's Kyle now, huh? Is he cute?"

"He's married with a kid, so eww." Tracy opened the plastic container set before her and took a sip of her egg drop soup. "Anyway, I'm seeing John tomorrow for lunch again."

"Again? Should I start dress shopping for your wedding?"

"Let's not get overly excited, but I do like him." A lot.

Tracy rubbed the churning sensation in her stomach. Any time she thought of John and Dak, her entity moved inside her. The reaction didn't seem negative. With any luck, it would stay that way. If Adonna didn't take to Dak, this was going to be hard on all of them.

As much as it freaked her out when Dak took John over, the entity seemed nice enough. And he was obviously interested in

Adonna. Hopefully not so interested that he'd take control again at an inopportune moment.

She shivered. How would she even know if he did?

If she and John ended up a couple, Dak would need to learn to give them the space they needed. She smiled to herself. She and John, that would be a pretty nice space.

A warmth spread through her. Could it be true, what Dak said: that John was on the way to falling in love with her? Tracy's stomach twitched, and she gently rubbed her skin, again. *Please give Dak a chance. This can be great for us.*

"Wow, girl." Laini propped her elbows on the table. "If you could see the dreamy look in your eyes. You've got it bad for this cop."

Tracy shrugged. Maybe she did.

Her roommate sat back. "Well, he'd better be good to you, or I'm going to serve him up with the ass-kicking of his life."

Tracy snorted. Let's hope she'd never have to bail her friend out of jail for assaulting a police officer.

30

"Thanks so much for meeting me again." Tracy placed her coffee down on the long table in Starbucks's back room.

"Hey, no problem," John began. "Your text sounded like you had some good news to share. I could definitely use some of that."

They settled into chairs on opposite sides of a small, round table. John's gaze roamed over the black curtain they used for a door. The thick fabric wouldn't do much to hide their conversation if anyone in the main lobby was listening, but it would have to do.

Folding her hands on the edge of the table, Tracy detailed standing in the middle of an executive meeting and pretty much telling off everyone in the room. "I think it was Adonna. She felt me get angry and gave me the boost I needed to speak out."

Damn, her eyes sparkled when she was excited. "That's awesome."

"But do you think I'm right? Do you think it was her?"

"It very well could have been her. Dak pokes at me all the time when he thinks I'm not going with my gut or doing the right thing. He gets pretty ticked at me sometimes."

You should listen to me more.

John stiffened, surprised to hear Dak after the day-long reprieve following the incident Sunday. *Bite me. I'm still mad at you.*

You missed me. Admit it.

John suppressed his grin, wishing he could hide the relief at hearing his friend's voice.

He returned his attention to Tracy. "Short movements like making us stand don't seem to be difficult for them, and she can read your thoughts. She must have felt your hesitation and given you a little extra encouragement."

Her face beamed. "That's the kind of encouragement I can get used to. I got a promotion."

"Get out. Really?" She nodded, and John hugged her over the table. "That's amazing. Congratulations!"

Tracy adjusted her blouse as she returned to her chair. Her gaze fixed on him, and she took a deep breath. "I wanted you to know that..." She gulped. "That I think I'm going to be okay."

John's gut twisted. If she was okay, she wouldn't need to see them anymore.

Tracy's expression faded. "I thought that would make you happy."

John blinked. "Oh, damn, yeah, it does. I'm sorry." He lowered his gaze. "It's great that you're feeling better about all this. I'm excited for you. And believe me, it only gets better from here."

She rested her chin on her raised palm. "With that in mind, I'd really like to discuss what Dak told me."

The falling-in-love thing. *Shit. You had to open your big mouth, didn't you?* Tracy wasn't some smitten little girl, ready to fall for the burly cop. She was a strong, independent woman. She didn't need anyone, let alone a guy to smother her, especially when her career was about to take off. "Listen, Dak gets a little overzealous sometimes. He has no idea how human emotions work. I mean, I like you, I like you a lot, but love? Hey, we've only known each other what, two weeks?"

She snickered. "That's not the part I was talking about."

"It's not?"

She shook her head. "I'd really like to know who Amy is."

Even worse. *Damn you, Dak.*

A sparkling heat flooded him.

Glad you find this funny. He took a bite of his sandwich and chewed slowly.

Amy. How could he explain the worst and best thing that ever happened to them?

He took a sip of his coffee. It needed more cream. He didn't care.

Tracy's eyebrow remained arched, waiting for an answer. At this point, he had no choice but to give her one.

"I was assisting with a trial in Philly when we met. Amy had an entity in her." He glanced at the shifting curtain, then back to Tracy. "Dak and Cowa felt each other from across the courtroom and drew the four of us together like Dak did with you and me." He shifted his weight. "Amy was great. An attorney. She understood what I went through as a cop. She got the long nights and the pressure. Most of all, she understood what it was like to have another voice in your head." He sipped his coffee again. "I thought it was perfect. Dak and Cowa even liked each other. Amy and I would walk holding hands and our entities did whatever it was that these things inside us do when we touch." He closed his eyes and cleared his throat. "I guess it was both Amy's and my fault. Neither of us fully understood what it was to have a host-alien relationship. We weren't a normal couple. There were four of us. Dak and Cowa loved us, so they never told us."

"Told you what?"

Dak wept deep within John. The pain still burned for each of them. "They were both male. They could talk and share, but…" John rubbed the sweat from his palms across his slacks. "When Amy and I made love for the first time, Dak drew so deeply into me that I thought he was gone. I didn't even think about it. I

175

thought he was giving me privacy." He threw back another gulp of coffee. "It was great for the first half hour or so, but then I felt Dak stir." John shifted his weight. "It was weird. He shook inside me. It wasn't anything I'd felt before, and then…"

Shit.

God, it was screwed up.

John tapped his finger on his napkin. "I woke up in the middle of the night and found Amy curled in a ball on the bathroom floor, crying. I tried to hold her, but she pushed me away. She couldn't stand the thought of touching me again." John rubbed the space between his eyes. "Dak had reached into her while we made love. Dak admitted to feeling Cowa's energy mingling with his own." He sat back. "Apparently, Dak didn't care that they were both male, but Cowa did." John gulped down tears just on the edge of forming. He couldn't say anymore. Hopefully, she understood. "Amy loved Cowa more than she loved me. I never saw her again."

Tracy grabbed his hands, looking deep into his eyes. "I'm not Amy. I'm not going anywhere. And Adonna is a female, right? There won't be a problem between us."

A sizzle reached from Tracy's hands and sank deep into John. Dak turned within, spun and cried out.

"Dak, are you okay?"

Warmth flooded him, but he didn't answer. The tingle slipped back through John's arms, wrists, and disappeared through his fingertips.

Tracy released him and stared at her hands. Her lips opened slightly before she looked up. "Was that Adonna?" She grabbed her temple. "Whoa!"

"What?"

She looked back to her fingers. "All this stuff is racing through my head."

"Anything you want to share?"

Tracy shook her head. "There's this flood of emotion. Happy and sad. Longing, but confusion. Fear. Lots of fear."

"Hold on a minute." He searched within him for Dak. *Anything happen between you two?*

Dak didn't answer, but the sensation John recognized as his friend swirled within, momentarily content.

"Dak seems fine. Maybe it's that new relationship thing. I mean, she's starting to wake up, right?" Shit, please let him be right.

Adonna had reached for Dak. She didn't cringe, she didn't shy away. Could it be possible? Did the four of them actually have a chance?

Tracy shrugged. "Maybe."

John glanced at the clock. Fuck it all. He really didn't want to leave now. But every second he sat here working on the rest of his life, a psycho was planning someone else's death.

But, God, did he want to stay. If Adonna and Dak kept getting along, John could spend the rest of the evening searching out Tracy's curves, seeing if she was as soft as he'd dreamed about the past few nights.

John blinked away the thought. He had to stop thinking from behind his zipper. He had a goddamn killer to put behind bars, for Christ's sake!

Tracy reached over, grabbed his sandwich, wrapped it in a napkin, and stuffed it back into the bag. She handed it to him, along with his coffee.

"What?" he asked.

"I can tell by the look on your face. Go ahead. You have a job to do. I don't want to get in the way."

"I'm sorry. I really want to continue this conversation."

"Me, too, but there'll be a time for that. Go. Make the world safe again. I'll be waiting for you." She straightened. "*We'll* be waiting."

He kissed her hand. "You know, you two might be the best thing that's ever happened to us."

She smiled. "Give Dak a kiss goodbye for me."

How about a real one?

Shut it. "I'll call you."

"We look forward to it."

We.

She'd called herself *we*. It hadn't been a typo on the text.

John's lip trembled like a wuss. He bit it back and manned up.

Tracy was perfect: kind, understanding, supportive. Not to mention that ass that he wanted to knead with his fingers while he… The little solder in his pants pressed against his zipper, making Dak fizzle with alien glee. They both knew Tracy was everything John wanted.

This time, John would make it work. He'd make it work for both of them.

31

Tracy sat on the ground in her living room, her back to the couch. She flipped through the last pages of *The Hobbit*, absorbing the words faster than she'd ever been able to read before. Finishing, she flipped the cover closed and threw the book across the room. The paperback slid down the wall and fell open over the pile containing every other novel in their house.

How many books had it been over the past few weeks: twenty, thirty? And that wasn't even counting the two books she'd read at the office earlier today, while she was supposed to be working on the new ad campaign.

She closed her eyes and let her head loll. Maybe Laini had more books hiding in her room? No. She'd checked yesterday.

More.

She pulled the hair at her temples. "There are no more!" What did this stupid alien think she was, a library or something?

Her hands fell to her lap. A library. That was the answer! There was one across the street from the Echelon shopping center. She could read for a while and then run over to the food court for dinner. Perfect!

As she grabbed her purse, the strap of her laptop bag fell, swinging over the edge of the kitchen table.

She was supposed to work tonight to make up for her lack of progress at the office today.

The right thing to do was to stop this ridiculous reading marathon and get back to the real world.

But what about all those wonderful books waiting for her at the library?

No. She needed to work on the new ad campaign. She had to dig into census data, buying trends, forecasts.

But that wasn't good enough to keep their mind off of the dull ache eating away at her.

Tracy bolted to the mirror in her living room. She stared into her eyes, studying the reflection of her face in her own pupils. "Listen. I really appreciate what you did for me on Monday, but what good is getting promoted if I get fired?" Her hands fidgeted, as if needing to grab something. "What's bothering you? Why are you trying so hard to lose yourself in books?"

More.

Her hands shot to her face. "You're driving me crazy, you know that?" She glanced back to the phone. Maybe she could call John. Maybe Dak could figure out what was wrong with her book-ravenous alien.

More.

And maybe they could explain why her Ambient learned a single word and repeated it over and over again and nothing else!

Trying to deny her entity seemed useless. Like a nagging child she couldn't send to her room, Adonna persisted until she got what she wanted. At the moment, that seemed to be books. Lots and lots of books.

She tapped her phone to check the time. Six thirty-two. She'd have plenty of time to whip through those forecasts tonight after the library closed. Yes. That was a perfect plan!

Picking up her keys, she headed out the door.

It had been years since she'd been to a library. She didn't even have a library card, for goodness' sake. She supposed that wasn't really all that much of a problem. She could grab a pile of books, sit in a chair, and let Adonna go to town. It would be senseless to take them all home. She'd have at least a dozen finished in the time it took to drive there and back.

Tracy entered the building and froze. Past the librarian's desk, rows and rows of bookcases lined the walls on either side of her and seemed to go around the corner as well. A smile burst from her lips.

"Can I help you, Miss?" a man behind the counter said.

What books should she get? "Do you have anything about aliens?"

He nodded. "Sci-fi. Row six on the left."

"Great. Thanks."

Her head spun and giddiness overcame her as she entered the row. But which should she choose? Did it really matter? She snatched the first five titles on the rack and dumped them on a desk in the back of the room where fewer people would view her freakish speedreading show.

Freakish. Is that what she was now, a freak? An aberration who had no choice but to succumb to the whims of an insane being who wanted to do nothing but read and speak one-word demands?

No. She couldn't think like that. Adonna had helped her, proven that they could live together. Tracy needed to realize that her Ambient was a completely separate person inside her. Once in a while, it was only fair to give in to her entity's whims. And reading never hurt anyone.

She sat down and grabbed the book on top of her pile and flipped through page after page. The words soaked straight into her subconscious with no more effort than her eyes scanning the paper. No human could read like that. It had to be impossible.

Mine!

Tracy blinked, startled by a word she didn't find on the page. "What?"

Someone leaned against the table. "Someone seems out of place here, and this time, darlin', it seems to be me."

Ho-lee-crap. "Sean?"

Duh. Obviously, it was Sean, with all six feet of him looming over her. He dropped a few books on the desk.

The desire to read fizzled from Tracy's subconscious. Her breaths came in rapid gasps as she envisioned him clearing the table with one arm and setting her atop the shiny wooden surface. Naked.

Oh, shit!

She pushed with her mind, trying to drive the entity inside her down. Her vision started to spin.

Sean's hand tapped against the side of his stack of books, as if he was having a similar struggle. Or maybe this was just a coincidence? Maybe he was a library regular?

Clearing her throat, she found her voice. "I wouldn't have pegged you for the literary type." True that. Someone that hot belonged on billboards, on movie screens. In her bedroom turning down the sheets. She fisted her hands as she envisioned stripping down to nothing and rubbing up against him like a cat on a scratch pole. Tracy stiffened as her body whirled, begging to touch him.

But that was just it. Touch. The more the better.

Tracy didn't want Sean. Adonna did. And it wasn't even sexual, at least not in the human sense. Adonna craved contact, and for some reason she wanted Sean, or whoever was inside him.

For the past several days, Adonna had warmed up to Dak, but there was something about Sean that drove her entity crazy. Now, instead of binge reading books to help her forget, Adonna was sizzling inside Tracy like a punctured soda can.

Snap out of it. You have to understand we don't want Sean in our lives. Please.

Her heartbeat increased. She needed to get out of there. Now.

Sean's scent reminded her of the night they'd met—a hint of beer and something metallic she couldn't place, mingling with the essence of what may have been women's perfume. Which wouldn't be a surprise if what he'd claimed about himself was true.

He slithered into the chair beside her. "I've had this strange need to read and I didn't have a whole lot of books in the house." He stared at the novels he'd chosen. His hands clenched, straightened, and repeated the movement. He stared at his palms. "Dogonit."

"What's wrong?"

He turned, his eyes dark and searching. "What is it about you? Why do I want to touch you so bad?"

So he *did* feel it. His entity wanted hers just as badly as Adonna wanted to reach out and make whoever was inside Sean her little alien boy-toy. Was this how it was between Dak and John? Was Dak constantly screaming, yearning, begging for his prim and proper cop to throw Tracy over the side of a couch and screw her brains out?

Because right now, all she could think about was climbing atop that table and spreading her legs. Librarians be damned.

Tracy forced herself to stand. "You know what, I need another book."

Good. Logical. Who cared if there were already a handful of books on the desk? He had no idea she hadn't read them yet.

She sprinted past the fantasy section to the far end of the building and slipped into the poetry aisle.

Poetry. Perfect. No one had probably been in that section for years. And damn did she need a few minutes alone to get herself— her *selves* together.

Panting, she grabbed her chest. Her heart throttled against her hand. She pushed, as if pressure would keep the raging muscle from ripping out of her chest.

This was crazy. Insane.

"You need to get a hold of yourself," she whispered, resting her forehead against the shelves.

"Darlin'?"

That southern drawl licked her like a rabbit on a salt block. Grasping the bookcases in front of her, she froze. Her panting increased. Deep, needy, and expecting. She didn't move. She wasn't sure she'd be able to if she tried.

Sean's hands encircled her waist. Tender, gentle movements stroked her sides.

Mine.

Lost in a stupor, Tracy ignored the word. Nothing mattered but the caressing fingers traveling across her waist, her stomach.

She imagined John standing behind her, the spicy sweet smell of his cologne.

Her shoulders relaxed, and a gentle tug drew her from the bookcase, easing her lax frame against his. John's breath tickled the back of her ear. Her head lolled, exposing her neck to a long drag of his tongue. God, she wanted this. She wanted him.

Tracy's body ignited at his touch. A sound slipped from her mouth that was barely recognizable as her own. She grabbed for his hands and pulled them around her. His body molded to her back. Firm, warm, and masculine.

His shallow breathing next to her ear strengthened the pressure growing inside her. Adonna twisted, reached, screamed. The fabric—she couldn't get through the fabric!

But Tracy ignored her pleas. The tease, the promises under John's touch drove her need deeper. She guided his hands to her breasts.

"There we go," he whispered, massaging, teasing, and kneading through her blouse.

Tracy turned her face toward her shoulder, where his waiting lips covered hers. She arched her back, forced her chest against his hungry fingers as he jammed his tongue into her mouth. He was rough. His touch felt angry. A deep, sinking sensation enveloped her. Her eyes sprang open and focused on long waves of blonde hair. Not John—Sean.

No! She tried to scream, but her body wasn't hers. Her mind whirled, lost in a tornado of twisting, focused need.

Each touch tingled, burned, pressed harder than the next. Her vision hazed again, and John came back into focus. Her body relaxed, and she opened herself to him. Drinking in all he had to offer.

She wanted to strip down to nothing, to offer more of her skin for him to explore, but that would mean stopping the gentle probing of his tongue across hers. The motion of his lips, the heat of his mouth, it was her new essence. Her new life force.

A slight grunt of dismay rumbled from her throat as his right hand left its intricate manipulation of her nipple. He fumbled with the button on her jeans.

She pushed his hands away, popped the button free and pulled down her zipper. Trembling, she guided his hand across her stomach. He circled her navel twice before easing over her curly mound, inching lower.

Adonna slammed down Tracy's torso, sizzling below their skin as he inched closer to her sweet spot. With a quiet sigh, Tracy eased her legs apart, giving him the access her body begged for.

He accepted the unspoken invitation, dragging his fingertips over her folds. "Damn, you're wet."

Tracy tensed, his voice seemed off, wrong somehow.

His finger slipped in easily, then a second. "You want this as bad as I do."

His digits hummed, tingled, heated inside her, and the sound of his accent slipped away, lost to the swirl of need swirling through her.

She panted with a ferocity beyond reason. She rocked her pelvis, jamming herself against him. Her body burned, ached, wanted. Adonna seemed to solidify inside her, tightening every muscle in Tracy's body. She trembled, swollen, needing.

Her eyes bolted open as he withdrew his touch.

"No, no," she pleaded, pawing at him, urging him to release the screaming tension he built in her core.

He spun her, pressing her shoulders against the bookcase before driving his tongue back into her mouth. She grunted under the harsh pressure, lips bruising under his, but all she could think of was wrapping her body further around him, giving them both what they craved.

He leaned away. His nose flared as he stared at her lips. "We shouldn't do this. You're not…you're not…"

"I don't care." The words sounded foreign. She did care. She cared a lot.

Something popped inside her. Her thoughts cleared.

Oh God!

Sean's hard, fixated eyes came into focus, as if she were seeing him for the first time. A wave of disgust and seething guilt rolled through her chest. What was happening? She placed her palms on his chest to push him away, but the pressure built inside her once again. Instead of shoving him, her fingers dug into his shoulders and pulled him closer.

Adonna, no!

A small, wicked snicker filled her world as he nipped her ear. "I am going to make you scream."

A growl erupted from a foreign place within her. Maybe from an alien place. Her thoughts mottled and fogged over again. She reached behind him, grabbed his hips and drew him even closer, rubbing herself against his growing erection.

"So eager," he whispered. "Maybe I pegged you wrong, darlin.'"

Something within screamed, begged to kick and punch and howl her way free. Instead, Tracy stood there, panting. Waiting. Wanting.

He grabbed her hand, dragging her out of the aisle, past the fantasy section and the pile of books they'd left on the table. The librarian glanced up from his desk as they passed by and Tracy giggled, realizing her pants were still unbuttoned. Like she cared.

But she did care.

Oh God! Where were they going?

She dug her feet into the ground, stopping their trot into the parking lot.

The cool breeze tickled her cheek and her partially bared stomach. It was like sensory overload. Adonna bounded inside her, pushing against the part of Tracy nearest to Sean. He tugged gently, and she followed past the empty handicap parking spot and a jeep. The frenzied beat of her heart bordered on the edge of terror and anticipation, or maybe a mixture of both. She needed to stop this, to let go of his hand and run home, but her legs kept walking.

Sean led her to the same sedan from the night they first met and pushed her into the passenger seat. Her heart throttled. She couldn't be there. She needed to get out of that car!

He glanced at her as he slipped the keys into the ignition. "Last chance, darlin'. No turning back if you don't get out now."

Everything that was Tracy sank deep, blotted out by a force she couldn't combat. She tried to scream, a prisoner behind her own eyes as she unwillingly dragged her fingers down her cleavage and unfastened the first button on her blouse.

"Less talking. More driving," her voice said.

No! She screamed, but her mouth didn't open. Her voice refused to react to her command.

He licked his lips. Adonna cupped and massaged Tracy's breasts as Sean's gaze stalked down her cleavage. She shifted, giving a teasing glimpse. The vivid image of his wet lips trailing over her nipples burst through her mind no matter how hard she fought it. Need took over and she sank further within her own body.

Sean's fingers shook as he turned away and started the car. He mashed his lips together. Adonna churned inside and Tracy's pelvis rocked in unison.

More.

A dark sense of energy built inside her. Tracy's body roiled in time to the movement of the entity. Adonna was ready and waiting, leaving Tracy lost in a void of near nothingness until they parked in front of a single-story white rancher.

Sean bolted from the car and opened her door. Adonna wrapped Tracy's arms around his neck, letting him lift her from her seat. His hands felt right, solid, knowing, like he'd touched her before. But then he had, hadn't he?

Tracy screamed without sound as Adonna fumbled for Sean's shirt, fluttering beneath her ribs as if desperate to feel his skin against hers. Only a small tingle of energy tickled her lips as he kissed her. She needed that jolt, the explosion he'd given her the night they met. So long. Too long.

Too long since what?

The thought faded to gray as he led her to the house. Tracy tried to dig in her heels again, but her muscles didn't respond. If she went into that house... *Adonna, stop! Please!*

The Ambient rubbed her body against Sean's back and ran her hands under his shirt as he fumbled with the keys. His skin trembled under her touch, his ribs expanded and contracted with his panting breaths.

She'd done that to him, given him such desire. The thought maddened her. How hard could she make him pant? What would it take to make him cry out her name? Thousands of options flew through her mind, each more delectable than the next. Her own hands began to shake. Her legs trembled in anticipation of wrapping about his waist.

No, no, no, no, no! Tracy struggled to separate Adonna's thoughts from her own, but the harder she pushed, the farther she sank. She floated, alone, yet completely aware. Lost.

When the door finally opened, Sean dragged her by the wrist

and flung her into the house. Her shoes tapped over the black-tiled floor before they met an onyx-mottled, Berber carpet. Odd décor, but the darkness matched the hunger in his eyes.

Her wrists throbbed from the severity of his grasp. So strong. Would he hold her down, make her beg? It didn't matter as long as there was contact. She needed to be part of him. He in her and her in him.

A trickle of doubt fizzled deep within her, a conscience effortlessly pushed aside, a trifle easily done away with. The world blotted out, nonexistent, leaving nothing but her and the swirling energy waiting beneath this man's skin.

Sean's eyes glowed. Intensity bordering on sheer fury called to her from his gaze. He yanked his shirt over his head and threw it onto a small wooden desk behind him. He stood before her, his chest smooth, already slick with sweat.

She darted toward him and traced his collarbone with her tongue. Salt and need filled her like an unquenchable thirst. But she'd take more. Yes, she'd take whatever she could get.

A growl rumbled from his chest as he grabbed her shoulders. She fumbled with the remaining buttons on her blouse before he helped her tug her shirt over her head. He dove into her cleavage, his tongue greedily lapping the soft flesh within her bra.

She reached behind her back, unclasping the hooks and freeing more of her skin to his wanton assault. She arched her back in offering, grasping his face and guiding his mouth where she wanted it.

A jolt of sweet joy crashed through her as he sucked her nipple deeply. Hard and rough—like a man with no cares other than his desire, and she loved every second. A new tension whipped through her, an essence meshing with her own. She moaned, reeling as his lips moved to her other breast and his teeth clamped down. Ecstasy exterminated the pain and she drew him more tightly to her. He bit down harder. The pressure intensified, heightened into a maddening mass.

The dark, explosive essence invading her body clawed at what it found within, stroking and fondling Adonna. The life that had now become a part of her own screamed for increased touch.

Tracy's fingers clutched Sean's hair, Adonna vibrated, as if desperate to find a way to get what she needed. Sean pushed Tracy back to the couch and shimmied off her pants. Adonna wrapped their legs around him, rubbing Tracy's swollen need against his jeans, soaking her underwear.

Sean's growl deepened as he ripped at the thin cloth. He painfully sucked more and more of her breast into his mouth as his fingers slipped between her legs and into her slick folds.

Her back arched and she cried out, her body and the entity inside her writhing, begging for release. Tears streamed down Tracy's cheeks as she molded her body to Sean's twirling fingers. The sensations were almost too much to bear. She wrapped her legs around him, trapping his hand between them and driving his fingers deeper. Her back stiffened and the roiling energy inside trembled and shook before a sizzling electric current exploded through her body, reaching out and touching every cell, every membrane until they cried out as one. She moaned as another wave hit her and she knew three other voices screamed alongside hers, but all she could hear was her own cries until her tremors ceased and Sean collapsed on her chest, gasping for air.

She held him for several moments as the energy inside them continued to spin, encompass, and share. Tears continued to stream down Tracy's cheeks as unimaginable delight eased through every part of her body until Sean's entity receded back into his host, and the part of Adonna that had apparently entered Sean returned where it belonged.

Sweet euphoria swept over Tracy before a melting sensation drifted over her body. She twitched and stared at her hand. Wiggling her fingers, she gasped as they answered her command. She was herself again.

Sean's weight pressed her down into the soft couch. She

gulped down the need to puke until he eased aside. His eyes had returned to a normal, human blue. The intensity in them turned to wariness.

He blushed. "I'm-I'm sorry."

The words, so simple, so caring. A stark contrast from the frenzy of moments before.

He stood, tugged his pant leg away from his skin and grimaced. "I need to change. I'll be right back." He headed for the back room.

Tracy hadn't even realized that his pants were still on until he stood. For some reason her mind envisioned him inside her.

Someone *was* inside her, but it wasn't Sean. Not his dick, at least. And it looked like he'd come in his pants when the four of them climaxed together.

Climaxed. Together.

Shit. What was she doing?

As Adonna slipped back into the recesses of her mind, Tracy became wary of her nakedness—of her own damp bottom moistening a black leather couch that she'd never seen before, in the house of a man she hardly knew. She didn't want to be here. She never gave permission. She only wanted to read. How could this happen? How could she have had no control over her own body?

But she had control now. She needed to get her life back.

She fingered her nipples expecting to find blood, but her skin seemed intact. Tender to the touch. Bruised, but not broken.

This would never happen again.

She slipped on her bra and shirt. She found her panties crumpled under the couch and put them on, wishing she could wash away the remnants of their, what? Certainly not love. Intensity. Desire. Lust. But nothing emotional. She didn't even want this asshole. She wanted…

Oh God, John!

Her stomach fisted and squeezed. How could she have done this to him? She blinked, and the foggy haze receded. This wasn't even her. She'd been taken over. Hijacked by a freaking sex-starved alien.

Had Tracy even been there? Of course, her body had, but she was barely conscious, pushed to the background, a prisoner unable to do anything but watch.

She slipped on her jeans and searched for her purse. She needed to get out of there. How could she even face Sean after the way she'd acted? The way they'd both acted, for that matter.

Tracy clenched her teeth. She'd been used. Adonna saw what she wanted, and she got it, Tracy be damned.

Was that what it was like for John when Dak had taken over at the restaurant? Pushed into the recesses of his mind while Dak did as he pleased with John's body?

John.

Her heart twisted within her chest. Her lungs refused to take in air. She'd been with another guy. A guy she barely knew, while the man she actually did care about was probably at work, saving people's lives. All because Adonna wanted to get her rocks off.

What kind of person had she become?

She pressed her palms against her temples. No. This wasn't Tracy's fault. She didn't even like Sean. There was no one to blame for this, other than the desperate slut who'd kidnapped her body.

Sorry.

The word came from deep within her soul. Adonna? Maybe, but her mind still whirled with the sense of energy slowly ebbing away inside her. If Sean were to touch her again, she wasn't sure she wouldn't explode from within if she didn't die from shame first.

She found her purse beneath an end-table and reached for the straps. She needed to get out of there. Now.

Tracy backed up until she hit the wall beside the door. Should she call out? Say goodbye? Make up a dumbass excuse that he wouldn't believe?

Taking a deep breath for courage, she grabbed the door handle and breathed a sigh of relief when it opened.

Just a few more steps and she'd be safe. She slipped out the door and ran-walked down the pavement and past Sean's car.

Shit. She didn't even know where she was! She glanced back to the house. Green shrubs lined the front windows. The eight from the house number thirty-eight hung below its counterpart, as if one of the screws were missing.

The door opened.

Sean tilted his head to the right, brow furrowed. "Tracy?"

"I-I'm sorry." Tracy turned from the house and bolted to the corner of the road.

Sean didn't follow, and she exhaled as the wind kicked up, rattling the street sign: Madison Avenue and Washington Lane. She'd never heard of either.

She continued her sprint down Madison, toward the droning sounds of a main road. Once she got to the street, hopefully she would see something that would help.

A droplet smacked her head.

Rain. Now? Seriously? Could this day get any worse?

She grabbed her cell phone and dialed Laini.

The line clicked when she answered. "Hey, girl. What's up?"

Tracy held back the sob brimming in her chest. "Hey. I need you."

A slight hesitation. "What's wrong? Did the cop end up being mistake number four? If so I swear I'm gonna break open a can of whoop ass!"

"No, no, no. It's not John. I just, I just." Shit. She just what? Glancing up into the darkening clouds, she entered a parking lot. "Can you come get me? I'm at the Wawa on Station Road in Erial."

"What the heck are you doing in Erial?"

"Could you please just come and get me?"

She sighed. "You're killing me, you know that?" Tracy imagined her putting the recliner's footrest down and setting her book on the table. "I'll be right there."

She clicked off the phone and stepped into the convenience store's vestibule. The rain dripped in uneven trails down the glass windows.

Tracy shivered as Adonna pulsed inside her.

The burning sensation of Sean's hands roaming over her, the heat of his mouth, forgetting this guy would be harder than shutting out any of the other assholes she'd dated.

She cringed. No, it wouldn't be hard to forget.

Adonna would have to get over it and get over him. Tracy had a great guy waiting for her and she wasn't about to let her Ambient screw that up.

She glanced through the doors, her gaze rolling over the people lined up at the counter. A double chocolate latte might help. At least for now.

32

John flipped on the wiper blades as he pulled out of Dunkin' Donuts. He washed a broccoli croissant down with black coffee. Dammit, he hated broccoli! Why couldn't Dak like chocolate like Adonna?

He shook his head and tried to focus on the case photographs he'd reviewed all afternoon, all of which he'd neatly tucked into the briefcase perched on the passenger seat. But his mind kept drifting back to Sunday: the horror on Tracy's face after Dak took him over and talked directly to her; and the fury he'd felt being pushed to the background in his own body.

I told you I was sorry.

"That doesn't change the fact that you did it. Or that you could do it again. Was it even hard for you?" John's eyes glared at his reflection in the mirror.

Dak sloshed like jelly, probably enjoying the broccoli, rather than answering the questions. But his silence was answer enough. If Dak had strained in any way to take control of his host, John would have felt it. John had governance over his own body because Dak allowed it. It was that simple.

You don't need to be afraid of me.

John snorted. "Really? You took me over, Dak. You had a conversation with a girl that I really care about and told her things I wasn't goddamn ready to tell her."

I didn't have the conversation. I suggested you should have the conversation, then I let you do the talking. Anyway, Tracy needed to know about Amy.

John stopped at a red light and looked into the mirror. "Yes, eventually, but not yet. You're rushing things. I know you're excited, but you're going to scare her. Hell, you've already scared me, and I'm used to you."

I'm only trying to help. Dak roiled. If he had a body, John imagined it slumping.

John caved. "I get that you're trying to help, but can you leave human stuff to me for a little bit? Please?" The light changed, and he started driving again. "She's already nervous about the whole entity thing. Now she knows something about my past that I wasn't ready to tell her. The time wasn't right. Can't you get that?"

No. But your anxiety is making it hard for me to enjoy this broccoli.

"Easy fix. Stop giving me anxiety."

I'll try.

Sure he would.

The only thing predictable about Dak was his unpredictability.

33

"Hold on a minute." Laini tucked her feet into the folds of their couch. "You gotta be out of your mind, girl. I mean, what are the chances of you happening to meet the creepy southern octopus at a freaking library, of all places. He has to be stalking you."

Yeah, either that or he is possessed by an alien. Oh, and by the way, I'm possessed by an alien, too. Tracy rubbed her eyes. "It's kind of complicated."

"Well, now that you're out of there and okay, dish out the dirt. Part of me doesn't even want to know why you would get into a car with him again. I freaking hope condoms weren't involved."

Tracy's eyes widened over the top of her latte.

Condoms. Shit. Would Adonna even think of that? Probably not. Even John still seemed to struggle with Dak over simple human common sense.

Dammit.

Monday she'd accepted her Ambient, finally experiencing the harmonious relationship John and Dak promised. But now, only two days later, everything was in upheaval again.

She rubbed her temples. There was no way she could live with the constant threat of being taken over.

But what would John and Dak do if they found out she got rid of her Ambient? Would they be able to forgive her?

A small smudge of froth outlined the opening of the plastic lid on her coffee. Two bubbles on the foamy surface popped.

They wouldn't take the time to forgive her because Adonna was what both of them were interested in. Dak wanted a girlfriend and John wanted to give him one. Tracy was only a convenience.

But the way John looked into her eyes when she told him about the promotion told her he cared. She knew he did. Or maybe she only hoped he did.

Sighing, Tracy set down her drink. "This is all so screwed up."

"Come on. How bad can it be?"

Tracy glared over the top of her cup.

Laini's eyes opened like saucers. "Holy, shit. You *did it* with that stalker, didn't you? Eww. I don't care if he was hot. That's just, eww!" She shook her head. "Damn, I can't believe things are already over with Inspector Gadget."

"No." At least not yet, they weren't.

Laini set her coffee on the table. "Hold the farm. Are you telling me little Miss Priss screwed a total stranger while her mild-mannered cop boyfriend was out giving people speeding tickets?"

Tracy rubbed her temples. "We didn't actually have sex." No, but she might as well have. "You make it sound…" Just as cheap and disgusting as it was.

Adonna rolled inside her, probably reliving her fantasy mash-up.

Laini leaned toward her. "Girl, you know I always got your back, but I think you might be a little under the weather, still. I mean, you walk around talking to yourself, you're eating chocolate like it's going out of style and not gaining any weight, which is really ticking me off by the way; and now you're *doing it* with a guy you barely know?" Her brow furrowed. "I know they gave you a clean bill of health after your accident, but I'm not sure you're all right in the head, yet."

Tracy looked up at her. God, did she want to spill it, but for all she knew, she was being watched. And what would happen to anyone if she told what was really going on? She looked up at the ceiling fan, the television. Were they watching her right now?

Leaning back, Tracy rubbed her forehead. "You know, you're right. I don't think I'm okay. I think I'm really stressed out and I did the stupidest thing I could come up with." Or that Adonna could come up with. Would Tracy ever be strong enough to deny the Ambient something she wanted? If John were any example, the answer was no. She could never completely trust that her body would be under her own control again. And she had serious issues with that.

She shivered. "I should have run my ass off the second I saw that freak the first time."

"Don't beat yourself up. The nut-job was hidden under a damn nice display of packaging." Laini rubbed her shoulder. "Hon, maybe you should call a doctor. Seeing a therapist isn't that bad. My mom goes twice a month. She says it's great."

A shrink, yeah, that would go over well. She'd probably be diagnosed with multiple personalities. "Thanks, but I think I can work this out on my own."

Laini pursed her lips. "Just promise that you'll call me the next time you have the urge to do something stupid. You and me, we can go down to the Rodeo House and ride that dumb mechanical bull again. That will kick that stupidity out of you well and good."

Tracy grabbed her back. "Ouch. We almost ended up in twin hospital beds last time."

"Which is much better than screwing the whole neighborhood, girl. So, promise me: Mechanical bull?"

Tracy exhaled. "Mechanical bull it is." But now, more than ever, calling Agent Clark didn't seem like a half-bad idea.

34

John sat in the parking lot outside the police station, rubbing his eyes. Deep veins seemed to feed puffy, sunken eye sockets. He turned from the rear-view mirror. If he didn't know better, he'd think he was doing drugs.

He slammed the door as he left the car. An entire morning casing the last known whereabouts of the two latest victims had turned up squat.

And then there was the waiting. No calls from dispatch last night, none this morning, and still none after lunch. The killer struck every week, like clockwork. Had he moved on to kill somewhere else? Changed his M.O.? Or had he struck again but no one had been reported missing yet?

Wondering—no—*knowing* some poor, innocent woman was out there, probably being tortured, kept a burning pool of bile eating a hole into the base of his throat. How many more would die because this maniac managed to stay one step ahead of him?

Art Commings met him outside the building, holding the *Office Space for Rent* sign. "I took care of this for you." He tossed the ripped cardboard behind the bush with the others. "You come up with anything?"

"All dead ends, as usual. How about you?"

"None of them had any new love interests. No new jobs. Nothing out of the ordinary. They have to be random marks."

John pushed through the door. "They have one thing in common."

"What?"

"They're all dead." *Because I can't find out this asshole's pattern.*

Staff Sergeant Biggs stuck his head out of his door. "Commings, Peters: In my office."

Art glanced at John. "He sounds pissed."

"Yeah. Let's see what's going on."

A tremor ran down John's spine as he entered the poorly-lit room. Other than the sergeant propped against the front of his desk, three more men stood in the center of the room looking like carbon copy cut-outs of each other. Suits. Suits were always bad news.

Sergeant Biggs looked up from his folded arms. "You guys are being taken off the case."

Heat flooded John's veins. Feds. Here they were, ready to sweep in, steal all his hard work, and make heroes out of themselves. "No way. We're getting close. I can feel it."

Biggs pushed away from the desk. "It's their jurisdiction now. There's nothing we can do about it." His red cheeks and grimace didn't match his words. "We need to hand over all the files immediately."

"This is bullshit," Art said. "Why is it their jurisdiction?"

John's veins turned to ice as one of the suits turned toward them: Agent Clark from the Ambient Custodial Division of Homeland Security. Shit.

Agent Asshole's gaze centered on John before turning to his partner. "We've come into new information on this case. This is now a Homeland Security issue."

"Homeland Security?" Art said. "This is a murderer, not a terrorist."

He seemed to disregard the comment. "When can we get the files?"

John lurched toward the agent's face. "When you tell me what this new nugget of information is."

"That's classified."

"Of course, it is." And if Clark was involved, 'classified' meant otherworldly. He'd met a lot of ACDHS agents over the last five years, but none out for blood like Clark.

Dak shuddered within, keeping quiet. Hiding. John didn't blame him. The last time they'd seen Clark, an Ambient died. No. An Ambient was executed and Clark seemed to enjoy it far too much.

Biggs moved between them. "The files and evidence will be ready within an hour."

"Like hell they will be," John said. "This is bullshit, Biggs, and you know it."

"It's out of our hands, Peters. Let it go. We have enough other cases to worry about."

"Enough other cases? Are you shitting me?" This *was* the case. These shitbags didn't care about South Jersey. These people were names and numbers to them, not neighbors. Federal agents had no business being here.

Art grabbed John's shoulder, giving him a tug toward the door. "Come on, man. Let's get out of here."

John's narrowed gaze latched onto Clark's. The agent's lips curled in a malevolent grin as Art ushered John from the room.

35

Tracy leaned over her laptop, holding her temples.

"Not feeling well?" Kyle Olson reclined on her doorframe, his brow furrowed.

She blinked herself from her stupor. "Oh, umm, no. I mean, yeah." She closed her eyes. "I don't know. I'm sorry." What was she supposed to say, that an alien forced her to be intimate with a total stranger? That her personal life was a complete mess?

He shrugged. "Don't be sorry. Even sick, you put out more work today than we normally see from your old department in a week."

"You're exaggerating."

"Only a little."

Something oozed across the plane of her diaphragm. The entity slithering inside her could still take hold at any time. For all Tracy knew, Adonna might decide she liked Kyle, and all of a sudden, Tracy would be attacking her boss right there on top of the desk.

She shuddered. There had to be a way to control her Ambient. There must have been others with this problem. Maybe she just needed to take some pills to keep Adonna sedated.

Sighing, she let her head fall into her palms, making it look like she was staring into the reports strewn across her desk.

Kyle stepped over the threshold and slid one of the charts toward himself. "Do you still think parents of grade schoolers should be our target?"

God, sales data seemed so inconsequential compared to everything else in her life. But things were finally happening for her. She was not about to let her wayward Ambient ruin her first big chance to prove herself.

Tracy straightened. "Definitely, and I had a great idea: add a stamp to every can saying *double box top points for your school.*"

His brow shot up. "Do you want to give my father a coronary? That's a lot of liability to hang out there."

She nodded. "But statistics show that even parents who buy groceries with the intention of cutting out the box tops forget all about it and throw them away." He didn't look convinced. "It can be a secondary campaign. 'Giving back to those who matter the most.'" She let the idea sink in. "I guarantee you, sales will increase, and you probably will see a minimal increase in corporate charitable donations."

After a moment, he nodded. "I like it. Why don't you prepare a pitch for Monday's meeting?"

She shuddered. Despite her unscheduled show of bravado last Monday, standing in front of McNulty and his stooges was far from her idea of a fun time. "The sales team will shoot me down."

"They won't. Not if I'm up there presenting with you."

Tracy fought her eyes from widening. If Kyle stood, giving his approval before the presentation even began, Daddy would certainly stomp any negativity from her jealous coworkers. This could be it: the chance she needed to prove she deserved this promotion.

Something swirled within her stomach.

But, first, she needed to make sure she was herself. Completely.

She considered Agent Clark's business card in her purse. Would her relationship with John and Dak be over if she had this thing ripped out of her?

If she did make the call, would she even be alive Monday to give her presentation?

Tracy rubbed her damp palms on her slacks. She couldn't live with this creature inside her, but there was also a chance that she wouldn't live without her. God, it was too much.

She needed to clear her mind. Focus.

A run: that's what she needed—a good, long run in the park.

36

Art shoved the last of the war room photographs into a manila folder. "You gotta stop stewing over this. It ain't anyone's fault."

No, it wasn't anyone's fault, but their case had been taken over by a government agency set up for the sole purpose of policing alien lifeforms.

He'd gone over every piece of evidence hundreds of times. If there were Ambient involvement, he'd have picked up on it. These women were raped and murdered. Ambients were sensitive to emotions. They wouldn't be able to cope with the fear that kind of violence would cause another. They'd lash out—unless it was a latent Ambient. Then there wouldn't be a goddamn thing the alien could do about it. Shit, just the thought of it was royally screwed up.

But there had to be something that linked all the cases, something that had drawn Agent Dickwad back onto John's doorstep. Whatever it was, it had been there, staring him in the face.

Shit. He slammed his fist on the table. "We missed something. Something important."

"John Peters doesn't miss anything," Art said. "You're a big pain in my promotion-less ass in that way." He smiled in that fatherly way that reminded John that Art trumped him in years of service, if not in detective skills. "Good cops get taken off cases all the time. You can't let it get to you like this."

Too late for that. Maybe if he'd spent more time on the job…

John closed his eyes and steadied his breathing. Second guessing himself wouldn't help, and being pissed off wasn't going to change anything.

Tracy's face eased into John's thoughts—the warmth of her hands when they touched, the relaxed way she made him feel. Yes, she'd been a distraction. A *major* distraction, albeit a pleasant one. How had she gotten so far under his skin in only two weeks?

Dak tingled beneath John's right shoulder blade, soothing the soreness.

Maybe getting off this case was a blessing in disguise. Tracy was a mystery he was more than ready to lose himself in. He could take her to dinner. Real dinner, not this fast food crap. He could give her the time she deserved, and if everything worked out, he and Dak would both be getting what they so badly needed.

As long as he didn't get another life-sucking assignment.

Art's cell phone rang. He glanced at the screen. "I gotta take this. Give me a minute."

John nodded as his friend strolled from the table with his phone to one ear and his finger in the other.

They'd been out of the loop for a while. John had no idea what kind of caseload Biggs had piled on his desk. While his adrenaline rushed at the thought of another, hopefully easier murder investigation, a nice, easy breaking-and-entering would be good, too.

His phone buzzed.

    Tracy Seavers: Hi! I'm at the park.
    Tracy Seavers: Just had a great run.

John's face flushed. He glanced at Art to make sure he hadn't noticed. Damn, the last thing he needed was for his partner to think he was whipped.

This was perfect timing, though. This was his chance to start over. He ran his fingers down the side of his phone. He should do it. Ask her out, let her know how he felt, no pussy-footing around.

The muscles in his neck tightened. It was Thursday. Statistically, they'd find another body any moment now.

But that wasn't his problem, anymore, was it?

He shuddered as a wave of guilt coated him. He owed it to those girls, to their families, to find the bastard that murdered them. He couldn't just stop because someone told him to.

He glanced at the door as Sergeant Biggs strolled by with Agent Dickhead and the younger one. What was his name? Brown? Whatever. Didn't matter. This was their problem now. Dak was right. He needed to get a life, and here he was, off the case and still letting his job get in the way of what he wanted.

And Tracy—damn. With those ample hips and that tiny pout that drove him crazy, yeah, she was definitely what he wanted. And John needed to act on that before someone else did.

Dinner tonight?

He double checked his spelling before hitting send.

Tracy Seavers: That would be great.
Tracy Seavers: I'd like to tell you something.

Tonight was definitely looking up.

Will pack you up at 7:00 OK?

Pack? Pick you up, you idiot. Goddamnit!

Tracy Seavers: Just enough time to get home and take a shower. Perfect.

She hadn't even noticed the typo. He smiled at his phone. Yeah, this was good. He'd make it work this time.

He tapped a 'K' and flinched as he looked up from his phone.

Art's brows were stitched together and sweat ran down the side of his face. "Mom," he said into his mobile. "Get a hold of yourself." He glanced at John then to the floor. "Can you put Dad on the phone? Can he talk?"

Art's face reddened. Shit.

"All right, all right," Art said. "Listen, I'm on my way. Hang up with me and call 911. I will be there in fifteen minutes." He lowered his phone and turned to John.

"Just go," John said. "I can finish up here. I'll tell Biggs."

Art patted his shoulder twice. "Thanks. I owe you."

37

Tracy finished stretching and eased onto her favorite park bench, perched atop the highest point in Gloucester Township Park. Refastening her ponytail, she breathed deeply, allowing the smell of fresh-cut grass to ease her tension. A run had been just what she needed.

She closed her eyes and listened to the soccer game in the fields at the bottom of the hill and the kids giggling in the playground somewhere far behind her.

The everyday. This is what she needed. This, and to talk to John and Dak again.

Somehow, someway, she needed Dak to help her get through to Adonna. She needed her Ambient to understand there were certain things that were off-limits. And taking Tracy over was definitely off-limits. And if that wasn't possible, then she'd make a date with Homeland Security. She *would* take control of her life again—any way she had to.

"Holy Hell. You actually *are* here."

Tracy opened her eyes and found Sean standing a few paces down the hill. Every embarrassing moment from the previous day flooded her thoughts.

Her lips parted, but she couldn't form a coherent thought, let alone a string of words.

He took another step toward her. "When we met at the library, I thought it was chance. But it was the same today: I felt this tug and my car just drove into the parking lot, and then I walked right up this hill. What in tarnation is going on?" He rubbed his torso and gulped like something had settled into his chest that he needed to dislodge.

Something *was* inside him, but a massage wasn't going to fix it.

His gaze returned to hers. "Yesterday, you just *left*."

A heaviness surfaced in her own chest. "I know. I-I'm sorry."

He piffed. "*You're* sorry?" He ran his fingers through his hair. "That whole afternoon is a blur. I mean, it was like having an out-of-body experience. I was on auto-pilot. I felt everything, but it was like I sat back and watched while…"

While their entities twisted, turned, and kneaded each other like taffy. Yeah, she knew exactly how it felt.

His lips thinned. "That's the first time I've felt out of control in a very long time." He kicked a mound of grass at his feet. "I can honestly tell you I have no idea what happened. I didn't like it." He looked up and grinned half-heartedly. "Well, I liked it, but you know what I mean."

Yes, she knew exactly what he meant.

Damn. He had to be even more confused and upset about all this than she was. At least Tracy knew what was going on. Sean was completely in the dark, and he didn't deserve to be. She wasn't supposed to talk about her entity to anyone, but this was different. Sean needed to know the truth.

"This is going to seem like a very strange question," Tracy began. "But have you by any chance had a near-death experience?"

He stepped back, nearly falling down the hill. "What are you talking about?"

"Has something happened to you recently? Were you hurt badly and recovered quickly?"

His nose flared, and his gaze traveled over his shoulder, back toward the parking lot below. "How-how did you know that?"

"I can explain, but I need you to have an open mind."

"I'm listening."

"This happened to me, too. I almost died, well, maybe I did die, and an entity jumped inside me and healed my wounds."

Sean's brow furrowed. "An *entity?*"

She nodded. "They're called Ambients. They're an alien race. They need our lungs to survive."

He folded his arms. "An alien, as in outer space? You have to be shitting me."

"I wish I was."

"Okay, I get it. I was an easy lay and now you're looking to get rid of me." He held out his hands. "It's all right. I do the same thing to girls all the time, but I don't make up cockamamie stories."

"It's not a story." But he was right about one thing, she really didn't want anything to do with him. His face would always remind her of what Adonna could do if she wanted something bad enough.

She shouldn't even be near him now. It wasn't her responsibility to tell Sean what he was. The government would find him, eventually. And she needed to get away before Adonna decided she wanted round two.

Tracy stood and started down the hill. "I think I should go."

"Wait." He grabbed her arm. "Do you really think you have something inside you?"

"An Ambient." She shrugged him off. "And yes, I do. I *know* I do. I realize it sounds crazy."

"Not too crazy." A chorus of cheers erupted from the soccer field below as Sean took a step toward her. "Do you hear this thing talking in your head, trying to get you to do things you don't want to do?"

Tracy smirked. "Like having sex with a guy I just met?"

He laughed. "So you really are a nice girl with a slutty alien inside you?"

"Yeah, I guess so." Adonna jittered, sliding along Tracy's skin. The movement was slow, encumbered. John said Ambients get tired after taking control of their hosts, and yesterday she'd definitely taken control, but it probably wasn't a coincidence that the entity's entire being seemed flattened as close as she could get to Sean. "So, you believe me, then?"

He pressed his temples. "Shit, I thought I was going crazy, hearing things. It makes sense now, all this weird stuff in my head." He squinted, as if trying to see the entity beneath her skin. "So, this feeling that I want to get in your pants again. That's all this thing inside me?"

Adonna quaked, spinning through Tracy's psyche. *No. Never again.* To Sean, she said, "Yes, but that's done now. I have someone special in my life. A really great guy. A cop. I'm not going to risk our relationship because my Ambient has a roving eye."

He shoved his hands in his pockets. "You didn't mention you had a boyfriend."

"Well, I do."

He clucked his tongue. "Damn. He'd be pretty pissed if he knew what we'd done yesterday."

A cold dread slipped through Tracy's gut. "I guess." Yes, John would be pissed. And he'd have every right to be. But then again, he was maybe the only one who could comprehend losing control of your own body. "John would understand. He has an Ambient, too."

Sean's gaze shot up. His expression hard, before he lowered his eyes. "I'm guessing this boyfriend thing is coming up now because this is goodbye. Are you saying we can't see each other again, ever? I mean, you just dropped a bomb on me. I have questions."

Adonna pressed against the inside of her chest. A sound similar to a hiss banged through Tracy's head like a ping-pong ball. Tracy ignored her. "It's better if we don't. I don't think the entities inside us could handle us being together without, you know."

"Fucking."

Tracy flinched. "Yeah."

Sean shook his head. "I'm usually the one doing the dumping when I'm done with someone." He sighed. "This is a pretty unpleasant feeling."

She reached into her purse and fingered Agent Clark's business card. She could understand needing answers, but she couldn't be the one to provide them.

"I have something for you." She pulled out the card and took a photo of it with her phone. Then, shaking, she handed the card to Sean. "These are the people who talked me through all this. They know all about the Ambients. They can probably answer your questions better than I could."

He stared at the creased card before plucking it from her fingertips. "The government ain't never helped me any."

She gave him a kiss on the cheek. A spark shocked her as her lips touched his skin. "Maybe you could try to find a real relationship. Put an end to the one-night stands."

He slid the card in his pocket. "Who in Sam Hill would want me?"

Tracy stepped away. "Give yourself a chance. You might be surprised."

38

Tracy jumped when a waitress tripped, and a tray of drinks splashed across the floor. John barely raised his gaze from the salad he'd been poking at with his fork. His furrowed brow twitched and reset to a deep line.

Had another woman disappeared? Stupid question. A woman seemed to die or disappear every day lately, but Tracy didn't remember hearing about a new victim being discovered. Not that she'd really been paying attention.

News of the first victim had horrified her. Now her thoughts about the murders seemed clinical, like no big deal. Adonna shifted, sparkling across her diaphragm, and Tracy shuddered at her callousness.

Another woman might be dead and all she could worry about was her own stupid problems. When had she become so cold? So much had changed in the last few weeks. Too much. She needed to make things right again.

John's gaze still roamed his salad. Something was definitely wrong.

"Do you want to talk about it?" she asked.

Gaping, he looked up and placed his fork down. "I'm sorry. I guess I'm not much company tonight."

She reached over and brushed his fingertips with her own. John or maybe Dak grabbed her hand, forcing their palms together. Dak leached on instantly, as if he were waiting beneath John's skin, hoping for contact. The Ambient seeped into Tracy, spinning, caressing, stroking—all soft, caring sensations. Nothing like the brutal, dominant force that had entered her yesterday.

This time, however, Adonna didn't respond. The only sensation running through Tracy seemed to be Dak. But the touch was so gentle, so kind. How couldn't Adonna want to wrap herself in such devotion?

John's eyes narrowed. "Dak said he wants to try something, and not to be scared."

"Huh?"

The swirl within her lurched and her lungs constricted. She tried to gasp, but the air wasn't there. A wave of panic throttled her core before Dak sizzled back out of her body and reentered John.

Tracy inhaled deeply, relishing in the aroma of fried chicken and sausage intermingled with the life-giving air.

John grabbed her arm. "What happened?"

"I don't know. I couldn't breathe."

John looked toward the table. "Dak, what the hell, buddy?" He nodded, as if listening, before he returned his gaze to her. "Dak was worried about you guys, so he did something to disconnect Adonna from your lungs for a second. Apparently without her, you still can't breathe." His lips thinned. "He says you should be healed by now and she should be talking. It's like she's exerted herself to exhaustion."

Tracy cleared her throat. Exerted herself? Yeah, rolling around rubbing your alien body all over a sleazy sex-starved entity will do that to you. Not that she would admit that. Not yet at least. "Is that bad? Are we going to be okay?"

"We think so. You're not having any trouble breathing now, right?"

She took in a deep, wonderful breath. "No, I'm fine."

"I guess we need to give her time, then. Maybe she was already weak when she jumped into you."

The unintentional underlying message set in: without Adonna, Tracy would die. Period. In one fell swoop, her get out of jail free card disappeared.

John rubbed his face.

"Are you all right?" she asked.

"Yeah. Damn, I'm sorry. I could really use some good news right now. What did you want to talk about?"

Tracy's jaw tensed. Good news? What she had was far from that.

His eyes softened, expectant.

Shit. He'd misread her text. He thought something *good* happened. And it looked like he'd had the mother of bad days. She couldn't tell him about Sean. Not now.

His brow rose.

Okay, she needed good news. There had to be something. "Umm, you know that promotion I got?"

He nodded.

"Well, things are going great. Kyle Olson loves my ideas."

He leaned toward her. "And?"

"No and. He loves my ideas."

His expectant look settled over her, warming the room. "Sorry, that's the cop in me. I'm sensing some trepidation in all this."

She sighed. "Well, yeah. I need to make a presentation on Monday morning. I'm kind of terrified."

He reached across the table and slipped his hand under hers. "You're going to do great."

Her lips trembled before rising. He had no idea if she'd do well or not. He didn't even know anything about her job. She relaxed as Dak danced across the edge of her skin. It was damn sweet of them, though, being so supportive.

The waitress arrived with their appetizers, taking away John's full plate of salad. He glanced at the fried green beans she placed before him but his gaze seemed to travel past the plate again.

Tracy waved her hand in front of his vacant eyes. "Are you still with me?"

"I'm sorry. This really isn't your fault."

"Okay, police-officer buddy hat is on." She tipped an imaginary chapeau. "I'm all ears." Hey, it was the least she could do after he sat through all her whining about her Ambient. Maybe it would be good to listen to someone else's problems for a change.

John took a bite of a green bean and chewed.

She imagined Dak poking him from the inside, trying to get him to open up. She stroked the back of John's hand with her fingertips, hoping to give Dak a little help in encouraging their favorite detective.

John took a deep breath. "I got taken off the case today."

She balked. "Why?"

He recounted what sounded like a particularly unenjoyable meeting. "We had to hand in all our files and tomorrow I get a new assignment." He rubbed his eyes. "And to top it all off, my partner's dad is in bad shape. He had to leave and I'm not sure when he'll be back."

Wow. Losing the case had to bruise his male ego. But she couldn't be all that upset about it. That assignment seemed to take a lot out of him. Maybe someone else could save the world, just this once.

"Well, look on the bright side. That gives you more time to spend on your social life."

A smile shot across his lips. Pure, genuine, and sexy as all hell. Yeah, she definitely wanted more time with her mild-mannered detective. More time to learn, love, and hopefully forget the last few days.

"You have no idea how happy we are to hear you say that." He entwined his fingers in hers. "Because I am very interested in taking this further."

A shimmer ran down her spine. "Further?"

His eyes darkened. "A lot further."

His gaze languished over her and heat spread across her skin. Yeah, overly-focused John was sexy. John without a case to worry about, with thoughts all centered on her, damn!

"We'd have to take it slow." He rubbed his thumb over hers. "Slower than I'd like, to give our entities time to adjust."

He spoke about this like other people might discuss using a condom. That was probably the detective in him, calculating all angles, all possibilities. She was usually the type to throw caution to the wind, but as that thumb continued to draw slow circles over her knuckle, she imagined that coarse, gentle touch slipping up her shirt, unhooking her bra. She shivered. Hopefully *slow* included a ton of foreplay.

John closed his eyes and puffed a laugh. "For the record, Dak is not onboard with taking it slow." When he opened his eyes, Tracy knew John was not completely committed to taking it slow, either. He licked his lips, his gaze filled with wanton promise, before he glanced away, becoming the cool, collected detective again. "What we need to know is, are you onboard? If you're not interested, let us know."

John flinched as if kicked from inside. But Dak had to already know her answer. John was right to be cautious, though. Things were a little more complicated than what she, Dak, and John wanted.

A flash of Sean overran Tracy's thoughts: his confused, somewhat shy demeanor at the park, his smile, and how his fingers had invaded her only the night before.

And she'd wanted it. At least the alien part of her had. Her stomach sank and churned, confused and ashamed at the mere thought of Sean touching her again, while Adonna tingled and rolled, as if relishing the memory.

Tracy dug her nails into her free palm. Warning bells had gone off the second she'd seen Sean. But Adonna, apparently, liked the danger.

She used her mind to grab hold of the foreign energy inside her. She focused Adonna's essence into her own eyes and stared at John. She traced his rugged jaw, sweet expression, and tousled hair. She lingered on the curve of his wide shoulders and imagined his strong hands holding her tightly to him.

If Adonna wanted danger, Tracy would serve it up to her in the form of a police detective. That's a sexy, dangerous job; coating a sweet, sensitive, and gorgeous guy. She wanted John and Adonna was going to like Dak—once she let him get his little alien hands on her.

Tracy released Adonna and the entity seemed to float within. Contentment and relaxation flowed through her. A positive response? It had to be. Finally!

Allowing her grin to break free, Tracy grabbed John's hand. Pressure flashed from her torso into her palm, but stopped, tingling her skin. John's hand heated and he pressed their palms together.

"They're touching," John said. "Not talking, just touching."

"Is that good?"

"I don't know, but Dak is happy."

Wow. Could it be so simple?

Tracy pulled back the tears forming in her eyes. Somehow along this crazy road, Dak and John had become the do all and end all of, well, everything. But with Adonna jonesing for the sleaziest guy she could find, Tracy wasn't sure she'd ever be happy. Yet, here they were.

She called up her best smile. "Do you think Dak would be happier if I took you up on that slow stroll to the next level?"

John's eyes softened, melting Tracy's heart. "I think that would make Dak *very* happy."

A lump formed in her throat. "Well, we wouldn't want Dak to be unhappy, would we?"

John's smile beamed. "Nope, we definitely wouldn't want that."

The clatter of the restaurant sounded around them. Customers arrived and left while she and John eased closer, enjoying a lazy dinner and a downright sloth-like dessert. She could drown in his eyes, melt into sweet oblivion as his gaze caressed her cheeks, hair, and shoulders.

What was he thinking; or what was Dak saying that she couldn't hear?

A deep warmth spread over her. Whatever his thoughts, the tides in their relationship had obviously changed. The simple admission that they wanted each other had made this modest silence a flood of connection, rather than her normal discomfort of filling a quiet void with meaningless consonants and vowels.

His expression spoke millions of truths words couldn't express, and she'd never felt so beautiful.

Tracy's heels tapped across the pavement as John walked her from his car to her front door. Funny, she'd planned on telling him about Sean, about how Adonna had used Tracy's body to get what she wanted, and about how she wanted to get rid of her Ambient once and for all.

At first, she didn't want to unload on him since he'd obviously needed her for a change. And now, with their relationship more official, she probably wouldn't tell him at all.

Her Ambient had settled into the background for the latter part of the date. By now, Adonna must know Tracy wasn't happy with her entity's recent exploits. Maybe she'd decided to play nice.

Tracy hoped so. Five weeks ago, Adonna gave her a second

chance at life. Until now, things had been shaky between them; but the fear and uncertainty was over now. That second chance re-started today, for both of them.

"Here we are." John slipped his hands into his pockets.

"I had a great time," Tracy said. "I'm really glad we could get together."

"Really? Because it seemed like I rattled about my problems all night."

"You didn't rattle that much. Maybe a babble or two." She gave his wrist a gentle tug toward the door. This was only their first official date, but they were past childish games. Tracy was more than ready to take the first of their slow steps to the next level.

John's gaze darted to the right, then back to her. Damn, she wished she could hear Dak.

"I'm glad I got your text." He closed his eyes and snickered. "Now, that sounded incredibly stupid."

"I don't think so." She stepped closer. "Why are you so nervous all of a sudden?"

He straightened slightly, his expression sliding back into the cool, confident visage of a hardened detective. "I'm not nervous."

Yeah, you are. She inched up and kissed him beside the ear. Red stains specked his cheeks as he removed his right hand from his pocket and slipped it around her waist. Hmm, maybe not as nervous as she thought.

Adonna fizzled in the center of Tracy's chest. That better be a positive response because anything that might have been there with Sean was now gone. *This* is where she belonged.

John's eyes dropped to her mouth. He licked his lips and eased closer. Her skin flushed as she leaned back, lips parted. He made her wait an eternity before his mouth closed over hers, sweet and tender at first. John's movements were slow, searching as his hand smoothed up her back to rest at the nape of her neck.

He deepened the kiss and Tracy sighed as he pulled her closer, opening her mouth to drink him in. He was all musk and heat with a heady mix of cologne. She dragged her nails through his hair, leaning up to take in more of him. Her body ached in all the right places, and she shifted her feet to steady herself. Damn, why had they waited so long to do this?

John turned to the right and gasped, leaving her open and wanting. Eyes closed, he held her at arm's length for three breaths before his gaze drew back to hers. "I want to come in, but I can't."

A spray of disappointment washed over her. "Oh, I—"

He held up his hand. "Dak is just…and I'm…" He shook his head. "God, this is killing me, but we need to take this more slowly. We need to make sure Adonna is okay with Dak before we even think about…" He swallowed hard. "Well, I know what *I was* thinking about."

Tracy wanted to reach out and touch him, let him know she was here no matter what. Hell, she'd do whatever she had to if it would wipe Amy's memory from him forever.

As he stood before her though, struggling, she wasn't sure that would ever be possible.

"Tracy." He ran his fingers along her cheek. A flash of pain darkened his eyes, something deep and cutting. "I want you. Let's make that perfectly clear. But there are four of us. Please understand we can't rush this."

But Adonna and Dak had talked. They seemed fine. Tracy opened her mouth to protest, but he kissed her cheek, then her lips sweetly. "Goodnight."

Her knees nearly gave out. Their night was over, just like that?

No. She wasn't okay with this. She needed to prove to John that Adonna was onboard with Team John and Dak.

Sweat broke across Tracy's brow as the entity pulsed inside her. Adonna seemed to expand with each unsettling beat. But what did that mean?

Tracy shivered. As much as she wanted John, she couldn't guarantee Adonna wouldn't be the cause of another alien-induced heartache.

Not yet, at least.

Tracy took a step back as John walked toward his car. Every cell in her body reeled in disappointment.

She needed to find a way to be certain about Adonna. And soon.

39

A steaming cup of coffee sat centered on John's desk blotter. Art reclined in the chair bedside his own desk, tapping on that infernal tablet computer.

"Didn't expect to see you today," John said. "How's your dad?"

Art looked up. "They admitted him. He had a minor heart attack. Doctor says he's stable, but they want to keep him under observation for a few days."

John nodded. Now probably wouldn't be the best time to mention the doctors said the same thing days before his own father died.

Biggs poked his head out of his office. His normally perfect hair stuck out in three places on the side of his head and his lips seemed cemented in a frown. "Peters, it's about time. I need you both in here."

John glanced at the clock. He was ten minutes early. As usual. He decided not to comment on the insinuation that he'd been late. Something was definitely up.

Art plopped into the seat in front of Biggs's desk. John stood inside the doorframe and folded his arms.

The Sergeant propped up his tablet and tapped the screen. "You remember Officer Giancarlo Doogan?"

A photo of the beat cop appeared on the screen: a formal head shot, probably a few years old from the noticeable difference in bulk.

"Yes," John said. "The cop who claimed to have shot someone fleeing the scene of Alexandra Nixon's murder."

Biggs nodded. "Doogan didn't check in after his shift last night. He was found dead thirty minutes ago in the woods behind Grant Lake Park."

Art closed his eyes and mumbled something under his breath.

"You think our killer caught up with him?"

"Uncertain. That's why you're here." The sergeant's frown deepened. "I hope neither of you had breakfast yet." He tapped the computer pad. The photo changed to a body lying on a bed of bloody leaves. Purple and red raised bruises covered his face, and a blood-soaked mass held his mouth open in what appeared to be a scream.

"Jesus," Art said. "What's in his mouth?"

Biggs straightened. "His genitals."

Art covered his lips and leaned away from the screen.

John pointed at the tablet. "Crime of passion. Look at the bruising. I'll bet some of that is post mortem."

"How the hell can you tell by looking at a computer screen?" Art asked.

Biggs disregarded him and turned to John. "I need you on this one. Agent Evans passed, said this is unrelated to their case."

"And how did the hotshot federal agent come to that conclusion so quick?" Art asked.

John furrowed his brow, contemplating the screen. "Did Evans know Doogan was the one who shot his perpetrator?"

Biggs shrugged. "I may have left a few details out. Funny how forgetful you can be on phone conferences when the people on the other end are shouting at you."

The sergeant's gaze remained stoic. John had never known Biggs to break the rules, but they'd developed a trust over the years. Maybe he didn't want the Feds anywhere near an investigation of one of his own.

"We're on it," John said. "Don't let them take the body until I get there." He turned to Art. "Call Emmerson and have her draw me up a standard roster of suspects. I want a list of every ticket he's given, or any domestic dispute call he's answered. Give me everything from his work files."

John's attention drew back to the screen, absorbing the bruising patterns. Evans was probably right. If their serial killer had found Doogan, he wouldn't have taken this kind of time. The cop's death would have been quick in order to efficiently eliminate the problem and get back to the woman he probably had tied up somewhere. This was something different. Someone hated Doogan. A lot.

He headed to the door. "And buy Emmerson a box of chocolate for me because I'll be asking for a lot more research before this is over."

So much for the simple breaking-and-entering he had hoped for.

40

A burst of cool air tickled Tracy's cheeks as she pushed open the exit door of her office building and headed for her car.

If the Olsons decided to start the new promotion over spring break, they'd only have two months before summer vacation. That's what McNulty would do—jump in head first—but it would be too early. They needed to wiggle their ad campaign in with everyone else's back-to-school advertising. They could get a head-start on September, and then have an entire ten months of fully-realized potential.

"Miss Seavers?"

Tracy jumped. Her laptop bag slipped from her shoulder and bounced off the asphalt, landing on the white painted line beside her car.

She spun to find a man in a dark suit with a familiar grin.

Agent Green held up his hands. "Sorry, I didn't mean to scare you."

She stared for a moment, no words rising to the surface. A day after finally deciding not to call the federal agents, one of them happens to show up outside where she works?

"What are you doing here?" she asked.

He slipped his hands into his pockets. "I was in the area and thought I'd check up and see how you were doing."

Tracy tried to control her gape by reaching for her laptop bag.

"Is everything okay?" he asked. "Is your new *friend* still running silent?"

A ball formed in her chest as she slipped the strap over her shoulder. This was her chance. She could tell him everything. Maybe they knew a way to get an Ambient out without killing the host. Maybe they could do it in a hospital so they could help Tracy breathe.

No.

Dak would never forgive her and it would drive a wedge between her and John that neither of them would be able to loosen, even if they wanted to.

Besides, Adonna had helped her on more than one occasion, and she'd been silent since the incident on Wednesday. It had only been a few days, but they had been *good* days.

And now that she and John were a couple, things would be better. Adonna had spoken to Dak or shared somehow. If they'd come to a mutual understanding, maybe they could all be happy together.

As long as Tracy kept away from Sean.

She could do that. She *would* do that. She had to.

Tracy cleared her throat and tucked her hair behind her ear. "Umm, yeah. It's been fine. I mean, weird, but fine. I think I'm starting to get used to the idea."

He nodded. "Can you sense any movement?"

Would it be bad if she had or hadn't? Agent Clark had said she might sense something, but that it was different for everyone. "Sometimes I think I feel her, but I don't know. It might be gas."

Green puffed out a laugh. He seemed so genuine, so *nice*. "Have you heard any voices? Felt any inkling at all to do something you didn't want to do?"

Oh, shit. He knew.

His expression remained serene, if not expectant, as if the idea held a hint of excitement for him. God, she wanted to tell someone everything. She wanted to trust this man that was supposed to be her lifeline. But for some reason, she couldn't.

She gulped as he stared at her, still waiting for her answer.

"Well, there's the chocolate."

"Chocolate?"

"Yeah. Normally, chocolate gives me a horrible headache, but since the accident, I can't get enough of it, and it doesn't seem to bother me at all anymore."

His head cocked to the left. "Interesting. I guess that's not all that bad a side effect."

Several witty comebacks came to mind, but she bit them back. Agent Green was not her friend, no matter how amiable he seemed. As much as she wanted to, she couldn't trust him. She couldn't trust anyone; except maybe Dak and John, but she couldn't even tell them everything.

She blinked away the thought. Maybe she really was alone in all this.

Green's eyes narrowed. "You sure you're okay?"

Her fingers dug into the strap of her laptop bag. "Yeah, there's a lot on my mind. I got a promotion and, you know, the pressure and all."

The agent's gaze wavered over her hands before returning to her eyes. "All right, then. I'll stop by again some time, if that's okay by you."

The word *no* simmered on her tongue. The invasiveness of him standing next to her car sank in, almost as if he had always been there, watching over her shoulder. Then again, maybe he had, and there wasn't a darn thing she could do about it.

She forced a smile. "I guess I'll see you around, then."

Green tipped his head and walked toward a plain, dark blue sedan. Somehow, his presence continued to press in on all sides, even after he'd driven away.

41

"This is what kept me up last night," Art said, pinning a photo onto the war room corkboard. "Why choke a guy with his own genitals?" He dropped his hands to his sides. "I mean, I get the anger and all, but *damn*."

John had never known Art to lose sleep over a case. "Did you know Doogan?"

"No, but he was one of us, ya know?"

"Yeah, I know."

The same sentiment trickled through the combined precincts. It didn't matter who did or didn't know him. Doogan was a cop. That's all that mattered.

John stood and pointed to the photograph. "Well, he didn't actually choke. This was done post-mortem. Our perpetrator was sending a message. Probably trying to substantiate their dominance."

"As in sexually, a lover's spat?"

"I don't think so. The rest of the bruising is a bit too aggressive. Too pointed. This perpetrator had a lot to prove." John rubbed his chin. "But let's see if Doogan was dating anyone, just in case." He leaned against the wall beside the war board and stared at the picture. "What *were* you trying to prove. And why?"

"That annoying sixth sense you got ain't telling you what this asshole was thinking?"

"Not this time."

Biggs opened the door and dropped a flash drive on the table. "Here are all Doogan's recent reports. Emmerson said if you want to print them, you can do it yourself."

John dragged his fingers through his hair. Electronic numbers and images didn't speak to him like the real thing. Hard copies were real, tangible. They couldn't be deleted with the swipe of a keystroke. They were something *more*. Not that he expected anyone else to understand that. He really needed those files printed. "I guess she didn't get the box of chocolate I sent her?"

"Actually, she was chewing on a caramel when she handed me the flash drive. She said thanks and that the printer is loaded with paper."

So much for good old-fashioned bribery.

Art flicked the memory stick toward John. "Tell you what: you start printing and I'll order take out."

John snatched the drive and headed out the door toward his desk. Nearly a dozen cops lined the walls and all chatter stopped as he stepped into the hall. He hadn't seen this many cops in one place since the layoffs started.

"You got a lead yet?" a beat cop asked, sparking a wave of blue uniforms shifting from foot to foot.

"Not yet," John said. "But we'll get him."

Someone murmured, "Pussy detective."

John froze. His grip tightened on the flash drive.

Had John been that much of an ass when he was on the beat? Maybe. He'd mouthed off a few times, too. Still did, for that matter. Gritting his teeth, he kept walking.

One of the cops sneered as he passed. "Hey, Peters, you gonna stay in here drinking coffee all day, or will you eventually go out and catch Doogan's killer?"

John spun and slammed the cop against the wall, pinning him with one arm. The guy looked barely out of the academy, all clean and neat, with fresh acne scars on his nose. That wasn't going to get him off the hook for being an ass-wipe, though. John stared into his wide eyes until the kid's cheeks reddened, and the he looked away.

Yeah, you better call uncle, you stupid shit.

He released him and turned. The rest of the cops stepped back, probably with good reason as John eyed each of them.

"Doogan was a good cop." His grip tightened on the flash drive. Hopefully the files inside wouldn't prove differently.

John took a steadying breath. They all knew he'd been removed from one of the last cases Doogan had been involved with.

"He would have wanted you all out there doing your jobs. I'll radio if we need any assistance." A few nodded as John turned toward his desk and let the door close behind him.

This was going to be a long day.

42

Tracy bolted up the hill, drawing on the last of her strength after running three full treks around the perimeter of Gloucester Township Park. Adrenaline coursed through her veins. She was unstoppable. Tomorrow, she would march into that presentation room, face the sales force, and—

She stopped a few yards short of the top of the hill. Sean sat on her favorite bench, smiling at her.

He stood. "You certainly can run for a long time."

Holy hell! "Were you watching me?"

"It's not like that." Sean held out his hands. "I was waiting for you to finish. I only wanted to talk."

She stared at him for a moment, at a loss for words. "How did you know I'd be here?"

"I drove by yesterday but I didn't get that tingling sensation in my stomach, so I figured you weren't here. Today, the pull started when I was a few blocks away. I guess this thing inside me is like a Tracy-meter."

Great. Just great. "Sean, I really don't think this is a good idea."

"I'm not looking for anything. I know you have a boyfriend." He shifted his weight. "Things still good with you and John?"

He tilted his head, his gaze intent, as if the answer interested him more than it should.

"Of course, things are good. Why wouldn't they be?"

His lower lip twitched. "I don't know. I'm sorry. I guess I'm actin' like a creep. I don't mean to. It's just that everything is different now and I wanted to talk some more."

Adonna sparkled along Tracy's diaphragm, but otherwise didn't react or fling herself against Tracy's skin. Maybe she'd finally listened.

He turned away. "I guess that's too much to ask and I don't blame you. Damn, I'm being a first-class jerk."

True, but it would be rude of her to agree with him out loud.

"You and me, the other day, that wasn't all this entity thing inside me. When you kissed me back, I couldn't believe that a decent woman was actually interested in an ass like me." He slapped his forehead with his palm. "Idiot!"

"Well, maybe if you tried getting to know a girl once in a while instead of going out and looking for a score, maybe you could find someone." Wow. That was harsh, but there it was: out there.

He shook his head. "I'm too far gone. All I know is how to use this," he motioned to his beautiful face, "to get what I want and move on to the next one."

Which wouldn't be her.

Ever again, at least.

But she couldn't help but feel sorry for him. He had a different woman every night, and still ended up feeling alone.

His cheek ticked. His gaze fixed on a white butterfly bouncing about the clover flowers in the grass between them. Something about his face changed, and a slight adjustment in his stance made him seem more vulnerable than before. What was that expression on his face? Regret?

"You look pretty disgusted with yourself."

He laughed. "Darlin', I'm the king of disgust."

She closed the space between them. "Why the king of disgust?"

Children laughed on the other side of the hill. Sean continued to stare at the butterfly.

"Are you okay?" Tracy asked.

His gaze latched to hers. His eyes quaked before he blinked and turned away. "It's nothing."

"Well, you sure are acting like it's something."

Walk away, Tracy. You don't want to have anything to do with this guy. But it wasn't like she was in any danger. There were dozens of people in earshot. And she felt bad for him in so many ways, not the least of which being that she had John to talk to about the Ambients. Sean had no one but her.

"Why don't you want to talk about it?" She shoed away a fly buzzing her hair.

His lips pursed. "No one ever listens."

Damn. One thing she'd always had in life was someone to talk to. Her mom had always been there, and when she moved out of the house, Laini had become her sounding board. Now she even had John.

Tracy had never understood the expression 'good friends are hard to come by'. It was a whimsical phrase, something to put on greeting cards. She couldn't imagine not having someone she could count on. How much of her success could she relate to others supporting her?

Probably everything.

She eased onto the park bench. "I'll listen."

What was she doing? This was incredibly stupid. Adonna's patience would only last so long, but Tracy sat there. Rapt. What would he say? What would drive a man to search for a different woman every night?

Sean's eyes rounded. "Trust me. You don't want to know my problems."

"Try me."

Sean laughed through his nose. He paced the grass three times before plopping beside her on the bench. "You really want to know?"

Probably not, but she nodded anyway.

He stared at the butterfly for a few more moments. An odd sense of peace seemed to spread over him. "I was a kid when it started." He cringed when the insect fluttered down the hill. "There are lots of places to go if this happens to you, plenty of people to talk to if, you know, you're a girl." He closed his eyes and took a deep breath. "If you are a guy, and you say you've been sexually abused by a woman, no one believes you."

Tracy's eyebrows inched up. Seriously? What guy would say no to sex? She shook the thought from her mind. That kind of sexism was exactly what he must have been talking about. And he said he'd been a kid. Maybe he'd been young. Shit. She was not prepared for a conversation like this. Then again, who would be?

The sun cast a shadow on the side of his face as he looked up at her. "The fucking psychiatrist they forced me to sit with every goddamn week didn't even believe me."

Her lips parted. "Couldn't you talk to your parents?"

He snorted. "Once I realized what was happening, I was afraid my father would kill me in one of his drunken stupors."

Oh. Crap. "What about your mom?"

"My mom?" His nose flared as if he'd smelled rotten meat. His eyes centered on nothing before he shook his head. "Screw this."

He stood and started down the hill. He turned when Tracy didn't move.

Every ounce of intuition she had told her to get up and jog in the opposite direction. This guy was seriously disturbed. He needed professional help, but suggesting another psychiatrist after the first one discounted his claims was probably the worst idea ever.

But what if she found out tomorrow that he'd put a gun in his mouth? How could she live with herself knowing that maybe she could have helped?

She tightened her grip on the edge of the bench. "I'm-I'm here if you want to talk about it."

His eyes narrowed. "You aren't a shrink, are you?"

"No. You just sound like you're hurting."

"I'm well beyond hurting, darlin'."

Tracy stared at him. Her fingers ached and sweat dampened her palms. "That's why maybe it would be good to talk it out."

His eyes softened. "Nobody ever wanted to talk. They blew me off, told me I was imagining things."

Her stomach twisted. He looked so tired. Alone. The dangerous edge had fallen from his shoulders, making him look more like a frightened child than the man who'd held her with such practiced hands. How long had he been alone like this, pretending a horrible past didn't exist?

"I'm here," she whispered. "I'll listen."

The butterfly found a friend and they swirled through the air together. Sean seemed to study the pair, concentrating. How could a past like that affect a person, having something so horrible fester that long, with no one believing him? His ribcage expanded before he sat back down beside her.

His eyes seemed to have lightened, now lost and maybe a little frightened. "I was about ten the first time my mom came to me in the middle of the night. I woke up and she was tickling me with her tongue. I had this funny feeling. It scared me." He paused, looked at the ground. "She giggled and left me there."

Oh. My. God!

"That was it for a few weeks, but then she came back. I woke up again in the middle of the night. I was already hard in her mouth. I remember that one vividly, the tenseness, the building, and then the explosion—and that look on her face—that satisfied, knowing expression." He trembled. "She patted my head, and said if I was a good boy, she'd do it again."

Jesus. "You should have gone to the police." But he was so young. Too young.

He shrugged. "At the time, I didn't know it was anything bad. And by the time I started to feel weird about it, dammit, I was scared. I didn't know what to do. I mentioned it once to my aunt, but she said I was having wet dreams. Said I was oedipal." He shook his hands, as if trying to cleanse the memory from his skin. "When I grew up and finally got away from her, my body was so used to coming every night that I started to go crazy. Masturbating worked for a while, but I wanted more." He leaned against the back of the bench. "So, I started to go to bars. I looked for slutty bleached blondes, just like her. And I used them. Like she used me."

Holy damn. Tracy reached for her hair and twisted the ends. She knew she wasn't blonde, but she checked just in case. "Sean, I think you need help. What you're doing, it's going to make things worse."

"Believe me, darlin'." He ran his fingers down her cheek. "I'm far past getting any help."

She remained perfectly still, letting him touch her skin. Her heart throttled but not in excitement.

He drew away. "And then there is you—a perfectly nice girl, nothing like my *mother*." He spat the word *mother* like a curse. "Normally, I would have walked right past you. I have my pick of sluts on any given night, but thanks to my new alien counterpart, I was drawn to you." He smiled a half-grin. "And you end up giving me the most intense sex of my life and I didn't even get my pants off."

She inched away. "But that's done now. You know that, right?"

He nodded. "John."

Tracy gulped. "Yes. I never tried to hide my relationship from you."

"I know." He stood, dragging his fingers through his hair. "I don't even know why I told you all this. I guess I thought…" His face hardened. "I don't know what I thought." He turned and headed down the hill.

This time, Tracy didn't stop him.

43

For the first time John could remember, he was the one handing Art a cup of coffee. His friend's sunken gaze rose to the cup before returning to his folded hands.

"You look like shit," John said. "Now I wish I added a shot of espresso."

Art choked a laugh.

John settled at the table. "Your dad?"

He nodded. "Long night. Touch and go for a bit."

"Then what the hell are you doing here?"

Art finally looked up. "I can't sit there and look at him lying in that hospital bed anymore. I need to work. I need to think about something else." He pointed at the war board. "I've reviewed all of the domestic disturbances and about half of the tickets Doogan issued. Anything that smelled of motive I printed and tacked up for you."

Dozens of papers hung at haphazard angles among photographs of the crime scene. That much data would have taken hours to go through with a team, let alone one man.

"How long have you been here?" John asked.

"You don't want to know."

But he did want to know. How awake had Art been while he reviewed those files? Was he in the right mindset to not miss anything?

Art walked to the war board and shifted one of the sheets that had partially covered Doogan's bruised face. "I think you were right about the aggravated assault. This bastard either hated Doogan, or hated cops."

"Then let's figure out which."

After three hours, names and traffic violations blurred together.

John rubbed his eyes. He needed a break.

Across the table, Art downed a fourth cup of coffee before grabbing another stack of papers. His partner would bottom out sooner or later. Hopefully later, once they'd sifted through all the files.

Things went nicely with Tracy on Friday.

"Friday?"

Art looked up. "Huh?"

John gaped before realizing he'd spoken aloud. "Sorry, talking to myself again."

His partner slid right back into his perusal of the documents before him: a testament to how often John spoke to himself on the job. It was a wonder John wasn't under constant psych evaluation.

Dak slithered below John's skin, just like he had when Tracy dragged her fingers through his hair. John licked his lips, relishing the softness of her kiss and the sound of her sigh when she tilted her head back.

John blinked, taking in the paperwork strewn across the table: the tangible things he was *supposed to be* thinking about. *Nicely played, Dak. But I need to get back to work.*

The entity chuckled inside him as John flipped over the last sheet in his pile then grabbed Doogan's moving violations from last week. Even the pages Art flagged before John arrived didn't spark any credible leads.

He tried to rub the sting from his eyes. Maybe if he took a few minutes away, he'd be able refocus and come up with something.

Grabbing his empty cup, John stood. "More crappy coffee?"

"Fill 'er up." Art handed John his mug.

The halls had returned to their normal, deserted quiet. Only a year ago this building overflowed with law enforcement officials and the lines for too-old coffee made a fix of java a social event. Now the café lay empty, the hum of a half-full coffee-warmer the only clue that anyone else had been there today.

John took a sip and pursed his lips against the bitter grinds. Maybe he didn't need coffee as bad as he'd thought.

The cappuccino he'd had with Tracy on Friday tasted gourmet compared to this, and they'd made fun of being able to chew it. Damn, she was beautiful when she laughed. She had a way of making him forget the job that consumed his life. She was patient enough to give him time to wind down, and not take it personally when he got lost in his own thoughts.

Tracy seemed to understand, despite having no clue what it was like to have people depending on you to save lives or solve deaths. Sitting with her, even in silence, drained the weight of his responsibilities away.

John stretched his neck, loosening the ache in his muscles. That kiss seeped back into his thoughts, the feel of her body pressed up against him.

The way Tracy had moved, the way she kissed, shit if she wasn't making her intentions more than clear. It had taken every ounce of his control not to draw her into his arms, push her through the door and give her what she wanted—what *he* wanted. Setting his mug down, he adjusted the stupid bulge in his pants.

This line of thought wasn't going anywhere. It certainly wasn't helping the case. But Tracy wasn't about the job. She was far more important.

John blinked and straightened.

Tracy *was* more important. They hadn't known each other long, but she'd become a distraction—a good kind of distraction. The kind of distraction he wanted more of.

"You coming with that joe?" Art called from down the hall.

John smiled. *Definitely a distraction.* He pulled out his phone and tapped Tracy's name.

Good luck on your presentation today. Knock em dead.

He pressed send and slipped his phone into his pocket. If she answered, she'd be even more of a distraction, and Art needed his coffee.

44

Tracy had barely gotten any sleep last night. Every time she closed her eyes, she envisioned a young boy and a mother with a far too knowing smile. How could a woman do that to her own son?

As hard as it was, though, she needed to push Sean out of her mind. Too much rode on today.

Her phone buzzed, and she drew the case out of her pocket.

Good luck on your presentation.

A warm tickle spread through Tracy's stomach as she headed down the hall toward the executive conference rooms. With everything on his plate, John still remembered how nervous she was about this meeting. She adjusted her slacks and straightened, feeling a touch taller than she had a few moments ago.

"Ready?" Kyle asked, grasping the handle on the conference room entrance.

"Ready as I'll ever be."

He pushed the door open. "Good afternoon gentlemen."

Everyone in the room shuffled, some taking their seats. How many times had she been in one of those chairs, waiting for the

Olsons to arrive? She never imagined arriving fashionably late with one of the bosses at her side.

Tracy set her presentation on the table, overly aware of the colonel at the far end of the room, tapping his pen on his leather-bound notebook. Even though he'd only entered the room seconds before them, she could feel his eagerness to get started.

She turned toward the easel, but the corner where she'd placed the tripod that morning lay empty. Everything they needed had been in the room. She'd triple checked, but McNulty had passed her in the hall after she'd left for lunch.

He wouldn't have. Would he?

She refused to turn toward him, worried her alien-inflated anger would start spurting curses at him, or worse.

Kyle reached for a marker in the tray below the dry-erase board but that was empty as well. His brow furrowed. Sweat soaked Tracy's blouse as his gaze trailed to her.

McNulty shifted in his chair. "That's okay, Kyle. Why don't you get started? Seavers can get anything you need."

Kyle stepped closer to Tracy. "You did say you'd stocked the room for us, right?"

She tried not to grit her teeth. "Of course, I did. Everything was here."

A slight twitch touched Kyle's lips before he turned. "You know what, McNulty, why don't you go grab the easel from my office."

McNulty sat up. "Me?"

"You have a problem with that?"

The egotistical ass's gaze flicked from the colonel to Kyle. "N-no, I guess not."

Kyle gave a curt nod. "Good. And while you're at it, why don't you run down to the warehouse and get us a box of dry-erase markers. Seems the ones I put in here this morning disappeared." He grabbed their presentation pad. "We'll get started so we don't waste everyone else's time."

Oh snap! Totally burned. Tracy hadn't known Kyle for all that long, but he was her new favorite boss ever!

McNulty grimaced before he stood. Tracy refused to meet his gaze as he passed and closed the door behind him.

Kyle plugged his laptop into the monitor and called up the PowerPoint they'd worked on. "While we are waiting for our supplies, let's go over some very interesting forecasts."

Everything worked as they'd rehearsed it, only backwards since they didn't have everything they needed. When it was time to make their pitch for the charity box tops, Kyle held up Tracy's posters since McNulty still hadn't returned with the easel. He kept quiet, but his eyes kept darting to his father, probably waiting for the expected blow-out over the fiscal liability of printing fifty million double-point box top labels.

The pointer shook in Tracy's hands; but a calm, swirling sensation spiraled from her stomach, around her ribs, and settled in her chest. *Thank you, Adonna.* "Even though offering double points puts the company at risk of a ten-million-dollar charitable payout, I am suggesting committing to this program for five years."

"Five years!" The colonel's face reddened. "We don't commit like that. We never have, especially harboring that kind of risk."

Adonna sparkled, settling the bile rising in Tracy's gut.

Kyle's gaze flicked toward her. His lips opened, but she shook her head. She didn't need him to dig her out of this.

"Let me explain, sir." Tracy balanced her presentation pad on the shelf below the white board and flipped to the last page. "I spoke with purchasing, and if we can make a bulk purchase of labels, buying a five year supply rather than four months, as is their current practice, plus hedging steel purchases, we will save eleven cents in packaging costs. That alone will pay for the charitable donation every year."

Her former boss, Miles, shifted in his seat. "We'd need more warehouse space. The labels aren't a problem, but the steel?"

Tracy nodded. Kyle had already proposed this question. "Remember, statistics show that only one in seven grade school homes, and even fewer in higher grades, bother saving box tops, even when they intend to use them when they buy." She turned to the colonel. "That means you will gain the extra sales." She highlighted the sales on her pad. "Plus, the prestige of being the first company to double their box tops, and the net after liability, will be an additional twenty-seven million dollars over five years." She pointed at Miles. "More than enough for additional steel trailers in the lot."

Her former boss's gape was wildly satisfying.

Tracy scrolled *$27,000,000 net profit* across her pad and underlined the words. "Twenty-seven million dollars of additional profit and one-point-five million donated to America's schools. It's a win for Olson's, and it's a win for the kids."

A harsh silence hung in the room.

The colonel leaned back, arms folded. His expressionless gaze carried over each person in the room before leaching onto his son. "You came up with these numbers?"

"Not me. Cost avoidance never even occurred to me. But I did check the math and I confirmed with purchasing. She's spot on. Those savings are real, and they'll go straight to the bottom line. And that's a low-ball figure. I think we'll annihilate those numbers with increased sales."

Colonel Olson stood. His hands fisted, then released. Tracy could almost feel him calculating the advance funding in his head. The silence pressed in on all sides.

What they'd proposed was huge for this quiet, conservative company. Olson's had become the second-largest soup manufacturer in the country by letting others take risks and adopting what worked. They were followers, not leaders. This had worked for them for generations.

Even though Tracy's numbers were sound, this was a very risky endeavor; at least in the eyes of the guy who was putting the money out. But he had to see the potential and the fantastic PR opportunity.

A smile spread across the colonel's lips. Tracy gasped. The man actually smiled!

"Nice work," he said. "I'd like to see you both in my office at noon tomorrow. We'll discuss this in more detail over lunch."

"Did I miss anything?" McNulty pushed through the door, a box in one hand and the easel under his shoulder.

The colonel grunted and left the room. Someone snickered.

Kyle shook Tracy's hand as McNulty dropped the easel on the floor.

"Your office was locked," McNulty said to Kyle. "And Rogers in the warehouse said he gave you the last box of dry-erase markers this morning."

Kyle's face remained serene. "He *did* tell me that was the last box of markers. I forgot. Sorry you had to walk all the way down there. Quite a trek, isn't it?" He gave McNulty a man-punch in the shoulder. "Good for the old cardio, though."

McNulty pretended to laugh, dropped the box on the table, grumbled something, and left with the others. The group had made it halfway down the hall before his voice boomed: "We're going to do *what?*"

Kyle held up both hands and Tracy double high-fived him.

Wait until John heard about this! They'd have to get together and celebrate.

She hesitated as she gathered her things. Anytime something good happened, she'd always called her mom or Laini. Was it weird to think of John first?

Her stomach fluttered, and she held her hand over her belly, allowing the smooth, comforting sensation to sink in. Maybe more than one of them was excited at the thought of seeing John and Dak again.

45

John's phone vibrated as he pulled it out of his pocket.

Tracy Seavers: Break out the bubbly! Col. Olson is even more excited about my marketing plan after today's meeting!

A smile burst free. He tapped out a message.

See? And you were worried. That's amazing.

John checked his spelling and hit *send*.

Tracy Seavers: We HAVE to get drinks tonight. Celebrate!

A night with Tracy? Damn, that sounded good. Everyone else had lives outside the precinct. There was no reason he couldn't, too.

He grinned, running his thumb over her name on his screen. For the first time in his life, he actually looked forward to his life outside the job. He started typing:

I'll take those drinks and raise you a dinner?

The longest ten seconds of his life passed before the icon flashed to show she was typing. Was he actually *nervous*?

Tracy Seavers: You're on!

John held himself back from fist-pumping in the air like an overzealous teenager.

Pick you up at 6:30.
Tracy Seavers: I'll be waiting. 😊

"Peters!" Agent Clark strode down the hallway toward John.

Agent Evans kept pace beside him. Agent Black or Brown—whatever the kid's name was—trailed behind them, tapping on his phone with a stylus.

"Agents." John inclined his head slightly. "Need some help with your case?"

"Just a few questions," Evans said.

Clark pushed within inches of John's nose. "Like why another woman wasn't murdered on Friday."

John tried to look surprised, as if he'd detached himself from the case and hadn't checked their progress, or lack of it, each morning. "I wouldn't assume there wasn't another murder. I'd be combing the missing person's reports."

Clark pointed to the younger agent. "Green has already done that."

So, the kid's name was Green. He knew it was a color.

"No recent disappearances match the profiles of the other victims," Green said.

John's eyes narrowed. "There's barely a profile between them. Other than eye color, we couldn't find a match."

The agents glanced between each other.

"What, you found a connection?"

Clark pointed at John, pushing him back. "We're really interested in why the murders stopped the second you were taken off the case."

Heat flooded through John. "What the hell are you getting at?"

Evans pushed toward him. "Has your Ambient manifested in any way? Spoken?"

"Other than craving broccoli, no."

"Have you had any episodes of sleepwalking?" Green asked. "Or waking up somewhere other than where you went to bed?"

"No."

Dak jolted, kicking John's bladder.

This line of questioning confirmed John's concerns. "You think an Ambient host did this?"

Clark's nose wrinkled. "Classified."

Of course, it was. "Nothing has changed since my last interrogation with you guys." He waited for a woman carrying a manila folder to pass out of earshot. "I barely know this thing is inside me."

"Have you noted any other Ambients in the area?" Evans asked. "We've found that they can be attracted to each other."

No sense in lying about that. "Yeah, Tracy Seavers. We ran into each other outside a coffee shop."

Green glanced at his phone. "That would be The Treehouse coffee shop, right?"

John's right hand formed a fist. He released it. "How long have you been watching me?"

Green shook his head. "Not you, but it is standard protocol to watch a new host for a set amount of time. If nothing manifests within a month, statistically, they're safe."

"So, you're watching Tracy."

Shit. Tracy had experienced some alarming issues with her entity, but nothing like this. Then again, how long had she been out of the Ambient Research Facility before the murders began?

"Our job is to make sure humanity is safe within the confines of the accord," Evans said.

Clark nodded. "And if we deem it's not safe, we act."

Dak shivered, and John worked at keeping himself from stepping back. They'd seen Clark *act* on an entity he'd deemed unsafe. Both he and Dak had nightmares for months.

Keep him away from Adonna. She didn't do anything.

How can we be sure?

She's too weak. There's no way she could take hold for long without Tracy knowing.

That was true. There was definitely something up with Adonna, but it was unlikely it had anything to do with murder.

What about the other host Tracy met? The entity that Adonna...

Dak fizzled and his words faded out.

John worked to quiet the flush of anger surfacing, imagining another man touching Tracy. But it had only been that: one entity attracted to another, nothing that sounded dangerous. Was it fair to sick these maniacs on a guy who was probably as confused as any other host?

Part of him wanted to say yes, to put Agent Dickwad on this guy's trail and get rid of the competition, but none of this was that poor sap's fault, and maybe not even the guy's Ambient's fault. They probably didn't even know Tracy was involved with anyone else.

No, he wouldn't throw some stranger under a bus. That didn't mean John wouldn't consider asking the guy a few questions, though, just in case.

He took a deep breath. "Well, if I run across another host, I'll be sure to let you know."

Green just blinked. Clark and Evans continued to scowl.

"If that's all, gentlemen," John tried not to spit out the last word. "I have my own case to get back to."

Clark called down the hall as John headed to the war room. "I find it interesting that the only person who saw our murderer ended up dead a week later."

John hesitated, his hand on the door.

Shit.

Please keep walking.

John turned. "Do you want to take over Officer Doogan's murder, too?" He eyed Evans, whose sneer took up most of his face.

Agent Green shoved his phone into his inner jacket pocket. "We don't think your case is related."

"That's what I thought." John pushed the door and headed into the war room. The bastards were trying to get him riled up for some reason.

Don't let them.

John unclenched his fists. "Working on it."

The papers on the corkboard shifted as he entered, calling attention to Doogan's final pose.

This crime scene *was* different. The women from the first investigation were raped. Two of them were tortured. The perpetrator had enjoyed himself.

The person who killed Doogan was angry. This was personal. They wanted to do harm. Kill. Emasculate. Or was the mutilation something else?

Art shifted in the corner. "You've got that scary detective look on your face again."

Scary? Yes. Terrifying. Doogan's sexual organs were removed after he'd been beaten to death. If stuffing the man's genitals into his mouth was a message, it wasn't for Doogan. The cop was already dead.

Who would get satisfaction from seeing Doogan that way? Did the perpetrator kill Doogan for someone else? But, who? And why?

Unless the motive was the most obvious one.

What if Doogan really had shot the killer? Maybe this was the perpetrator's way of keeping the investigation off-kilter while getting rid of loose ends.

The photos from the women's murder scenes flashed through his mind. He centered on the people gathered against the barricades outside Melissa Harpoona's house.

Tracy was there. Why? Morbid curiosity over a dead schoolmate she hardly knew?

And she seemed so interested in the case, always asking questions.

John's stomach clenched. He jumped when Art's hand appeared on his shoulder.

"Hey." His partner frowned. "You okay?"

John blinked and nodded. "Yeah." He glanced back to Doogan's photo. "I'm feeling a little nauseated all of a sudden."

He grabbed his phone and brought up Tracy's last text. He tapped his finger beside the happy face emoji.

No. The Feds had been watching her. They'd have picked up on anything strange.

He was overthinking this. He had to be.

46

"I'm telling you, you should have seen his face." Tracy propped her elbows on the edge of the table, soaking in John's bemused gaze as he leaned across his plate, waiting for her to continue. He barely flinched when a waitress dropped a tray of dishes a few booths away.

When was the last time she had a guy's complete attention like this? Her cheeks heated. Probably never. In the past, she'd felt second fiddle to her date's phone, or a pretty waitress, or the flat screen broadcasting the game.

Tracy's stomach clenched, and she shifted her weight. "I don't think the colonel could believe that a higher charitable donation could possibly lead to more profit."

John stared at her for a moment. She gulped. Should she have said something else?

His eyes narrowed as if deciphering some grand puzzle before his posture relaxed. "Well, that's why he gave you the promotion, right? Sounds like you really know your stuff."

She released a breath. He actually *was* listening. It was invigorating and horrifying all at the same time. Tracy drank in the lines of his shoulders, the virile cut of his jaw. Shit, he was hot and attentive. What in God's name was he doing here, with her?

A tiny dimple appeared on his cheek when he smiled. Warmth wrapped her up and drew her heart slowly, lazily toward her stomach. She imagined those strong arms encircling her, those hands removing her clothes.

Flushing, she ran her fingers over the top of her wine glass, regaining her composure and bringing her back to the conversation about her business meeting. "I was so nervous, but once I got going, it felt right. Like I was always meant to be up there."

John raised his glass. "To the future CEO."

"I don't know about all that, but thanks." She clinked her glass against his.

Before withdrawing, John ran the side of his hand along hers. She shivered, and it had nothing to do with their Ambients. He was so sweet, so perfect.

But so was break-up-with-you-on-the-answering-machine Jason.

Part of her tried to put up a wall to brace herself against getting hurt again. But she couldn't. She didn't want to. Not this time.

John sipped his drink and set it down beside the last scoop of the *Triple Chocolate Meltdown* they'd been sharing.

"Are you going to eat that?" Tracy asked.

He folded his hands. "No. If I do, the date will be over. I'm not ready to say goodnight."

She warmed. Sometimes, the end of the date was just the beginning.

John had said he wanted to take this to the next level, but what did that really mean? Was it safe for her to open up and let him in? God, she wanted to. Now, more than ever.

Yes, her life was upside down, but things had leveled since she met John. Maybe things were even better than before.

This relationship was right in so many ways. Meeting John had been the tipping point that brought her back from the edge of a dark, frightening place she didn't want to remember. She needed him, and she was pretty damn sure the feeling was more than mutual. All she needed to do was break through the chain-mail armor he seemed to wear around his heart.

"I had an awesome time tonight." She cringed at her own words. How many times had a guy said that to her, followed by a sleazy line to try to get her in bed? Was she doing the same thing to John? Maybe.

To hell with maybe. She was. She totally was.

And to hell with taking things slow. Everything about their relationship was right. She just needed John to see this as clearly as she did. She'd never have a normal relationship with a non-host. Adonna had cut Tracy's options down from a million eligible men, to a few alien hosts. It was unlikely she'd ever meet another host she liked as much as John. She'd find a hole in that armor if it killed her.

Tonight had been great. Pressure-free. She could relax with John, as if they'd known each other forever. Being with him was like being swaddled in a blanket: warm and protected. Not that she needed to be protected, but it was nice to know he was there, just in case.

Tracy uncrossed and re-crossed her legs as Sean's shirtless form flashed through her mind.

No. That was not what she wanted. *And, Adonna, you better wipe that thought from your mind forever.* Tracy steadied herself with a deep breath.

Never again. It wasn't about Sean, anyway. It was about the entity inside him.

Adonna rolled, but nothing more. Good.

Tracy understood that Adonna was her own person with her own needs. If Tracy wanted to make it work with John, she needed Dak to show Adonna that he could make her feel the way

Sean's Ambient had. Tracy needed to be sure that Sean would never be an issue between her and Adonna again.

"I had a great time, too," John said. "That's why I don't want it to end."

He rotated his grip on her hand, not holding it on one place for more than a few seconds. There was no sense of the now-familiar touch of Dak seeping into her skin because John wasn't giving him a chance. How horrible it must be for the poor alien, being so close, but unable to touch.

"You're teasing Dak."

John smiled. "I certainly am. He's not being a good boy. I don't want him anywhere near you, but I want to hold your hand."

Sean's entity had exploded through his host's skin to get inside her. Hard, fast, and strong. Frightening. Was that what Adonna wanted? Could Dak give that to her?

Tracy's gaze carried along John's shoulders, up his strong neck, and settled on the adorable dimple. It would be so much more intense being with someone *Tracy* wanted—connecting with John on her own terms while giving their Ambients the contact they so desperately wanted.

Maybe Dak knew this. Maybe that was why he was struggling to get to Tracy. If Dak was ready to show his stuff, if he could give Adonna the intimacy she wanted...

John continued his small touches, denying his entity entrance. But maybe that was a good thing, because tonight wasn't about the creatures hiding inside them. It was about Tracy, John, and whatever this little spark was that had ignited between them.

She settled her hand over John's. Thankfully, Dak kept to himself. "I'm not afraid of Dak, and I'm definitely not afraid to take this further."

John's eyes darkened. He broke her gaze.

"Are *you* afraid?" she asked.

"No!" John bolted upright, then settled himself. "I mean, no, of course not. I told you, I'm interested." He smiled before he took her hand again. "I'm *really* interested."

He closed his eyes for three beats before opening them. His face remained turned toward the menus tucked in the clip beside the window.

Damn, she wished she could hear the argument probably going on between John and his Ambient. For maybe the first time, she hoped Dak would win—as long as the entity would agree to give them some privacy. Which was probably unlikely, but she hoped he would.

She and John hadn't been together all that long—just a few weeks, but he'd bounded over the friend zone like an Olympic athlete. He'd become a part of her life, slipping in effortlessly, as if he'd always been there, belonged there.

He did belong. The intensity brewing inside her may have something to do with the Ambients, but she didn't care. This was real, and she wasn't about to let it go.

His gaze flicked back to hers.

"Everything okay?" she asked.

John turned his hand beneath hers and squeezed her palm. "Yeah. Actually, I think it's great. I think maybe we're both great." His long fingers dwarfed hers, and there was no extraterrestrial sizzle in their contact.

"Dak's keeping to himself."

"For once, he's being smart." John gestured to the melted ice cream and soggy cake still between them. "Do you want any more of that?"

"No. I think I'm ready to leave."

His grip on her tightened as their gazes locked.

What was going on in that head of his? Was Dak poking at him, or was he lost in his own thoughts?

She squeezed his hand back. "Laini is at her book club tonight. Do you want to come over for a bit?"

His lips parted, showing a brief flash of his teeth. "Yeah, I think we'd like that a lot."

The sound of John's radio kept Tracy company most of the ride home.

John gripped the steering wheel with both hands. His cheek ticked, and he grimaced more than once. Despite the quiet in the car, the conversation between Dak and his host seemed quite heated.

Adonna remained silent, as always. Maybe she realized that Tracy and John were finally going to be alone. Maybe she was gaining her strength, anticipating an evening with Dak.

Tracy adjusted her seatbelt, imagining John's arms around her, loving her—not just taking what he wanted, but giving, too; and Dak giving the same to Adonna. Her skin ached and her Ambient twitched beside her heart, over her stomach, and lower.

Had there always been this many red lights from Applebee's to her house?

John parked in her driveway and sprang from the car. Tracy chuckled to herself, wondering how much of that haste was Dak's doing.

If things did go well, hopefully Dak and Adonna could be discrete. She really wanted this moment to be about her and John, if that were even possible.

Tracy fumbled for her keys as John walked her to the front door. He kept back a few paces as she jiggled the lock. She pushed open the door and stepped inside but John remained two steps down from the porch, again.

"Aren't you coming in?" she asked.

"I'm not sure that's such a good idea anymore."

She furrowed her brow. "Why not?"

"If I walk through that door..." He closed his eyes and took a deep breath. "Dak is pushing me really hard to walk up those steps."

Tracy smiled, folding her arms. "And that's bad because?"

He puffed out a laugh. "I'm serious. What's going on in here..." He tapped his temple twice. "...he's like a raving lunatic, I swear." He slipped his hands in his pockets. His eyes swept over her, devouring her inch by inch until his gaze returned to hers. "Are you getting anything from Adonna? By now she has to know that we're thinking about... I mean, she'll know if you're..."

"Turned on?"

His lips thinned. "Yes." He made his way up the steps, then stopped. A battle raged in his eyes, a hunger that would have startled her if it had been anyone else, mixed with fear and heartbreaking dread.

Amy must have been his last real relationship. John had probably been devastated. But Tracy wasn't going to live in another woman's shadow. She knew what she wanted.

She slipped her hand into his and lazily coaxed him through the door. "There is no chance in hell that she doesn't know exactly what I'm thinking right now."

The heat in his eyes twisted her own need into a dull, throbbing ache. And Adonna... Tracy searched inside her, looking for a sign, but the entity hung like a balloon, silent in her chest.

She nodded. "We're *both* very ready for this."

A small growl sounded in John's throat. "You have no idea how happy I am to hear you say that."

In one fluid movement, he slipped his hand into her hair and brought his lips down to hers. The kiss was hard, demanding, and she melted into him, relishing the feel of his soft, eager lips. His hands smoothed over her shoulders, her sides, igniting her skin and making her body cry for more.

Drawing a slow, long line up her throat with his tongue, John snickered into her ear before drawing her earlobe into his mouth.

Squirming, reeling from the sensations, she grabbed his wrist and placed his hand on her breast. He granted her one gentle squeeze before his fingers moved to the top of her blouse. His mouth claimed hers again, his tongue forceful and searching as he released the top button, then the second.

The cool air heated as he dragged his fingertips down her cleavage. She bit her lip, trying to deny her quivering skin. God, she wanted this. She wanted him.

She raked her teeth against the slight stubble shading his neck as her blouse fell to the floor. Fisting her hair in his fingers, he leaned her head back again, his mouth claiming her greedily as she removed his shirt one agonizing button at a time.

The room heated as he eased her against the wall. She felt trapped, but her skin ignited as he pushed against her. She wanted to steer him to the TV room, where they could sink into the couch, or even better, the bedroom, but the wall, shit, the wall would do just fine.

John pulled her leg up to his waist and pressed his erection against her. She groaned and sucked his tongue into her mouth, taking control and staking her own claim as she brushed the shirt from his shoulders.

He released the kiss. "Wait." He stepped back, exposing a clean, well-muscled chest and abs to die for. She had to contain herself from running her fingers across the ridges on his stomach before he reached for his shirt.

Tracy frowned. "What's wrong?"

John shifted and the change in light revealed three deep, round scars centered over his heart. Tracy gasped. Bullet wounds?

He fumbled with his shirt, slipping one arm back through the fabric, but she pulled the still-warm cotton from his hands. Now that he was bared to her, she didn't want him hidden from her ever again.

"Don't cover up," she said, moving closer.

John paled, clutching the fabric in his left hand and holding it over his heart, covering the scars. Tracy took his hand and gently drew it downward.

He tensed, stopping her. "Don't."

"What are you hiding from me?"

He lowered his gaze. "Bad memories."

He relaxed, and she eased the shirt away from his chest. The whitened indents stood proudly on his otherwise flawless skin. A long, white line trailed between them, maybe a surgeon's doing; a mark of courage. Survival. She reached toward the indents, but he grasped her hand. His fingers were cold.

"That's where you were shot?"

He nodded, looking away.

Her gaze traveled back over the indents. They were too close together to be an accident and all centered over his heart. Whoever shot him had intent to kill. She tugged lightly against his grip and he released her to explore the marks with her fingertips. The whitened skin seemed softer than the tanned flesh surrounding it.

He trembled slightly, his eyes closed. "I know it's awful. Let me put my shirt back on. I don't want you to have to look at this."

She ignored him, continuing to explore the scars with her fingertips. John's eyes remained closed.

"They're far from awful." She moved closer, placing a kiss on each circle.

John eased her away, holding her face between his palms. His shirt fell across the tops of her feet. "How can you say that? They're a constant reminder of that night."

His eyes quaked. So much pain. So much uncertainty. She wished she could whisk the hurt away, so they could truly be alone without the past wedging between them.

A gentle tug brought his hands to her lips. She kissed the backs of his fingers. His lips parted, his face worn, sad. She slipped her hands around his back, drawing him closer, and dragged her tongue along the surgical scar. He trembled with each movement.

She met his gaze. "They're beautiful. These are the reason Dak came to you. They're part of who you are, and without them, we never would have met. How could I ever think they were something awful?"

His face softened; his hands smoothed up her back. Despite her mentioning his name, Dak still left them alone. Part of her loved the Ambient a little more each second he gave them to explore each other.

"Tracy?" John's voice came as a whisper, a tentative sound that didn't match the intensity that had resurfaced in his eyes.

She leaned up, her lips parted, inviting. She could take a kiss, force it, but she wanted him to break through this pain. She wanted to feel that he wanted her enough to push away the past, step away from his fears and into her heart.

His lips closed over hers. Warmth shot through her: firm, demanding, but gentle and honest at the same time. She relaxed into his embrace, soaking in his strength as he drew her closer. His tongue worshiped hers as her hands explored the curves of his sides, his back. His palms roamed her in turn before hesitating on the clasp of her bra.

"This needs to come off." He unhooked her hands from his neck and slowly spun her. She held her hair up and shivered when the clasp released. His hands roved over her naked back, pushing the garment from her shoulders and to the floor. Suddenly bare, her skin drank in his heat, combatting the chill of the air conditioning. He kissed her cheek. His hands explored her stomach as he held her from behind. She lolled her head back and he rewarded her with a deep, searching kiss.

Humming with delight, she drew him deeper into her mouth. They'd waited too long to reveal this much desire to each other. Now that they'd started, she didn't ever want to stop.

John pressed her back to his chest and she tensed, sure Dak would take advantage and reach out for Adonna, but only safe, sure, human heat met her skin. All John, all hers.

His hands inched up, stopping teasingly close to her breasts. She arched her back in offering, still languishing in the heat of his kiss. He swallowed her desperate whimper as his hands rose, worshiping her soft flesh.

"So beautiful," he whispered, ushering her toward the couch.

He eased her back, placing soft kisses on her stomach while he unzipped her pants. She raised her hips, giving him easier access to shimmy the fabric down her legs and off.

She lay before him, naked except for a thin, lacy thong. His lips parted, and his glossy gaze traveled over her body. It was as if his eyes touched her, her skin shivering as he drank in all she had to offer.

Tracy reached for him and he eased his body over hers, pressing their chests together. He tensed as a fire erupted between their skin.

Dak.

The alien's essence tingled across Tracy's stomach, as if there were a cavern between her and John for his play area. Her nipples hardened as John pressed her more closely. "Are you all right?"

She nodded. It wasn't as if she didn't expect Dak to join in sooner or later. The intensity, the pressure and kneading force of the Entity reaching through her skin and into her body tensed every cell Dak touched. Her body arched. Her skin tingled as a deep ache enveloped her.

John's lips closed over hers, tightening his grip on her and searching her with his tongue. He sighed and trembled, and they moaned together as Dak seeped deeper into her. Tracy's stomach fluttered, and pressure built inside her. So much, almost too much to bear.

Her body froze. Completely immobile, the heaviness shook within. She couldn't breathe. She tried to cry out when the pressure turned to pain, but her voice didn't respond.

John's brow furrowed. "Tracy, are you okay?"

Her hands shook. "Bad!" Her voice shattered the moment. She pushed John away with strength she knew she shouldn't have.

John cried out and clutched his torso. He buckled over, choking. Had she hurt him? Hurt Dak by breaking the contact?

Tracy rolled off the couch, crouching on all fours in nothing but her underwear. She took a predatory pose or was it defensive? And why was her body moving without her control?

"Wrong," her own voice gurgled up her throat, but not her words. Holy shit!

John took a few deep breaths and held his throat as he looked up at her. His eyes radiated pain. "Tracy?"

"Not right." Her body rocked back and forth. She felt like a praying mantis about to snatch its prey...or maybe rip the head off its mate. Oh God!

John reached for her and she hissed.

Sweet Lord! Why did she hiss?

John? John help me!

John pulled his hand back. Tracy's body relaxed. Control came back in a flood and she crumpled to the floor. Tears streamed down her cheeks.

As she held her head, John touched her shoulder. She batted him away.

John held his hands up as in surrender but remained kneeling beside her.

If he touched her again, she'd kill him.

Wait, what?

"Tracy, are you there?"

She opened her mouth, relieved when her own words answered. "Yes, but I don't know what's going on."

She wanted to reach out to him, hold him, shelter herself from whatever this was, but the pure anger churning within left her frozen in place.

"Adonna?" John whispered.

Her head jerked up.

Had she done that, answered to another name?

His hand moved tentatively toward her. "Adonna, I don't know what's wrong, but Tracy is really scared."

"Not right," her voice growled. "Wrong."

Oh God, was that Adonna?

John grimaced. "Yeah, everything's wrong. I get that." He shifted his weight. His eyes seemed to search, as if hoping for some sign of Tracy in her eyes. "Is it me? You don't want me to touch you? Do you want me to go?"

I need you. Please don't leave me! Tracy tried to move, blink. Nothing happened. Her body didn't move at all.

John took a deep breath. "Is it Dak, then?"

Tracy's body swayed to the left. "Not right. Wrong."

What does that mean?

A slight whimper escaped Tracy's lips, the only speck of emotion not trounced by this invasion.

John inched closer. "Adonna, you can feel Tracy. I know you can. You know how scared she is. Please let me hold her. Dak promises he won't touch you."

"Wrong," Tracy's voice said. Colors mixed and faded in her mind. Rusty-red, then grayish-purple. The essence in her pushed the thoughts, like the contrasting hues should mean something. But they were only colors!

The weight inside her seethed, dripped with a pure hatred Tracy couldn't bear.

John's hands formed fists and released. "I'm getting all that wrongness, but Tracy needs me. She's your host. She's given you her lungs, you can't deny her comfort. Now, let me touch her. If Dak goes anywhere near you, you have my permission to crack his stinking non-corporeal head open. Okay?"

The pressure in Tracy's chest dissipated and she collapsed to the floor. John gathered her into his arms. She muffled her sobs against his chest, her tears moistening his scars.

4 7

Tracy shook against him. John held her lightly at first, and when Adonna didn't protest, he cradled her, stoking her right arm with his thumb. Gentle touches. Nothing to reawaken the entity inside her.

The lighting from the foyer cast shadows through the living room, leaving dark, foreboding corners.

Tracy's head bobbed against John's chest. Dak swirled inside him, hovering at the edge of John's skin, just millimeters from Tracy, way too close for comfort.

Don't you dare, buddy. We promised.

The entity juddered. *I didn't do anything. I swear it!*

Tracy clutched at John's chest and squirmed into his lap. John tightened his grip, wishing he could transfer some of his strength into her.

Her trembling didn't dissipate, and he wished he knew how he could squelch her fears.

When Dak had taken control of him the first time, John had blacked out. He didn't have to experience it firsthand. John stroked her cheek. He couldn't imagine how terrified Tracy must feel, how invaded. All he could think of doing to help her was being there. A rock in reality. Strength and understanding.

The pulsing and shaking near his heart deepened. He imagined Dak slapping his head, if he had one, wondering what went wrong. He could sense his friend's need to reach out to Adonna, to soothe, to understand. But if John even thought Dak would try to touch Adonna now, he would have broken contact with Tracy. Anything to avoid Adonna's anger.

In time, Tracy's quaking stopped. She wiped her nose and pushed back hair damp with tears. "What happened? Why did she do that?"

He kept his hands on her shoulders. "We don't know. Is Adonna talking?"

"I heard the words *not right* in my head. Why does she keep repeating that?"

"We don't know that either."

She hugged her knees, covering herself. John handed her the slacks behind him and her bra.

"Thank you." She replaced the garments and settled onto the couch. She looked at the carpet, the ceiling, everywhere but at him.

He wanted—no, he *needed* to fix this. He just had no idea what *this* was.

John handed Tracy's blouse to her, slipping his own shirt over his shoulders. He shuddered as the lamplight caught the tears still streaking her cheeks. Visions of Amy curled up on the floor, sobbing, rushed back to him.

He'd lost her because of Dak. He wasn't about to let that happen again.

Tracy affixed the final button on her shirt. A forced smile appeared. "This isn't quite the evening I had planned."

That was an understatement. "It's okay."

"Is it?" Her hands formed fists and she pressed them to her

thighs. "She took over my body. She pushed you away. Is Dak okay?"

"He's fine. He's hurting, though. He doesn't understand this, either."

Tracy's gaze fell to her lap. She hugged herself. "I can't take this. She barely talks. I only feel her, and, and she *took* me. I had no control, she forced me to the background, and there was nothing I could do about it."

"I understand."

"How can you take it, John? How can you let Dak violate you like that?"

John reached for her. "I don't think they realize how it affects us emotionally when they take control. It's got to be hard on them, too. They never have control."

"Are you making excuses for her?"

John slackened. Was he? At this point, he wasn't sure what he was trying to say.

She buried her face in her knees.

John slid beside her and pulled her into his arms. Regret, hurt, and shame rolled through the essence spinning inside him.

Tracy leaned on his shoulder. "How can you live like this, never knowing when he might do something to you that you don't want?"

A deep breath did little to settle him. "Honestly, he's only done it about three times total, and one of them was with you. Now that he knows how it makes me feel, I doubt he'd do it again."

She lifted her head and gazed into his eyes. "You actually trust him, even though you know how easily he can take advantage of you?"

"Yes." The answer came more quickly than he expected. Maybe if he hadn't lived with Dak for so many years, if he hadn't shared his hopes, dreams, and every emotion with him—maybe then he would feel differently. But it was true. He trusted Dak with his life.

Tracy shook her head. "I can't be so gracious. I can't live like this."

A weight formed in John's chest that had nothing to do with Dak. "Once you can talk to her, things will be better."

Tracy stood, grabbing her temples. "You keep saying that, but it doesn't get better. It keeps getting worse!"

John reached for her. "Tracy, come on."

"No." She stepped away. "God forbid I touch you or this ungrateful bitch in my head might hurt someone."

"Tracy—"

She held up a hand, stopping him dead.

"I like you, John. More than any guy I've ever met, and I'm not letting a freaking alien stowaway decide who I can and can't be with." She gathered her hair over one shoulder, spinning it into a rope as she paced the room. She stopped, nodded to herself, and turned to him. "I'm going to have her extracted."

John stood as Dak turned to stone in his gut. "You can't do that."

"Watch me. I can't live like this. It's not fair."

"And how is extracting her fair?"

She pointed at her chest. "I never asked for this. I never asked to have this thing inside me."

"She saved your life!"

"I didn't ask her to. I'll go to the hospital. They'll be able to help once she's out of me."

"Tracy, you don't know what you're saying."

"I do. I want this thing gone."

John grabbed her shoulders. "It's murder!"

Tracy's eyes widened. "What do you mean?"

"She can't live outside your body."

"I know that. She can go find another one."

John released her. His eyes dampened. "They won't let her. That's not how it works." He rubbed his face with his hands and sat on the couch.

"What are you talking about?"

John's hands shook. Was it Dak's terror or the horror of his own memories? He looked up.

"I saw an extraction once. Our good friend Agent Clark had this whitish rod." He motioned with his hands, as if holding the horrid instrument before him. "He used it to rip the entity out through the host's pupils." He closed his eyes, every muscle in his body tensing. "When they got it out, they could have let him go, let him find another host, but they didn't."

Her brow furrowed. "Why not?"

"It's not what they do." He stood. "The entities, they can breathe our oxygen, but carbon dioxide is poison. When their host dies, or if they are extracted, they need to move at the speed of light to avoid the impurities in our air until they find another host." A shiver overtook him. He folded his arms. "But they don't let them. They hold them. They keep them still."

Tracy's brow furrowed. She moved closer. "Why?"

"Any entity that is forcibly extracted is no longer covered under the accord. They hold them still until they suffocate." John covered his face with his hands. How could he make her understand? "I still have nightmares about it. The entity looked like clear vapor at first. But the more impurities he absorbed, the darker he became. He twisted and writhed, and even though he didn't have a voice, I could tell that fantastic, beautiful, eternal being was pleading for mercy." He looked at Tracy. "I screamed at them, begged them to stop, but they held me back. One of them said, 'This is the best part,' right before the entity became solid, like smoked glass. Then Agent Fuckwad released the trigger on the extractor and the entity dropped."

John reached out to the floor, the need to catch the falling creature still strong within him. He lowered his hands. "Its body shattered when it hit the ground. They laughed as the pieces turned to dust and blew away like nothing ever existed. No memory, no proof."

He gritted his teeth. "How could they do that? How could they senselessly destroy an eternal life and laugh about it?"

Tracy touched his arm and he jumped. "It sounds horrible."

"Don't do that to her, Tracy. I know you're upset, but you need to give her time so she can explain. Don't kill her just because you're scared."

Tracy folded into his arms. "I didn't know. They told me they could get her out. They never said what would happen to her."

"They never do." He drew her to him. "Give me your word you won't call for an extraction."

"I've never even squished a spider, so I sure as heck can't kill something that can talk, even if I don't like her very much."

John ran his fingers through her hair and stroked the back of her neck. He wished he could be sure she was telling the truth.

"I just wish I understood why." Tracy whispered into the crook of his neck. "Why would she seem so angry? Why push you away?"

"I'll say it again. Give her time. If you can keep her from overexerting herself, maybe she'll find the strength to explain."

48

Tracy cuddled into the sheets. She smiled as John tucked her in like her mom used to when she was little and had a temperature. But this was far more than a fever. More than something she could cure with some acetaminophen.

His lips brushed against her forehead. Soft. Gentle. Loving. Part of her had to recognize this one blessing the entity had given her.

Would someone so kind and wonderful have even noticed her on the street in front of the coffee shop that day? Doubtful. She had Adonna to thank for that.

The bedding shifted as her detective in shining armor sat beside her. His fingers trailed across her forehead and brushed back the hair at her temple. "Do you think you're going to be able to sleep?"

Tracy shrugged. "I don't know. It's so much to take in."

"I know. Do you want me to stay?"

God, yes.

How could she ever be alone again, not knowing if this thing was going to take control and do goodness knows what to her body? But that wasn't John's problem. He was a cop. He needed his sleep, and sitting there all night with her wasn't going to give him the rest he needed.

"Go ahead." She tried to keep her voice from quaking. "I'll be fine. I need to learn to deal with this sooner or later."

"You sure?"

No, of course not, but she nodded anyway. A heaviness overcame her, and she was vaguely aware of John's weight lifting off the bed sometime later. The door clicked behind him.

Someone gasped in the hallway. Tracy's eyes shot open, but the line of light shining from below her door stung her eyes.

"Sorry, I scared you," John's voice said. "You must be Laini."

"Inspector Gadget? I mean, John?"

"Yeah. Good to meet you."

"Whew, yeah, same here. Umm, listen, don't let me bother you guys. I'll slip into my room and put my headphones on. I won't hear a thing."

Tracy hugged her pillow. If Adonna hadn't interrupted, Laini would have had something real to worry about. But now, Tracy and John would be stuck in a holding pattern until this freak inside her finally started talking.

"It's not like that," John's voice said. "Tracy isn't feeling well. She's in bed."

"Well, shit, that sucks, 'cause damn, you're even hotter than she described."

Oh, no. She didn't.

"I mean, well, umm, could you, maybe pretend I didn't say that? I tend to have diarrhea of the mouth. It's a certified medical condition."

John puffed a small laugh. "It was nice meeting you." Heavy footsteps tapped on the wood flooring.

"Yeah, back at you!" And then Laini whispered, "Damn nice ass, too," hopefully out of John's earshot.

Tracy rolled over, suppressing her grin.

It seemed like only seconds had passed before the sound of

Laini's alarm clock down the hall startled her awake. The nightstand clock read 6:35.

Tracy clutched her pillow and listened to the rain pummeling her window. Eventually, she'd have to get up, even if it was just to call out of work.

But she couldn't call out. She needed to start mapping her action plans. There was so much strategizing to do, so much planning.

She tried to sit but the weight of the blankets pulled her back down. How could she even think of marketing? How could she focus on anything, wondering when this God-awful parasite inside her would wake up again and use her body as a puppet?

But Kyle was counting on her. He'd put his own neck on the line supporting her concepts. Now she needed to prove she could do more than sell her ideas. She needed to bring the concepts to fruition.

She slumped to the bathroom, removed her nightshirt, and let the cold water in the shower incite goosebumps across her skin. Her body trembled. She needed to jump out of the frigid stream, but she held herself there, focusing on the sting.

If it came down to it, would she be able to call Agent Clark and end this nightmare? If Adonna were a human being, would she even consider sending the Ambient to her death?

No. Of course not.

The water warmed, soothing a dull soreness in her neck and shoulders. There had to be a way to figure this out.

"Please talk to me," Tracy whispered, leaning her forehead against the cold tiles.

Her chest seemed to thicken and weight her down.

She pounded her fist on the tilework. "Talk to me!"

The chill of the tiles crept up her arm despite the warming shower. She was alone, but not alone.

And the entity inside her was getting stronger.

49

John slapped the snooze button on his alarm clock. Rain pummeled the window beside the bed. It would be a great morning to sleep in, but he needed to get to the precinct.

He sat up and rubbed his face. He had to start looking at Doogan's murder from a fresh perspective. As illogical as the evidence made it seem, it was completely logical that Doogan's death was related to the case the Feds had taken from him. He needed to concentrate. Focus.

He picked up the shirt he'd dropped on the edge of his bed last night. The scent of wild berries and spring breeze wafted from the fabric.

Tracy.

God, what a horrible evening. Adonna was another mystery he needed to figure out. What the hell had happened last night?

Good morning.

John stretched. "Good morning, buddy. Sleep well?" Their everyday exchange seemed a bit forced this morning. Silence echoed within. "I'll take that as a no." John slipped out of the sheets and into the bathroom.

She pushed me away.

"Yeah, I was there." John rubbed his chest. "My body, remember? I'm surprised I'm not bruised."

But I still don't understand why.

John closed his eyes. God, the terror in Tracy's eyes when Adonna took over, the hatred in Adonna's voice when she'd pushed them away. He blinked, but the memories refused to fade. "Are you sure you didn't misread her? Maybe she wasn't in the mood."

How could she not want to touch?

John smoothed shaving cream over his face. "You had a little more in mind than touching, Dak. Admit it."

She floated, John. She was waiting for me, but the second I touched her, she just—

"Freaked out."

Dak's energy shook, sending prickles across John's arms.

Everything had gone perfectly. Far better than John had planned.

Going back to Tracy's place last night hadn't even been on his radar, but the food, the conversation, the chemistry—dammit, even their entities were in sync.

At least he'd thought they were.

Dak rustled beneath his skin as John dragged the razor down his left cheek. "You are the resident Ambient expert. What could have happened? What did she do right before she pushed you away?"

She flinched.

"Flinched?"

Yes.

"Is that normal?" A long pause grated against John's soul. He placed the razor down. "Dak?"

No. It isn't normal. And when I started to touch her, she stiffened instead of...

"Spit it out. Instead of what?"

Sharing. Opening.

"But you still kept going?" He didn't answer. "Dammit, Dak. Do you realize you may have completely ruined our chances with both of them?"

The entity seemed to harden. *You're wrong. I would never force anyone.*

John's eyes narrowed in the mirror. *Like you did to Cowa?*

His stomach sank and the whole-ness inside him dissipated. Crap, that was low.

"I'm sorry, buddy, you know I didn't mean that." John rinsed the razor in the sink. "Tracy is the best thing that's happened to me in a pretty long time. I thought this was it and we could both be happy."

And then your entity blew it to shit.

"I didn't say that."

You thought it.

Had he? Maybe subconsciously. "I think we're both a little angry and confused right now. Let's just call Tracy later on and see how they're doing. And work on keeping that Ambient ego in check, because as soon as Adonna starts to talk, I want you groveling at her feet. Got it?"

Understood.

John brought the razor back to his neck and winced as the blade nicked the skin. He reached up to dab the blood with a tissue, but his hand froze. He watched the bead turn into a line and run down his neck. He tried again to stop the bleeding but his hand wouldn't respond.

"Umm, Dak, buddy, what are you doing?"

The blood. It is so important to your life, but it drains so easily.

"Which is why I'd like to keep it inside me." The line reached his breastbone. "Dak!"

His hand sprang free and he placed pressure against the wound.

"What the hell, Dak?"

Sorry. You haven't cut yourself in a long time. I don't have blood. It fascinates me.

"This coming from the guy who can't stand it when I case a crime scene."

That's different. You weren't going to die. Your body was clotting the cut already.

"Okay, well, next time you want to study blood, leave my bodily fluids out of it." His cell phone rang, and he snatched it from beside his bed. Biggs's name flashed on the screen. "Detective John Peters," John said into the phone.

"We've got another body," the sergeant said. "Same M.O. as Doogan. I'm texting you the address."

John sighed and wiped the rest of the shaving cream off with a towel. "I'm on my way."

The showers had tapered off to a light drizzle by the time John drove up to the yellow *Police Do Not Cross* tape surrounding a light blue rancher.

Art got out of his car holding two steaming paper cups. "Cut yourself shaving?" He gestured with one of the cups toward John's neck.

John fingered the wound. "That's why you're a detective. Can't get anything past you."

"Smart ass." He handed John a coffee. "You might want to finish this before you go in." He pointed toward the entrance to the house, where an unfamiliar member of one of the forensics teams pushed back a cotton mask and sat on the front step, breathing deeply. "The body's been dead a few days. Neighbor called 911 because there were a lot of flies buzzing around an open window. He figured his neighbor's dog had died while he was on vacation."

John took a sip of his coffee. "Vacation?"

"Yeah. He was supposed to be on a hiking trip. That's why no one called to report him missing. Poor bastard never even left the house."

"And there's a dog?"

"Yeah. He's at the Pamper Paw down on the highway. The victim checked the dog in Sunday night."

"So, he dropped the dog off at the kennel for vacation, came home, and never left."

Art set his coffee on the roof of his car. "Yeah, and it gets worse."

"How so?"

"This one's a cop, too."

Giancarlo Doogan's former partner, Herb Simon, leaned over the meeting room table, holding the back of his neck. For the fifth time, he glanced toward the photos on the war board. "I don't know how anyone could do something like that."

"That's not what I asked you," Art said.

"Nothing's changed since you talked to me last week. I can't think of anyone who'd want to kill Gian."

John flinched. With Simon's light accent, Doogan's first name, Gian, sounded far too much like his own.

"Or J.J. McCartney?" Art tacked a picture of the second victim to the board.

Simon grimaced. "I didn't know him."

"Could your partner have known him?" John asked.

"I don't think so. Not that he mentioned, anyway." He sat back in his chair. "We were imported from the Deptford precinct. I think I heard someone say McCartney was from Echelon or maybe Evesham. We're all still getting to know each other after the goddamn district consolidation."

John nodded. The recent changes had made investigations as a whole harder. Too many crimes and not enough cops, let alone medical examiners and the like.

Simon seemed to study the back of his hands splayed on the edge of the table. "Is this guy aiming at off-duty cops? Are we all targets?"

"We don't know enough to speculate, yet." John sat beside him. "If you can think of anything, anything at all, I need you to call me."

"Of course. This asshole killed my partner. I want him as bad as you do."

Biggs poked his head into the room, mouth open as if he were about to speak, before his gaze centered on Officer Simon. "Everything okay?"

"Just finishing up." John reached out to the officer to shake his hand. "Thanks for your cooperation."

"Anytime." He nodded to the sergeant before leaving the room.

"What you got?" Art asked Biggs.

"McCartney died Sunday night." Biggs opened a manila folder and set it on the table.

John tapped the edge of the computer printouts, digesting the notes. "McCartney's genitals were mutilated before being inserted into his mouth."

"Yeah, 'cause cutting off a man's package ain't bad enough." Art crossed his legs, shifting in his chair.

"The bruising on the face and abdomen is far more extensive." *Interesting.* John rifled through the pictures.

"So, what? He was more pissed this time than he was with Doogan?"

John rubbed his chin. Serial killers didn't always seem logical, but they were very logical, very calculating, in their own minds. The perpetrator knew exactly what he was doing. He had purpose. Strategy.

"It's possible he's superimposing someone else onto his victims." John paced the room. "A parent, an authority figure. In his mind, he's trying over and over to kill the same person. He's getting angrier because the person isn't dead.

"Or he's just targeting cops," Biggs said.

"It wouldn't be the first time." Art sat back, folding his arms.

"No." John scratched the back of his head. "I keep telling you. This is personal."

"The only connection so far is they are cops."

"There's something else," John said. "It's here. We just need to find it."

50

Tracy's soul wandered through the dark. A speck: lost, alone, and insignificant. She seemed weightless, yet her feet tapped across the pavement, toward a house she didn't recognize.

A scream drummed through the air, piercing from every angle. Tracy spun in all directions, but the sound echoed, bouncing off the walls. Her hair dripped with sweat and she ran.

Pressure built up from behind. Another scream. Sirens blasted in the distance. She changed directions and stopped, pushing her soaked, matted hair out of her eyes.

"Wrong!" she cried out, her own voice shattering the night and shocking her awake.

A wave of cold slapped her wet face. A clash of thunder momentarily drowned out the roar of pummeling rain. Tracy shook her head to clear the fog. Drenched hair slapped her cheeks.

She grabbed for her hair and lost her balance. The world spun. She gasped, seizing the windowsill.

The windowsill?

The haze around her mind cleared. She was leaning out her bathroom window with one leg on the sill. Her hair, arms, and shirt hung saturated and dripping with water. Was she climbing out the window or back in?

She scrambled inside and slammed the window closed. Water streamed from her pajama pants, soaking her already wet socks. The clock on the vanity changed from three-fourteen to three-fifteen. Had she been sleepwalking? And had a terrible need to jump out the window?

Her wet socks slapped against the linoleum. She turned the shower to hot and tugged off her sopped clothing, leaving it in a heap beside the toilet. Slipping through the glass doors, she allowed the heat to overcome the goosebumps coating her skin.

She'd been hanging out the window. In a rainstorm. In the middle of the night. She could have fallen!

Tracy turned off the water and propped herself against the cool tiled wall. Her world had already turned upside down, but now sleepwalking? And what the hell possessed her to climb out the window?

She grabbed a towel and dried herself. She didn't need to worry about *what* had possessed her, but *who*.

Thunder boomed outside, rain streaming across the bathroom window in torrents. This wasn't something she could ignore. There was no way she'd been sleepwalking.

She slipped on a pair of warm flannel PJs and stood in front of the mirror. Dark circles highlighted puffy rings under her eyes, like she hadn't slept in weeks.

Squinting to see within her pupils, she leaned toward the mirror. "Where were you going?"

Silence stirred within her mind, as if she were alone. As if she were normal.

Tracy knew better.

She stretched, her muscles aching like she'd spent the night working out. She glanced at the window and the water pooled on the floor. What *had* she been doing all night?

She threw her towel over the puddle and dragged her fingers

through her wet hair. "Listen," she whispered. "John says to give you time, that you need to rest and maybe you'll be able to explain things." She bit her lip. "How can you have the strength to climb out a window but not enough to talk to me?"

Sorry.

The word slapped her like a hand across her cheek. "Adonna?"

Sorry.

Holy shit.

Tracy's heart throttled against her ribs. "Sorry for what?"

Wrong.

Tracy closed her eyes and let her head fall back. "Can you please tell me *what's* wrong?"

She grabbed her arm. Three raised, red abrasions stung her skin. Scratches…probably from the bushes outside the window. So, she *had* been outside.

Holding her head, Tracy paced the bathroom floor. How could John stand living like this, knowing your body may have gone somewhere and done God knows what, while you were sleeping? How was it possible for her muscles to be moving without her even knowing it?

John certainly didn't like Dak controlling him, but he seemed far more accepting, at least on the outside. Was that all for show—to make her feel better; or did he really trust Dak as much as he led on?

Over and over, he'd said that it would be better once Adonna could explain herself, but these one and two-word answers were driving her crazy. This entire experience had been a nightmare, and she wanted to be done with it.

She should call Agent Clark right now and get this over with before John and Dak could try to talk her out of it again.

A flash of ice followed a whispering jitter inside her tummy.

Who was she kidding? As annoying as this thing inside her was, it was alive. Now that Tracy knew extraction was a death sentence, she'd have to find a way to make this work.

They were going to have to find a way to make it work.

"But we're going to have to live within some boundaries. You owe me at least that much."

Did she, or was it the other way around? Tracy had been dead. Period. End of story. Adonna had saved her, but did that give her the right to do anything she wanted with Tracy's body?

No. It wasn't right. They had to learn to live together. They had to find a way to communicate.

Clearing her throat, Tracy closed her eyes. "Okay, maybe we should start over. Thank you for saving my life. I appreciate it."

She resisted the temptation of adding the word *bitch* to the end of the sentence. Could Adonna sense her bitterness, even though she was trying to take a step in the right direction?

Nothing but a warm feeling swirled in her chest. That had to count for something.

"My name is Tracy. Yours is Adonna, right?"

A giggle burst from her lips. Tracy covered her mouth. Where had that come from? An involuntary reaction? A manifestation of her entity? If only she could tell the difference, maybe she could make some sense out of this insanity.

Tracy rubbed her palms across her lap, steadying herself. "So, how are things going in there? Have you ever been inside a human before?" Damn, did that sound stupid.

A voice rose from deep within her. *Yes.* A deep whisper. Her own voice, yet not her own.

Okay. Good. That's a start. Tracy trembled. "Okay, wow, so..."

What the heck do you say to an alien living inside your body?

"Are you done with that whole healing-me thing?"

No.

"So you're still tired, huh?"

Yes.

"Sorry about that. I guess you didn't plan on this much work when you jumped inside me."

No answer.

"John says that when you're stronger, we can have conversations with more than one word. Not that there's anything wrong with one word." Damn. Why did this have to be so hard?

Yes.

It was probably improper to ask but she needed to know. "I was wondering about last night. Did you go somewhere?"

No.

"Then why was I climbing out the window?"

No answer.

Tracy flopped against the wall behind her. "Okay, then can we talk about what happened with John? I was enjoying his touch. You pushed him away." Silence lingered. Maybe she needed to ask an actual question. "Do you like John?"

Yes.

Well, that's good. "Then why did you push him away?"

Not right.

But he was right. Every stinking inch of him. She was damned if she'd finally found the man of her dreams and have it screwed up by something out of her control. "What's not right about John?"

Not John.

The warmth ran from Tracy's face. "Dak? Why don't you like Dak?"

Wrong.

What the frig does that mean? "You need to give me more than that. They're a package deal. What's wrong with Dak?"

No answer.

Tracy gritted her teeth, waiting. "Adonna? Adonna talk to me!"

It wasn't fair. She couldn't say that Dak was wrong and not explain. Dak was part of John. There was no having one without the other. Yes, Dak was a bit overbearing, and God knew was self-centered, but, but...but everything.

"Please give him a chance," Tracy whispered.

The silence berated her until she fell into tears.

51

John showered, dressed, and checked his voice mail. No messages from Tracy. Then again, it was only 6:00 a.m. Sane people were still asleep.

He slipped into his blazer and reached for his shoes, but they weren't beside the closet where he always left them. His brow furrowed. He'd been exhausted when he got home the night before. Maybe he left them somewhere else?

Retracing his steps, he checked the bathroom, the kitchen, and finally found his shoes beside the front door.

Odd. He had no recollection of leaving them there.

John slipped the right shoe onto his foot and balked at the caked mud stuck in the heel and now all over his hand. Why were his shoes filthy?

Lightning struck outside. The weather could certainly be to blame, but had it been raining before he got home last night? In the morning, yes, but not last night.

He must have stepped in a mud puddle earlier and not realized it.

Staff Sergeant Biggs's office was closed when John arrived at the precinct, so he eased into his chair and drummed his fingers on the desk.

Two dead cops. They wouldn't be able to keep the details from the media much longer. The last thing they needed were copycats looking for a reason to kill and mutilate police officers.

But this didn't have anything to do with cops. Deep in his gut, he knew it. But on the off-chance he was wrong, Biggs would have to keep the patrols on extra alert. It wasn't fair not to have everyone as prepared as possible.

Art Commings pulled his chair up alongside John's desk. The artificial leather squeaked as he sat. "You wanna tell me what the hell is going on?"

"What do you mean? You know everything I do."

Art looked over his shoulder before leaning closer. "I was just grilled by the Feds. They asked tons of questions. Wanted to know if I'd seen anything out of the ordinary—about you."

John gripped the edge of his desk. "What did you tell them?"

"What do you think? That you're an annoying pain in the ass with great instincts and I'm pissed off that I'll always be trailing in your footsteps."

John cracked a smile.

"Seriously, man. I—" His cell phone rang, and he checked the screen. "Shit. It's my mom. Give me a sec." He stood and walked toward the coffee machine.

John stared at the nearly-filled carafe, wishing he'd poured a cup before Art got here. Not that the coffee here was that good, but he needed a serious dose of caffeine. He hated it when Art didn't show up with Starbucks.

Art shouted into his phone, "Mom, just hold it together. I'll be there in fifteen minutes."

John stood as Art walked over. "What happened?"

"My father is on a respirator." His lower lip trembled. "They don't... They can't..."

Sergeant Biggs pushed open the door to his office. Dark lines accented sunken eyes. "Peters, I need you, pronto."

"Yeah, I'll be right there." And to Art, "You okay to drive?"

"No. I ain't going anywhere." He pointed toward Biggs's office. "Whatever is going on here is bullshit. I can't let you walk in there alone. I got your back."

"No, you don't." He turned to Biggs. "Commings needs a vacation day. His father took a turn for the worse."

Biggs glanced at Art, then to John, then back to Art. "How long do you need?"

Art shrugged. "I can be back tonight."

"Like hell," John said. "I wasn't there when my dad died, and I've never forgiven myself. You're not making the same mistake. You get a vacation. Take it, goddammit."

Art's nose flared. He spoke between clenched teeth. "Someone is out for my partner's ass. How many times have you been there for me?"

"This is different. I can handle Biggs. Your mom needs you."

Art pressed his lips together before he nodded and grabbed his coat. He slapped John's back twice. "If they start shoveling shit, call me."

John snorted. "You got it."

Biggs watched Art slip out the door. "I didn't know it was that bad."

"Yeah, well, it is."

The sergeant's grim visage hadn't changed.

"What's the big emergency?" John asked.

He motioned to his office.

John followed and a chill coated his skin as the door closed behind him, leaving him alone with Biggs and Agents Clark, Green, and Evans: the three dimwitted musketeers.

"What's going on? Did you finally realize you still need me on your case?"

Agent Clark pushed off the edge of the desk. "In a way, yes, Detective Peters."

Green nodded, while Evans glared.

Clark narrowed his eyes. "New evidence makes you intrinsic to the case, as a matter of fact."

John shrugged. "So, go ahead, spill it. What's the new evidence?"

Agent Green rested his hands on the back of a chair. "Where were you last night, Detective Peters?"

Huh? "Working. I have a case, too, remember?"

"You were here at the precinct all night?" Clark asked.

John's stomach sank. "No. I left around eleven p.m."

"And then what?"

"I went home and went to bed. It was a goddamn long day."

"Where were you around two a.m.?"

"Sleeping. What's with you?"

Biggs towed him back and John realized he'd advanced toward Clark.

"There was another murder last night, John." Biggs's voice sounded sad, fatherly, repentant.

"What does that have to do with me?"

Clark cleared his throat. "This one was different. It looks like the victim fought back, and the unconfirmed suspect punished her for it."

John's face flushed. This maniac had cut up every victim viciously before he killed them. If that wasn't punishment, he couldn't imagine what was.

"Amelia Smith, age twenty-four." Agent Evans drew a photo out of a file. "Cause of death, excessive blood loss due to removal of limbs," he said, with all the sensitivity of ordering a hoagie for lunch.

"What?" John reached for the grizzly photo, but Agent Evans yanked it back.

"Her wrists were broken from the pressure of her assailant's grip."

John clenched his fists. *Bastard.* "Murder weapon?"

"His hands. He's found a new way to make them bleed. He ripped her arms right off, so she couldn't fight back anymore."

John cringed. The cuts had become successively deeper with each victim. More blood each case. This maniac was getting off on it. And now this?

A shudder ran through him. That kind of strength, it wasn't natural—not without an Ambient.

Shit.

Dak rustled below John's navel as Clark plucked the photo from Evans's hand and shoved it in John's face. The remains were barely recognizable as a body with all the blood and dismemberment.

"Forensics believes the unconfirmed suspect held her to the floor with his foot, and from the blood spill, they think he ripped both arms out at the same time." Clark seemed to study John's expression.

"That's impossible," John said. "Even if he was drugged up."

But they knew that. And they knew that John knew it, too. That's why he was here. They wanted firsthand information on Ambient-induced strength, and he was one of the few hosts with a documented case of super-human ability.

He focused on the girl's face. Did she have a family? Children of her own?

"Can anyone vouch for your whereabouts last night, Detective Peters?"

What little blood still flowed through his veins froze. Each agent's emotionless gaze had locked on him. Biggs looked at the floor.

Shit. "You can't possibly think this was me."

Agent Green's attention switched to the screen of his phone. "It says here, four and a half years ago, September fifteenth, you ran into a burning building. Firefighters reported you pulled a two-ton beam out of a doorway, freeing the family trapped inside."

"Yeah, well, I probably had some leverage, and what does that have to do with anything?"

"The last two crime scenes and victims' remains show signs of enhanced strength, detective. The kind of strength no man alone should have."

"Sure, I get that, but it wasn't me. Sergeant, you know me better than that."

Biggs looked up. "I have complete faith in *you*, John." He rubbed his eyes. "When you ran into that burning building you reported blacking out. You had no recollection of saving those people."

That was true enough. But he'd protected people that day. Saved lives. This was something completely different.

Biggs had been the only person in the precinct that John had told about Dak, and only after the sergeant had been cleared by the FBI. Biggs had been nothing but supportive and hadn't mentioned John's *situation* since.

John turned to his superior, his friend. "My Ambient didn't do this."

"I'd like to believe that, John, but we have no way of being sure it wasn't involved."

"How about my word? Don't you think I would know if someone had used my body to kill people?" He glanced down at his shoes and the mud still caked on the heels.

Crap.

Dak, buddy, you're being awfully damn quiet. Help me out here.

Nothing.

Agent Green slipped his phone into his suit jacket. His lips pursed slightly, and his eyes showed a faint quiver before he recovered his blank expression. Evans moved behind John as Green revealed a set of handcuffs.

John struggled against Evan's grip as Green walked toward him. "This is ridiculous. You're arresting me? You have no evidence."

Green clicked the cuffs around John's wrists as Clark picked up a long white cylinder from inside a box on the desk.

An extractor. *Shit.*

Dak swirled inside him, slamming against his back as if trying to escape the body he'd attached himself to. **John, help me!**

The cylinder began to hum as Clark twisted a dial in the center of the device. "Article fifty-one of the Ambient Accord states that any entity believed to have committed a crime shall be extracted and nullified."

John twisted against the other agents' grip. Could he use Dak's strength to take them both out? Probably, but what would it say about Dak's innocence if he did? Or his own, for that matter.

Clark pointed the rod at his face.

"No!" John shut his eyes and gritted his teeth. He turned his face into his shoulder. They weren't taking Dak without a fight.

John, I'm scared.

"Open your eyes, Detective Peters. I can pull that thing out of you without your cooperation, but it will be a lot less painful if you let us take it."

"You have no proof."

"We have just cause. That entity is a suspect. We can't risk it killing another human being."

I didn't hurt anyone. I swear it!

Where were you last night, Dak? Where did you take my body?

I would never hurt anyone! Please!

Dak pulsed within him, filling John's body with his vapor-like spirit and easing back. Almost as if he were gasping for air.

"This isn't right. Dak didn't do this."

At least he hoped he hadn't.

No. He *knew.*

Dak was part of him. He felt what Dak felt. There was no pride emanating from Dak seeing those bleeding, cut-up bodies. He mourned for them, maybe even more than John had.

A hand grasped his chin, forcing John's face forward. He dared not open his eyes to see whose.

Think, John, think.

What reason would Dak have to murder people?

He has a fascination with blood.

No, but there's more. This perpetrator has a fascination with pain. With control. With women. *Human women.* None of the women had Ambients inside them and they'd all been raped.

They'd. All. Been. Raped.

"DNA!" John shouted. "I can prove Dak is innocent. Take a DNA sample. If my DNA matches what you found on the victims, I'll lay here and let you rip him out of me. No struggle."

"It will take a month to confirm." Agent Clark's breath wafted across John's face. Way too close. "I'm not taking a chance it will kill again."

"Fuck that!" John scrunched his eyes tighter. "That's just red tape and you know it. They can do it in a week, two weeks tops. Throw me in jail until the results come back. I'll come willingly."

His skin began to prickle along his jawline. His cheek began to shake.

Deep within, a blade seemed to cut along the edge of his lungs, searing and burning a line beneath his ribcage.

John, it hurts. John!

"Don't do this. Please!" The sensation of a thousand needles pierced John's mouth. He cried out and his eyes flared open.

"Gotcha," Clark mumbled.

Crimson light seared John's retinas.

He fell to his knees, blinding red immobilizing him. A scream echoed through his brain. His or Dak's? Maybe both.

"Please!" John sobbed. "A week. Just give us a week to prove he didn't do this."

Something popped in his chest, like his own grasp on life shattered within him.

Can't. Breathe. Dak's voice seemed faded. Distant.

I'm sorry, Dak. I'm so sorry.

One of the men holding John released his grip. The light disappeared abruptly, leaving ghostly, blinding orbs in its wake. The pain and pressure stopped.

"Dak," John whispered, falling to the floor and grabbing his chest. "Dak, please tell me you're still in there."

The sting subsided in his eyes but a mass seemed to hang within him, as if Dak had tensed every muscle and died clinging to his host.

Dak?

John's eyes cleared.

Clark pushed Agent Green away from him. "What the hell are you doing?"

"He's right," Green said. "We're supposed to uphold people's rights, not be judge, jury and executioner without all the evidence."

"The accord clearly states that even the hint of suspicion is punishable by nullification."

"The accord is wrong," Green said.

Dak, answer me. Please.

"So, what would you have me do, let that thing go free?"

"No. I expect you to do the right thing. We have no leads other than Peters. None."

"Which is why I want to end the problem. Now."

Agent Green stepped between John and the man holding the extractor. Why was this Fed protecting him?

A sharp pain riddled his chest, as if the killer had claimed his next victim by cutting out part of John's ribcage. A dull, aching cry shrieked from his lips as his vision succumbed to erratic bright starbursts. The pain faded into pressure and an intense need. John opened his mouth and breathed as if he'd never tasted air before. He released the breath and took another as his sight slowly returned.

"That thing just latched back onto him," Clark said. "I almost had it out."

Green yanked the extractor from Clark's hands. "If we find proof this alien is the murderer, I'll extract him myself."

"And who makes sure it doesn't kill again in the meantime?"

Green straightened. "I will, and he's not going straight into lock-up. I have questions." He glanced down at John, his brow furrowed, his eyes glossed with concern. "Not to mention that now he has some extra incentive to help us."

That was the understatement of the century. John coughed, holding his chest.

John, are you all right?

Dak! Thank God.

Just keep breathing deep like that.

Like he had a choice.

John took in another breath. His head reeled as Agent Clark dragged him from the Sergeant's office and into an interrogation room.

52

Something crashed downstairs, jolting Tracy from her stupor. She stuck her head out the door and called, "Laini, are you okay?"

"Yup. Dropped a plate. Sorry."

"You're cooking?"

"A girl's gotta eat. You want a Pop-Tart?"

Tracy grinned. Cooking, apparently, was a relative term. "Sure. I'll be down in a minute." Sitting on the edge of her bed feeling sorry for herself wasn't doing her any good, anyway.

She threw on a comfortable pants-set and headed downstairs.

Laini's eyes widened as Tracy entered the kitchen. "You look like you got hit by a truck." Her jaw dropped. "Oh, shit on a cracker. Please tell me I didn't say that to a girl who actually *was* hit by a truck a couple months ago." She held out a napkin with a Pop-Tart perched on top. "That earns you the last chocolate frosted. I can have a strawberry."

Tracy slumped into a chair and waved her arms. "It's okay. I probably do look like I was hit by a truck."

"You didn't break up with the cute cop, did you?"

"No." Not yet, at least. Tracy rubbed her forehead. "Laines, things are so weird. I went to sleep last night and everything was fine, but I woke up in the bathroom with my head hanging out the window."

Laini set a cup of coffee in front of Tracy. "Let me get this right, you're sleepwalking now?" She sat down. "Hon, this is getting to be too much. I wish you'd see a doctor. Post-traumatic stress, or whatever, isn't anything to mess with."

"It's nothing like that."

"Yeah, that's what they all say on the cop shows, and the next thing you know, the roommate is locked in a closet calling 911."

Tracy laughed. "Maybe I *should* talk to someone." But she couldn't talk to the federal agents, and John wouldn't hang around long if she was so negative all the time. He'd been a dream about it all, but what guy wants to take on such baggage? She took in a deep breath and let it out slowly. Hopefully Dak wouldn't give up on Adonna. Otherwise, she and John were through.

Tracy grabbed the coffee and took a sip.

No. She wouldn't tell John about this. Not yet, at least. She was a grown woman and this crying and feeling bad for herself had to stop. Things could be worse. She could be in a casket right now, but she wasn't. She had a second chance. She needed to re-learn how to live, knowing that she wasn't only one person anymore.

Like John said, he was proof it can work out. She needed to accept her new normal and move on.

She straightened and a sense of calm settled over her. If that came from Adonna, it better be real because Laini was right. If she didn't get a hold of herself, she was going to need a psychiatrist. Or worse.

53

John picked at his nails and shifted his weight on the uncomfortable chair. He glanced at the mirror on the wall to his right. Who would be watching from the room hidden within? Sergeant Biggs? The Feds? And who would they send in to interrogate him? If it was Clark, the asshole was about to get an earful.

He drummed his fingers on the long, simulated wood table. How many times had he left people waiting in this room to make them uneasy before they were questioned? He took in a deep breath, enough for both him and Dak, then let it out slowly. He wouldn't give in to the anxiety this room was created to promote.

"Dak," he whispered, but glanced at the mirrors. They could be listening already. *Where'd you go last night? What did you do?*

His friend's essence twisted within.

Come on. Before they come in here, we need to get our stories straight.

You think I killed those girls.

Tell me that you didn't.

I didn't!

Then where did you go? Where have you been going every night?

Why do I wake up in the morning feeling like I haven't slept in a week? He slammed the desk and sat back.

I'm sorry.

John tensed. *For what?*

Making you tired.

Was he talking around the question on purpose? *I'm still waiting for an explanation.*

I didn't mean for it to happen.

John's stomach plummeted. *God, Dak. Please tell me where you've been.*

I've been watching her.

John straightened. *Watching who?*

Adonna. Well, Tracy, but I was there for Adonna.

I'm still waiting for that explanation.

She's mine. It's my responsibility to protect her while she rests.

John rubbed his eyes. *Are you telling me you went to Tracy's house and watched them sleep every night?*

Yes.

"Why, exactly?"

Until we can lie together and join properly, one should watch over the other while they rest. It's what my kind does.

John rubbed the back of his neck. *And you've been hijacking my body to do it?*

I'm sorry. I didn't think you would understand.

Why the hell didn't it knock you out every day? I thought it was hard to take someone over?

Not so much when they're asleep. Dak twitched twice. **I didn't think it would be that long. I thought she'd be stronger by now, and you and Tracy would be cohabitating.**

Cohabitating? You mean sleeping together.

Yes. If you embrace while you sleep, Adonna and I can meld.

Meld? A conversation for another time. Okay, I get that you're attracted to Adonna. I respect that, and I don't pretend to know what your kind does when they're dating or whatever. But can you honestly tell me that's where you've been every night?

Yes. I swear it.

John wasn't sure what an alien would swear on but the force within him swirled naturally. John couldn't sense anything that would make him think Dak was lying.

I sure hope it was worth it.

Dak roiled. *She yelled at me. Told me to leave. That I wasn't right.*

What? Who?

Adonna. She leaned out of Tracy's window.

John shook his head. No wonder Adonna was struggling to regain her strength. She'd been trying to fend off Dak every night.

I never tried to touch her. Not without you. I guess I just hoped...

The door opened, and Agent Green entered. He held up a white cotton-headed swab. "I'll need to get that DNA sample."

John nodded and opened his mouth. Green wiped the swab along the inside of his cheek before clicking the sample into a plastic box. He handed it through the door before pushing against the lock until it clicked.

"Why'd you help me?" John asked.

"Because extraction is wrong. That being inside you is a US citizen, no matter what Clark thinks of their species." He sat opposite John. "I'm interested in getting your insight on our case."

"Why? I'm a suspect."

Green pulled out his cellular and swiped his thumb across the screen as he read. "You majored in criminal psychology before you joined the police department."

"Yeah, so?"

The agent glanced at John, then back to his phone. "Decorated five times while still considered a rookie cop. Recognized three times for your assistance with ongoing investigations, hailed as a hero twice, at least one of which we could tie in to your Ambient."

"Entity."

Green raised his brow.

"He prefers to be called an entity."

The agent seemed to ignore the comment but John knew better. He could sense the guy's wheels turning.

What are you looking for, Green?

"You were promoted to detective at twenty-nine and your partner seems to think you walk on water."

John stared at him, waiting for the punch to the chest that would take him off guard.

The agent smiled and set his phone down on the table. "You've spent more time studying the unknown suspect than anyone else. Taking you off the case was a mistake. I want you to look over the new case files. You might see something we missed."

Now *that* was unexpected.

John paused, waiting for a "but" that didn't come. He had his own doubts, though. The case the agents had taken from him was no longer his chief concern. "You have my complete cooperation, but I need to ask you—when that DNA test comes back negative, is Dak out of danger?"

Green glanced at the mirrors and edged closer. "I doubt it. Clark is a great agent, but he's not too fond of sharing Earth."

John sat back. "Not good enough. I want it, in writing, that Dak and I will both be cleared by that DNA sample."

Sighing, Green tapped the edge of the desk. "Even if I get that for you, it's only a piece of paper and you know it. We have seven days to prove without a shadow of a doubt that the being inside you was not involved. Then you have my personal guarantee that I will do everything in my power to keep Clark and Evans at bay."

But Green was low man on the totem pole. This kid had no authority. John might as well be making a deal with his neighbor's lapdog. He could feel the tendons in his neck harden.

Green leaned closer. "I know what you're thinking, but this is your only option."

John glanced at the mirror and exhaled. The kid had their balls in a vice.

Can we trust him?

"Dak wants to know if we can trust you."

The agent's eyes widened, and he shuffled closer. "You can actually talk to it, just like that?"

He nodded. "Answer the question. Can we trust you?"

John latched onto his gaze. He wanted to look into the kid's eyes when he answered. The words meant nothing, but intent always surfaced in the pupils and in the body language if you knew how to look for it.

Green met his gaze. Steady. Unwavering. "Right now, I'm probably the only person you *can* trust."

54

Laini slammed her fist on the number pad beside her keyboard. "Dagnabbit!"

Tracy slipped into the seat across from her at the kitchen table. "I may be wrong but I'm pretty sure that's not the way a keyboard works."

Her roommate massaged her temples. "I stinking hate this program. My boss asked if I could do a pivot table and like an idiot I said, 'sure, no problem.' I have no freaking clue what I'm doing."

"Did you Google it?"

"Of course. Google is my life. I just can't figure out what to drag where to get the results I need."

Something fluttered within Tracy's chest and she stood. "Well, how hard can it be?"

Very hard, she knew that. Why so many people still insisted on using spreadsheets over databases was beyond her. But her mom always called her a natural-born button pusher, so she might as well give it a try.

"Let me see." Tracy leaned over Laini's shoulder and perused the mish-mosh of undecipherable numbers on the screen. "Yeah." She nodded. "I think you're doing something wrong."

"Tell me something I don't know."

Tracy's right hand twitched then twitched again. The second time it moved toward the mouse, but sprang back, as if thinking better of it. Was it possible that…

Adonna, have you done pivot tables before?

Her chest fluttered again.

Tracy hadn't exactly been nice any time Adonna made herself known. Was she in there now, wanting to help but afraid of Tracy getting angry again?

I'm not afraid. It's okay. Show me how to fix it, if you can.

After three heartbeats, she reached for the mouse with her right hand and the keyboard with her left. A few strokes later, Laini's pivot table was gone. Adonna highlighted the base data and clicked *Insert Pivot Table*. Tracy's hands became her own again. Wow.

She cleared her throat and turned to Laini. "What are the results you need?"

"I need the sum of purchases and quantity of purchases to a given vendor."

Tracy's fingers started to click. Ten seconds later, the data appeared.

Laini gaped. "No friggin' way! I've been sitting here for two hours, and all this time you knew how to do that?"

Adonna whirled while Tracy shrugged. "Lucky guess, maybe. It works off the same principles as a database. You just need to tell it what to do." Which seemed logical enough. More logical than an alien inside her, anyway.

"You've saved me a crapload of work! Thanks so much!"

Adonna jittered, shimmering toward Tracy's stomach.

Tracy grabbed the edge of the table. Would she ever get used to such an odd sensation? She stepped back from the computer. "You should save this and refer to it later. Just drag what you want to calculate into this field." She pointed at the screen. "It's not really that complicated." And it wasn't, now that someone else showed her what to do.

Slipping back into her seat, Tracy sipped her latte.

"Rock on!" Laini fist-pumped into the air. "I can change the data, too. This is awesome!"

Tracy exhaled, releasing some of her tension. This was the kind of relationship John had with Dak. *This* she could live with: an unseen friend, someone with different life experiences and willing to help. But the Jekyll and Hyde stuff still made Tracy want to run for cover. She needed explanations. She needed to understand this non-corporeal person inside her.

There was probably a perfectly good reason to be hanging out of the window during a torrential downpour. At least she hoped there was.

She ran her hands through her hair. In a year, she and Adonna would probably be laughing about all this together. At least she hoped they would be. But part of her still needed reassurance.

She grabbed her cell phone. "I need to make a call," she told Laini, and walked toward the front of the house.

55

John opened a manila folder and sifted through the crime scene photos.

Agent Green scrutinized his movements, probably watching for a reaction to the pictures of the murdered women: looking for signs of disgust, pride, or eroticism. John would do no differently.

"Wait a minute." John slid a picture of Alexandra Nixon away from the others. She stared back at him through long, parted *blonde* bangs. "Where did you get this picture?"

Green looked over John's shoulder. "From her parents. This was taken two days before she died."

John held the photo between two fingers. "She was a brunette when we found her. Are you telling me she dyed her hair just before she was murdered?"

Had that even showed up in the report? How had he and Art missed that?

"So?"

"The perpetrator probably marked her when she was blonde." He threw the photo on the table. "He *is* looking for blondes. He probably figured she was trying to hide from him when she changed her hair."

"How is this helpful?"

John dug his fingers into his scalp. "He's fixated on blondes. There's probably a reason. Whatever that reason, that's his trigger." He sat back and looked at the ceiling. "But why change to killing two cops?"

"If the cases are related."

"They are." He could feel it.

"But the victims in case one are all women," Green said. "Case two has a pair of male off-duty cops. Gian Doogan was linked to the case, but J.J. McCarthy had nothing to do with case one."

"Call it a sixth sense." John pointed to the photographs on the war board of the two officers in their dress uniforms beside Forensics' shots of their beaten bodies. "What I don't understand is the change in M.O., and then going back and killing another woman."

"All right," Green said. "Let's consider this." He tilted his head as if contemplating. "The perpetrator who killed the cops is a man scorned. He reeks of vengeance or deep, loathsome purpose. The serial suspect is a super strong, woman-hating, Ambient host." Green crossed his arms. "All data says your instincts are usually spot on, but I think we should continue to treat this as two separate cases."

John nodded. "Yeah, maybe."

His phone rang. Tracy's name appeared on the screen and he tapped to answer.

"Hey, you."

"I'm so glad you're there. You're never going to believe it but Adonna is some sort of computer expert. Well, maybe not an expert, but she helped Laini concoct this seriously detailed spreadsheet."

How was it possible that the sound of someone's voice could

have the ability to melt away the troubles of the rest of the world? He could listen to her forever.

"John?"

He blinked. "Oh, yeah, well, you know, it's completely possible that her former host worked on computers. It makes sense that whatever knowledge she's learned would move with her to the next host."

Agent Green had his phone out and tapped his stylus against his lips. However, from the lack of eye movement, he was concentrating less on the screen and more on John's conversation. His interest didn't have the sinister feel of the overbearing Evans or the homicidal Clark, though. He was more like Agent Fox Mulder, perpetually in awe.

Green glanced at him then returned his eyes to the screen.

"So," John continued, "you guys are getting along, then?"

"Mostly, yeah, but something weird happened last night."

John flinched and glanced at Green. "I'm listening."

"I know you're busy, but can we please have dinner, tonight?"

John's eyes returned to Green. "Dinner tonight? Ummm…"

"It won't be long. I need to…" She sighed. "Have you ever sleepwalked?"

Sleepwalked? He bit back the question as Green continued to feign perusing his phone. "Tonight's going to be a little hard." *Because I am under house arrest, and everywhere I go, this pre-pubescent kid in a suit has to go with me.* "But maybe in a few days?" *Or a few weeks, after the DNA tests come back and prove their innocence.*

Dak didn't butt in on the conversation. They both knew the clock was ticking. Clark might try to extract Dak no matter what the test results showed. They needed to find the killer and prove without any doubt that he and Dak weren't involved.

Green frowned and placed his phone on the table. "If that's Tracy Seavers, we can meet her for dinner. It's either that or take-out."

Huh? "Tracy, hold on a second." He muted the call and turned to Green. "What, I'm supposed to take you along with me on a date? That will go over well."

The agent smiled. "I'll tail you and sit in another booth. I'm actually a little interested in seeing how two hosts communicate. I'm sure the Ambients get excited to meet one of their own kind."

You have no idea. "But you'll stick out like a sore thumb."

"Me? I've been trained in covert surveillance. I can keep a low profile."

John pursed his lips. "You're wearing a cheap polyester suit that looks like you borrowed it from your dad. You stick out, kid, trust me."

Green fingered his lapels. "It's polyester, but it wasn't *that* cheap."

John snorted. Dragging the kid around wasn't the worst thing he'd ever had to do, but the case was more important than anything else. Dak's life was in his hands. Then again, his instincts and intuition weren't up to par in the last few days, as Green had pointed out. Maybe a break was what he needed. Just an hour to refresh his batteries.

Tapping the mute button again, he brought the phone back to his ear. "You know what, I changed my mind. How about I pick you up at five o'clock?" Dak swirled and shimmered between John's lungs but remained silent. "It will have to be another quick one, unfortunately. This case has some unforeseen deadlines, but we can take an hour to eat."

"That's fine!" Glee reverberated in her voice. "We want to see you guys."

"Then we'll see you in ninety minutes." He glanced at Green. *All three of us.*

56

John helped Tracy out of the car. She tensed as John slipped his hand into hers but Adonna had sunken deep into wherever it was the alien hid.

Was that acceptance, or was the Ambient still so disgusted with Dak's *wrong-ness* that she forced herself as far away as possible?

The cool evening air teased at the edge of her skirt as they entered the restaurant. Something above the knee was probably not the best choice for fall, but she wanted to look nice. She needed to get John's mind off work for a while, even if it was just to remind him that she would still be here when he solved this new string of horrible crimes.

The scent of garlic and marinara wafted from the tables as the hostess seated them in a round booth with a wonderful view of the super-romantic parking lot. Not that many places in South Jersey had a great view, but after that first date on the terrace of Villari's, John had set her standards high. Serene, quixotic settings were a little much to ask, of course, when they only had an hour to eat.

"So, do you really expect to spend the entire night at the precinct, again?" Tracy asked.

"Pretty much. There's a whole lot to do and not much time to do it in. I need to figure this out before someone else dies."

Tracy shivered.

God, how could he stand it? And how could she keep him here, knowing he should be out trying to catch a maniac? "We didn't have to meet tonight. I'm sorry. We should have rescheduled."

He grabbed both her hands and kissed them. "Hey, I needed a break anyway, and Dak and I wanted to make sure you guys were okay."

"We're fine, I guess." But she understood him asking. Their last date had gone so horribly, horribly wrong. She unfolded and refolded her napkin. "Dak has no hard feelings, then?"

"No. He's still hoping that Adonna will come around." He shifted his weight and looked away.

John always looked to his right when Dak talked to him, as if the Ambient were sitting at their table. She'd probably develop similar gestures when Adonna animated. Hopefully, she'd find a way to be equally discreet.

"We were both really happy you called," John said. "I'm sorry it has to be a short date. Dak and I are really motivated at this point."

"Motivated for the date or for the case?"

A warm smile brought out the dimples in his cheeks. "Both. Wrapping up this case means more time for us." He squeezed her hand and closed his eyes briefly.

There was something else. Something maybe even more important but she couldn't quite place her finger on why John seemed suddenly uncomfortable.

Three tables down, a baby screamed, reaching for a cup on the table. The mother threw a handful of french-fries on the high chair. The fistful of food worked as good as a pacifier.

It all seemed odd with the two of them—no, the four of them

—sitting here with regular lives going on around them, like the two shouldn't mesh together. Maybe that was the source of his discomfort, always harboring Dak's secret.

The waitress appeared and started to review the specials. John pulled out his badge and showed it to her. "Listen, I don't do this often, but can you help us get out of here fairly quickly? I have some important business to get back to."

Her eyes widened. "Do you want everything to go?"

"No, we'll eat here."

She nodded and took their orders. What must be going through the poor girl's head?

If John had been any other guy, Tracy would be insulted that he wanted a speed-date. If he was trying to prove how much he cared by making time for her, then home run.

A shiver crept up Tracy's spine. A real home run would only be in their future if Adonna allowed it. Tracy needed to find a way to make her icy interloper warm up to Dak and maybe ask Dak why in God's name Adonna had gone out the window.

To her left, a man sitting alone in a booth glanced at her over a menu. He looked up when his waitress approached. Tracy jumped, nearly knocking over her glass.

What was Agent Green doing here?

The meeting at the parking lot hadn't been the end of it. He was still lurking… and while she was on a date, for goodness' sake! Was nothing sacred with these people?

She eased toward John. "That guy in the booth over there. He's one of the federal agents who did my orientation. He's been watching me."

John looked over his shoulder and groaned. "Yeah, about that. He's not actually watching you at the moment. He's watching me."

She straightened. "What?"

"It's kind of a long story, and we only have an hour, but consider him my new partner for the week. We're going to be joined at the hip."

A coppery smell whisked through the air. Adonna sparkled while a deep heaviness overcame Tracy.

John turned back to her. "Unfortunately, wherever I go, he goes."

"Seriously? Why?"

"I'd rather not get into it right now. We—"

The seat beside Tracy shifted as someone slid into the booth beside her. She gasped as sparkling blue eyes met hers.

"Hey, darlin'," Sean drawled. "How've you been?"

Adonna writhed. *Mate!*

Like hell you're going to mate!

Every ounce of Tracy stiffened. This was *not* happening. "What are you doing here?"

"You know me, I was driving along doing nothing, and suddenly had this urge to get something to eat."

So, his entity drew him here. Shit. Was he going to pop up everywhere, now?

"Hey, I'm Sean." He reached across the booth to John.

Sweat broke out across Tracy's brow. She needed to get Sean out of here. What if he said something? What would she do?

John's brow furrowed as they shook hands. "John."

Sean's cheek ticked. His nose flared as he held onto John longer than necessary.

John yanked his hand free. "How do you know Tracy?"

Sean blinked, his annoyed expression melting into a friendly smile. "Awe, we're old friends, aren't we?" He placed his arm around Tracy's shoulder.

She cringed while the energy whirling inside her warmed at the touch.

Taking a deep breath, Tracy pushed down with all her subconscious might. Adonna twisted into a ball and spun, as if trying to thwart Tracy's control. The entity wouldn't win. Not this time.

"So, you are the big, strapping policeman she's been bragging about?" His lips tightened. "I thought you'd be taller."

Tracy tugged, and Sean released his hold.

John's jaw set. Enough testosterone flared between the two men to fill a football stadium.

"Sean, this isn't a good time. I'm…"

John's phone rang. He glanced at the screen. "Dammit." His gaze ran over Sean. "Tracy, I need to take this. Are you okay?"

Her jaw froze shut. She tried to cry out "No!" but her head nodded instead.

Shit, Adonna, don't do this again!

Tracy shivered as Sean's hand cupped her knee.

Glaring at his phone and then at Sean, John stretched across the table and kissed her cheek. "I'll be right back."

His eyes continued to bore through Sean, sending a very clear, territorial message that would have infuriated Tracy if she weren't trembling inside and begging him not to leave. Sean just smiled back. Bastard.

Both John and the federal agent slipped into the vestibule and out the front door. They might as well have been miles away.

"Alone at last."

Tracy tried to shimmy farther into the booth, away from Sean, but her body didn't respond. "We are not alone. There are about a hundred people here."

He moved closer. "A hundred hungry, preoccupied people that couldn't care less what's going on in this booth. Why so tense?"

"You shouldn't be here."

"I wanted to see you."

"I told you I'm with another guy."

"Him?" Sean gestured to the window where John watched them from the sidewalk while talking on the phone. He shifted and paced like a German shepherd, his gaze not leaving Tracy. Agent Green stood beside him, also with a phone to his ear.

"If he were really into you, he wouldn't have left you alone with the competition."

"You are *not* competition."

"Really?"

His hand slid up her thigh. She tried again to shift away but her body remained frozen. Sweat dampened her brow and underarms. *Adonna, don't. Please let me go!*

"John will be back in a minute."

"Then I better speed things up."

Tracy bit her lip as his hand crept higher. Damn that stupid short skirt!

His fingers tickled the edge of her underwear. Her body heated, and she hated herself for it.

"Isn't it exciting," Sean said, "to have your big, burly, law-abiding boyfriend right outside the window while we're in here, thinking of all the dirty things we can do to each other?"

She managed to shake her head. "I'm not thinking anything like that."

He snickered. "Then tell me to stop."

Her voice froze again as she tried to form the words. Dammit!

He skimmed his fingers further up and Tracy gasped as her legs spread without her consent. Sean snickered. "There we go."

The energy building inside her shot down her side, meeting Sean's hand at the top of her thigh.

Dammit, Adonna, stop!

Sean froze. His face twisted, as if he struggled under a huge weight.

Tracy thrashed and screamed, stuck inside her own body while Sean's hand shook on her skin. His fingers skated down toward her knee, then back up her thigh, and back down again. Was he fighting his Ambient, too?

He blanched, and serenity returned to his features. He smiled, eyes darkening. Tracy clawed at her shadowy prison, a specter within her own body. Her head lolled back, and she sighed.

No! Adonna, stop!

"You're getting off on it, darlin', aren't you? Knowing how close I am to your sweet spot, while your dickless boyfriend watches, completely clueless of how close I am to his precious little puss—"

"Please, stop." Tracy turned to the window and caught John's gaze. Her expression must have conveyed her horror because he bolted toward the door.

Sean withdrew his hand and slithered to the side as John and Agent Green came through the entrance. Adonna shrieked when the contact ended.

John barreled into the restaurant and hauled Sean out of the booth, lifting him by the collar of his shirt with one hand. "What did you do, you little piece of—"

"Peters!" Agent Green appeared at his side. "You've already declared yourself a police officer. Do you really want to do this here?"

Sean leered, his eyes fixed and wide. "Lots of people looking. This should be great fodder for tomorrow's headlines, Johnny boy. Police brutality. They'll eat it up."

John mumbled under his breath, released Sean, and turned to Tracy. "What happened?"

Her hands trembled on the seat cushion. What should she do? What could she say? *Sorry, honey, but I just let another guy feel me up under the table.* Yeah, that would go over well. He already looked like he wanted to snap Sean in two. Not that the asshole didn't deserve a good beating.

Sean eased back into the booth before returning his darkened gaze to Tracy.

She cringed and scooted out the other side toward John. "I want to go home."

"That's okay, I need to get back to work anyway."

Sean drew his toothpick holder out of his pocket, shook it until a wooden shoot appeared, and set the box on the table. He poked the stick into his mouth, holding it like a cigarette. "Why don't you leave Tracy here? I'll give her a ride."

Tracy tensed. The innuendo hung in the air like a weighted

veil.

She swallowed down the lump forming in her throat. This wasn't funny. If his entity really could find her, how long would it be before he figured out where she lived?

John slipped his arm around her shoulder. The vein in his neck pulsed. "No, that's all right. I'll get her home."

The left side of Sean's mouth lifted in a grin. "All right. I'll see ya real soon, darlin'." He tapped the table, glided out of the booth, and headed for the exit.

Agent Green waited for him to leave and followed him out the door.

The grip on Tracy's shoulders slackened as John took a deep breath. "Dak said he felt an entity. Was that the guy from the bar?"

Nodding, she looked away. "I really want to get out of here."

Tracy's skin crawled, an odd sensation alongside the spiraling, writhing entity within her. Why, why, why couldn't Adonna react this way with Dak?

John brushed his hand along her cheek. "Why didn't you warn me? I never would have left you alone with him."

"I tried to. I couldn't get the words out. Adonna—"

Agent Green reappeared. "I paid both our checks and got our meals to go." He inclined his head to Tracy. "Sorry to steal him away earlier than expected, Ms. Seavers."

She nodded, her eyes catching a gold glint beside a crumpled napkin. Sean's toothpick case. She glanced to the door, but he was already gone.

Tracy grabbed the intricately painted metal container and rubbed her thumb over the embossed peach.

"Leave it," John said.

She should.

No. She should throw it across the room; break it into a million pieces.

But the tin had been in his family for generations. He wouldn't have just left it there.

Unless he left it on purpose.

Her veins iced. "Oh, God. He's going to use this as an excuse to see me again."

Adonna billowed out, sizzling inside her.

"Like hell, he will." John's eyes brimmed with fury. "Give it to me."

She clutched it closer to her. "He'll still come looking for me."

"I don't want you within a mile of that piece of shit."

Agent Green's phone rang. He answered, thanked the person, and turned to John. "I ran Casanova's plates. He has a few parking tickets but everything else came up clean."

John piffed. "Yeah, I'll be wanting to look at more than his misdemeanors. You have a full name and address?"

Green nodded.

John held out his hand to Tracy. "I'll shove it in his mailbox."

The agent's gaze flashed from John to Tracy. There was obviously something the agent wanted to say without her hearing, but she couldn't bring herself to move.

How long had Sean been driving around in circles, hoping to feel that pull that drew him to her? He was a deeply disturbed guy, but this?

At least she knew that he wasn't wanted for assault or anything. Assholes with parking tickets she could deal with; but John was right. It was probably better if she didn't go anywhere near Sean.

She handed the toothpick case to John.

There. Done. She'd never have to think of that jerk anymore.

She shuddered. Never, ever again.

57

The breeze kicked up as John walked Tracy to her car. He didn't button his coat.

That fucking asshole walked in on their date and tried to... John took a deep breath, tightening his grip on Tracy. Now he wished he'd said no to dinner when she'd called him earlier. If they hadn't been in the restaurant, this wouldn't have happened—unless that ass was stalking her. With an Ambient involved, who knew what he was capable of?

Agent Green waved. "I'll catch you back at the precinct."

John would have smiled if he wasn't so pissed. Green wouldn't be going back to the precinct. At least not right away. He'd tail a car behind so Tracy wouldn't notice, and after John dropped her off, they'd go back to the precinct together.

But that's not what John wanted to do. This Sean guy had crossed the line with Tracy. He and the little shit were going to exchange some words. Fists, if necessary. Fists would definitely be good.

"If you and Agent Green are partners now, why didn't you drive together?" Tracy asked.

John laughed, allowing her warmth to quiet his desire to beat and dismember. "That would have been awkward, picking you up for a date with another guy in the back seat."

"He could have gone to a different restaurant and met you later." She shivered. "I don't like feeling like people are watching me."

Did she mean Green or Sean?

Maybe both. Green, he could steer away. Sean was going to be a problem. He knew the type. Loud, proud, and territorial. His Ambient probably amplified the little shit to a super big shit. Yeah, he and Sean were definitely going to have a talk.

The traffic light turned yellow in front of him with plenty of time to get through but he stopped anyway, giving Green a chance to catch up. The kid would lose his badge if he lost the ACDHS's number one suspect in this killing spree. John wasn't thrilled with the current situation, but the kid had saved Dak's life. There was no reason to make this hard on the guy.

Green's car coasted up behind a sedan and a minivan before the light changed. He appreciated the agent's discretion. He was surprised Tracy hadn't asked more questions already. The less she knew at this point, the better.

Beside him, Tracy fidgeted and looked at the floor. She was a smart girl. She had to know something was up, especially since he'd been using her as a crutch for the past week. Damn, she was easy to talk to. Something about being with her made everything *right*. Maybe that's why his blood boiled when that jackass put his arm around her.

"So, what's really the deal with Sean?" John asked. "Anything I should know about?"

She flinched.

Crap. There *was* something between them. His pulse quickened.

She adjusted her purse strap on her shoulder, set the bag on the floor, then picked it back up before meeting his gaze. "It happened a few weeks ago."

A few weeks ago. When she and John had already been together? His knuckles tightened on the wheel. He counted back from ten, glanced in her direction, and then back to the road. "I'm listening."

Tracy took a deep breath. "I think we were drawn together, like Dak drew you to me."

I told you that entity was focused on her.

Quiet. This is hard enough.

She gulped. "I think Adonna pushed away Dak because she wanted whoever is inside Sean."

Dak flipped over in John's chest three times, expelling the breath from John's lungs. Jealousy was a new, very uncomfortable sensation that he hoped he'd never feel from Dak again.

Gasping for air, John pressed the brake and turned into the first parking lot he saw. Green shadowed, parking a few car-lengths away. He'd have to thank the kid for that later.

John turned off the car and faced her. He did his best to pipe down the heat burning his face. "What happened between you two?"

Tears filled her eyes. "I didn't want anything to happen. I was there, but I had no control. I screamed for her to stop. It was like I was a puppet, and someone else had the strings."

Dak's angry rolling stopped as if he were shot dead. The entity sank from John's chest down toward his stomach.

John rubbed his forehead. "Adonna made you have sex with him." Bile rose in his throat.

"No." Tracy grabbed his right hand. Her eyes seemed to search within him. "It didn't get that far. We kissed."

His grip on her tightened. His hands shook, more from Dak's screaming than his own brewing jealousy.

He steadied himself with a deep breath. "The entities are very tactile. If she had control, you didn't just kiss. They like contact. And lots of it."

Her eyes widened, speaking thousands of words he didn't want to hear.

A sound emanated through his mind that started as a growl, grew to a scream, then ended as a whimper. John tried to keep a level head as Dak bounced against his organs. One of them had to keep themselves together.

And Tracy, dammit, the regret in her eyes.

John knew very well what it was like to be controlled. He'd felt an Ambient's craving for touch. It was undeniable. He needed to understand that this was Adonna's doing, not Tracy's. That didn't help Dak much, though.

Tracy closed her eyes. "I'm so ashamed."

John forced the image of her in Sean's arms from his mind. Maybe it wasn't as bad as he thought. "Tell me what happened."

"We didn't have sex, I swear it. I guess she didn't need to."

"They only need their hosts to touch."

She nodded. "I wasn't wearing much. He still had his pants on. I guess that was enough skin for her to get what she wanted." Tracy covered her face. "Shit, I feel so used."

It could have been much worse. He drew her into his arms. "It's all right. I understand."

She leaned back and looked into his eyes. Hopefully she couldn't see Dak's pain.

"I didn't want to do it," she said. "Please believe me."

He nodded but gritted his teeth at the same time. "I do. It doesn't stop me from wanting to pummel that jackass."

"Sean didn't mean it, either. He was as confused as I was."

"He didn't seem so confused tonight."

"No. Tonight he was just being a jerk."

John drew the metal toothpick container out of his pocket. "You don't know how badly I want to throw this out the window."

"Please, don't. He's going to come looking for it."

"He doesn't know where you live, does he?"

Tracy shook her head. "It's always been chance meetings." She flinched. "Well, not really chance. He seems to be able to sense me from a distance."

"From a distance?" John stifled the growl in his throat. "Dak, what do you think?"

The Ambient pulsed twice. *I can't sense anyone past a few hundred yards. But I'm not all that strong a tracker.*

"Is it possible for him to sense her from a mile away or more?"

Dak shuddered. *With concentrated effort, yes.*

Shit. Sean being able to find her didn't bode well for them. He needed to keep Tracy as far away from this prick as possible. The first step was to return that stupid tin and keep himself from knocking on the door and punching the bastard's lights out.

He squeezed the box, denting the metal. Returning that piece of crap kept Sean away from her. That's all he needed to do. In time, Adonna would forget about whoever was inside that scumbag and realize there was a decent Ambient waiting for her right here with open arms.

The entity fizzled like John had taken a drink of soda.

We can still make this work, buddy. You'll see.

John slipped the toothpick holder back into his pocket. "You don't need to see him ever again. I'll shove the tin in his mailbox tomorrow. Then we're done with him."

"Thanks for understanding."

The swirling within him continued. Dak's movements seemed erratic. *You okay, buddy?*

The entity's essence shook. Maybe it was better to leave him alone, for now. John wondered how he would feel if he'd set his heart on someone, spent his nights watching her, protecting her while she slept, only to be shoved aside for the first piece of alien ass that sauntered by.

Visions of Tracy, half naked and rolling on the floor in Sean's arms, flashed before him. He believed her when she said that she wasn't in control, but she never said she didn't enjoy it. Was he really in a different position than his alien friend?

"Are you all right?" Tracy asked.

"I'm fine."

He wiped his cheek and stared at his damp fingers. Were they his tears, or Dak's?

"None of this was your fault." He returned his gaze to Tracy. "I'm not happy, but I understand. Keep away from that guy, okay?"

She nodded. He hated the pain in her eyes. What was Adonna doing inside her? Gloating? Laughing? Would there ever be a future for the four of them, now that she'd tasted something she apparently liked?

Dak formed a ball and the spinning slowed. John wished he could comfort his friend, as the entity had done for him so many times.

"I'm not so sure Dak is going to get over this all that quickly. I've never felt him this upset."

A half-hearted smile crossed Tracy's lips. "Tell him I'm sorry."

He ran his fingers along her cheek. "You're not the one who cheated."

Tracy trembled. Her eyes widened and searched a faraway space. Had Adonna spoken to her? "I don't think she meant to hurt Dak. I don't think she was really thinking about anyone but herself."

Typical.

John bit back the thought. He didn't know Adonna yet. He didn't have the right to pass judgment. But at the moment, all he felt was Dak's pain.

"I'm sure she didn't mean to hurt him." He turned on the car. "We'll get through this."

Taking care not to lose Green, John drove from the parking lot. He really didn't need this extra crap on top of everything else going on. Personal problems weren't a luxury he could afford, but this was the life he chose. He was damn lucky that Tracy was willing to work with his insane job. Any other woman would have bolted by now.

After pulling into her driveway, he walked her to her front door and held her for nearly a minute. Dak tingled beneath his skin, not reaching out for the touch John knew his friend craved. A pang of guilt twisted his gut. It seemed wrong to enjoy the warmth of a woman while his friend suffered within.

Tracy pushed up on her toes and kissed the side of his mouth. He turned, drawing her back for a full kiss. Her mouth opened and her heat, her taste flooded him. He drew her tongue into his mouth and she relaxed as he tightened his grip. He groaned, sensing her acquiescence, her agreement, her willingness.

Shit, he wanted her. Needed her. He needed to pull her inside and make her forget Sean ever existed. He could do that for her. Clear her mind. Show her what she already had. Cover her body with his and protect her from that fucking asshole.

He blinked and released the kiss. What was he thinking?

No. Not like this.

She dropped back on her heels and opened her eyes. "That was nice. I wish I could convince you to come in."

John cleared his throat. "You don't know how much I would like that."

But she deserved better than him screwing her to make her forget about Sean. John wasn't thinking about her right now. He was thinking about himself and his bruised ego.

Dak twitched, startling him. He needed to refocus. Dak's life was still at stake.

He glanced over his shoulder to the dark blue sedan parked a few houses away. "I really need to get back to work."

He kissed her fingers, then leaned down to her lips. Her kiss started sweet but deepened. She opened her mouth like a woman promising more. And goddamn, did he want to give it to her. But that would take time Dak didn't have.

He gently pushed her away. "When this is all over, we'll pick up right where we left off."

Disappointment marred her features before she nodded. "I'll be looking forward to it."

Biting his lip as he turned to the car, he ignored the raging hard-on pressing against his zipper. Dak shook within. *You all right, buddy?*

I thought you might go in. You wanted to.

"I sure as hell did." He opened the car door.

I don't want to mess this up for you. I won't touch Adonna if you want to go back.

"Finding the killer is my first priority. It has to be. Not because it's my job, but to get you safe again. We'll have time for our relationships later."

She wanted you, John. You could have...

"I know what I could have, but I didn't. I'm getting you off the suspect list. Period. No more Tracy and Adonna until that's accomplished. Got it?"

John?

"Yeah." He slipped into the driver's seat.

Thank you for not letting them take me.

"Don't mention it."

He pulled out and headed back toward the highway. Tracy's kiss still burned on his lips. Why did he have to meet her now, when his time wasn't his own? Making love would be so much more fun than spending the night mulling over more case files and...

Making love?

Had he actually thought that? He'd only known Tracy for what, a few weeks? He couldn't possibly be in love, but he couldn't ignore the attraction between them. And for the first time, the idea of waking up in a woman's arms every day didn't spook him.

He shook the thoughts away. Happily ever after would never happen unless he got his head in the game.

His grip tightened on the wheel until his knuckles whitened.

Maybe Dak was right. He should have stayed with Tracy. He wanted to go in, stay with her, *be* with her.

Shit, maybe he should go back. Maybe she was scared. Maybe she wanted him to come in, so she wouldn't be alone.

But could she ever really feel safe with that rat bastard around?

Maybe not, if the other Ambient was seeking her out and pushing her and Sean together.

The wheel squeaked beneath his grip. No. That wasn't even an option. He needed to put a stop to the stalking, now.

John pulled into a convenience store and parked in the back. A lone streetlamp lit up a single red doorway and a stockade fence hid the dumpsters from residential housing. Agent Green parked alongside him. They both got out of their cars.

"What's going on?" Green asked.

"Give me lover-boy's address."

The kid raised a brow. "You're not serious."

"I'm dead fucking serious. Give it to me."

A cat mewed nearby.

Green's voice remained settled. "I don't think you're in the right mindset to talk to anyone right now."

"Who the hell do you think you are, telling me what kind of mindset I have?"

"I'm the guy who sees the look on your face." He held up his hands. "I don't believe you're our killer, but don't lie and tell me you're not angry enough to strangle that guy."

A syrupy, decayed smell wafted from the dumpster. The cat's call heightened to a howl, and someone behind the wooden fence shouted for it to shut up.

John took a step back. The kid was right. What the hell was he thinking?

He hadn't been thinking. Not with his head, at least.

Green's hands remained splayed at his sides, nowhere near the gun he had tucked in the back of his imitation leather belt. The kid did trust him, but he was right not to trust John with Sean. Not until he calmed down.

"How about you give me that family heirloom, and I give it back to Sean tomorrow when we question him? Maybe I can also hint that it would be in his best interests to keep away from Ms. Seavers."

"You're going to question him?"

"Of course. He's a host. I may not have an Ambient inside me but that doesn't mean I can't spot the symptoms." His expression turned stony. "I'm surprised you didn't mention it, knowing what we were looking for."

Dammit. The kid was smarter than John gave him credit for, but there was no sense in lying at this point. "Tracy told me about him, but I didn't want to go in guns blazing on a hunch."

"Unlike tonight?" A crooked smile crept across his lips.

John stifled a laugh. "Okay, you're right. Me and Sean face-to-face is not a good idea, but I'd like to observe if you're bringing him in."

Green nodded. "You got it."

An agonizing three more hours of reviewing evidence at the precinct turned up nothing. Exhausted, both John and Agent Green headed out for the night.

Dak had grown quiet, probably giving John more time to think. The Ambient depended on his friend's lungs for life and now he also depended on John to catch this criminal to avoid being eradicated like a common pest.

Agent Clark couldn't possibly understand what it was like to have another life inside him. Anyone wielding an extractor should be required to host an entity first. Just because Ambients didn't have bodies did not make it okay for them to be exterminated.

Part of him felt sorry for Sean and what he would face during the interrogation tomorrow. But only a small part.

John pulled into his driveway. Green parked right behind him, blocking his ability to leave.

The agent leaned his head out. "I'll hang here until an overnight surveillance team arrives."

"Like hell you are." John lifted his take-out bag. "We still have left-overs and I want to discuss the cases some more." He walked to the agent's window. "I have a comfy couch. Sleep here, plus have agents watching the house. That way there is undeniable proof that I didn't leave."

Green's wide eyes were almost comical. "So much for my fluffy down pillows back at the hotel."

"Yeah, well, my lumpy pillows will put some hair on your chest, kid. Now get out of the car."

58

Pans rattled in the kitchen and Tracy's mother laughed when Laini said she didn't know where the cooking spray was. Her mom was beginning to make Saturday breakfast a habit. Not that either she or Laini minded. Pop-Tarts were great and all, but there was something dangerously adult-like about eggs and bacon.

Tracy knew she should be in there helping, or pretending to help, but she couldn't keep herself from jumping when her own voice sounded in her head, speaking words that were not her own.

She closed her eyes and the swirling gray-purple cloud encompassed her thoughts. She steadied herself for what she knew would come next.

"Don't say it. I don't care what you want. Unless it comes wrapped in a nice, respectable police detective, you're shit out of luck."

Need.

"I don't care what you need."

Mom walked in from the kitchen, placing two paper plates of

eggs onto the coffee table between them. "You're talking to yourself again."

"Yeah, except I'm not my own best friend." And maybe she never would be.

Why couldn't her entity be more like Dak? John seemed happy, comfortable with someone inside him. Why did her Ambient have to end up being such a one-centric, myopic pain?

"I know you've been through a lot but Laini is very worried about you."

"True that." Laini plopped on her recliner, balancing a plate piled high with bacon.

Tracy covered her eyes. "What did you tell her?"

Her roommate shrugged, scooping food into her already packed mouth.

"Enough to know that things aren't back to normal yet," Mom said. "Do you want to talk about it?"

Little did she know that things would never be normal again. There was no way to make her understand that. "Lately, I've been two people; two people who want completely different things."

Mom giggled behind a bite of her eggs. "It's called being young. There are so many choices out there for you. Far more than when I was your age."

"When you were my age you already had a teenage daughter." Tracy cringed when the words left her mouth. Attacking her mother was the furthest thing from her mind but it was too late to take it back.

Her mother stared at her plate. The air seemed heavy.

Clearing her throat, Laini stood slowly. Her gaze darted between Tracy and her mom. "You know what? I just remembered, I've got that thing in the…" She gestured over her shoulder with the plate. "Well, you know." She grabbed her purse and headed for the front door, plate still in-hand. "Thanks for the breakfast, Ms. Seavers."

Tracy's mom watched her go. "Wow. Mention teenage pregnancy and she bolts faster than your father did."

Tracy cringed but her mom just took another bite of egg. Why couldn't Tracy be so poised in an uncomfortable situation?

Her mom swallowed and placed her plate on the table. "I made a big choice when I was fifteen years old. Everyone said I should get an abortion. I've never regretted my decision, no matter how bad things have gotten." She folded her arms and reclined, as if their discussion was about nothing more serious than the laundry. "Now, what are we really talking about here?"

Tears formed in Tracy's eyes. Thirty years ago, her mom had transitioned from child to adult with one decision and in that instant, she'd grown up more than Tracy could imagine.

She covered her eyes. "Oh, Mom, I'm so confused."

Within moments, her mother's arms engulfed her. "Whatever it is, I'm here for you."

Tracy soaked her mom's shoulder with tears as her mother rocked her like she'd done when Tracy fell and skinned her knee at her mom's best friend's high-school graduation party. Tracy didn't actually remember but there was a picture on her mom's nightstand. She'd always wondered, why that picture? Why that moment, out of the last thirty years?

Maybe that moment was significant to her mother. All of her friends were there, celebrating a normal teenage event, but her mother was aside, taking care of Tracy.

Her mother had given up so much for her. How could Tracy turn around now and try to hurt her? Why would she say something so heartless, something she didn't even mean?

Mom patted her head and smiled. "Tell me. Whatever it is, I've probably been through it."

Tracy bit her top lip. How exactly does one explain having an alien inside you without actually saying so? "Remember that guy I told you about?"

Mom's eyes widened. "John, right? So, you *do* have a

boyfriend." She clapped her hands once. "Fess up. Tell me all about him."

Tracy smiled as Mom retro-spiraled into a teenager again. Maybe that's what she needed: a friend. "He's wonderful. You'd love him. Handsome, polite, honest."

"Sounds fantastic. What's the problem?"

That was the million-dollar question. "I think I may be falling in love with him."

"I'm still waiting for this problem."

And what a problem it was. The problem of the century. "I met this other guy, too. I can't stop thinking about him." Or at least the other me can't stop thinking about him.

"Ah, choices. Tell me about this other guy."

"He's nice-looking." God, she hated admitting that. "But he's such a dick. I knew I should keep away from him."

"But you didn't?"

She lowered her eyes. "No." But she wanted to. She shivered.

"It's not unnatural to be tempted, honey. It's called hormones."

"I want to think about John. I want to be with John, but the other me can't get this other guy out of my head." She tugged at her hair. "I hate the other me, sometimes. I swear it!"

"Well, I might not be the best person to ask for romantic advice, but I think you need to get the second guy out of your system."

"What do you mean?"

"You love one guy, but you're tempted by the other. Give your hormones what they want. I guarantee you, they'll stop asking."

Tracy balked. "Did you just tell me to sleep with a guy I don't even like?"

"Believe it or not, I did."

Adonna did somersaults along Tracy's diaphragm. The Ambient and her mother would probably be great friends under other circumstances.

Mom rested her elbows on her knees. "Chances are, the sex

will suck, and you will want to puke afterwards. You'll realize that the grass is not greener over in hot-jerk-land, and you'll never look back." She raised a brow. "If John is meant to be your guy, a quick fling isn't going to do anything to change that."

"This isn't the sixties, Mom. If I cheat on my boyfriend, he'll be pissed." But would he be pissed? He seemed to understand that it was Adonna the first time. Yeah, he was upset, but he respected that there was someone else involved.

Wait, was she talking herself into this?

Adonna slithered below her ribcage.

Whose thoughts was she thinking, hers or Adonna's?

A vision of swirling, grayish purple flashed through her mind. *Want.*

Tracy shook her head. No. No want.

The very idea was ludicrous. If Adonna wanted to get it on, she'd have to re-wire those alien hormones to sizzle for Dak. That's the way it had to be. Tracy was not going to sacrifice herself or take a chance at losing John just to placate an over-sexed alien.

59

John dragged a razor across his face. Images of each item in evidence flashed through his mind. What was the missing link? There had to be something.

They're going to extract me, aren't they?

Dak's perpetual question did little to settle John's nerves. "How about you quit worrying and help me think?"

The killer in the first case left huge amounts of evidence at each scene, the biggest of which was his DNA. He made no attempt at hiding it. Didn't even use a condom. Of course, that was good news in that it would clear him and Dak eventually. DNA evidence also proved there were no copycats. It was the same guy every time. But the rest of the clues he left seemed to mean nothing. Was he planting them on purpose, leaving a rabbit trail that always led to an empty hole?

And then there were the cop murders. So different, but the crime scenes had the same feel. The same resonance. Not that a feeling was the kind of evidence that would hold up in court, but his intuition had never steered him wrong. Whatever it was, it was big and bold and blaring, yet just out of their reach.

John's jaw tightened as he finished dressing and slid on his blazer. Maybe he was overthinking the clues. Maybe they were all left behind to keep him off-kilter. But it wouldn't last for long. Eventually, this creep had to make a mistake.

The stairs squeaked as he made his way to the kitchen, past the neatly-folded bedding on the couch. He had to hand it to Green, the kid was a great house guest. The room was probably neater now than when they got home last night.

"Yeah, we're on our way," Green said, speaking into his mobile. He shoved the phone into his pocket and handed John a cup of coffee. "We have to go. Agent Clark just called for backup. We got the asshole."

The ACDHS had their suspect cornered. John couldn't believe it. What an incredible break!

His ego puffed a little, but he ignored his own idiocy. It didn't matter who caught the scum bag, as long as the creep was behind bars. The women of South Jersey deserved to breathe a sigh of relief.

Tapping the glove box in front of him, he willed Agent Green to drive faster. Screw the residential signs. Fifty didn't even cut it at a time like this. "Turn left here," he said, and grabbed on to his seat as the car skidded onto Teardrop Lane.

Holy shit.

At least a dozen marked and unmarked police cars congregated at the end of the street. Flashing red lights reflected off vinyl siding in the early dawn light. They pulled behind the last of the cars and jumped out.

Uniformed officers loitered by their vehicles as John passed with Agent Green. John's shoulders turned to stone. Was it over already?

Sergeant Biggs tapped incessantly on his phone as he exited the house from the front door. He flinched when he saw John.

Something was definitely up. "What happened? Did we get him?"

Biggs shook his head. "No. The bastard got us." He glanced at Green. "Sorry."

"Sorry?" Green said. "Sorry for what?" The agent continued into the house.

Slipping his phone in his pocket, Biggs gestured to the door. "Please tell me that kid had you under surveillance all night."

"Yeah, he slept on my couch. Why?"

"Then I guess you are officially off the hook. The Feds can't blame you when they had their own man on you." He continued toward his car. "Get your ass in there before the Feds trample more evidence. I'll check on the perimeter teams. We might still be able to catch the perpetrator."

So, the asshole got away, anyway. The Feds were more useless than he thought.

John continued up the walkway. The thickness of the air gave him pause. A coppery tang stung his nasal passages.

Dak shook and twisted, as if trying to hide from the smell.

Ignoring the solidity gripping his chest, John strode toward the door, but was blocked by a black suit.

"This is a Federal case," the man said.

"Let him in," Green called from further within. "He's with me."

John passed the forensics team carrying bags from the scene and moved into the living room. The once light-colored carpet was splotched with crimson stains: footprints in a disjointed, erratic pattern. The creep had never been that sloppy before.

To his left, agents taped markers around a severed arm lying beside the body of a blonde woman. Another man placed tape on the floor around her spread legs.

Another life lost. When would it end?

He moved to the other side of the room, where most of the agents seemed to be gathered.

Green crouched beside a red puddle, rubbing his temples.

There was no sign of the carpeting beneath the crimson stains on his half of the room. The rug had become so saturated that the blood had pooled in places.

"The computers say it was fired off but there is no residue," one man said. "Where is it?"

"Where is what?" John asked.

All eyes turned to him. The few who had been crouching, stood.

"Why don't you tell me." The man who had spoken clenched his fists and stepped toward John.

Green appeared by John's side. "Peters didn't do this. He was with me when Clark called for backup."

The first man asked, "Are you certain of his whereabouts?"

Green's nose flared. "Yes. I was on-scene and had two agents stationed outside. Peters is clean."

"Then how do you explain this?" He motioned behind him, and the agents parted, leaving a full view of the carnage.

Body parts littered the floor without reason. Blood splattered up the walls and across the furniture. John counted at least two severed heads.

He gulped down the need to puke as Dak twisted and rolled within him. "Who was this?"

Green pointed to the head on the right, perched on the remains of a man's buttocks. "That was Agent Clark." He pointed to the left, where another head lay turned away in the middle of the couch. "That was Agent Evans."

John's eyes narrowed. "That's impossible. We were here within twenty minutes of Clark's call for backup."

"We were here within twenty minutes of the *precinct's* call to us."

Meaning the dispatch didn't happen fast enough. Dammit.

But that still wasn't enough time for any normal assailant to do this.

Green covered his mouth as if holding back a wretch. "We

need to officially label this an Ambient attack." He stood. His face shone a pale yellow. "From what I can tell, Clark and Evans called for backup as they moved in to engage. I guess the killer had other plans."

"Everything is accounted for but the Ambient extractor," another agent said.

That's good, right?

John nodded. With the extractor gone, Dak was safe. For now, at least. Unless they had another one.

Unfortunately, the disappearance of the weapon came at too high a price. He wasn't fond of Clark or Evans, but neither of them deserved to be mutilated.

John turned from the scene and followed the footprints out the back door. They ended in the sand a few feet from the house, right before the grass started.

"They say he made off into the woods." Green moved behind him. "Seems to be his M.O."

"But not this time. He left another way. The front door or maybe the garage."

Green's brow furrowed. "But the prints are right there."

John crouched over a red print in the sand. The color had already faded to a hue closer to brown. "Look at the doubling of the image here," he pointed. "And here."

"I don't see it."

"That's because you're green, Green." He stood. "The killer walked out this far and then doubled back on his own footprints." He pointed to the grass. "See here? There is sand in this print. Like the other cases, he made it look like he went one way, while he took off another." He nodded. "He did a damn good job of it, too. I wouldn't have noticed if he hadn't done this before."

Green motioned between the smaller footprint and John's size-13 boots. "At least this will rule you out as the killer."

John pursed his lips. That wasn't enough to save Dak, and the kid knew it.

The agents mulling around the bodies talked and glanced in their direction. Their eyes darkened, their movements quick, their hands hovering close to their weapons. They wanted Ambient blood.

Green pushed John toward the front door. "I think we'd better get you out of here."

But getting him out of there wasn't going to change anything. They needed to feed those rabid dogs another bone.

"Sean had plenty of time on his hands after he left us last night," John said.

The kid pursed his lips, nodding. "I can get a warrant within fifteen minutes."

60

Tracy tugged the hair at her temples and banged her forehead against the cool sliding glass door leading to the backyard. The vision of a hideous gray-purple cloud erupted in her mind.

I need.

The words repeated. Adonna had moved from one-word demands like *want* to nearly complete sentences. I need. I want. Her insistence had grown worse since Tracy's X-rated conversation with her mother. Leave it to Mom to accidentally start an unstoppable chain reaction and then leave Tracy alone a few hours later with no distractions to keep her Ambient from driving her crazy!

She grabbed a glass from the dish drain beside the sink and drew herself a glass of water. There had to be a way through this. Adonna needed to understand that there was more than one person's needs and wants involved.

Tracy finished the water and slammed her cup onto the countertop. The glass shattered, slicing her hand.

"Dammit!" She turned to the sink and ran water over the blood. She relaxed her fingers and let the stream cleanse the wound as the being inside her pulsed. "Can this day get any worse?"

She dabbed the laceration with a paper towel and affixed a Band-Aid on the small cut. If she survived a car accident, she could endure this.

Stepping on the bottom of the trash can to open the lid, she tossed the paper towel inside and froze. Her towel lighted atop dozens of others, all stained with blood. Had her mother cut herself while cooking? Laini? Why hadn't they said anything?

Her stomach rolled—or something inside her stomach rolled. She shivered and leaned her forehead against the cool glass door.

The sun peeked over the trees along the back of her property, shining down on the rabbit hole in the corner of the yard beside the garbage cans. Two brown bunnies chewed on the grass. Such a normal scene. Nothing special. Except for the incessant twitching and pressure jabbing from within.

Want mine.

Tracy growled, staring at her reflection in the glass. She needed to take charge. She wasn't a child anymore. This was her life, and she wasn't going to let it be run by anyone else. "I told you that the only option on the table is John and Dak. You need to get over this."

No over. Mate.

Well, at least the thoughts were getting easier to comprehend. Then again, it could have been the repetition. "You need to understand that if I give you what you want, it will hurt me, and it will hurt John."

No hurt. Hold. Touch. No hurt.

Tracy rubbed her eyes. If she really believed that, she'd find Sean and take a long stroll in the park holding hands. But she didn't believe it. Not at all. Yes, Adonna wanted touch, but lots of it. The naked kind. The kind that could end her relationship with John.

The Ambient pulsed within her chest. Tracy could feel the

entity getting stronger, as if someone had placed a balloon in her chest and slowly inflated it over the past week. "Are you done healing me? Is that why you can speak?"

Almost. Done soon.

That was some consolation at least, but the pressure inside her continued to build. How could John stand it?

Give. Now you give.

"Give what?"

The purple cloud returned to her thoughts. A color she'd equate to Sean for the rest of her life. Not like Tracy expected another answer. Adonna pretty much had a one-track mind. One could only hope she'd change her focus.

No change.

Tracy flinched. Adonna could read her thoughts, just like John said. So much for privacy. "Why can't you give Dak a chance? He seems like such a nice guy. And he really likes you."

The purple cloud changed to a brilliant green, as if that was supposed to mean something.

None of this was fair. This was her body, not Adonna's. She had the right to be with who she wanted.

Debt.

Debt?

Tracy shivered. Maybe she did owe Adonna a debt. The entity had saved Tracy's life, but in return, she shared her lungs. Wasn't that enough?

Adonna rolled and shook within her. Apparently, her lungs *weren't* enough.

The rabbits outside chased each other across the yard. Did animals have these kinds of problems or did they mate with the nearest possible prospect when the time came? How much easier it would be if she didn't care?

Could she go to Sean? Give Adonna what she wanted?

Yes.

Tracy snorted. Dumb question.

It wasn't that Sean wasn't attractive. He was just… She shuddered. How could she even consider letting that seriously disturbed man touch her again?

No. She wanted nothing to do with him.

And the thought of hurting John, of losing her chance with him, it wasn't worth it. She took slow, steady breaths as the pressure inside her increased.

Don't tell.

There was always that option, but then she'd have a secret. Her relationship with John would be based on a lie. That wasn't what she wanted.

The essence inside her thickened. John said she'd be able to feel Adonna's emotions. Was this anger or disappointment? Maybe a mixture of the two. But Tracy had to wonder, with Adonna getting stronger, why hadn't she taken Tracy over again? She could make Tracy do whatever she wanted. Why not now?

Trust.

Trust? Interesting. Okay, yes, she and Adonna would have to live together for a long time. Probably the rest of Tracy's life. Trust would be good. Is that what Adonna was doing? Trying to gain Tracy's trust?

Yes.

She flinched. Having her mind actually answer her own hypothetical questions was definitely going to take some getting used to.

At least Adonna was making the effort. Maybe Tracy needed to make the effort, too.

The thickening inside her dissipated and became a sparkle, like sipping a freshly opened can of soda.

So, the matter on the table was still Sean. How could Tracy give Adonna what she wanted, but still save herself for John?

The gray cloud returned. *Just touch. Just touch. Please.*

But she'd learned that Adonna lost all sense of reason around

Sean. It was stupid to even consider going near him. She couldn't. She wouldn't.

The essence within her swirled and her concerns fizzled, fading to the background. She'd always played it safe. Stuck to harmless, nice guys. Not that this was a bad thing, but there was something intrinsically intense about Sean, and maybe a touch dangerous. What would it be like to be with someone like that? Someone so sure of himself. Direct. Unafraid of taking what he wanted.

Yes. Yeeeessss.

Adonna writhed as the mental image flashed in both their minds. Tracy winced at the thought. Adonna sparkled, stroking her from within. A haze grew over Tracy's thoughts.

Being with Sean would certainly give Adonna what she wanted. But what about Tracy? How could she do such a thing and then face the man that she really cared about the next day?

Please. Please.

Adonna would never give up, she was certain of it. Tracy needed to fight her.

A wave of effervescence shimmied through her throat before spinning behind her eyes. Tracy grabbed the edge of the table, steadying herself. The fizzle in her head intensified before settling back into her chest. The tension in her muscles seemed to slacken.

She blinked her eyes and caught her reflection in the picture frame beside the window. Her face skewed before coming back into focus.

Adonna had saved her life. Tracy had a debt to repay.

Her vision blurred again before becoming clear. Crisp. Like looking in a mirror.

Her Ambient wasn't asking much. Just a few minutes. Maybe she only wanted to say goodbye? How could Tracy deny her that? Her Ambient deserved this.

Yes! Thank you.

"Once," Tracy whispered, touching her reflection in the frame. "Once, and then never again. Do you agree?"

The swirling began to pulse again. Was Adonna thinking? Considering all options? Looking for an exit clause?

Agreed.

Tracy released the breath she'd been holding. "And then you give John and Dak a chance?"

John.

"Not Dak?"

John.

Tracy closed her eyes. At least she was half way there. Hopefully, someday they'd find a way to make Dak right, too.

Turning from the sliding door, she passed the shattered glass and grabbed the broom hung inside the pantry. She'd have to vacuum, too, or one of them were bound to find a stray shard while walking in bare feet.

As she swept the shattered glass, the depression in the countertop caught her attention. She ran her fingertips over the indent: the exact size of the base of her cup. Had she done that—slammed the glass clear through the laminate?

Her gaze carried back over the shards, some of them stained with blood, before drawing back to the indentation.

How was that even possible? She wasn't *that* strong.

61

"You're letting him go? You've got to be kidding me!" John threw his hands in the air, nearly knocking over a picture on Sergeant Biggs's desk. "We haven't questioned him."

"Sean's lawyer was here waiting for him," Green said. "There's nothing we can do."

"What do you mean there's nothing we can do?"

Biggs rubbed his face. "Peters, did you really assault your suspect in a public restaurant?"

John's cheeks cooled. "Assault? He's charging me with assault?"

"And he's using you as part of his alibi. He says there's no possible way he could have been at the restaurant with you and abducted last night's victim in the timeframe her parents said she disappeared."

John's eyes widened. "Are her parents sure what time she went missing?"

The sergeant shrugged.

"This is bullshit. We can still question him."

Biggs shook his head. "His lawyer is using article six of the consolidation code."

"What the hell is article six?"

"It went into effect two weeks ago as a kneejerk reaction to overcrowding caused by closing so many precincts. It was in your consolidation paperwork."

"There's only a handful of cops left. Who the hell has time to read a shitload of paperwork?"

Green folded his arms and leaned against the back of a chair. "That lawyer is certainly well versed. We can't hold Sean unless we produce concrete evidence. I can't even overrule it with Federal jurisdiction."

"But he's a goddamn host for goodness' sake."

"He has the right to remain silent," Biggs said. "And he's claiming your warrant is a personal attack since he and your girlfriend…"

Fire burned in John's chest as he held up his hand. "I got it."

This wasn't right. Laws that protected criminals were bullshit. If Sean was keeping his mouth shut, he knew something.

John punched the desk. "Let me talk to him. Just ten minutes."

"Too late." Green pointed to the small window overlooking the outside offices. "His attorney has already signed him out."

Sean and a guy wearing a suit that probably cost more than John's car walked through the cubicles. John shoved through the door before Biggs could argue.

The bastard had the gall to smile. "John, buddy, nice to see you again."

"Don't give me that shit, Sean."

The little prick turned toward his lawyer. "See what I mean? He was like this last night, too."

"You little piece of—"

Green gripped John's arm. "He's baiting you."

The attorney pulled off his spotless glasses and pretended to clean them. "Do you intend to assault my client again, Detective Peters?"

"Don't," Green whispered.

John took in a deep breath to calm himself, but his pulse continued to pound in his ears.

"I didn't think so." The lawyer replaced his spectacles. "We will be on our way, then."

Sean took two steps before looking over his shoulder. "Oh, by the way, tell Tracy I said hello."

Son of a...

Green's grip turned into a vise. "He's not worth it."

Maybe not, but pummeling him sure would feel good.

The entrance door shut behind Sean and his lawyer.

John shrugged out of Green's grip. "I still can't believe the ACDHS let that guy go. They have to consider him a suspect. You guys are suspicious of everyone."

Green ushered John in the opposite direction. "Definitely. He'll have a caseworker nosing up his rear by morning. If he even thinks about doing something illegal, we'll know about it."

"But they still could have kept him here."

"With that lawyer? Unlikely. Besides. They still have their number one suspect under close observation."

John stopped short. "Me?"

Green nodded. "They're not giving up on you. They probably think your Ambient has us both under mind control."

"Dak."

"Excuse me?"

"His name is Dak."

"Dak." Green nodded. "Do you think he'd let me question him? He could provide a unique perspective now that we're certain we're looking for a host."

John steadied himself against the rolling in his chest.

We don't have a choice, Dak. Your life is on the line.

And to Green: "Yeah. Both he and I will continue to cooperate."

My kind didn't do this. Life is sacred. All life.

I know. But we have to make them believe that, too, or when we catch this creep—whoever it is—the entity inside him is toast.

"And can Dak help us look over the evidence?" Green asked.

Does he think I went out for coffee every day? There's nothing in those pictures.

"Yes," John answered. "Dak said he'll give it his best shot."

John shifted in his chair and placed his elbows on the table as Agent Green positioned his phone between them and called up the voice recorder. They'd chosen a private room normally reserved for sensitive meetings. No windows and no observation mirrors. Despite the certainty of Dak's innocence, the walls seemed to press close, unsettling him.

Green tapped on a blank pad with the back of a pen. "What's it like?"

"Huh?" That wasn't quite the question he expected.

"What's it like having an alien inside you? Can you *feel* him?"

John furrowed his brow. "Sometimes I can feel him. Most of the time I forget he's there, unless he's in a chatty mood."

Green leaned across the desk. "So, he can really talk to you: full conversations in English?"

"Yeah. How is this helping the investigation?"

"I'm sorry." He pushed back. "That's just my own curiosity. I'm fascinated by the whole idea."

John nodded. Green's fascination was probably the only reason Dak was still alive.

The agent pressed the record button on his phone screen. "We've concluded that it is possible for the alien to take over your body without your knowledge. Can *you* do anything without him knowing?"

Only if I fell asleep, but I'm pretty much awake when you are awake. It's hard to sleep with your host's eyes open.

"Dak says no. At least I haven't found a way to shut him down. He's always aware of me."

Green scribbled a note on his pad. "Could the alien stop you from doing something it didn't like?"

"Well, you know he can take control, so I suppose so."

"That would mean that the Ambient is an accomplice. He's letting the perpetrator kill people. Either that, or it is all the alien and the human doesn't even know."

John straightened. "Now wait a minute. I'm not prepared to accuse this entity without all the facts."

"But you said that the alien can take control when it wants."

Not really. I couldn't control you now even if I wanted to.

John glanced at the desk. "Why not?"

Your neurons have been shooting off erratically since Biggs said they were letting Sean go. It itches. I wouldn't be able to concentrate hard enough.

Sorry. He took a calming breath "Apparently, anger makes it harder for an Ambient to control a human. I don't know if that little nugget helps at all."

"You never know." More scribbling. "But if the suspect went to sleep, the Ambient could take over either way, right?"

John tensed, glancing down at his muddy shoes. "Yeah, he could."

Green nodded. "So, again, if the Ambient wanted to stop him, it could. The entity could walk its host into a police station while the perpetrator is asleep and confess."

Unless the host takes medicine to help him sleep.

John straightened. "What?"

I had a host that took Temazepam before he went to bed at night. It was horrible; like being paralyzed.

"What did he say?" Green asked.

"Some drugs knock them out. The perpetrator might be drugging the Ambient every night as a safety measure."

Agent Green tapped the side of his stylus on the edge of his computer pad, nodding to himself. "Is there anything we should be looking for that would tell us if the murderer is the Ambient or the host?"

What is he looking for, phantom cell residue or something? We're not corporeal.

"He doesn't think so."

"Is there anything that drives them crazy? Anything that could compel them to murder?"

Don't say it, John.

But he had to. Even if it meant pointing his finger at another alien, he had to save Dak. "They are really tactile. Seeing another Ambient makes them very touchy. Dak tripped me into Tracy when he first saw her."

Green shook his head. "Good to note but none of the victims were hosts—at least not officially on record. If they were, we'd have gotten involved from the onset."

John brought his fingers to his lips. "We're still missing something."

"What do you mean?"

"I don't know. I feel like there's something right under our noses."

Green tapped the *off* icon on the recorder app. "Well, we'd better figure it out. The clock is ticking. If he keeps to his M.O., he could be picking out his next victim right now."

The conference room door opened, and Biggs walked in. "I know you didn't want to be interrupted but I thought you might want to know that the medical examiner confirmed that Gian Doogan and Jonathan McCartney were both killed by the same man."

No surprise there, but John's eyes narrowed. "What did you call the second cop?"

Biggs's cheek twitched—a rare change in expression on the normally stoic sergeant. "Jonathan," Biggs clarified. "He was known as J.J. in his precinct. His father and I went to school together. I always knew him as Jonathan."

Jonathan. Gian. Sweat dampened John's shirt. The similarity, it couldn't be a coincidence.

"I see your wheels turning," Biggs said. "What is it?"

The murderer had cut off the genitals, shoved them in the victims' mouths. The ultimate sign of power and dominance over another man. A sign that he was better. Worthy.

Of a woman…a woman the other man had.

Shit. Why hadn't he seen it sooner?

"It's Sean. He wasn't killing random cops. He was looking for me. He only had a first name."

"What are you talking about?" Biggs asked.

"He wants Tracy. He must have known she was dating a cop named John. Gian and Jonathan. He was going down a list and slaughtering the competition."

Green narrowed his eyes. "What, like the terminator in that old movie, taking out everyone with the same name? That's a little crazy."

"I'm telling you, this makes sense. We have to bring him back in for questioning."

Green shook his head. "Even if I thought you were right, we still have no evidence. They will continue to hide behind the law and say you have it out for him because of his history with Tracy."

John stood, shooting his chair back on the tiled floor. "Then let's get out of here and find some evidence." Because now that asshole knows exactly which John he's looking for.

62

Tracy's hands trembled on the steering wheel as the sun set behind Sean's house. The last time she was there, Adonna had been worked up into a heated frenzy and Tracy had been screaming, begging her to stop.

The broken numeral eight beside the front door still hung by its last screw, warning her that nothing had changed. If she got out of the car, there was no reason to think Adonna wouldn't take this as far as she could.

Coming here was insane. She couldn't face Sean again. What was she thinking?

Adonna swirled within her stomach and moved into her chest. Tingling, but not insistent. Maybe the Ambient really did want to build trust between them. Otherwise, she'd have taken over and marched Tracy's body up to the front door half an hour ago.

Trust. It seemed such an odd concept, sitting in front of a house she'd never wanted to see again. A house she wanted to forget and a man she wished she'd never met.

Adonna jittered and lowered in her abdomen.

Tracy's hesitations were selfish. Adonna was finally building a rapport with her. This is what Tracy wanted: the same symbiotic connection John and Dak had. The relationship would be work, like a marriage. They needed to compromise and learn to live together. Adonna wanted to see this other entity one last time. Tracy had agreed, and she couldn't withdraw her promise now. In a few minutes, this would all be over. At least she hoped it would.

Shit, this was insane!

Tracy rummaged through her purse and grabbed her phone. She rubbed her thumbs over the edge of the case, concentrating on each curve where the rubber met the touchscreen. John wouldn't approve. He'd be sensible, find another way. Maybe that's what she needed right now. The voice of reason.

She tapped on his name in her favorites and waited four rings before his voicemail picked up. It shouldn't have surprised her that he didn't answer. It was a miracle she'd seen him at all in these past few weeks.

If he'd answered, maybe he could have come; sat with them to make sure Adonna didn't get out of hand. But that option was gone now. She'd have to face Sean alone, but she didn't have to do so in the dark. John needed to know what she was doing. It was only fair.

She settled herself with a deep breath as the voice she'd grown to care so much about faded into a beep. "Hey, it's me. Listen, maybe it's better that you aren't there to talk me out of this. I'm at Sean's. Don't be angry. Adonna is crazy about his Ambient, and I'm sure you of all people know what it's like to have an entity in your head that wants something." Tracy paused. How could she make this not hurt so bad? "Adonna promises that if I give her one more time with him, she'll let you and I be together." She gulped. "I-I'm going to try to hold hands. That's all you said we needed to do, right?"

Crap. John wasn't stupid. He knew just as much as she did that Adonna wanted more than hand-holding.

Tracy shuddered again. She needed to get this over with. Now.

She spoke into her phone. "Please don't freak. I really care about you. I'm doing this to give us a chance. I hope you'll understand." Tears trailed down her cheeks as she hit the red button, ending the call.

Adonna reeled inside her, but not in the happy, sparkly way she had for the entire trip. She seemed more solid. Like swallowing a crust of bread and not washing it down with water. Maybe she finally understood how hard all of this was on a human.

The walkway and the door loomed before her, but staring at them was not getting her any closer to being done with Sean. She slipped from the car, tugged her shirt to straighten the wrinkles, and headed up the walkway, avoiding an uplifted crack in the cement.

The door swung open before she knocked. Sean smiled. "This is a nice surprise."

Tracy gasped and took a step back. A little part of her wished he wasn't so damn good-looking. She lowered her gaze to the concrete patio.

Now that she was standing here, she had no idea what to say. "I-I'm surprised to find you home."

He propped himself against the door frame. "Well, that's doubtful, darlin', otherwise you wouldn't be here." His body made a perfect, posed angle, as if he'd jumped off a perfume ad.

She forced herself to make eye contact. "Oh, well, I wanted to see you."

"Now that, I believe. Want to come in?"

Like she had a choice. Adonna's entire essence pressed against the front of Tracy's body, almost as if her host's skin was the only thing keeping the Ambient from leaping out and taking Sean on her own. Tracy slipped past him without answering.

Sean closed the door behind him. "So, do you have something to give me?"

"Excuse me?"

"My toothpicks. I left them at the restaurant."

Damn. He *did* leave them on purpose. "Actually, no. John was going to put them in your mailbox this morning."

"Well, let's add dependability to the list of things your wonderful inspector is lacking."

He sprawled back on the couch, the same couch he'd eased her onto while Adonna got her rocks off with his entity. Adonna tingled as the memory surged between them. Part of Tracy longed for the explosion that had erupted through their bodies.

She shook the thought away. So many times in her life she'd been alone, even when involved in a relationship, leaving her feeling unappreciated and deficient. John had broken through that, lifted her up and made her feel special, wanted, understood. Tracy didn't want Sean. She was done with him and every other guy like him she'd ever been with. She straightened as warmth spread through her. John wasn't lacking, not at all.

Tracy touched her chest as her breath hitched. She needed to go find John and beg him to forgive her for even considering this.

"I'm going to take a wild guess here, darlin', and say that you didn't come here on your own."

"What makes you say that?"

"I'm guessing that this electrical energy between us is driving you crazy and that alien inside you is going absolutely batty over it." He shifted his weight. "You see, this dude inside me, he wants to jump your bones like no tomorrow. I keep telling him I don't like brunettes, but he can't stop thinking about what it was like touching you." His gaze dragged over her. "I think he got off more on me running my fingers up your skirt in the restaurant than I did."

Tracy shook her head. "That wasn't me."

"I didn't think so, but it was your body. That was your heat, not your ghostly gal-pal."

Tracy gritted her teeth. "Alright, this is the deal. My Ambient wanted to see you again. I told her one time only to say goodbye. That's it. I'm serious about John."

Sean laughed. "Come on, darlin'. If you were serious about the cop, you wouldn't be here. You know what that thing inside you wants and I think you need to admit that maybe you want it, too."

She stepped back, hands shaking. "Well, that doesn't matter, right? You don't like brunettes."

"You know, I think I owe my little alien tourist a favor. He did save my life and all. Maybe just once, I'll make an exception."

Tracy backed against the wall as he approached. He dragged his fingers through her hair.

"We don't have to do anything. Just touch." She turned away.

Sean leaned down. "Funny. My little hitchhiker is having second thoughts now, too. He wants me to leave you alone." His breath tickled her cheek. "But I don't think I want to. I liked the way he squirmed when I roved my hands over your skin. I liked the way my fingers tingled as I twisted them inside you. And I *know* you liked it, darlin'."

No. God, no. "I'm in love with someone else."

"But you *want* me." He grabbed her chin and forced her to face him. "That's a heck of a pickle, isn't it?" His mouth closed over hers.

Tracy tried not to respond, but Adonna's excitement surged through her veins. She kissed Sean back, welcoming the suction that drew her tongue into his mouth. He pulled her from the wall. She should stop this, demand a light touch, but her body succumbed to the whirling within her.

Adonna sparkled around Tracy's lips. The Ambient teased with light touches. Sean growled, his hand tightening around her waist. Tracy trembled as his other hand slid under her shirt.

A small part of her screamed, but the emotions flooding from Adonna tromped every uncertainty. His touch kindled a rushing fire across her skin. Every pore ignited, flared, exploded, and shrieked to be covered in everything that was him.

Adonna was going to get more than touch. She would get it all, and Tracy was powerless to resist this drowning need, this unbearable pressure bearing down on her soul.

She didn't argue as Sean eased her onto the couch.

6 3

"I still see no reason to think there is a connection between the murders of the women and the cops." Green grabbed a jar of peanuts out of his bag.

John just glared at him, rearranging photos of the Alexandra Nixon crime scene. Art had learned to trust John's instincts over the years. This kid was far too green to understand the power of going with your gut.

"You sure you don't want to check out that call for backup in Pitman?" Green asked, shaking a handful of nuts out of the jar.

John leaned on the table in the war room. "It's not our guy. Dispatch mentioned minors. He's never involved kids before."

Green threw a peanut in the air and caught it in his mouth. "What about the shooter in Deptford mall?"

"Too public, not his style. We don't have time for a wild goose chase."

John clenched his teeth as Agent Green munched on the nuts. Apparently, crunching helped the kid think, but after a few hours, the sound ground through what remained of John's nerves. Why couldn't he just chew gum?

Refocusing, John considered a picture of the first victim:

Diana Worth, twenty-six, from Haddon Township. Single mother of two. No family in the area. That first crime scene had been clean other than the perpetrator's DNA. No blood and no sign of struggle. Their killer had become more violent with each murder. Only one victim had resisted: the first woman to have her limbs ripped from her. He scanned pictures of the grizzly scene tacked up on the war board. It wasn't natural. It wasn't human.

Dak shivered. *You can't still be thinking that one of my kind did this.*

No, John didn't believe Dak could do something like this, but what about another Ambient? Was Green right? Would the entity and the host have to be in cahoots to pull off a murder?

John rubbed his temple. "Am I stronger because of you or would you have to give me strength?"

"What?" Green asked. He tossed the finished peanut can into the trash and wiped his hands on a paper towel.

"Sorry, I was talking to Dak."

I think you are probably always strong since I'm living inside you. But maybe you can't conceptualize that strength, so you don't use it.

Green stretched. "Please tell me you two have had some kind of epiphany."

"No, I'm still coming up dry. I wish I knew if I was dealing with a psycho alien or a psycho human."

"The answer is here." Green picked up an evidence bag containing a dead flower found outside the door of the third victim's house. "He's telling us a story. We just haven't figured out the plot yet."

John shook his head. "No. I don't think so. If he were, he'd be straightforward, boastful. He'd place the clues on the body, like he did with Melissa Harpoona. He'd be taunting us with them." John rifled through the evidence, fingering a bar receipt dated nine months ago. "I think he's dropped random things to keep us off balance."

"Well, it's working."

John stood and placed his palms on the table. "No. It's not." He gathered the photos and placed them to the side. "It's not about the victims right now, it's about him. It's about the things he's left." John carefully spread the evidence across the table between himself and Green.

"I don't get it. We looked at all this already. Clark and Evans had their top people on it."

"But they weren't looking for what I'm looking for."

Green cocked his head. "Care to enlighten me?"

"They were looking for the common denominator. They were trying to piece together the puzzle."

"Isn't that our job?"

"But our psycho would know that. He dropped a bunch of clues that meant nothing. He did it on purpose."

"To send us on a wild goose chase?"

"No. To cover his own ass—just in case."

"Just in case what?"

John picked up the smallest bag on the table. The wooden splinter he'd picked out of Melissa Harpoona's garden. "In case he screwed up."

Green's brow arched above puffy red eyelids. "That stick could be anything. It could have come in the mulch for all we know."

John brushed his fingers over the Forensics note. *Wood from a clingstone peach tree.* Could a peach tree have been mulched? Of course, but not likely when all the other mulch around it was black. Every other clue had to do with dating. A flower, a bar receipt, a movie ticket stub, and then this single sliver of wood.

Tilting the bag to avoid glare from the overhead lighting, John furrowed his brow, taking in the red and blue ink on the splinter. Could this be it, the one piece of the puzzle that didn't fit? He could be reaching for straws, but straws were something when nothing else made sense.

Across the table, Green picked at his gums. He shrugged. "Sorry. I have a nut stuck between my teeth."

John tensed. The toothpick container in his jacket pocket suddenly weighed him down. He grabbed the case, turning the embossed metal into the light. His hand trembled as the image of the peach within a red and blue circle burned into his brain. He flipped the canister over.

Made from 100% recycled clingstone peach trees.
Carington Farms, Fort Valley, Georgia.

Bile pooled in John's stomach.

Sweet Jesus. This is what he'd been looking for.

John tapped out a toothpick. His stomach clenched, seeing the red and blue stripes on the ridged end. He held it beside the evidence bag.

Green stood, inching closer. "Holy shit."

Dak squirmed, deepening John's sense of dread.

Sean had shown up out of nowhere at the restaurant, almost as if he'd been stalking Tracy. Or maybe that wasn't Sean at all. Maybe the Ambient saw something it wanted and took Sean right to her. The Ambient wanted Adonna but Sean wanted…

Tracy!

John fumbled for his phone. Tracy's missed call appeared on his screen. He tapped on the message. Little pieces of his soul chipped away as he listened to her recorded voice. Every nightmare about finding someone he loved dead crept to the surface, weakening him. He shut the visions out. He couldn't be weak. Not now. Tracy's life depended on it.

He sprang from his chair and bolted toward the door. Dak rattled within him, suppressing an ungodly scream.

"What?" Green asked, slipping through the door behind him.

John shoved his phone in his pocket as he raced toward the exit. "That shithole has Tracy."

64

Adonna slammed at Tracy's chest. *I need. Why blocked?*
Tracy had no idea what Adonna meant. Her blouse slipped off her shoulder and fell to the floor as Sean lapped her neck and collarbone. She waited for the sensation of Sean's entity entering her body to touch Adonna, but it didn't happen.

Adonna's swirl glided up into Tracy's mouth and reached for Sean's tongue as they kissed. The sensation tingled, driving the Ambient into a heated fury. Tracy slipped further away, trying to shut the flood of sensations out.

Straddling Sean, Adonna tensed as his jeans kept her from what she wanted. She fumbled with the button as he unclasped Tracy's bra. His kisses deepened, became more demanding.

Adonna stretched, reaching into Sean. The deep, undeniable desire throbbing through the Ambient subsided before she slingshotted back inside Tracy's body.

The jolt knotted her stomach. Her breath hitched.

No!

Tracy's hands shook and formed fists before pushing Sean back with such force that Tracy landed on the floor. Her bottom stung from the sculpting in the Berber carpet.

Sean wiped his arm across his mouth. "What's the matter, darlin'? Things were just getting good."

She dragged her fingers through her hair. "I-I don't know. That wasn't me. My entity, she pushed me off you."

He said stop. He said run.

Who said? I thought this is what you wanted?

Afraid. Leave. Now.

Her heart began to pummel as Sean walked across the room to the desk he'd thrown his shirt on last time she was here. "I can't believe your little gal pal changed her mind after all this." He took something out of the drawer.

"Umm, well, she's not interested anymore. I guess that means you and I are off the hook."

"Really?" Sean's body blurred as he charged toward Tracy. He grabbed her wrists and clamped them in cool steel.

Before she could even think of fighting him, he yanked her arms over her head and hung her on a peg beside the entrance. He kissed her cheek. "No, I think you're definitely still on the hook."

Her breath hitched. Adonna flexed and sank as Tracy pushed up on her tiptoes trying to release herself but the peg was too high. "What are you doing? Let us go."

Sean grabbed for her legs. She kicked, slamming him in the face. Barely swayed, he laughed and held her steady with his shoulder while he bound her ankles with a zip-tie.

"What's the matter, darlin'? Haven't you ever tried anything a little kinky?"

Her stomach hardened, Adonna balled inside. This was far beyond kinky. Why hadn't she listened to her flight instincts and stayed away?

"Sean, you're scaring me. I really want to leave."

He folded his arms. "So that's it. You're done with me? Just like that?" He walked back to the desk and fumbled within the drawer. He turned toward her before tucking whatever he found into his back pocket.

"I want to go home. Please."

"I thought you were different. Maybe not." He picked up a long, plastic-covered roll that had been wedged between the desk and the wall and stripped the wrapping. The packaging fluttered to the floor as he walked back to her. "You know, you are the only one who I told about my mother. The only one who listened, at least." He picked at the end of the roll before unfurling a long sheet of opaque plastic.

Tracy's eyes widened. A drop cloth? "Sean, this isn't funny anymore. Please let me down!"

Stretching out a puddle of plastic beneath her, he tucked the tarp into a crevice in the wall. She tried to kick him but only managed a weak swing of her bound ankles.

The plastic crinkled as he began to draw the sheet up behind her. "Those midnight blow jobs went on for years, but when I was seventeen, I wanted more."

She cringed as he kissed her cheek. The smell of plastic caked inside her throat as he hung the roll over two smaller hooks above her shoulders—hooks just the right size and spacing to hold the reel.

Her heart throttled. The plastic swished as she toiled with the hook securing her handcuffs. "Sean, please."

His eyes finally met hers. "Sorry for the delay, darlin'. If I knew you were coming, I would have had this all ready for you." He smiled, almost sweetly. "Now we can get on to the good stuff."

He grabbed Tracy's hips, immobilizing her as he nibbled at the tender flesh beside her nipple. Adonna trembled, an odd mix of yearning and fear quaked into a confused fury. Without Adonna's desire flooding her, Tracy succumbed to a building horror mixed with the bewildering deluge of sensations erupting from her Ambient.

Sean stepped back as his gaze dropped over Tracy's half-naked form. He smiled, dragging his palm over her bare stomach. "One night, when my dad was passed out drunk on the bed, I snuck into their room. Boy was my mother surprised to see me. She told me no—*that I should go*, but that didn't stop her from spreading her legs with a big fucking smile on her face." He moaned a deep guttural groan from deep in his chest. "Damn, did she scream when I fucked her. I loved it. Daddy never budged." He kissed the side of Tracy's neck. "Would you like that, Tracy? Would you like me to make you scream?"

Tears streamed down her cheeks. "Please let me go."

"She said that too once, when I tied her up. She said she didn't like it. She clamped her legs shut, so I hit her." He slapped Tracy across the cheek.

Stars flashed before her eyes before the sting settled across her skin, searing even as he stepped back. The room fuzzed, and two Seans stood before her before molding back into one.

"She liked it when I hit her. She got so damn wet, writhing and begging for more. I gave it to her. I gave it to her good and hard." He laughed, dragging his fingers through his hair. A hiss escaped his teeth. "Oh, it was soooo good."

The entity quaked in Tracy's chest. *He's going to hurt you. This is my fault!*

Tracy shook the fog from her head. She needed to do something. She needed to gain control. "I'm sorry about what happened to you. I understand, you're upset; but, please, let me go and we can forget about all this."

Sean placed his hands on either side of her head, crinkling the plastic. "It was her fault, you know. For years, she sucked me off every night. By the time I was a man, I wanted it. I *needed it*. And I had to find new ways to make it more intense."

His hand eased behind his back and revealed a long carving knife.

"Oh, God!" A cool sheen of sweat coated Tracy's face. She pulled, twisted, and stretched against the hook holding her.

"She said *oh God*, too. She liked it when I cut her. Made excuses to her friends as to where the marks came from. It became a game between us." He licked his lips. "Do you like games, Tracy?"

"Please, you don't have to do this. We can get you help."

"I don't need help!" He screamed in her face before stepping back. A composed expression swept over his features. "We're not so different from these things inside us, you know. We have needs, desires. We want to screw just as much as they do. We want pleasure." He glanced at the knife. "Any way we can get it."

"But our entities don't want each other anymore. Mine wants to leave."

A smile touched his lips. "The one inside me is begging me to let you go, but he's lying. He's got a little alien hard-on just thinking about us spreading your legs and pile-driving into you."

Adonna shivered before thickening. *I'm sorry. I'm so sorry.*

Sean stared at the knife, tilting the blade to catch the light from the lamp beside the couch. "One night, I carved a heart on her chest. There was blood everywhere. She moaned, twisting her hips with every turn of my blade." His gaze traversed to Tracy. "I'd screwed her at least ten times that night. She smeared the blood all over her, begged for more. Yelled at me because she wasn't coming. Blamed me for not being man enough for her. She begged for me to hurt her, to make her scream like never before." His eyes darkened. "So, I plunged a knife into her stomach." He mimicked the move, a look of pleasure coating his face. "Oh, she screamed. She cried, cursed me when I climbed on top of her, but she was wetter than ever before." He licked his lips, his eyes wild. "Oh, how she howled as I screwed her. I liked that scream. It was different from the others. Real. Hard. Meaningful." He pointed the knife at his chest. "I did that to her. I was man enough to make her scream like that." He raised the blade. "So, I plunged the blade in her chest again and again until she stopped screaming." He lifted his chin. "Then I knew I'd finally satisfied her."

Tracy's whole body shook, shouting at her to run. She yanked at the handcuffs above her. "Oh, God. Oh, God. You're crazy." Blood streaked her wrists.

"You like blood, too, I see." His eyes glazed, looking at the shackles.

"No, I don't. You killed your mother. You killed her!"

He shook his head slowly, as if they were discussing nothing more important than the weather. "No, my father did. The police found the knife in his hands. He was passed out drunk on the couch as usual. A crime of passion they called it." A smile crossed his lips. "They were right about the passion part."

"You're sick. You are really, really sick." She choked back a sob. "Please let me go. I can try to help you. There are people you can talk to."

"Talking doesn't help. My first foster mother tried to talk it out with me." He feigned a pout. "Tragic the way the blood soaked her beautiful, blonde hair." He took a step closer. "Someone broke into the house and killed her. Such a loss. They never found the guy."

I should have listened to you! Pull harder on the handcuffs. I'll try to give you strength.

Tracy tugged but nothing happened. A whimper escaped her lips.

"Don't cry, darlin'. I won't make you wait much longer." Sean placed the blade under her breast. "Are you ready to scream for me, Tracy?"

His nose flared as he flicked his wrist. Only the sensation of cold steel touched her, at first. Then a stinging fury lanced across her ribs. She bit her lip, holding in tears.

There was so much she hadn't done. So much she needed to do. Adonna had given her a second chance, and she'd wasted that gift. Her vision blurred with tears, but she wouldn't give him the satisfaction of a scream. She wouldn't be his plaything.

Sean ran his fingers through her blood, smearing bright crimson across her navel. "So beautiful. Do you know how beautiful you are when you bleed? Would you like to bleed more for me?"

She clamped her mouth shut and stared at the ceiling. *I'm sorry, John. I'm sorry I didn't listen. I'm sorry I wasn't more careful.* She blinked the sting from her eyes. *And I'm mostly sorry I never got to tell you I love you.* Tears ran down her cheeks.

"You want me to cut deeper, darlin'?"

A sob broke free.

"Good. Let's play."

65

"I'm telling you the killer is *not* in Pitman. I gave you the goddamn address!" Green yelled into his cell phone.

The siren atop their car wailed as John turned the steering wheel, screeching around the corner.

"I don't care that all available units have been dispatched. Reroute them here, now!" The agent threw the phone onto the center console. "Idiots!"

"I take it our friends aren't going to make it to the party?"

"They think they have the killer cornered in that house in Pitman. Everyone else has been dispatched to a live shooter at Deptford Mall. How can there be no one else?"

John piffed. "Layoffs. That's what happens without funding."

John turned off his siren before pulling off the highway and into the residential section. The streetlights cast an eerie glow across the recently paved asphalt—a street Sean probably used every day—the road Tracy drove to meet him.

His knuckles whitened on the wheel. He had precious minutes, maybe seconds to get to her. He needed to keep his calm. He'd get there in time.

Dak roiled within. *Are you sure?*

"Of course, I'm fucking sure!" John blinked at Green's wide eyes and parted lips before turning back to the road.

Whatever happened tonight, John was to blame. If he'd only pieced together the puzzle sooner...

No. Second-guessing himself helped no one.

Focus. Center. Detach. Keep calm, like any other take-down.

He drew a deep breath and let it out slowly. *I'm coming, baby. Hang in there.*

After speeding past a Wawa, he turned down a partially-lit street and parked three houses away from the address. He opened the door. "You ready?"

The kid's eyes widened. "We *are not* going in there without backup."

John got out of the car and strapped on his bullet-proof vest. "Watch me."

The agent muttered under his breath but grabbed his own vest and followed. The smell of damp mulch faded into freshly-cut grass as they moved in tandem toward the side of Sean's porch.

Frogs chirped from the trees overhead, but the otherwise resounding silence vised through John's resolve. What if he was already too late?

Dak jittered *Don't say that.*

I don't have time for you. Get scarce, now.

His friend faded and sank away. Tracy was fine. She had to be.

Green peered into the window and mouthed, "*Can't see.*"

John pointed to the right and they darted past the bushes to a window on the side of the house. Inching up to the glass, John froze. Tracy hung like a piece of meat beside the front door. Blood smeared her stomach. Tears streamed down her cheeks.

Agent Green grabbed his shoulder and whispered, "Focus. You're no good to her distracted."

John nodded, but clenched his teeth. Tracy was hurt, bleeding.

The bastard would pay for this. Screw it if John lost his badge in the process.

Crouching, he followed the thin-framed agent back to the entrance. The kid wasn't exactly the partner he would have asked for to raid the den of a killer, but Tracy could be dead by the time the cavalry arrived.

He settled himself with another deep breath, pointed to the agent, and held up two fingers.

Green nodded, raising his pistol beside his face. His gaze shot from John, to the door, and back. A bead of sweat ran down his temple.

Had this kid even fired a gun outside of a shooting range? Looked into the eyes of a killer? Made an arrest? John was running into an active crime scene with an unknown at his side. It was suicide.

A scream echoed from within.

It didn't matter how inexperienced the kid was. They were out of time.

John kicked the door. The frame buckled but didn't give. They'd lost the element of surprise. *Dammit, Dak, where are you?*

The Ambient spiraled down toward John's ankle. His hip and leg heated.

Ignoring the lancing pain in his shin, John crashed against the panels again. The door gave, dropping him inside.

"Federal agent," Green yelled. "Put your hands—"

A thudding clang cut him off. John pushed to one knee as Green crumpled beside him.

Shit! John ducked as an object passed over his head, barely missing.

"Police! Freeze!" John held up his gun.

Sean stood before him, bare-chested with red stains trailing down his right arm. Tracy's blood.

The dickwad raised his hands, a mocking smile crossing his

lips. "Hi, Inspector. I guess you finally got my invitation. So glad you could make it."

John's finger twitched over the trigger. He nudged the agent on the floor. "Green, you okay?" The kid's hand lay empty. Where was his gun?

A snicker echoed through the house. "Mr. Federal Agent seems to be unavailable at the moment."

John glanced to the ground a few paces away from him. An iron lay on its side, water leaking on the black-tiled floor. A blunt force object. He'd slammed the iron against Green's head and then thrown it at John. If John hadn't ducked, he'd be lying beside his new partner.

The sound of tears permeated the still-open door shielding Tracy from his view. John kicked it closed, keeping his eyes on Sean. "Tracy, you okay?"

"Please get me down."

"Hold on." He gestured to Sean with his gun. "Put your hands on your head!"

Sean's smile infuriated him. "Are you going to tie me up, Inspector? That sounds like fun, doesn't it?" He lowered his hands slightly. "Do you like boys, John? I haven't tried it myself, but—"

"I said, put your hands on your head."

Sean shrugged. "Can't. Sorry. Not finished with your girlfriend, yet."

The man became a blur, launching at John with unfathomable speed. John pulled the trigger but he doubted Sean was even still in his sights when the bullet left the gun.

Sean slammed John against the door, creaking the damaged wood.

The wind whooshed from John's chest. Stars riddled the room. His gun bounced across the tiles.

Snickering, Sean backed up a step and kicked the weapon away. "We don't need this, Inspector." He held up his fists. "Come on. Whoever's left standing gets to finish off the girl."

Blood coursed through John's temples as he swung. He was mildly conscious of Dak's presence racing to his bruises and healing him. Sean ducked and backed away. His chuckle fueled John's anger as he throttled the psychopath with successive hooks and uppercuts.

Sean stumbled and rubbed his jaw. He grimaced. His bruises didn't seem to be healing as fast as John's.

Whoever's inside him doesn't like him very much.

Remind me to thank him later.

"Give it up, Sean. It's over."

His maddening smile reminded John of Norman Bates. "Nah, I don't think so."

In a flash of movement, Sean reached behind his back.

John rushed toward him. A hum filled his mind, nearly drowning out the bang of a gun.

Burning, stabbing heat riddled John's upper arm as he hit the floor.

"John!" Tracy cried.

Sean's shoes tapped across the tiles. "Oh, I'm sorry, John. It looks like I shot you. How inhospitable of me."

John tried to get up, but Sean kicked his wounded arm. John's world swirled with blinding colors and pain. *Dammit!* Deep within, tremors of emotion roared that were not his own. Dak's voice bounced between his ears but the pain blotted out the words. He shook his head. Tracy. He needed to…

Agony exploded anew as his arms were hauled over his head. This wasn't going down this way. He needed to get control.

John twisted and kicked as Sean dragged him across the floor and attached him to a hook on the opposite side of the door from Tracy.

"There we go," Sean said. "A matched set." He turned to Tracy. "See, he's not all that. What kind of man lets a little bullet hurt him?"

Little bullet.

Asshole.

John tried to unhook himself, tried to ignore the pain, but his vision blurred again.

Hold on, John. I think I can push the bullet out.

Thanks, buddy.

Don't you die on me, John. Don't you dare die on me!

Working on it.

The Southern scumbag sauntered back toward Tracy. She leaned in John's direction as Sean whispered something in her ear. Hope left her eyes. *Stay with me, baby. I'll figure this out.*

Sean clapped his hands and kicked Green's body before he strolled back to John. "For a big, strong, strapping cop, I'm a little disappointed. I guess you aren't the man Tracy thought you were."

The bullet is moving. Just another minute.

"I'm a thousand times the man you'll ever be."

Sean laughed. "Oh, you could have been, if you took advantage of your situation. But you didn't, did you?"

"What the hell are you talking about?"

"Your little alien friend, Inspector. You see, as soon as Tracy clued me in to what was inside me, I started working at controlling it."

The cuffs clanged as John tugged against them. "You can't control an entity. They are beings, individuals."

Sean nodded. "And, like human beings, you can make slaves out of them."

"Impossible. They are too strong."

Almost there.

"Not if you take away what they need." Sean pressed closer, assaulting John with the stench of beer and stale ashtrays. "It took all of fifteen minutes of me smoking before it begged for mercy."

That would be torture, like having acid poured into your lungs.

I doubt that's a problem for him. How's that bullet coming?

"Now all I need to do is pick up a pack of menthols and this thing does whatever I want."

"Like, what? Helping you mutilate innocent women?"

Sean chuckled deep within his throat. "No. My alien enhanced me, made me stronger, faster—all the things your entity is racing to do for you now, while exhausting itself trying to heal you. But it's a little too late for that, Inspector."

It's detective, you stupid shit. And at least I didn't have to torture him to get help.

Sean's eyes darkened. "Anyway, now I have a chance to try out my new toy."

New toy? Wonderful. As Sean walked to the back of the house, John glimpsed a butcher knife laying on a serving tray on the couch. Dark crimson still stained the blade.

His gaze shot to Tracy. The long gash along her upper abdomen drizzled with five lines of blood that joined into one before streaming down her leg. Her life drained from her, dripping onto a plastic tarp at her feet. She panted; her eyes glazed and fixed on nothing. Sean had cut her like a piece of meat. And now the bastard was getting something new to torture them with.

You're half-healed. See if you can get free.

John yanked. Agony blazed through his shoulder. He cried out, more out of frustration than pain.

Sorry. I'll try again.

Dak spun around the wound. Quickly, at first, but his speed began to dwindle. Dak was getting tired. John and Tracy were running out of time.

Sean called from down the hallway. "Now don't go hurting yourself, Inspector. You'll spoil my fun."

Bite me, bastard. John yanked, clenching his teeth. The metal hook above him bent.

Dak, it's working!

Just another minute. I almost have it.

Pressure from within pierced his shoulder. A stabbing pain broke through his skin before smoothing over. Something metal bounced on the tiled flooring.

The bullet is out. Pull free, John. Pull free!

John yanked, but the bent tip of the hook wouldn't budge. He pushed up on his toes, trying to scoot the handcuffs over the edge. The pain in his shoulder seared like he'd lifted weights and forgot to stretch.

A blur appeared before him and a fist smashed into John's gut. John gasped for air.

Dak went limp inside him for a second before shooting his healing essence down to John's stomach.

Sean shook his hand. "You know, punching you isn't as much fun as hitting a girl. You hurt."

"Sorry to disappoint you."

A smile burst across Sean's lips. "No worries. I have other ideas for you." He propped himself against the door beside John. "You know what the best part of this is?"

"The best part of what?"

He waved his hand in the air. "All of this. I mean, hearing people scream, knowing I have the power to do that… What a rush! But the best part is always when they give themselves to me, when they admit that I am worthy, that I'm good enough to give the ultimate gift."

Dak darted back to John's injured shoulder. *Keep him talking.*

"And what exactly is that?" John shook his handcuffs. They came a touch closer to the edge.

Sean tilted his head. "Why, their lives, of course. They give their lives to me because I am worthy." He eased closer. "Because they want to please me. Because I am better than them."

John grimaced. "You're not better." *You're just your average, everyday sicko.*

Sean pressed closer. "You're going to give me a gift now, John. The biggest gift of all."

"I'm not giving you anything, asshole."

Dak shimmered around John's biceps. John could almost feel them getting larger, stronger.

Buy me some more time.

"Do you smell that, Inspector?" Sean inhaled. "That's fear. That's a gift in itself. It means you are ready to give me what I want."

"Why don't you tell me about it? Tell me what you're going to do to me. Make me good and scared."

"I don't need to tell you. You already know." Sean drew a silver rod out from behind his back.

The missing extractor. *Shit.* He wasn't after John. He wanted Dak.

Sean chuckled. "I wish you could see the look on your face. It's priceless."

Dak, can he force two entities inside himself?

No. He'd have to be dead, and the second he died, his entity would leave to find another host.

Unless he found a way. *Keep trying to free us!*

John kept his voice steady. His gaze traveled over the horrific cylinder. "You have no idea how to use that thing."

"Oh, but I do. The first agent refused to teach me, but the second agent got chatty after he watched me rip his partner's head off."

Shit.

Shit. Shit. Shit. Shit. Shit.

Sean turned the lower dial. "It's over, John. Give me your alien. I want it."

John scrunched his eyes shut, turning his face away. The rod hummed. Sean's rancid breath warmed John's face. He gritted his teeth. *Dak?*

The Ambient sparkled in John's chest. *You're as strong as I can get you. Free us!*

John yanked against his handcuffs. The sheetrock gave. Dust fell on his face and the hook tumbled to the floor. John rolled away.

Sean pushed the extractor under his arm and clapped his hands. "Exciting stuff, Inspector. But now what?"

John toiled with the cuffs. No key.

Sean looked toward Tracy. "Johnny needs a bobby pin, darlin'. Do you have one?"

She looked up before her head fell limp. The blood beneath her had begun to pool.

If John had only figured this out sooner, she'd be home, safe.

"Dang those modern haircuts." Sean turned back to John. "I guess you're on your own."

Keep trying! You should be strong enough to break the cuffs!

John yanked. The restraints squeaked but didn't give. Sean inched in his direction, extractor in hand. Out of time, John thrust upward, kicking Sean between the legs.

The cylinder rolled across the floor, landing beside Agent Green's arm. Sean grunted and doubled over, buying John a second. He tried to get to his feet.

"Watch out!" Tracy screamed.

Face red and eyes blazing white, Sean lifted the coffee table with one hand and smashed the wooden surface onto John's legs. Pain shot from John's knees into his spine as he slammed back to the floor.

Sean picked up the extractor and cleared his throat. "Well, you made this more interesting, but I'm ready to be done."

A white light emanated from the instrument's tip. John closed his eyes. *Buddy, we're in trouble. How bad am I hurt?*

Bad. I don't know what to do. Dak bounded between John's chest and stomach. *Don't let him take me!*

John's head spun. He took in deep breaths, trying to stay conscious. He could sense Sean crouching next to him, but he couldn't do more than shift his weight.

"Eyes or ears, Johnny-Boy? Your choice. I hear pulling it out through your ears hurts more, so I'm fine with that."

Tracy's voice shot through the darkness. "Why are you all about him, now? I thought you wanted me. I'm waiting for you."

"You'll have your turn," Sean said.

"I'll have my turn now." Tracy's voice boomed like a parent scolding a child. "You made me a promise. I want to scream. I want *you to make me* scream."

Sean backed away.

What is she doing?

Buying us time. I can't move my legs. Fix whatever you can. Help me fight him.

Dak's heat spiraled through John's limbs. The pain deepened but John bit down the desire to whimper like a child. Sensing Sean was no longer near, he opened his eyes. Sean pressed against Tracy, kissing her deeply.

But where was the goddamn extractor?

Tracy leaned her head back as Sean kissed her neck. "Yes, I want you. Please, Sean." Her gaze flicked to John. Her brow furrowed as her lips twisted in disgust. She must have been in agony, but he loved her for it.

A surge of energy coursed through John's body.

That's it—that's all I can give you.

It would have to be enough. John sprang to his feet and propelled himself toward Sean. Tracy cried out as the shithole pushed away from her.

John and Sean crashed and rolled to the floor, bunching up the plastic beneath Tracy. Twisting, John tried to use the handcuffs as a weapon, but Sean rolled and pinned him to the ground.

"Stupid move, Inspector. You should have seen this coming." The extractor appeared in Sean's hand. The light turned orange before John could force his eyes shut. The glow pierced his retina, latching on to something deep within him.

John?

John's senses deadened. His limbs became weighted, useless masses. He stared into the light, helpless.

John!

"Let them go!" Tracy screamed.

Dak lurched in his chest, not the soothing, gentle roll John had become accustomed to, but a shuddering, staccato tug. John's lungs burned as if Dak clung to the fragile tissue with claws. The entity shook. A scream echoed within John's ears.

Hold on, Dak, hold on.

Sean dropped close to John's ear. "Give in, Inspector. Give in to me. Give me everything."

"Stop it," Tracy cried. "You're hurting them!"

Something inside John's chest popped.

Dak tightened. *Can't breathe.*

Don't you let go, Dak. Don't you dare!

John?

The essence inside him relaxed, almost as if Dak had passed out.

Come on, Dak! Snap out of it. Fight this!

John's retinas burned. He willed himself to cover his eyes in a last futile attempt to hold his friend inside, but his arms only jerked in response. Pressure built behind his sinus cavity and then abated with a whoosh. The air between his face and the extractor blurred as if he was looking through gas vapor or heat coming off a blacktop on a hot day.

No.

It couldn't be.

A sense of dread replaced the intense life that had become a part of him.

Empty.

Alone.

Lost.

Sean laughed as he stood. "Yes. Yes, it's mine!"

Dak was gone, ripped from the body he'd called home, and now a prisoner, just like John and Tracy.

But what would Sean do? How would he get Dak inside him?

John's arms jerked again. He bent his leg and tried to push himself up. He didn't know if he could get Dak back, but he could still keep his friend out of Sean.

The psycho held the extractor in front of him. Dak's nearly clear, swirling energy yanked and pulled, as if trying to get away from the cylinder. If Dak got free, would he know how to get back inside John? Or would he have to shoot for another host?

John clenched his jaw. It didn't matter, as long as Dak wasn't forced inside that laughing maniac. Pushing up to his knees, John cursed the handcuffs, the dizziness, blurred vision, and the pain lancing his legs. He straightened as much as he could. "Let him go."

With a ruthless kick of Sean's heel, John fell back. His entire body tingled, engulfed by pins and needles. Somewhere distant to his senses, Tracy sobbed. Numbness overtook him. His limbs failed to respond. Was this what life was like before Dak? So empty? So weak?

Sean eased the cylinder closer to his face. His chin blurred behind the struggling entity. "It's magnificent, isn't it? They're eternal, you know. They can live forever." He took in a deep breath and stood taller. "So much power. So much knowledge. And it's mine. Mine to do with as I please."

Dak's color darkened to a pale, ghostly green. His movements slowed.

"Let him go," John pleaded. "He can't breathe."

Sean's eyes widened as if marveling as the entity solidified before his eyes. "No, he can't. Because I control everything. Its life is in my hands." His gaze flicked to John. "You gave it to me, John. You gave me this power."

Oh, God, no. Sean didn't want Dak inside him. He wanted to watch him die, just like the women he cut to pieces. "Let him go! Don't do it!"

"Let him go!" Tracy echoed.

Dak changed to the color of smoked glass. His essence took shape, shook, and reached for John.

John stretched his cuffed hands toward his friend. "Dak, I'm sorry. I'm so sorry." The shape formed a mouth that opened in a silent scream. "Fight him, Dak! Get away! Run!"

A crevice gouged through John's soul as Dak's shaking ceased. The form solidified to a shiny black-smoked cloud and stopped moving.

"Nooo!"

This couldn't be real. It had to be a dream.

No, a nightmare.

Dak.

Not just an entity. Not just a thing. John's friend.

The only one who ever completely understood him.

The only one to stand beside him no matter what.

With him when John needed him, easing to the background when he wanted to be alone.

Annoying him like a brother.

Loving him like a best friend.

Gone.

Dead.

For nothing more than some maniac's amusement.

The emptiness inside John burst into a scream of agony. His ears drummed, overshadowing the sound of Sean's laughter.

"Did you see that?" Sean cooed. "Did you see it give me its life?" He ran his fingers under the tendril that had reached for John. "I can still feel the power. Eternal life, given to me. To me!"

John gritted his teeth. Tears blurred his vision. "I'm going to gut you, I swear. You killed him. You killed him for nothing!"

Sean turned to John, his eyes wide. Soulless. "Not for nothing, John. I killed him because I could."

He tilted the extractor and Dak's body slipped free. The glass-like form glistened in the lamp light. It spun twice as if floating, then crashed onto the tiles and shattered.

Erased. Riddled to dust.

John slipped to the floor, shaking. The void in his chest widened. There was nothing left. Nothing. Dak had saved his life, shared his dreams, lived his world. How could he be gone?

Sean stepped on the dust, grinding the pebbles into the grout framing the floor tiles. "You will never know the rush of this kind of power, Inspector. I can have anything." He turned to Tracy. "Anything I want."

66

Tracy barely noticed Sean walking toward her. Dak had been alive, spoken to her through John. He was an entity, a person, a friend.

The dust splayed across the tiles as Sean walked through Dak's remains—the final assault on what was left of someone that didn't deserve to die.

A groan sounded through the room. Agent Green's hand moved.

He's alive, dammit!

Tracy blinked at the sudden sound of Adonna's voice. "What?"

A pressure built within Tracy's chest, as if her heart had inflated like a balloon. The entity inside her pressed to the surface, consumed. The fabric of Tracy's will began to unravel. "Adonna, what are you—"

Tracy stretched her neck. She stared at Sean and licked her lips, but she wasn't the one moving her body. A cage formed around her, pushing Tracy deeper into her mind than ever before.

Her eyes settled on Agent Green's twitching fingers. He'd lived. Imbecile. Why couldn't he have stayed dead?

Anger sizzled through every cell in her body. What had Agent Green done to Adonna that she wanted him dead?

Adonna's power scorched and controlled, driving Tracy to the depths of near-nothingness. She banged against the bars inside her own body, lost, unable to fight an alien will so much stronger than her own.

"What did it feel like?" Tracy's voice said. Her body strained against her handcuffs, leaning toward Sean. "Holding an Ambient in your hands as eternal life ended?" She looked at him through damp, matted bangs. "Could you really feel his power ebb to nothing?"

The edge of Sean's lips curled. "You are *not* Tracy."

"Tracy's gone."

I am not, you bitch! Give me my body back!

Sean ran his fingers along the side of her cheek, her breast. "Good. You're the one I liked better, anyway."

Adonna tilted Tracy's head back. "Touch me again, touch me again with those hands that take what they want."

Sean pressed against her chest. Pain ricocheted through the cuts along her ribs. "Did you like watching it die?"

"Oh, yes." Adonna writhed under his touch. Traitorous whore. "Is that what it was like when you killed the humans? Was there blood? Could you see their lives drain from them?"

Her gaze drifted to John. He'd barely moved. His pale face stared back into Tracy's eyes, expressionless, defeated, lost. Tracy couldn't even console him. She couldn't even console herself.

Sean ran his fingers through her wound. Tracy cried out in agony, while Adonna moaned.

He rubbed his crimson-stained digits together. "Do you like the blood?"

Adonna stared at his fingers. "It flows so easily." Her gaze shifted back to John.

Tracy shuddered deep in the recesses of her being. A hole bore within her, a deep sense of foreboding. Her body moved without her permission, her chin rising toward John's vacant form.

"Can you make him bleed for me?"

No! You bitch!

Sean laughed. "You want me to put him out of his misery?"

Adonna shook Tracy's head. "No. I want you to put him *in* misery."

Light flashed in Tracy's eyes before Sean yanked her head toward him. His tongue invaded her mouth. She willed her teeth to close, her jaw to tighten, but Adonna was too strong. She drank in the kiss. Enjoyed it. Savored it like fine chocolate.

Tracy's mouth tingled as the entities collided. That was all Adonna wanted, wasn't it? She wanted the entity inside Sean and nothing else mattered. Not Tracy, not John. Not even Dak.

She mentally pounded against Sean's chest, kicked her legs, but her body no longer did her will.

Relax.

The word rolled over Tracy, echoed in her mind as Sean moved away from them.

Relax. Sure. Easy for that psycho bitch to say when she was puppeteering a stolen body.

Let me go, Tracy demanded.

Not until I get what I want.

Tracy screamed inside. What Adonna wanted was blood. Blood and Sean. Either one ended in death.

The hilt of the knife flashed as Sean stood above John. He glanced back toward Tracy. "If I slit his throat, there will be a lot of blood. He'll die quickly."

Adonna arched Tracy's back. "No. Not fast. I want him to suffer. I want to watch his eyes while he bleeds."

Monster!

John winced, his eyes vacant and staring. He didn't move or acknowledge he could hear them plotting his death.

Tracy wished her eyes closed but Adonna forced her to watch

Sean rip away the Velcro fastening John's bullet-proof vest. The black padding slipped to the carpet with a thud.
John, fight him. Please!
Sean's body hid his actions but not John's cry. Subliminal tears flowed through Tracy, while Adonna sparkled with excitement.
A red circle emerged in the center of John's chest as Sean sauntered back to her. The growing stain encroached on the stark white material with a sickly crimson sheen.
Smirking, Sean held up the knife. A long drip hung on the edge of the blade before tapping against the plastic at her feet. Adonna writhed as if being stroked by a lover.
Sick alien bitch.
"Did you hear him scream?" Sean said, dragging his tongue along the side of her neck. "Did you hear him scream for me?"
The handcuffs jiggled as Adonna shifted Tracy's weight. Her tongue rolled inside his mouth. Tracy cringed.
"Let me do it," Adonna whispered. "Let me cut him. I want to feel what it's like. I want to see blood flow because of me."
No, no, no, no, no!
Sean brought the blade to Tracy's cheek, smearing John's blood across her skin. "And what does Tracy say?"
Adonna smiled. "She's screaming at me. Cursing. Scratching."
You bet your ass I am!
"But she's weak. She doesn't understand. She'll never understand."
I'm going to kill you. I swear it! Don't you touch him!
John moaned a dull, weak sound. Why didn't he struggle? Why didn't he fight for his life?
Maybe because he'd lost part of his soul. Dak was gone. They'd become one, like a marriage. Losing him must have been worse than losing a limb.
Tracy couldn't imagine having someone become a part of her and then have them ripped away. There was no chance of her and Adonna ever forging the type of relationship Dak and John had. If

she could get her hands on that extractor, she'd rip the bitch out herself.

Adonna shivered, her gaze falling on the extractor nestled near the arm of the couch. Could Tracy do such a thing? Could she rip Adonna out? Watch her suffocate?

Adonna tensed her muscles, probably feeling every thought.

Yes, bitch, I want you dead. How does that feel? I suddenly have the strange desire to chain smoke.

Of course, she'd have to take control of her body first.

The plastic crinkled as Sean shoved the knife between Tracy's ankles, slicing her skin as the cable tie dropped onto the bloody tarp. Her arms burned as he jostled the handcuffs over her head. The metal popped and her arms fell. The ache in her shoulders numbed Tracy's mind, but barely slowed Adonna. She reached for Sean, swallowing him in feverous kisses, rubbing her blood-soaked chest against his.

Sean pushed her against the wall, fumbling with the button on her pants.

Adonna growled as the zipper loosened. Tracy's double-crossing body reacted as Adonna's need flooded her.

No. She couldn't. She wouldn't.

"Wait." Adonna grabbed Sean's hands. Her gaze delved through him before drifting to John. "I want the last thing he sees to be you taking this body he loves. I want him to see me give myself to you."

Sean assaulted Tracy's mouth again. She tried to spit, bite, anything, but it was like watching a horror movie from inside her own body. Sean pulled the knife out from behind his back and placed it in Tracy's hands.

Adonna raised the blade before her eyes. "Show me. Show me how to kill him."

No!

Moving behind her, Sean placed his hands on her hips. His erection snugged into the crook of her ass as he molded his body against her. He drew her earlobe through his lips, sucking the tender flesh. The sound echoed through Tracy's helpless mind.

"You are so much more fun than your human." He fondled her breasts from behind.

Adonna trembled, arching Tracy's spine in response. She leaned back. "Tracy has a secret. Her body aches. She wants you. She's always wanted you."

No, I do not!

"Let her go," John's voice sounded a dry garble. He seemed to struggle to raise his head.

Sean shifted the knife in Tracy's hands, angling the blade downward in her fist and tightening her grip. They moved toward John.

"Fight them, Tracy." Struggling in his handcuffs, John pushed backwards, but slipped on the tile. "You're stronger than her. Fight it. Fight them."

I'm trying! Tracy thrashed, kicked, but her body wouldn't respond.

"Stab him in the heart," Sean whispered, nuzzling Tracy's ear. "His body will pump the blood right out of him like a gift to you."

Oh, God, no. Please!

Adonna dropped to Tracy's knees and steadied the blade.

Think about what you are doing. I'll give you anything you want. Anything. I promise. We can leave with Sean. I'll go gladly! Just, please, don't do this!

Adonna grinned at John. "Hooold stiilllllll." She sang the words as if playing a sick game. That's all humanity was to these things: a game. Temporary housing. Something to live in and discard.

Tracy's soul hardened when John grimaced, seeming to fight for breath. "Screw you, bitch."

Her heart crumpled as his words echoed her own thoughts. The last thing he would see was Tracy's face and her hands holding a knife. The hatred in his eyes bored through her. How had something so wonderful gone so wrong?

Adonna raised the blade and clenched Tracy's teeth. Tracy screamed a shattering cry of agony as the blade plunged down with strength she shouldn't have. The knife paused on contact before slicing deep. A popping sensation rebounded through Tracy's mind.

Somewhere in the distance of her senses, Sean laughed. A monomaniacal, continuous banter. "Yes!" he shouted. "Look at him bleed!"

Adonna raised the blade again, staring directly into John's eyes. John reached for her.

No, he reached for Tracy.

She flung her soul toward him, desperately trying to force herself between John and the knife, but the blade continued to fall. Over and over.

Tracy shrieked, a sound overshadowed by Sean's incessant laughter.

"Watch," Sean cooed. "Watch the blood spread. You did that. You did!"

Thankfully, Adonna closed Tracy's eyes. "Is he dead?" she asked.

A snicker sounded near her ear. "Maybe. But his eyes are open. He could still be watching."

Adonna placed the knife beside her as Sean shimmied her pants down. Her hand shook.

He flipped her on her back, drenching Tracy's body in John's blood. Liquid warmth spread beneath her shoulders but quickly cooled. A metallic tang wafted around her: Sean's scent mixing with the life of the man she cared for. Love and merciless hate smothered her like a filthy blanket.

Tracy's soul heaved, but she had no body to retch with.

"How does that feel?" Sean asked, his voice sweet, as if he'd trailed a flower across her skin. "Drinking in the ecstasy, the power of the life freely given to you?"

Freely? You son of a bitch!

Adonna smiled. She shifted beneath Sean, spreading her legs.

No. God, no!

"Take me," she whispered. "This body is his last gift to you."

Sean wiped his hand along his lips, smearing blood across his face before sinking his tongue into Tracy's mouth. Copper flooded her taste buds. Blood. John's blood. Tracy screamed, wishing she could cry as Adonna wrapped her legs around the horror holding her down.

What was left of her soul died, leaving her behind. Broken and lost.

Tracy's arm made a punching motion and Sean reeled up. Adonna unhooked her ankles, letting Tracy's heels fall beside his hips. His eyes widened before his gaze dropped to his stomach. The hilt of the knife stuck out from above his navel. Tracy's hand shot out again and pulled the blade free.

Sean stumbled back and Adonna thrust once more. Had she gone completely insane? Mad for blood?

She twisted the knife through his gut. "Let him go," she grunted.

Backing into the wall, a chuckle gurgled up Sean's throat. He drew his bloody hands away from his stomach, considered them, and laughed.

His gaze returned to Tracy. No, to Adonna. "I knew you and I would get along."

Tracy's body inhaled deeply and sprang toward him with a dizzying speed. The knife slashed across Sean's throat. Blood flooded from the incision, instantly drenching his clothing. He hit the floor before Adonna righted herself. A pool of crimson spread across the Berber carpet as Sean's swollen eyes stared toward the ceiling.

Tracy stumbled and fell to her knees. "Tracy," her voice said. "I can't. I'm too tired."

A whoosh flooded through her. Tracy brought her hand to her forehead and her body responded. She wiggled her fingers in front of her face as the energy coursing through her body receded.

Tracy shifted her shoulders. They reacted. She was in control again. The overwhelming force that had pushed her deep into her own mind lay dormant. Asleep.

"Tracy?"

Pushing back the fog, she spun toward the voice. Her hands instinctively flew in front of her, warding off an attack. But there was none.

The blade of the knife, still clutched in her numb fingers, came into focus. A trickle of blood clung to the hilt before dripping to the carpet.

The haze behind the knife cleared. Agent Green's wide eyes came into focus. He reclined on his shoulder, holding his head.

So, he *was* alive. Too late to help John. Too late to help Dak. Maybe too late to help her.

A spasm in her arm unlocked her fingers and the blade dropped to the floor. For the rest of her life she'd see John's imploring eyes, the horror stretched across his features. She'd sense the knife piercing his heart. She'd feel his blood splatter across her face.

It hadn't been her, but she'd felt it. Every single slash, every unforgiving stab.

She'd killed him. The one guy who listened and understood. The person who accepted her despite her idiosyncrasies. The man who reached into her soul and made everything right.

The man she loved. Dead. Because she wasn't strong enough to stop it.

Tracy staggered to her feet and hobbled toward John's body. She folded into a heap beside him.

Vacant. Hollow. Everything was gone. What was left of her was a shell. Not human. Something less. She hauled John's torso into her naked, bloodstained lap.

She needed to keep him comfortable. Needed to keep him safe.

Leaning against the couch, she gathered him in her arms, refusing to allow her gaze to fall on the horrendous holes she'd cut into his chest.

She'd only known him for a short time, but it was enough for her to know it was right. Maybe even meant to be. But now he was gone. Dead by her own hands.

Agent Green staggered to his feet. His right hand remained riveted to his temple.

He squinted as he limped toward her. "Miss Seavers, are you all right?"

She blinked. Was she all right? Odd question. She was sitting on the floor in the living room of a serial-killer, naked and drenched in her boyfriend's blood. She may never be all right again.

The federal agent lifted the silver cylinder from the corner of the couch. His gaze carried over Sean's footprint embedded in the dark dust covering the floor. The quake in his eyes told her he knew that an alien had lost his life. "Who?" he asked.

Tracy shivered. "Dak." One body. Two deaths. If Dak had still been within John, would the entity have been able to save him? Would they have been strong enough together to stop Adonna?

A sticky ooze slid within Tracy's chest, creeping about her body, using her like a parasite. An abomination. A sick, deceitful creature that didn't deserve the air Tracy's lungs filtered so it could live.

Her gaze drifted to the extractor and then to Agent Green. "Take it out of me. This thing inside me killed John."

Green stumbled and eased to the floor beside her. His head lolled against the couch. "I don't think I could hold the chamber up long enough."

Sirens sounded in the distance. The agent laughed and shot his hands to his head again. "Glad they could make it. I think I'll include in my report that this freaking county needs more police. No wonder so many people died before we caught this asshole."

We? Tracy tightened her grip on John's body. Not that Green's comment mattered. Sean was dead, but at way too high a cost.

Brakes screeched in the streets. Shouts sounded through the closed windows. Could one of them help her, rid her of this invader—this unwanted guest? They'd have to. Tracy couldn't live with a murderer inside her. She wouldn't.

John's body jerked. Death pangs. She held him tighter. Her stomach turned. None of this was fair. None of it.

John's body quaked as if startled. Tracy screamed, releasing her grip.

Green knelt beside her. "What happened?"

"He moved."

John's eyes bolted open as wraithlike, white, lifeless orbs. His mouth splayed, his jaw stretching his lips into an unnatural, wide O. An inhuman, latex-like squeal riddled the room, as if someone slowly released the air from a balloon. But John's lungs expanded, rather than contracting. The ghostly intake pierced Tracy's ears, lashing and gouging—berating a soul no longer capable of absorbing any more horror.

The door kicked in. Legs in dark trousers moved about the room. Voices shouted indiscernible words.

Tracy trembled as John's eyes rolled, the whites replacing themselves with dilated, lifeless pupils. His mouth closed slowly. He stared into a void of nothing. Would his torment ever end?

Green held out his arms, shielding John's body from the cacophony of intruders.

Someone covered Tracy's naked shoulders with some sort of light cloth.

A man crouched beside Green, rubbing a stubbled cheek. "Jesus Christ. It's Peters."

Green glanced over his shoulder. "I need a code-seven medical team now!" He turned back to John. "This one just picked up an Ambient."

Tracy gasped, the quick intake burning her lungs. "What are you saying?"

"The scream and the white eyes… That's what happens when they latch on. He's got another entity in him." He lifted John's tattered, blood-soaked shirt and grimaced. "Let's hope it's a damn strong one."

67

THREE WEEKS LATER

Light seared through John's eyelids, but the peaceful sensation of floating lulled him into keeping his lashes closed. An incessant beep berated his ears, but it wasn't his alarm clock. What the hell was that?

He lifted his lids. White walls. Television hanging in the corner. Cheesy striped curtain on his right.

Dammit. A hospital.

Did he get shot or something?

He reached inside himself, seeking the warmth he'd grown to depend on more than the air he breathed, but his search came up empty.

Dak?

The rest of the room came into focus. Tracy sat beside him, reading a book.

Her gaze darted to him, her novel slipping to the floor. "John!"

She threw her arms around his shoulders. He tried to return her affection, but his limbs wouldn't move. Leather bands buckled his arms and legs to the side rails. What the hell?

Tracy covered his cheeks with tear-filled kisses. Whatever put him in that hospital bed must have been pretty bad.

"You're okay," Tracy said, wiping her own tears from his cheeks. "You're really okay."

John shifted his weight. A dull ache gnashed through his back. "I guess." He smiled, his gaze drifting over her eyes, her lips, and the tiny indent in her brow that appeared whenever she was worried. "Do you have any idea how beautiful you are?" His heart trembled within his chest. For a moment he thought it was Dak, but the quake wasn't followed by one of his friend's snarky comments. Where was he?

Agent Green pushed the curtain aside. A red patch tainted the white in his right eye, and the faded yellow edge of a bruise marred the same side of his head and face. "Well hello there, partner. How are you feeling?"

John shrugged. "Like I was hit by a truck." John mustered half a smile. "Was I?"

Green didn't return the grin. "Can you tell me your name?"

John blinked, glancing at the bindings around his arms. What was going on? "Peters. Detective John Peters. You wanna tell me why I'm tied up, kid?"

The agent stared at him for a moment. His nose twitched and he swallowed, looking away. He nodded to Tracy, tapping her shoulder as he left. Why were they acting so weird?

"Thanks, Alex," Tracy said.

When did they end up on a first-name basis? John raised an eyebrow. "Alex?"

"He's been sitting beside me for almost three weeks. Did you expect me to keep calling him Agent Green?" Tracy settled on the edge of the bed. "Art Commings was here, too. He felt guilty for not being there to help when…you know."

A small spot in his chest twisted. "No, I don't know."

The last time he'd seen Art, his father was in the hospital. John and Agent Green were working on the murder investigation. That had been three weeks ago?

Tracy's eyes darted to the floor. "How much do you remember?"

He yanked against the bindings. Why hadn't Green removed the ties when John told him his name? "I guess I'm not remembering a lot." He leaned back his head. *Dak, help me out, buddy. What's going on?*

Something tickled inside him, reaching out with a soothing motion. The sensation warmed him slightly, a sensation both familiar, yet completely foreign.

John's jaw clenched. "Something's wrong with Dak." His chest fluttered. "Jesus, something's wrong with Dak!" The bed creaked as he pulled against the bars. "Someone, get us some help!"

Tears streaked down Tracy's cheeks, dripping from her chin as she stood.

What was wrong? What had happened?

"I'm so sorry, John. I can't even imagine…" She turned away, hugging her shoulders as she looked out the window.

A vision of her tied up, hanging from a wall flashed through his mind. The agony of his own arms wrenched over his head echoed through his shoulders. The pain, the…

Sean. It had been Sean all along.

The night flooded back to him. The fighting, the screams, the blood—the anguish of having his best friend yanked from his body.

John stiffened.

Sean had taken him—dragged Dak out, ripped him from the protection of John's body and the security of John's lungs.

A cloudy vision of Dak's body shattering on the tiles replayed in his mind. A succession of horror and helplessness as he reached out to catch his falling friend. Each echo cut a hole deeper into John's heart, as if he were being stabbed repeatedly with a butcher's knife.

The muscles in John's arms tightened. His jaw clamped shut.

Like being stabbed repeatedly with a butcher's knife.

His gaze fell on Tracy as she turned from the window. Her eyes. So beautiful, yet they had been hollow. Horrid. Ugly.

"You stabbed me."

She shook her head, easing into the chair beside him. "No. It wasn't me."

John knew it wasn't, but it was still her body, her face he stared into while Adonna plunged the knife through his chest. He clenched his fists. "Did they pull that bitch out of you?"

Tracy's hands dropped to her lap as she lowered her eyes. She wiped her nose before returning her gaze to John. "No. They didn't."

"What?"

"She's not considered a threat."

John sat up as much as the bindings allowed. "Not a threat? The bitch nearly stabbed me to death."

"She wasn't trying to kill you."

"Yeah, well, the blade told me otherwise." He shifted toward the curtain. "Green! Green, get your ass in here. Tracy needs an extraction. Now."

She touched his shoulder. "I'm fine, John."

"Like shit you're fine. She pushed you out. She gave herself to Sean and they stabbed me." John closed his eyes and gritted his teeth. Sean's cackle echoed through his mind. "God, that laugh, I don't think I'll ever forget it."

He bit the inside of his cheek, but it did little to control the shiver that ran through his veins. Fresh tears dampened Tracy's cheeks.

"Shit, Tracy, what happened? How'd you get out of there?"

John's stomach fluttered and fizzed. He'd first felt that strange sensation about five years ago, when he woke up from being shot —tied to a hospital bed—with federal agents asking if he knew his name. The warmth trickled from his face. "Adonna did kill me, didn't she?" Each nod of Tracy's head throttled him like a sledgehammer. "There's another one inside me."

She continued to nod. "His name is Jace."

John's muscles began to shake. His legs rattled the bars around the bed. "You know its name? How the hell do you know its name?"

Tracy rubbed her hands across her face. "Adonna killed Sean."

What? John flopped back onto the pillows. "I don't understand."

"Adonna seduced Sean to get contact, so she and Jace could come up with a plan. She was originally going to kill Sean so Jace could jump into Agent Green."

John glanced at the curtain. "But Green is still alive."

Tracy nodded. "That's why Adonna had to improvise."

"By killing me?"

Her lips thinned as she nodded. "Dak was already gone. She made a flash decision. I'm not saying it was a good one—"

"She killed me!"

"Because she was going to kill Sean. She needed somewhere for Jace to go. She thought it would make us happy."

"Happy? Are you out of your mind?"

Tracy rubbed her face. "I've had a few weeks for all this to sink in. I was pretty upset at first, too, but—"

"Upset *at first*? She killed me. You should have had that bitch extracted the first chance you got."

"She never wanted you dead, John."

John threw his weight against the bindings. The entire bed shifted toward Tracy. "How can you say that? I watched her plunge the knife into my chest over and over. And, dammit, I had to look into your eyes the entire time." And, God, the coldness in that expression, the absence of emotion inside eyes he'd gazed into for warmth, for refuge. "I watched you kill me, Tracy. Not that psycho alien bitch—*you*." He closed his eyes, trying to ward off the memory. "I had to watch the woman I love cut my freaking heart out."

She stuttered over a sob. "It wasn't me."

"No. It wasn't. That's why she has to go."

Tracy reached for him, but he drew back.

Those hands had been covered in blood. His blood. She needed to understand that they could never be together until that thing inside her was gone.

She lowered her hand, steadying herself. "Adonna feels my emotions. She knew I loved you. This was a way for all of us to be together."

"What are you talking about?"

"Jace is her mate. That's why she was so drawn to Sean." She leaned toward him, folding her hands. "They lost each other years ago when their hosts were killed in a car crash. They've been jumping closer and closer ever since, hoping to find each other again. She wasn't strong enough to explain before."

"I guess she's talking now."

Tracy nodded. "She's explained everything. I don't agree with what she did, but I understand."

John clenched his fists. "You understand. Well, that's just ripe."

Tracy straightened, but not with any real conviction. "Adonna asks that you give Jace a chance. She thinks you'll learn to love him as much as she does."

John closed his eyes. Nothing flowed through him. No strange voice echoed through his mind. No one reached to him from within his being. No one consoled him, or kicked him for being stubborn. He was alone.

But maybe not for long. One day this Ambient, Jace, would be strong enough to talk. And then what? Take Dak's place?

His hands shook on the rails beside his mattress. "I don't want this. I can't. I can't have another one inside me." He swallowed hard. "Green! Green, get in here."

The kid leaned around the curtain in less than a second. Had he been on the other side, waiting?

"Take it out of me," John said. "I'm not going to ruin Dak's memory by being a convenient host for another one."

Green's gaze hit the floor. "That's not really a valid reason for an extraction."

John's hands shook. "This thing was helping Sean. The psycho admitted it."

"He was being tortured," Tracy said. "He never hurt anyone. He just made Sean stronger."

"Stop it!" John lurched toward her. The bedrails rattled. "You may be happy harboring a murderer but I'm not. This thing could have stopped Sean. He could have saved Dak but he didn't."

"He couldn't." Tears welled in Tracy's lashes. "Sean was too strong. Like you told me, Dak couldn't control you when you were angry. Sean was always angry."

John pushed back against the pillow. His gaze focused on the yellow stains in the ceiling tiles. "Take it out of me, Green. You know there's just cause."

The kid reached around the curtain and returned with a silver cylinder.

Tracy stood. "No. You can't kill Jace. He didn't do anything."

"I didn't do anything to deserve this, either," John whispered.

Green held up his hand. "I can extract the entity and then let it go. There's a real hospital ten minutes away. It shouldn't have a hard time finding another host."

"But we don't want another host," Tracy said. "And John's not completely healed. He could die."

"Then let me die." John's own words sent a shudder down his spine because he meant it. He couldn't live like this. Empty. Alone.

Dak would have been here for him, talked him through this. Guided him. How could he even force himself awake each morning without him?

433

"Tracy has a point." Green lowered the cylinder. "You might still need the entity to survive."

"I don't care. Do it."

It wasn't fair. They'd allowed another entity in without his permission. They didn't have the right, but John did. He didn't have to live with their decision.

Green turned the lower dial and the light on the tip of the extractor began to glow. He'd keep his eyes open. Make it easy. Hopefully this Jace person wouldn't put up a fight.

Jace *person*... He didn't have a body, so it wasn't a person. Just some sort of parasite. A liquidy gas that couldn't even live without a real person's help.

Tracy's voice begging him to stop faded into a haze as the light turned orange. It didn't matter. This thing wasn't human. It shouldn't even be on this planet. John's chest began to tingle.

Was Dak a parasite?

No. Of course not. He loved old movies and broccoli. He had an odd sense of humor. And boy did he love to touch. More than all that, he loved John. Dak would have done anything to make John happy. Even give up the chance at his own happiness when John had fallen for Tracy.

His lungs began to burn. The alien inside him convulsed as the light seared through John's pupils. The horror of Dak's extraction flared through him. Had Dak been in as much pain as John was? Did he know he was going to die? Was he afraid?

Was this new alien afraid? Did he feel guilty about what he'd done, or was he really under Sean's control? Was he decent—nice like Dak, but lost, crushed under the thumb of a psychopath?

A rolling ooze moved through John's chest. He missed Dak, but did that give him the right to discount another life? What would this do to his relationship with Tracy? Would Adonna ever forgive him? Not that John cared, but Tracy did. She had to live with the entity inside her twenty-four seven.

This Jace could never replace Dak, but who says he couldn't

find a place in John's life? And how great would that be to have Tracy *and* a bond between the entities inside them? A haze appeared in front of John's face. The alien hadn't put up a fight. The last tendril holding to John's lungs released.

"Wait." John held up a hand. "Stop. Turn it off."

Green furrowed his brow and clicked the lower dial. The essence slammed back through John's eyes with dizzying intensity. A stabbing jolt seared his left then right lung as the alien latched on.

Tracy held her hands to her temples. Her eyes shone with tears.

John stared at them. Adonna hadn't taken control. She could have pushed Tracy down deep into her psyche and yanked that extractor out of Green's hands like snatching a lollypop from a toddler. The Ambient had stood there and watched as her mate was pulled from the man she purposely put him into. Interesting.

Green lowered the extractor and folded his arms.

John clutched the cool bedrails.

Silence lingered as if someone had paused time.

Is that what he'd done, paused time, postponed the inevitable?

Blood coursed through John's temples. Why didn't he let Green finish? Why did he let the Ambient slip back into his body?

Dak.

Five years ago, waking up and finding out about Dak had terrified him. Left him in a world of uncertainty. But uncertainty had grown to something stronger than John could ever have anticipated. The relationship he'd forged with his entity had been the best thing to ever happen to him.

Dak shouldn't have died. But there was nothing John could do to change that. Dak had given John an incredible gift: a second chance.

He would have wanted John to do the same for someone else.

"M-maybe we should leave it inside for a bit. Let's make sure I'm completely healed, first."

Tracy sprang to life, falling on John and crying into his shoulder. Her warmth spread through him, filling the voids left by the untimely death of his best friend.

Life continued.

No one said moving on without Dak would be easy, but his friend's life was worth living for, if only so someone could remember who Dak was, and what they meant to each other.

68

TWO WEEKS LATER

Tracy stared at John's front door. If he were anyone else, she would have walked away by now. But she couldn't. She wouldn't.

The police psychiatrist warned her that John would have good, as well as bad, days. His mood swings had been wild, maybe due to the stress of losing Dak, or his body assimilating to a new entity. She'd stand by him, though, no matter what.

Even if he didn't want her anymore, she still owed him her life. None of this would have happened if John hadn't tried to save her.

The door opened as she approached. Alex stepped out. The bruise on the side of his head had finally faded, leaving only the red stain in his eye as a constant reminder that they all nearly died on the whim of a killer.

"How's he doing?" she asked.

The agent shrugged. "Hard to tell. He's talking more today. That's a step in the right direction."

She gave him a kiss on the cheek as she slid through the door. John waited for her in the foyer, his arms folded.

"Did you know I was here?"

John didn't look up from the floor. "I felt a little tug in my chest. Figured you were close by."

Tracy hung her jacket on a hook beside the door. "So Jace is moving around more?"

"Only when you visit."

"It's been over a month. He should be talking by now."

John looked up. "I seem to remember telling you the same thing." He dragged his fingers through his hair. Tracy followed as he walked toward the kitchen. "I'm not used to being alone. It's starting to drive me insane." He leaned against the countertop. "I appreciate you guys coming to stay with me all the time, but it's not the same as having someone always babbling in my head."

Tracy ran her fingers along the side of his face. His cheeks had sunken in. If only he'd eat more. "You're not even getting emotions from him? Nothing at all?"

He shook his head. "It's my fault. I'm trying hard to accept having another entity, but he knows deep down that I resent him for what happened to Dak. I can't help it." He tapped twice on a pile of unopened mail. "If he'd talk to me, we might be able to get somewhere."

Let me try.

"Adonna is offering to see if he'll talk to her." Tracy reached out her hand. "Do you mind?"

John offered his palm and she grasped it.

A slight itchy sensation tingled her skin before Adonna skidded through their touch and into John. With a sudden pop, the entity ebbed back almost before she'd entered. Adonna trembled.

"What's wrong?" Tracy asked.

The entity didn't answer with words. Instead, a flood of negative sensations oozed and quaked within Tracy.

She raised her eyes. "Guilt. He's feeling incredible guilt. He knows how much you cared for Dak and he doesn't think he can live up to that. He doesn't feel like he has the right to even try."

John closed his eyes and rubbed his forehead. He turned away. "Jace, I'm not asking you to be Dak, but I am your host. I'd at least like to know if you're okay once in a while." He held his hand steady before slapping his palm on the veneer. "Nothing. It's like he's not even in there." John shoved himself away from the counter. "How am I supposed to get to know him when we can't communicate?"

"I have an idea." Tracy tugged him to the couch and sat him down. "Let's see if we can coax a reaction out of him." She unbuttoned her blouse and let it slip to the floor. She shifted her weight, giving him a good view of the deep green Victoria's Secret special.

John smiled. "I don't know what it's doing for him but it's definitely working for me." His gaze lifted from her chest to her eyes. "I told you, though, I'm not ready. My mind wouldn't be with you, and you deserve better." He ran his fingers along the pink line under Tracy's breast, a souvenir of Sean's handiwork. "And I'm so damn afraid of hurting you."

Within a week, her wounds had healed a year's worth, and he knew it. Entities didn't take chances with their hosts. But the sentiment probably ran deeper. She ran her fingers up his chest to his collar and unbuttoned his shirt.

He stopped her near his navel. "I told you I'm not ready."

Tracy continued unfastening until his shirt lay at his hips. "Relax, Detective. This isn't about you." Well, not completely anyway.

She yearned for his touch as much as ever, but right now, her priority was Jace. At the moment, she needed Jace just as much as Adonna did. Jace was the key to bringing John back to her. She needed to convince this new entity to communicate.

She ran her hands up John's sides and across the flawless skin over his heart. If anything, Jace had proven his healing strength. John barely had a blemish on him, not even the original bullet holes. She moved her hands over John's well-muscled shoulders. "Anything?"

John shrugged.

Can we hold each other?

My thoughts exactly.

Tracy inched closer to John and smoothed her hands along his back. Her brassiere crushed between them, the stiff lace teasing her hardened peaks. John trembled. His eyes darkened. His reaction or Jace's? Not that it really mattered. Adonna laying just below the surface of Tracy's skin, ready to pop, reminded her that if one of them got turned on, the other would follow.

John kissed the edge of Tracy's cheek, placing short, sweet pecks along her jawline before claiming her lips. Adonna rolled, shaking, waiting. A small electrical shock danced across their skin.

John snickered. "You're driving her crazy, Jace. She's right there. You know you want her."

Adonna rolled and jolted, skating across Tracy's skin.

"I feel him," John's eyes widened. "Oh, shit."

His entire body quaked, his skin heating beneath hers.

Adonna went rigid within Tracy, her very essence tingling with anticipation. John tightened his grip, flattening their bodies together. The jolt flashed from John's skin, sizzling into Tracy, burning and twisting until it found what lay in wait for him.

Tracy threw her head back and moaned as Jace's essence soaked through Adonna. So tender, so caring, so gentle. A sense of calm overcame her entire being before pressure began to build.

John pulled Tracy to him and kissed her, his own lips trembling as the entities spun, flashed and devoured each other. Such heat, such need, Tracy fought not to explode. Tears streamed down her face as John continued to claim her lips, their tongues mimicking the frolicking of their entities as they immersed themselves in each other. Taking, but also giving with no regard to the outcome, other than making themselves one.

A small whimper escaped Tracy's lips, the tension within her too much to bear. John released their kiss as he cried out.

An explosion of energy rocketed between them and she echoed John's cry as her body ignited, as if succumbing to liquid flames.

The onslaught subsided and Jace's energy slowly seeped back toward his host. John leaned Tracy down to the couch and collapsed atop her, gasping for air.

"Holy shit," John whispered. He looked up. "Are you okay?"

Tracy nodded, wiping growing tears from her eyes.

Damn. She hadn't even gotten his jeans off.

She forced a smile through her panting lips. "I think it's safe to say Jace is in good form."

John's laugh cut off as his eyes sprang open. He looked to the side and sat up.

Had Jace finally spoken?

John held his head, massaging his temples. An eternity seemed to pass.

"I understand," he finally whispered. "No, I don't expect you to be Dak." His moist eyes darted to the window. "I believe you. You're right. Maybe this was better." He laughed, holding his head.

What do you think they're saying?

I don't care. As long as everything is okay.

John turned to Tracy. "Yes, I *am* in love with her. I think I have been since the day we met."

Tracy's stomach flipped and centered itself.

Love.

She'd felt it from him, but was never sure it wasn't her imagination. And here he was, expressing his heart to the one person he couldn't lie to: the entity who could read his thoughts.

We're going to be together!

Shush.

John smiled and lowered his gaze. "I will."

He seemed to be collecting his thoughts. Either that, or counting the pile in the carpet. Tracy left him to his task. Even though they'd coaxed the entity out, Jace talking after so long had to stir up a lot of memories. How John dealt with those ghosts would define their future together.

With a nod of the head, he looked up. "We're going to be okay." He turned to Tracy. "Yeah. Definitely okay."

Tracy didn't bother wiping her tears away. She climbed into his lap and buried her head in his neck. "I love you so much."

She bobbled against his chest as he laughed.

"Careful," he said. "I seem to remember these things being horny twenty-four seven. You don't want to start the engine going again."

Tracy inched up for a deep kiss. This time, meant for John and only John.

Their entities left their hosts to themselves, leaving their humans to seek and find each other again. Their rediscovery broke time itself, leaving them in a glorious void of learning and relearning. Tracy trembled with each stroke of John's hands, each touch of his lips.

Yes, they were going to be okay.

All four of them.

PLEASE REVIEW

A note from the author: If you enjoyed INVADED I'd love it if you took a few moments to leave a short review of the book on your favorite book retailer's website. Reviews are like fine-spun gold to authors, and your opinions could help others make decisions on which books to consider reading for themselves.

    Not only that. It would make me REALLY REALLY happy.
    (And no one wants an unhappy author.)

Things can't get any worse than being snatched by a dragon, until Anna is dropped into a bloodthirsty battle for the Draconic crown.

Turn a few pages to enjoy the first two chapters of Jennifer M. Eaton's #1 Best Seller DRAGON MOUNT

ACKNOWLEDGMENTS

Invaded was a lesson in perseverance for me. I started this book on March 27, 2014 and finished the first draft on June 6, 2014. It was 56,000 words (about half its final length). Soon after this, something magical happened... I signed a three-book deal for FIRE IN THE WOODS. Wonderful news for me, but not good news for INVADED. My life turned into a whirlwind that day, and writing became a job rather than an outlet. The manuscript sat, forgotten, as I wrote five new novels.

In 2016, scrolling through my manuscript file, I came across a mystery file called "INVADED". To be honest, I barely even remember writing it. The manuscript was a shell of what it is today, filled with problems and plot holes, but I rediscovered the spark that had driven me to write a novel at twice my normal speed. The concept resonated with me, and I found myself falling back into the world again.

The challenge of writing a thriller and a romance with six personalities living in three bodies was a huge undertaking. I received a lot of professional feedback on this novel and revisions went on for an additional two years before I started submitting to publishers (Thus, getting even more feedback).

Invaded is still, and will probably remain, the "odd duck" in my catalog. I know it is a strange blend of genres. There aren't too many urban science fiction paranormal serial killer murder mystery romances out there. Still, I send it out to the world hoping readers will enjoy it. As grueling as this experience was, over time it became a labor of love, and words on a page mean nothing until they are read.

As far as acknowledgements go, I always like to start by thanking my husband, who puts up with my crazy need to write. Also my kids, who've grown up with the insanity of having an author in the house.

Special thanks to the following people who gave personal and professional advice on this novel over the years: Anna Simpson, Claire Gillian, JK Ford, Julie Reece, Sheryl Winters, Melissa Crispin, Kelly Said, Sharon Hughson, Jocelyn Adams, Terri Rochenski, Entangled Publishing, and The Wild Rose Press. Thank you so much for your little nuggets of wisdom along the way.

Finally, thanks to my official editing team who helped slap this manuscript into shape for publication: my developmental editor, Latoya Smith; and my proofreaders, who were the last sets of eyes on this twisted tome: Chelsea Clemmons Moye, and Tandy Boese of Tandy Proofreads. Without them, my i's would have no dots, and my t's would never be crossed. (There would also probably be 50,000 more commas.)

And, of course, special thanks to *you* for reading. I know this book was *out there*, but I sure hope you enjoyed it. And if you start hearing little voices in your head, or craving odd food, beware the FBI agents in black suits.

Alien Kisses!
—Jennifer

ABOUT THE AUTHOR

Jennifer M. Eaton hails from the eastern shore of the North American Continent on planet Earth. Yes, regrettably, she is human, but please don't hold that against her.

While not traipsing through the galaxy looking for specimens for her space moth collection, she lives with her wonderfully supportive husband, three energetic offspring, and a duo of poodles who run the spaceport when she's not around.

During infrequent excursions to her home planet of Earth, Jennifer enjoys long hikes in the woods, bicycling, swimming, snorkeling, and snuggling up by the fire with a great book; but great adventures are always a short shuttle ride away.

Read more from Jennifer M. Eaton
www.jennifereaton.com

PREVIEW OF DRAGON MOUNT

DRAGON MOUNT

USA TODAY BEST SELLING AUTHOR
JENNIFER M. EATON

Chapter 1

Anna didn't need a man. What she needed was a dragon—a big, hulking, nasty dragon fully capable of biting the head off of any jerk who even thought of hurting her. As she breathed in the essence of moonflowers drifting on the breeze, she knew this would be the place to find what she was looking for.

Well, she might not exactly find a dragon in New Zealand, but maybe enough magic to help her forget and start over.

A woman on the street corner spun a rack of postcards

displaying pictures of the country's pristine landscape. Anna's stomach soured as she tucked back the dark hair that blew into her eyes. She and Andrew had dreamed of sitting in a little café, filling out postcards just like those, writing *Wish you were here, suckers!* over and over again. A hint of a smile touched her lips, before it fell away.

When they first started planning this vacation it was a pipe dream—the mutual *coup de gras* of their bucket lists. It was supposed to be their honeymoon.

Until a honeymoon was no longer needed.

"Stop thinking about him." Her sister didn't even look up from her fistful of pamphlets. "I can smell you brooding from here."

The sun slipped toward the peaks in the distance, ending a day filled with terminals, planes, and busses. Anna shielded her eyes as the sky exploded with an orange and pink glow.

"It says here that those mountains you're staring at are called *Aoraki*." Sybil pointed to the text. "The original settlers believed that the sons of the sky god got their canoe stuck on a reef. They froze to death and became the mountains." She smiled. "That's kind of creepy. Right up your alley."

Anna took a step toward the postcard vendor and stopped herself. Postcards were meaningless, but fun. They'd always been a favorite part of every vacation. But maybe not anymore.

She closed her eyes. How many things would she have to give up because they reminded her of *him*?

"Right now these Maori people are celebrating some sort of ancient fertility festival called the Seventeen Year." Sybil snorted. "Fertility, huh? Sounds like my kind of party."

Of course it was. Anything her sister could relate to sex was a good time. How could she be so flippant about things like that when guys…

Sybil lowered the pamphlets. "Stop. Thinking. About. Him."

Anna sighed. How could she stop? She was standing on a street in New Zealand, where they'd dreamed of going since forever.

A fistful of brochures slapped Anna's cheek. She stood stunned, gaping.

"You are going to enjoy this vacation if it kills me." Sybil pointed the pamphlets at her like a sword.

Leave it to her sister to drag them both back to elementary school tactics.

A laugh popped out of Anna's mouth as she splayed her hands. "I'm sorry. This is just harder than I thought it would be." That was the hugest of understatements. "But I'm okay." She nodded to herself. "I need this."

More like she needed *to do* this. New Zealand wasn't only her and Andrew's dream. It was her dream. That didn't change because he was out of the picture.

"What you need is a nice, stiff drink."

Anna smiled. It probably couldn't hurt. "I think I need some time for all this to soak in."

"Then let's call this a good start." Sybil raised her hand into the air. "Taxi!"

"Wait. Where are we going?"

Her sister glanced back at her. "Like I said, to get a drink."

"Is there something wrong with the hotel bar?"

Sybil waved at one of the approaching yellow cars. "Yes, it's packed with tourists. I want to meet some New Zealanders."

Her sister, the quintessential party girl. "We haven't even unpacked and you already want to go bar hopping?"

"Oh, come on." Sybil was inside the cab before Anna could argue. "Believe me, once this vacation is over, you'll be a new person."

Was there something wrong with her old person? Anna didn't think so.

Well, not her *old*-old person. Growing up, she'd been ready for anything. She and Andrew were going to take on the world together.

Until she caught him in bed with someone else.

PREVIEW OF DRAGON MOUNT

Mom had always called Anna a miniature explosion, ready to take on the world. The firecracker inside Anna had extinguished that night, and she hadn't found a way to rekindle the spark.

She closed her eyes and swallowed the painful ball building in her throat. She was here to forget—to erase the bad and come home as a clean slate, ready to start over. This started by proving to herself that life no longer revolved around one guy.

In the distance, a large black bird soared toward the mountains. It circled as if it flew for the pure pleasure of feeling the wind in its feathers. That's what she needed, the confidence to spread her wings and glide toward the horizon.

Sybil glared at her. "Don't make me drag you into this car."

Anna sucked in a deep breath before she slipped onto the worn, black seat beside her sister. "One drink. Promise."

Her sister made a spectacle of rolling her eyes.

"Where to?" The driver's accent made it sound like *Wayer-tou*.

Sybil leaned up and handed a brochure to him. She pointed to a handwritten note on the top of the page. "Do you know where this is?"

He snorted. "Kinda off the beaten path for a couple of Sheilas."

Sybil flopped back in her seat. "Sounds perfect."

Off the beaten path? Was she out of her mind?

Anna leaned closer as the cab pulled from the sidewalk. "This is crazy. We are in a foreign country with—"

"Not a care in the world." She tapped Anna's knee. "Relax. Trust me. We're going to see where real New Zealanders hang out."

Great. Just great.

Anna stared out the window as they left civilization behind. The approaching dusk cast a deepening haze over the hillside as clean, undisturbed green stretched out as far as the eye could see. The tension eased from Anna's shoulders as she lost herself in undefiled nature.

She hated to admit it, but those rolling fields reached inside and mended part of the hole torn in her heart. She couldn't imagine living somewhere with so much incredibly beautiful *nothing*.

"I have a surprise for you." Sybil nudged her shoulder. "We're not taking the movie site tour tomorrow."

Anna spun toward her. "We're not?"

"Nope. I changed our date to Monday."

"Why?"

"Because tomorrow morning, you and your favorite sister are taking the plunge off Kawarau Bridge."

Anna nearly choked. "What?"

"Yup. It's all set up. They're picking us up at our hotel at 8:30."

"Are you out of your mind? I am not bungee jumping!"

"Yes, you are. It's already bought and paid for. No refunds, no excuses."

No excuses? Anna had a great big gaping excuse. Even back home in the US she erred on the cautious side. She really didn't have a choice.

Eight years ago, she woke up after a car accident and found out she had a rare blood type. The hospital had to have plasma flown in from another state, and the delay almost killed her. Ever since, she'd been warned to take it easy and cautioned against foreign travel, but here she was, vacationing in New Zealand with a nutty sister who wanted them to plummet to their deaths tied to the ends of rubber bands.

"There is no way I'm jumping off a bridge."

Sybil snickered as the cab pulled to a stop. "We'll see."

Her sister paid the cabbie as Anna stepped onto worn, colorful cobblestones. The black sconces encircling the weathered rock buildings and the matching streetlamps flared to life simultaneously. Anna jumped as one of them blew out.

"Surprise!" Sybil said.

Anna looked up and down the deserted street. "Surprise what?"

"Don't you recognize it? This is the street they modeled Bree after."

Anna looked again. "It is?"

"Yup. I found it on Wikipedia under little-known *Lord of the Rings* sites." She narrowed her eyes. "One of these places is supposed to look just like the Prancing Pony inside."

Anna took in the gnarled, wooden signs. She could barely read the names on some of them. At the far end of the road, four men in long coats entered a bar with a carved rooster hanging above the door. It seemed warm for coats that long. Must be a Kiwi thing.

Sybil grabbed Anna's wrist and tugged her along the bumpy, colorful walkway toward a worn, timber door with wide, black hinges. "This place looks as good as any to start."

Anna pulled out of her grip. "To start? I agreed to one drink."

Sybil held her chest, feigning hurt. "Of course we'll only have one drink." She pulled Anna through the door. "Per bar."

Anna sighed. With Sybil, there was always a loophole.

Inside, the tavern looked nothing like the Prancing Pony. It looked more like the bar in that old show *Cheers* that her father watched on Netflix. A circular bar dominated the center of the room. Its white-tiled surface clashed with the dark paneling. Flickering candles on cherrywood tables nestled against the wall cast a yellowish glow throughout the room. Inside the serving-circle, a dark-skinned man placed a glass into a huge wooden fixture hanging precariously over the bar.

"Welcome, ladies. Please, have a seat." He gestured across the nearly empty bar and the mostly open tables. So much for meeting the locals.

Anna had to admit the tavern had its charm, though. The hotel bar had all the appeal of a meat market, while this place oozed culture.

An old man wearing a multi-colored, patchwork shirt sat alone at the table closest to the door. His tunic matched the vibrant weavings hanging from the walls like he was a part of the decor.

Combine him with the dead animal heads mounted above the entrance, and Anna felt as if she'd stepped back in time. If she could convince them to trash the plasma television screen, this place would be the perfect retreat.

She and Sybil settled on stools at the bar and ordered drinks. From the opposite side of the serving circle, a very light-skinned platinum-blond guy flashed a smile. His eyes mirrored the overhead lighting, making everything about him seem paler, as if he were dusted in white powder. Anna quickly looked away. She settled her eyes on the Malibu Bay Breeze the barkeep handed her, forcing her gaze to remain there so she didn't stare.

"Is it always so quiet here?" Sybil asked the bartender.

"You missed the happy hour crowd. People have been staying in after dusk the past few days."

Sybil frowned. "I guess we'll have to come back earlier tomorrow."

Or not.

Sybil had to notice that this *wasn't* the Prancing Pony. Absorbing culture was fine and all, but Anna had her first taste of New Zealand on the car ride over here. She wanted to see more, not spend her time drinking.

The bartender walked to the other side of the counter and spoke to the blond guy. After a moment, they both turned toward Anna. She nearly choked on her drink before she looked away.

Her cheeks heated. The blond must have mentioned that she'd been staring at him. With skin that pale, he must have people stare at him all the time, and here she was, the gawking American, jumping on the bandwagon.

Anna concentrated on the ice cubes in her glass, trying to not look like she was aware the two men were still chatting.

About her? No, of course not.

But what if they were?

If she and Sybil had stayed at the hotel bar, like she'd wanted, she could've just caught the next elevator to her room and hid from all this awkwardness.

She leaned toward her sister. "This obviously isn't the right place. Maybe we should go."

"Come on, Sis. There's more to sightseeing than movie locations. There's a lot about the local culture I'd like to sample, too." She spun her stool toward a table of three guys near the wall and sipped her drink through the thin, red stirring straw. Her lips turned up in a wry grin.

Anna's eyes widened. "You came all the way to New Zealand to get laid?"

"Well, not only to get laid. But it's on my to-do list."

"What's wrong with the guys in New Jersey?"

Sybil shrugged. "I might run into them again. I hate that. This will be more fun. No strings attached." She smacked Anna playfully. "Not to mention New Zealand accents. Yum."

Anna shook her head. "You're crazy."

"Me? And it's not crazy to sit home every Saturday night?"

Hanging out at home was a perfectly respectable thing to do on the weekend. She and Andrew…

Anna cringed, closed her eyes, and refocused. There was no more *she and Andrew*. Not since she left for college. Not since she came home to surprise him on his birthday.

College had become her life after that night. Classes and studying. Nothing more.

Nothing more than lying awake at night, crying.

She gritted her teeth. She was not *that girl* anymore. She didn't need a guy, and she didn't need to go out on the weekend to look for another shitfaced, lying bastard. Anna worked her tail off studying all week. She needed to decompress and relax on her days off. Alone.

Anna cringed, then straightened. She didn't want to be alone. Not really. But she wasn't ready to get out there and date again.

Andrew had been her world since middle school. She didn't know how to be with anyone else.

Sybil would never understand that. Her sister's plan was to play the field and be married to her cushy corner executive office for the rest of her life. There was nothing wrong with that, for *her*. Anna wanted the best of both worlds—a family and a job. She wasn't going to find that hooking up with a guy she'd never see again.

"I don't understand how you can even think of sleeping with a guy you've just met." Anna sipped her drink and set it back on the bar.

"Believe me. It's a heck of a lot easier than getting tied down in a relationship. Guys get crazy when they hang around too long. They get all protective and..." The word cheat hung on the edge of her lips before she copped out by sipping her drink.

Anna crumpled her napkin and threw in on the bar. "I don't know, I think I still want what Mom and Dad had—the love of my life, job, and two point five kids?"

"Point five?"

"Yeah, my dog." Anna watched the condensation drip down her glass. "Is it so wrong to want a guy that will do almost anything for me?"

"You're dreaming, little sister. He doesn't exist. I gave up looking for him years ago."

But Dad existed. Could it be true that their generation hadn't spawned any great guys?

The bartender adjusted the volume on the television.

A news reporter brushed back a lock of her dark hair and brought a microphone to her lips. "So there you have it. This small village, the third in as many nights, now lays in shock after this morning's gruesome discovery. The identities of the women have not been made public yet, but NZN News has learned that two of the victims lived here in Wellington, and the third was a Norwegian tourist. Neighboring towns have called for a seven o'clock curfew tonight, as all of New Zealand prays for an end to this senseless killing spree."

"They were disemboweled, just like the last two," one of the guys at the table said. "I saw it on the internet. This bloke is a sadist or something."

Last two? Holy crap! Were they anywhere near Wellington?

The bartender changed the channel. "I hope they catch him soon."

"There be no one to catch," the old guy in the colorful garb mumbled. "They look for a man. They need to turn their eyes to the sky. They seek what they are not prepared to find."

A shiver ran down Anna's spine. The tavern was oddly reminiscent of an old horror flick, and this weathered, creepy guy was the trope old codger that knew the truth, but no one believed him until they were running for their lives. If he was about to say that all of New Zealand was haunted by ancient bloodthirsty spirits, she was *so* out of here.

The guy at the other table turned in his seat. "What are you talking about, pop, some Maori legend?"

The old man's eyes darkened. "Is no legend. We in a Seventeen Year. They should not be looking for a man."

The table of guys laughed. "So what are they looking for, a dragon? I think you've had a few too many."

"Every seventeen years the dragons fly. They search New Zealand for mates." He pointed to the television. "This be the work of a gray dragon, the worst of them all."

"Yeah, and Aoraki and his brothers got stranded on a reef and became the mountains." One of the guys laughed into his beer.

Anna took in the old man's colorful attire, remembering the brochure Sybil read to her. It seemed crazy that people still believed that kind of folklore.

The elder remained stoic. "How do you know they did not become the mountains, if you were not there?"

Anna bit back her smile. The ominous cloud in the room lifted as the table of guys snickered. It was sad they made fun of the old man, though. He couldn't help what he'd been brought up to believe, no matter how ridiculous.

The bartender leaned across the counter toward her. "The bloke on the flipside would like to buy you a drink."

Anna cringed. The guy she'd been staring at? She glanced around the barkeep. Blondie smiled at her.

"Umm, no thanks. Tell him no offense, I'm just passing through. I'm not going to be here that long."

Sybil elbowed her. "What's wrong with you?"

"He's not my type."

"What, he doesn't have a pulse?"

"Shut up."

Someone settled beside her, and Anna tensed. She turned her head slowly until her gaze met eerie, light blue eyes and even lighter skin.

Blondie smiled. "Hello, I'm sorry. I heard you turn down my drink. You're not from around here, I suppose?" The New Zealand accent dripped from his pale lips. The package didn't seem to fit together.

"Um, no. We're from New Jersey."

He tilted his head. "In England?"

"No. New Jersey as in the United States."

His eyes widened. "Oh, that makes sense. You didn't look or sound English. Anyway, in these parts, it's customary for a man to buy a woman a drink to say hello. I was only being courteous. I didn't mean to offend you."

Sybil left her chair and sat on the other side of Blondie. She scribbled something on a napkin.

Anna shifted her weight. "In America, a guy buys a girl a drink if he's trying to pick her up."

"Pick her up?"

"As in a date."

His eyes widened, showing more of the creepy glass-like

pupils, which maybe, now that she looked closer, were eerily beautiful.

"That would be a bit presumptuous of me, wouldn't it?" he asked. "I don't even know your name."

Sybil held up the napkin she'd been toiling over. It read:
Platinum blond babies are beautiful

Anna laughed. Well, no, it came out more like an embarrassing snort, but Blondie didn't seem to notice, thank goodness.

She offered him her hand. "My name is Anna."

Instead of shaking, he flipped her palm down and kissed her knuckles. Who in God's name was this guy?

"It is a pleasure to meet you, Miss Anna of the great continent of America. My name is Joesephutus."

She shuffled her feet, trying to ward off the odd tingle in her toes. "Wow, that's quite a name. Do you mind if I just call you Joe?"

His smiled seeped into her. "Only if you allow me to buy you that drink."

Sybil gave a thumbs up over his head, and then returned to her place beside Anna.

Yeah, little sister Anna getting picked up in a bar would make Sybil's day. Anna would never hear the end of it.

As she gazed into Joe's haunting, crystal eyes, though, she couldn't help but want to know more about this interesting man. She'd gone from being completely freaked out about his appearance, to enthralled.

Too bad 11,000 miles was too far for a long distance relationship. She needed to nip this in the bud before it went any further. "I'm sorry, but I'm really not interested." An ache welled in her belly. She bit her lower lip to keep from retracting her words as Joe lowered his eyes.

His lips thinned. "No problem. Enjoy your time in New Zealand." He bowed his head and returned to his seat.

Anna nearly stepped off her chair to stop him. After all, it was only a drink, and he seemed nice. Shoot, why couldn't she be more like Sybil and okay with things like this?

An elbow in the back returned her attention to her sister. "What's wrong with you?" Sybil said. "He was cute."

"I don't know." And she didn't. Anna's stomach continued to whirl. Her skin ached, as if tugging her toward the other side of the bar, nudging her back to where Joe slipped into his seat and cradled his drink between his palms.

He'd been sweet and didn't come on too strong like the asses in bars back home. The poor guy was probably just shy, and she'd totally turned him down.

Sybil was right, what *was* wrong with her?

A cool breeze whipped in when someone opened the door. Anna was glad for the touch of chill as she turned toward her sister.

"Holy hell," Sybil whispered, her gaze fused to the entrance.

A man walked, no—slid through the entrance, but not in a slimy, snake-like way. It was more like gliding across the surface of a pond. He towered over everyone, well over six feet. Stopping in the center of the room, he placed his hand on his chest and bowed to the old man, who straightened, beaming.

The newcomer turned back to the bar, and Anna's heart triple beat as his gaze brushed over her. His long, dark hair shifted slightly as he walked, coming close to falling over one eye, but not quite covering it. Anna had seen this man before, on the cover of hundreds of romance novels. He seemed painted; perfect, as if molded by an artist. She quivered, warming in all the most embarrassing places.

He smiled at Anna, before turning his attention to Sybil. As soon as his gaze left hers, a sweep of relief flooded Anna, as if she'd been held by something, but then let go.

Sybil blanched, her eyes wide as the stranger slipped his fingers over hers.

"Please forgive my forwardness." He kissed the back of her

hand, just like Joe had. "But you are the most beautiful thing I've ever seen." He leaned up, still holding her fingers. "You must allow me the honor of your company."

His gaze darted over the bar, where Joe leaned back on his stool with a dumbfounded look on his face. The hot guy smiled before returning his attention to Anna's sister.

Sybil blinked as if waking from a stupor. "Of course, please, sit."

The man eased onto the seat beside them, his gaze never leaving Sybil's. How was it that no matter where they were in the world, her sister managed to be a beacon for beefcake? It wasn't fair. Well, not like Anna wanted to be eaten alive by a guy's eyes, but damn, did her sister wear *come and take me* perfume or something?

"I'm Sybil. This is my sister, Anna."

He lowered his head. "Miss Anna, a flower equally as lovely."

Sure, but you went for the one that looked and dressed like a runway model. Hot guys never went for the plain ones. Not that she wanted him to leech onto her, but, you know.

"My name is Quenor." He kissed Sybil's knuckles again, this time hesitating as his lips touched her skin.

Sybil cleared her throat. "Quay-noor? You mean, like, Connor?"

His eyes bored into her like he hadn't eaten in a month and she was a hot fudge sundae. "Connor sounds lovely with your accent."

Wow, his own accent sang from his lips. Anna could listen to his voice forever. She had to tear her eyes away from him. Taking a deep breath, she placed her chilled glass to her temple to try to cool herself down. She definitely needed to get a grip.

"Can I get you something to drink?" the bartender asked Connor.

"Whatever the lovely Sybil is having is fine for me."

Their gazes remained locked. Sybil seemed tongue-tied.

Icy fingers itched up Anna's back. Something wasn't quite

right about this guy. There was hot, and then there was *too hot*. And then there was Connor. The attraction Anna felt when he looked at her, the attraction she still felt, even when he'd obviously chosen Sybil, bordered on hypnotic.

The bartender reached up and grasped a wineglass from the fixture hanging over the bar. As he pulled the cup down, the contraption tilted. Several of the glasses slipped from their housing and fell, shattering on the bar top.

Sybil cried out, and Anna gasped as a strong shove sent her stumbling off her seat. The bartender stood, gaping at the mess, while Blondie's right knee angled up on the bar, and his other foot balanced on the stool that Anna had occupied. His left hand still held her from harm's way, while his right held the fixture from falling at the same time. How had he gotten across the bar so quickly?

"I have this end." Connor reached up, his long arms easily grabbing the other side of the fixture.

"Thanks," the bartender said, helping them ease the wooden frame safely to the floor. His face contorted and reddened with the effort, while Joe and Connor lowered the fixture to the floor without difficulty.

Sybil held her hand to her chest, but her eyes remained glued to her new date.

Don't worry, sis, no glasses hit me. No reason to check and make sure I'm all right or anything.

The barkeep grabbed a dustpan and saluted Joe and Connor with the sweeper brush. "Your drinks are on the house, mates."

"Thank you, but that's not necessary." Joe turned to Anna, and his eyes widened. "You're bleeding."

She blinked in surprise. "What?"

He grabbed her hand, raising her red, glistening fingertip. "You've been cut."

"It's not that bad."

His gaze centered on her fingertip. His brow furrowed as a red bead dripped down to her palm.

She trembled. "Umm, you can let go of me, now."

His gaze flicked to hers and held. He leaned closer. Her pulse throbbed in her ears like she was underwater. The room spun, but dizziness didn't overcome her. The beat of her heart seemed to slow while every inch of her yearned to lean closer and breathe this beautiful stranger in.

Breathe him in? What in God's name had gotten into her, and why was this guy still holding her wrist?

She tried to push him away, but slipped, smearing blood across his cheek. He hardened his grip, as another red droplet beaded on her fingertip.

Her gaze drew back to his light blue, crystalline eyes. She needed to scream, to slap him in the face, to run. She couldn't move, though. Her breaths came shallow and raspy. Part of her longed to kiss away the crimson stain that tainted the edge of his pale lip.

Wait. What?

The brightness of the blood against his milky skin caused flashes of Edward Cullen to run through her mind. The idea was ridiculous, of course. No one believed in vampires. That was almost as stupid as believing in fairies.

But he was fairy-like, now that she thought about it, with those icy blue eyes and white hair. He actually pulled off his albinism with an air of sex appeal. Well, not the dripping screw-me sexy like Connor, but there was definitely something about this guy who was still… fixating on her bloody cut like a deranged lunatic.

He released her.

She nearly stumbled, but grabbed the edge of her stool instead. "What is wrong with you?"

He blinked as if clearing his eyesight. "I-I don't know." He stared at her finger like it might bite him.

Okay, so, yes—this guy was cute, but he obviously had some serious issues.

She grabbed a napkin and wrapped her wound. "In case you were wondering, that is *not* the way to get an American girl's attention."

"I know, I-I'm sorry." He rubbed his temples. "I-I didn't mean to offend."

Connor left Sybil's side and grabbed Joe's shoulder. "Joesephutus, are you all right?"

He wiped the blood from Joe's face with his bare hand and then stared at his fingers.

"Wait, you two know each other?" Anna asked.

The taller man whipped his face in her direction. His gaze focused on her with an intensity that made her want to cower in the corner. Connor leaned closer and drew in a deep breath. Was he... smelling her?

Joe became pale. Well, pale-er if that was even possible. He took a stilted breath before elbowing Connor's considerably larger bulk out of the way and taking Anna's uninjured hand. "Anna, I would really, really like to buy you that drink."

His grip tightened. Not painful, but strange. Possessive. Every part of her screamed to tug her hand from his, but all she could do was stare into those glassy, light eyes.

Connor laughed, tapping Joe on the back. "I can't believe it. You are one lucky little..."

The door to the bar flung open and slammed against the wall as if it had been kicked.

The cool breeze thickened the air.

Connor nudged Joe.

"I feel it," Joe said.

Holding Sybil's shoulder, Connor glanced at Anna, then Joe. "We need to get your little lass out of here."

"I'm aware of that." Joe turned to the barkeep. "Do you have a back exit?"

"Too late," Connor whispered.

Joe grumbled under his breath, tightening his grip on Anna's arm. He leaned close to her ear. "If you get the opportunity, run like your life depends on it." He glanced at the door. "Because it does."

Chapter 2

Four men entered. Their long, gray jackets shifted with a life of their own.

Two of the men remained on either side of the door, as if standing guard. One walked to the table of guys that had made fun of the old man. Anna expected him to strike up a conversation. Instead, he stared at them.

An itchy sensation crawled up her spine as the guys at the table fidgeted and cast panicked glances at each other. After a moment, one stood, threw a few bills on the table, and scurried between the two men standing by the door. Seconds later, the other guys at the table followed.

The fourth newcomer stopped mid room and drew his fingers through his short, brunette hair as he scanned the tables.

The old man's lips thinned before he stood. "You are not welcome here." His accent tripped over a marked shake in his voice. His hands formed fists.

The guy in the center of the room lifted his nose into the air and sniffed as the third shoved the old man back into his seat.

Asshole. Anna moved to intervene, but Joe drew her back.

"This is a Seventeen Year, elder," the third guy said. "We'll search where it pleases us."

"Enough." The one in the center of the room set his gaze on

Sybil. "The elder deserves honor, whether or not his tongue is forked."

The old man shifted in his seat. His gaze jumped between the two newcomers. "You'll not find the South's hopeful in these villages. They are at the base of *Aoraki*. You waste your time here."

"We'll see." The one who seemed to be the ring-leader sauntered toward Sybil with a gait not unlike Connor's. He reached out and fingered one of her curls.

Sybil gasped, but didn't move until Connor edged between her and the lead asshole, who probably had six inches on her date's already impressive height. "This one is mine, Galeptopnor. You can look elsewhere."

The guy—was his name Gale Topner?—laughed. His dark gray coat shifted around his waist. "Brave words, for a twilight born." He leaned past Connor, taking a deep breath, as if smelling Sybil behind him. "Luckily for you she is nothing." He straightened. "Unlike the careless, languid greens, the children of the mountain take the Seventeen Year seriously. We'll entertain ourselves once the hunt is over."

Connor reached back, shoving Sybil further behind him. "Then get on with it, and let the rest of us enjoy our night of freedom." He pointed his chin toward the old man. "As the elder said, the offerings are on *Aoraki*."

Gale stepped back. "As they always are, but it has been ten cycles since they've presented anything of value."

Offerings? Value? What in goodness name were these people talking about?

The newcomer stepped toward Anna, and Joe jumped between them in an awkward recreation of Connor's protection of Sybil. Gale towered over him by over a foot. Anna smashed against the bar as Joe backed into her.

"We-we're not in the hunt," Joe said. "Just leave us to our entertainment."

Anna cringed. Entertainment? She was no one's entertainment, thank you very much.

Anna pressed her palms against Joe's back, ready to shove him away, but he didn't budge. She could feel the sculpted ridges of muscle beneath his T-shirt, and her attention drew from the man advancing, to the one standing between them. His skin warmed under her hands as if his body reached toward her, beckoning. Her sight blurred before refocusing on Joe's back, and his thick, distinct platinum hair.

Gale smirked. "What are you hiding back there, runt?"

Joe straightened, trying to make himself bigger.

Where did he get off trying to be her protector? She'd dealt with assholes before. She didn't need some guy to jump in like a knight in shiny platinum armor.

"Cain." Gale's word came out as a command, and the jerk who'd scared off the guys grasped Joe by the shoulders, picked him up, walked him across the room, and set him down beside the empty table.

A chill swept through the door, sending a shiver across Anna's skin as Gale gazed down on her.

She was vaguely aware of Cain pointing at Joe as he shouted: "Stay."

Joe's eyes saddened before he lowered his gaze to the floor. Part of her felt naked without him sheltering her; which was ridiculous since they'd only met a few minutes ago.

Her breath hitched as the tall stranger reached for her. She willed her hands into fists. She tried to punch, but her body didn't react. She stood frozen as Gale twirled her hair around his fingers.

"That one's just a child, a plaything," Connor said. "Leave her to the runt. Maybe she'll keep him busy and out of your way."

"I have no need to keep a runt out of my way." Gale continued his perusal. "His participation in the Seventeen Year is a waste of his people's meaningless hope." He leaned closer to Anna, his nose grazing her neck as he breathed her in. "You, though, precious one." He cupped Anna's cheeks. "You are *very* interesting."

The pupils in his eyes seemed to swirl, dragging her to infinity. Something deep in her mind prodded that she wanted to push him away, to stand up, pull back her shoulders and tell this asshole that she wouldn't just stand there and let him... let him...

Let him what?

Damn, he was handsome, and his hands, so warm against her skin. She could melt under his touch. Anna eased toward him, but someone batted Gale's hands from her. The room instantly chilled.

"Back off," Joe said. "She's mine."

The two men guarding the door snickered, while Gale's face twisted into a snarl.

"He's right," Connor said. "The boy found her. He has first rights."

"Really?" Gale shoved Joe, slamming him against the bar as if he weighed no more than a loaf of bread. "Are you willing to fight me for her, runt?"

Joe lunged for the taller man, but Connor shoved an arm between them, grabbing Joe.

"This is not the place," Connor said.

Gale crossed his arms. "Would you rather we challenge on the mountain? I can humiliate him now, or eviscerate him later. It makes no difference to me."

Joe twisted in Connor's grip. "Let go of me."

"Calm down, little one," Connor said. "There's no reason to die today."

All three of them glanced at Anna, and she could tell from the looks on their faces that there was probably a perfectly good reason to die today, as far as they were concerned. Whatever it was, she didn't travel all the way to New Zealand to get in the middle of some stupid pissing match with the locals.

She shuddered, eyeing the door.

If you get the opportunity, run like your life depends on it.

The other two men still blocked the exit. Had the bartender answered when they asked about a back door? Why were they all still staring at her?

"Enough." Gale turned to Connor. "Keep your little pet grounded or I will ground him for you." He grabbed Anna's wrist and wrenched her toward the exit.

The soles of Anna's shoes slid along the slick hardwood. "Wait. I'm not leaving with you."

Gale didn't turn. He just pulled harder.

"Stop!" Sybil cried out. "That's my sister."

The night air chilled Anna's face as the tavern door closed behind them. "Please let me go. I don't have any money."

Well, not much anyway, but she'd give it to him, if he'd just leave her be.

Gale pulled her behind the building and shoved her against the wall beside the dumpster. He pressed her shoulders into the cool brick. A huge, flattened courtyard sprawled out behind him, big enough to house a bazaar or a circus, but now lay eerily empty. Damn that freaking curfew.

He stared into her eyes, and the tension slipped from her muscles.

He ran his nose up the side of her neck, again. "Your scent is intoxicating."

Her scent?

Gale held her face. A trace of smoke carried on his breath. "You are special, did you know that? Your blood is very hard to find."

"My-my blood?" Her blood was a hindrance, a curse. What was he talking about?

"But now that I've found it, you will be mine."

Anna's head lolled to the side. She groaned as he dragged his tongue along her collarbone.

Something deep within her screamed. This man was insane.

471

Yet she eased closer to him, languishing in his touch. She slipped her hand behind his neck and ran her fingers through his soft hair. Voices shouted somewhere in the distance, but she tuned it out, soaking in only the sound of Gale's breath, heated to a pant.

"For the next ten months, you will be queen." His eyes consumed her. She couldn't move. "Would you like that," he asked. "Do you want me?"

"No, she doesn't want you."

A bored expression crossed Gale's face before he turned and faced Joe standing in the courtyard behind him. "Haven't you learned, runt? Bugger off before I put you down."

"Let her go. This isn't right."

The cold air swept through her now that she was devoid of Gale's warmth. She pawed at the back of his coat.

He slipped his arm around her shoulder, and she cuddled into his embrace.

"See," he said. "Does she look unhappy?"

Unhappy? How could she be unhappy with such strength around her, such warmth?

"She has no idea what she feels. You're compelling her." Joe stepped closer.

Anna smiled at him. He was sweet, but she didn't need him anymore. Gale was what she needed, no one else.

Sybil appeared, screaming Anna's name while Connor held her back. She must be jealous. She must want Gale, too, but it was too late. Anna had already given herself to him.

"Let her go," Joe repeated.

Gale snickered, walking behind Anna. "Here she is," he said. "Come and take her."

Anna swayed, lost like a dandelion puff drifting on the breeze as an odd sweeping crackle sounded in the darkness behind her. Any other day she'd be terrified of the courtyard's darkness, but Gale was here. She belonged to him. He'd protect her.

A scream shrieked from Sybil's lips. Still in Connor's grip, she reached for Anna, pointing.

Anna blinked, startled when the cool air touched her cheek.

What were they doing outside?

A deep, guttural growl echoed through the courtyard. Anna spun toward the sound and froze. A huge figure loomed inches from her, dwarfing her slight form. Monstrous gray wings fluttered on the edge of the darkness before two bright, yellow eyes fixed on her.

Time froze for a moment while her mind took stock and tried to separate fantasy from reality.

What she saw wasn't possible. It wasn't real.

That certainly didn't change the fact that something huge and sinister stared back at her.

Heart racing, she ran, passing Connor and her sister, heading back toward the front of the tavern.

As she cleared the corner, Cain snatched her in a vise-like grip. "Don't leave now," he said. "The excitement has barely started."

He shoved her back toward the rear of the building, where the huge gray beast reared up, bellowing in fury over a smaller, silvery-white... God, could she even say it?

They were DRAGONS.

Cain's grip on her tightened. "Do you know how few human beings have seen dragons spar?" He whispered in her ear, "You should be honored."

Honored? Was this asshole out of his mind? Two more gray dragons dropped from the sky, one on either side of the small, pale dragon.

"When they disembowel the sniveling runt, Galeptopnor will offer you his seed to seal your union."

This was insane. She must have gotten a spiked drink at the bar.

Connor leaned out from behind a stack of empty vegetable

crates and beckoned to her. She struggled, but Cain's grip dug deeper into her biceps.

Further inside the courtyard, the smaller dragon snarled and snapped, whipping one of the larger creatures with the edge of his tail. The gray howled, backing away, while the first dragon lashed out with one muscular, clawed arm.

A dull thud sounded through the air as the largest gray slammed its reptilian arm into the little dragon's chest. Cain yanked Anna back as the small dragon stumbled, but its wing hit them with the force of a baseball bat. Cain lost his grip and Anna thudded to the ground.

She ignored the pain, scrambled to her feet, and sprinted toward the stack of crates.

Connor held out a hand to her while dragging Sybil behind him. He grabbed onto Anna like a vise.

"Dra-dragons," Anna whimpered.

"So I see." Connor yanked, propelling her into a sprint beside him.

Sybil grunted with each clop of her chunky heels on the pavement. Anna thanked God for the foresight to wear sneakers.

As they slipped from the alley, Connor skidded to a stop a few feet from a line of three more men in gray fanned out in front of the tavern. The door opened, and the bartender stuck his head out. "I've called the police."

Connor didn't even glance in his direction. "Fine. Get inside and pull down the shades."

When they were alone, one of the gray-clad men smiled. "Hello Quenor."

Connor's nose flared. "Zeph." He backed Anna and Sybil up a step.

"So, that's your game, is it?" Zeph walked toward them. "Wait until Gale is busy with the runt, and you slip out with the prize? That's not playing fair."

Connor tugged the women closer. "That's not what's

happening here." He glanced at Anna. "She's too young for my tastes."

Zeph held his hands out to his sides. "Yet here we are."

The silence seemed to echo along the sidewalk as Connor's gaze roamed the streets. If he was looking for a way out, Anna prayed he'd find it.

Zeph's face morphed into a feral sneer. "Hand the girl over. You know this won't end well for you, my friend."

Sirens sounded in the distance, drawing Zeph's attention away from them. Connor shoved Anna and Sybil down the alley opposite the tavern. "Run. Don't look back."

The wood and brick walls provided little protection from the biting wind, and even less from the roaring snarls that filled the night behind them.

Anna and Sybil stopped beside a dumpster.

"Oh, God. What were those things?" Sybil clutched her chest. "Who were those guys?"

Anna shook her head. She didn't give a damn about the guys, but she'd gotten a damn clear look at the creatures fighting behind the tavern. And no, she hadn't been hallucinating. There were actually dragons in New Zealand!

Sybil started to hyperventilate, and Anna grabbed her shoulders. "Stop. I need you to focus. Can you do that?"

Tears streamed from her sister's eyes. "Those things, they were monsters."

"I know, but we have to get out of here. Panicking isn't going to save us." She looked over her shoulder. No one else came down the alley, but the roars of the creatures heightened, as if there were even more of them now. She turned back to her sister. "We need to get to those sirens. I need you to run with me."

Sybil gulped, then nodded.

"Okay then, let's go."

They sprinted down the alley. Pungent smells from the dumpsters rose through the air, turning Anna's stomach. She ran faster, dragging her sister behind her. Their only chance was to find protection, and the sirens seemed as good a chance as any. She darted to the right, and down a deserted street.

Whooting beats filled the air, sounding like someone repeatedly snapping a towel. Anna blotted out the sound and concentrated on the sirens. If she dwelled on what might be flying toward her, she might succumb to a sobbing hysteria.

Something dug into her shoulders. She cried out as sharp claws punctured her flesh.

This wasn't real. This couldn't be happening. Why wasn't she waking up?

Her stomach flipped as the ground dropped out from below her. Sybil screamed, falling to her knees, looking up and reaching for Anna as she rose into the sky.

I really hope you enjoyed the preview of
DRAGON MOUNT
You can pick up your copy of this and other great adventures by
Jennifer M. Eaton at your favorite booksellers

By the way,
Thanks for reading!
I hope you enjoyed the book.
Alien and dragon kisses!

Made in the USA
Middletown, DE
03 October 2018